The Saddest

Princess

By

Leah Toole

The Saddest Princess

For
my beautiful daughters
and their incredible dad.

Prologue:

I used to think about dying.

There were days I would imagine floating up to heaven to finally meet the God I have been having one-sided conversations with my entire life.

In my darkest days, those moments would bring me peace and I would often wonder just how long God would make me suffer before He called me to Him.

But now, as I ride into London, I realise that every struggle had been a test.

Tests to gauge my commitment to my own fate and whether I would be worthy of the destiny He had intended for me. A destiny even I had far too often lost sight of throughout the years.

But in time I overcame them all and I have finally been rewarded; and for that I shall be eternally indebted to God and to the one true faith.

As I ride into London to a great sea of people waving and cheering, I almost forget to remain composed. As their new monarch – and England's very first Queen Regnant – I must remember to keep my feminine emotions hidden from my people and from the world, for nothing said weakness like the tearful blubbering of a woman.

The great crowd of people who had come to witness my arrival stand holding banners over their heads, and as we make our way towards the Tower of London, I take in all their cheers and calls of joy. Women are weeping and children stand tall on walls and barrels to get a better view of me, their new queen.

Never have I felt such acceptance and love in all my years, but I keep my composure as the sergeants-in-arms walk before us and lead us through the city. Even with my half-sister Elizabeth riding beside me with a huge smile on her face, her long red curls flowing down her back, I am not vexed, for this is my day. And I shall remember it until my final day on this earth.

I was later told that there had never been a public rejoicing such as on this day, and with that I believed that God was with me, and that the misery and pain from my past would no longer haunt my future.

I used to think about dying.

But now I realise what a waste that would have been...

November 1558

As I lay in bed, my great, swollen belly allowing me no rest as it throbbed uncomfortably before me, I contemplated my pitiful existence.

To this day, after forty-two years of life, I could not even begin to imagine what the purest kind of joy felt like. The joy one would expect to feel on their wedding day to their beloved, or upon holding one's child in one's arms...

What I felt at my coronation is perhaps the most joyful time I can claim to know, followed perhaps by the day I arrived in London, when the people of England had loved me.

But now I was left with nothing, my life having passed me by utterly without meaning.

The marriage I had so longed for had been lacklustre and loveless, resulting only in horrific failures. Perhaps I am, after all, more like my father than even he knew...

"Your majesty," a voice whispered, and I know it is one of my ladies. I turn my head in her direction and open my eyes only to find her much closer than I expected. I recoil from her and groan, "What is it, Cecily?" I ask even though, in truth, nothing mattered anymore.

"Forgive me your majesty, but Cardinal Pole is here," my lady-in-waiting said.

I try to turn away from her, but my body is too weak and frail, and my painfully swollen belly keeps me from moving freely.

"What shall I tell him, your Highness?" she persisted.

In response I lifted my arm and waved her away.

In the distance I heard her muttering to the Cardinal that he may return later, then the door closed, and I listen as her weightless footsteps return to my bedside. I did not turn to look at her.

Instead, I continued staring blankly at the wall before me and listened as she picked up the bible she had lain down on the chair and sat back down before turning a page and mumbling under her breath as she read.

I knew that death was close, I could feel it in every fibre of my body as it pulsated in pain, and I was suddenly unable to contain the question I had long feared to ask. But as a new wave of pain pierced through my bloated belly like a dagger, I could no longer supress my need to know.

"Was I a just ruler, Cecily?" I whispered quietly enough so that only she would hear. But when she did not immediately respond, the shame and humiliation engulfed me and as soon as the words left my mouth, I regretted them.

I felt my face redden with embarrassment and self-loathing. How could I doubt myself in these final moments when I had sacrificed so much to achieve this much-desired fate!

Cecily licked her lips, her eyes wide as she stared back at me,

"Of – of course, your majesty," she stammered unconvincingly.

Her pathetic stuttering quickly turned my humiliation into anger, and I unleashed my shame in the only way I could.

"I am anointed by God!" I shouted, "I know my divine calling, and my soul is free of sin! There was never such a just ruler as I!"

Suddenly my chest felt heavy, and I gasped for air as I tried to heave myself into a sitting position. Cecily simply sat frozen and stared at me bewildered.

My other lady, who had been reading by the fireplace, rose from her chair and hurried towards me to aid me upright and once I was made comfortable, she returned to her seat by the fire once more. I sighed deeply then to regain my strength, but instead I began to cough violently.

Cecily stood and held a cup of wine to my lips. I sipped it and let the warm liquid soothe me, but it did very little to comfort my mind, for in truth I had often wondered of late if my failures, as well as my ill health, were punishments from God Himself.

"Forgive me, your highness," Cecily said as she sat back down in her chair, her face hard as stone.

I did not reply but instead turned my face away and watched the flames flickering in the fireplace.

After some time, soothed by silence and the gentle dancing of the flames, I suddenly felt my eyelids become heavy, and I allowed sleep to take me.

But even in the final moment of consciousness, I knew that sleep would bring me no peace, for there was no escaping my tainted conscience. And as soon as I drifted off to sleep, I was suddenly engulfed in flames.

Standing on top of the pyre, begging for my life as the flames licked closer and the smoke filled my lungs, I knew that I was dreaming, for this was not the first time that this hellish nightmare had haunted me.

I was bound tightly with rope, my hands tied behind me so that I could not escape, and all the while I was screaming. Screaming in pain, screaming for forgiveness, and even screaming for my mother. But far worse than the pain was the smell of my own burning flesh.

It filled my nostrils and entered my throat with every shriek. But I could not stop screaming.

For dozens of nights this nightmare had tortured me, the burning pain and the smell becoming worse with each night that passed.

But tonight, the dream was different.

Where I had always been surrounded by complete darkness before, tonight I was not alone.

This time there was a crowd of people witnessing my demise.

Hundreds of my subjects stared up at me, faces I had never seen before, people I had never met. But I knew who they were. I knew.

I squeezed my eyes shut to block out their cold, dead stares and I felt my eyes melting from within the sockets as the flames licked higher and higher. I let out one last, long, guttural scream, and with that my burnt body slumped forward and I knew that I was dead.

I awoke with a jolt, and I was safely back in the comforts of my royal bed. I looked to my side and Cecily was still there beside me, reading the bible as always. Although I was sweating, I pulled the sheets over me and clutched them to my chest, breathing in deeply to calm myself.

"Read to me, Cecily," I commanded. The words of God have always comforted me, and I needed Him now more than ever.

Cecily began to read the passages of the Holy Bible aloud, but somehow the words did not console me, for the faces watching my fiery death danced before my eyes and I could not shake them from my mind.

I shivered and began to cry silently. As the hot tears rolled down my face, I knew that God must have forsaken me, for if I could not draw comfort from His holy teachings, then I knew that I must be lost to Him.

But no – they had been heretics! Condemning them to the stake was doing God's work! All three-hundred and twenty-seven of them had denied the true faith and forsaken their souls.

I was doing God's work, and I should not feel guilty for it.

I righted all my father's wrongs when he turned his back on the Pope and the catholic faith simply to shun my mother and marry that harlot, Boleyn! Those heretics got what they deserved when they denounced God's laws and turned their backs on their church, and if I could, I would burn them all over again!

I revelled in my thoughts for some time, but even they could not comfort me for long, for now that I was leaving this world without a catholic heir, and only my heretic half-sister to succeed me, was that not proof that God was not by my side?

I must get Elizabeth to agree to follow on in the Catholic ways and reign as a Catholic queen. I cannot have all my work be undone, for it had been the only success in my meaningless life!

Despite all my other failures, my mother would have been proud of the queen I have become: a fighter for the laws of God, as her mother, Isabella de Castille, had been before her.

Very much like my Spanish grandmother, I had warred against those who would do my country harm, and I had fought to save the souls of my loyal subjects.

Her battle may have taken place outside of the walls of her kingdom, while mine had been a deeply festering tumour that needed cutting out from within, but the battle for what was right remained the same.

Why else had I been my mother's only surviving child? Why else had God taken my brother Edward from this world before he could marry and produce a Protestant heir? Surely all that has happened must hold some meaning…

I was born to be Queen of England.

I was born to do what no one else was strong enough to do. Yes, I was a brave warrior queen like my grandmother before me; and all that was left to do now was pray that I be remembered throughout history as such.

Chapter 1

February 1516
Greenwich Palace, London

It was evening when the queen of England first began to feel the familiar tightening that signified the decent of the baby.

Katherine of Aragon heaved herself up from her chair by the fire and informed her ladies to fetch the midwives and Dr Vittoria. Her ladies curtsied and left the birthing chamber, whispering frantically to one another, but Katherine paid them no mind, for tonight she would do anything to make sure the birth of her baby would be a safe and successful one.

The queen made her way towards the bed, her heavy belly before her filled with hope and fear.

She inhaled deeply as another tightening coursed through her and she doubled over in pain, her long black hair falling over her shoulders and into her face, "Take my hand, your highness," said Maud Green, her chief lady-in-waiting, as Katherine straightened up and slowly waddled towards the bed, groaning as the wave of pain continued.

"The pains are coming quickly," Katherine said in her strong Spanish accent, "I pray the prince will be born soon."

Maud offered her queen a reassuring smile and as her pain began to ease, she was able to lay back on the bed to regain her strength momentarily before the difficult ordeal of giving birth worsened.

The queen's ladies returned with the midwives in tow, but Katherine furrowed her brow, "Where is Dr Vittoria? I requested that he be present."

"Your Grace," said one of the midwives, her creased face suggesting she was the one with the most experience and therefore in charge, "it is forbidden for a man to be present."

Before Katherine could respond, another contraction came, rendering her unable to utter a single coherent word. The pain was so intense that she could do nothing but hold her belly and breathe while the midwives rushed around her, busying themselves in preparation for what was to come.

As soon as the pain began to dissipate Katherine lifted herself up on her elbows and spoke firmly as Maud dabbed a cloth on her queen's clammy forehead.

"I am the queen of England," she said in between gasps as she glared at the midwife in charge, "and I have England's prince and heir in my womb. I *insist* that Dr Vittoria be present at the birth of this child! I cannot lose another one of my babies, I cannot!" she closed her eyes and gritted her teeth through another contraction, but she spoke on, "I will not put this child's life in danger. So help me *God*, the doctor will be present."

The midwives exchanged a nervous glance but sent out one of the ladies to summon the doctor.

Katherine lay back on her pillows and moments later the doctor entered the birthing chamber.

"Your majesty," he said as he bowed quickly, "How may I be of service?" he asked, his old face calm and reassuring.

"I beg you to do all that you must, doctor," Katherine breathed, "I cannot in good conscience bring another baby into this world only for it to be ripped from me too soon. You must instruct the midwives as well as you can."

With that the doctor bowed his head and began whispering with the midwives and after some quiet discussion, the doctor turned back to Katherine, "Your majesty, we have concluded that the midwives will continue observations of your majesty during the proceedings. Should there be any complications I

12

shall be present to guide the ladies verbally and from behind your majesty's closed door, to safeguard your honour."

It was not what Katherine had wanted to hear, but with the pains intensifying and drawing closer together, she knew her time to push was near. The doctor excused himself and retreated while the midwives examined the queen, "Your grace must hold onto the birthing ropes now, your time to push has come."

Katherine heaved herself up onto her knees, held on tightly to the ropes that were tied to the bedposts in preparation for the birth of the prince, and with one deep breath she calmed her nerves, tuning out her mind's fears.

The queen's screams rippled through the birthing chamber with every push as the midwives muttered words of encouragement and the ladies prayed in quiet murmurs in all corners of the chambers. But as the hours ticked by it was clear that it was not to be an easy birth.

Despite it being her fifth time labouring a baby from within her, Katherine felt that it was no easier than the first, and as she pushed and screamed to bring this new child into the world, she envisioned her first-born baby boy.

He had been born a perfect and robust baby, a strong and healthy heir for England, and he had brought with him so much hope and joy for the future. But God had seen fit to take him away, and after only fifty-two days of life, Katherine and Henry's world had crumbled. What followed had been nothing but misery and darkness, one stillbirth after another.

But this time would be different, Katherine thought. This child would be another healthy boy, and he would live to become the future of England, Katherine could feel it in her very soul.

"Something is wrong," the old midwife suddenly said to another in a rash whisper, "Bring in the doctor," she ordered.

13

"Her majesty is losing a lot of blood," the midwife told Dr Vittoria as he approached quickly, "the baby is stuck inside her."

He simply nodded and then spoke to his queen, "Your majesty must lie back."

She did as he commanded and watched as he gently waved the midwives out of his way and took their place at the foot of the bed, where Katherine's feet lay apart.

Katherine of Aragon looked around the room, at the midwives and at her ladies, and saw complete and utter horror in all their faces. Her ladies stood by the window, their hands clasped tightly in prayer, some crossing themselves at the unusual situation, and the midwives watched in awe at what was happening before their very eyes. For never before had a man attended, or indeed aided, with the birth of a royal child.

But of course, this was not any child, this was the future Prince of England, a prince Katherine had fought too hard to keep safe in her womb, and this day would not end in sadness and despair like so many others had. This birth would bring her and her husband the ending they had dreamed of for so long. This child would be their heir.

As another strong contraction swept through the queen, the doctor spoke quietly to the midwives and their eyes widened in shock.

"… it is not safe!" Katherine overheard one of them reply in horror but when the midwife in charge nodded briskly in agreement, one of the younger ones scurried away.

"Your majesty must stay strong. The prince will be born soon," said the old midwife as she moved to Katherine's side and took her hand in hers.

The young midwife returned with something in her hand and passed it to the doctor, "Your highness," he said then, "When your next contraction comes you must push as hard and as long as you can, and you must remain constant throughout the pain that you will feel."

Katherine nodded and immediately felt her belly tighten, "It's now, doctor."

"Then push now, your majesty! Push!"

Katherine gritted her teeth and pushed with all her might, releasing one long, animalistic wail and suddenly, quite unexpectedly, she knew that she had been cut. The agony she felt in that moment was unlike anything she had ever experienced, and she could feel herself losing consciousness from the overwhelming pain. But then, as the corners of her mind slowly began to darken, her baby was born in one slithering gush.

She fell back against her pillows, breathing heavily, as everyone flew off in a frenzy to get a glimpse of the new baby. But as each second passed, the silence grew louder and louder.

"What is it?" Katherine asked, her voice begging, but no one answered.

In that instant – much to Katherine's relief – her babe squealed. She could see its little pink body wriggling in the midwife's arms, and she knew that her baby was alive and that she had been blessed with a healthy child… at last.

Queen Katherine held out her arms and tried to smile, "What is it?" she asked again.

But in her heart, she already knew, for the quiet that had spread throughout the room spoke volumes.

The midwife came closer and handed Katherine her baby, "It's a healthy and beautiful baby girl, your majesty."

Katherine nodded and looked down at her new-born child as disappointment flooded her to her very core, replacing all the intense relief and joy she had felt but moments ago when she had heard that delicious new-born cry. Katherine looked into her little baby's face and tried to feel what she ought to feel at the birth of a live child after so many that were not. But all she felt was emptiness, and there was no love for this useless baby girl.

Katherine closed her dark brown eyes in frustration. After all she had been willing to sacrifice in pursuit of a male heir – her body, her sanity, her reputation, her own *life* – none of it had mattered.

And for all the sacrifices she had made, God had not granted her the one thing she had wanted most, and all her efforts had been in vain. For despite having borne a healthy child at last, Katherine had failed, and she knew that there would be consequences.

It was as if she had summoned him with her fear, for within mere moments Katherine heard heavy footsteps approaching at a deafening speed, and suddenly the doors to her chambers were flung open.

Her king and husband stood before her, his pale face giving away nothing as he looked upon her and the inadequate child she had produced.

"My lord… she is healthy – " she began but he looked away and rested his pale blue-eyed stare at Dr Vittoria, who bowed deeply as if in defence for his presence.

The king looked back at his queen, cleared his throat, "We are both young," he said slowly, "it was a daughter this time, but by the grace of God the sons will follow."

And with that he turned and left, leaving his queen and his daughter behind without so much as a second thought.

King Henry VIII banged his fist upon the table and raged, "A girl! A useless girl, Charles! What am I to do with that?"

Charles Brandon was the king's closest friend, as well as his brother-in-law by marriage to the king's younger sister, Mary Tudor.

Having known Henry since childhood and been by his side throughout all his endeavours and fits of rage, he knew not to answer him when his anger ran hot, and so instead he sighed and allowed his king to continue his heated rant.

"Five pregnancies, Charles," Henry continued, holding up his open hand, "and all have resulted in dead babies and now a girl who will likely not make it past childhood either!" Henry ran his hand through his dark red hair as he paced the room, "What am I to do?" he shouted rhetorically, "A king needs a son. *Two* sons! My father had two sons and look what happened! And here I am, king of England, and NO HEIRS!" in his fury he swiped his arms across the table before him, sending everything crashing to the ground.

Charles simply watched his friend calmly, and after several minutes of angry pacing, Henry stopped and stood by the fireplace, staring into the flames.

"What am I to do, Charles?" he repeated, and with his anger subsided and replaced by disappointment, Charles took a step towards his friend and spoke openly.

"Your majesty must take the positive from this live birth," he said, "The queen has delivered a healthy child, a girl yes, but a child that lives is proof that the queen *can* produce a living heir. The princess is strong. She will bring with her an alliance upon her marriage one day, and in the meantime, you now know that you and the queen are able to have more living children," Charles took a deep breath and steeled himself for what he said next, for he knew that the future of England, as well as the king's sanity, hung in the balance, "The next child no doubt will be a living boy."

Henry looked at his friend, "I pray you are right Charles. I pray for a son every day," then he sighed deeply, "But until that joyous day comes, I must busy myself with other matters, namely the princess' royal baptism."

Henry then rubbed his hands together and proceeded towards the door with a newfound spring in his step, and Charles knew that his ever-changing mood had turned the tide once more, "There is much to do!" the king called over his shoulder, "I want only the best for my daughter," he said as he left the room.

"Of course, your majesty," Charles Brandon replied as he bowed, pleased with himself for diffusing the king's rage yet again.

20th February 1516

Although this girl child was not the prince everyone had prayed for, she was a princess of England nonetheless, and much preparation had been made for this merry occasion.
Crowds of people gathered to see the fine tapestries that hung from the court gates to the Church of the Observant Friars' door and the path that had been gravelled and scattered with beautiful flowers. But above all else, the people gathered for a glimpse of their new princess.
As the procession began the crowds' hubbub dissipated, their eagerness to gossip suddenly blown away with the wind, and the little princess emerged, carried safely in her godmother's arms.
The Countess of Devon began her slow walk along the wide path towards the church as she cradled the three-day-old princess in her arms, followed by the Lord Chancellor Thomas Wolsey, and Agnes Howard the Duchess of Norfolk, all of which would be the royal baby's godparents.
The priest was waiting for them at the church door and as they approached, he took a step towards the Countess of Devon, who presented the princess to him so that she may be blessed.
The priest gently opened the princess's little mouth and rubbed salt onto her gums, "I hereby exorcise any demons that

may prevail onto thee, and bestow upon thee the reception of wisdom," he said, and they entered the church.

Throughout the length of the aisle, on their way towards the baptismal font, hung beautiful tapestries that had been hand stitched and decorated with pearls and precious stones.

Upon their arrival at the silver font the priest took his place beside it as the king's chaplain began singing Te Deum.

"I ask you, oh Lord," he said above the singing, "to bless this water so that this child may be cleansed of sin," he touched the water with his right hand and completed a prayer over it. He then carefully sprinkled the water over the princesses' dark red head three times as he said, "I baptize you in the name of the Father, the Son, and the Holy Spirit."

He then turned to the crowd of lords and ladies within the church, and as the Countess of Devon held the princess up high for all to see, he called out, "This child has been reborn in baptism and is now a child of God. She has been reborn and will forever be known as Mary, her royal highness, the Princess of England."

As the city of London celebrated the birth and christening of the new royal princess, queen Katherine recuperated in her chambers, where she would remain until she had been properly churched by a priest.

It was custom for a woman to be hidden from the world until she had stopped her bleeding and had been cleansed of the sin of giving birth, and while Katherine would typically become restless to re-enter society, this time was different, for she felt nothing but emptiness after the birth of her daughter.

Whenever she thought of that little innocent babe, Katherine could not help but shudder with distaste and she felt nothing but disappointment towards the child. Which was why, when she had handed her to the wet nurse only moments after her birth, Katherine had commanded for the princess not to be

19

returned to her, choosing instead to complete her period of confinement alone.

But during the nights Katherine found herself letting go of her frustrations towards the poor girl and realising that it was in fact she herself who was to blame, for Katherine had failed in her one true purpose as queen: to give the king a healthy male heir.

The queen knew that her age for producing heirs was coming swiftly to an end, and she was also painfully aware that when the time came, the king would no longer wish to share her bed if it meant no heirs were to result from their couplings.

She winced in agony then as her heart ached at the thought of her beloved husband abandoning her for his whores.

Katherine let herself wallow in her guilt and sorrow while she was alone, as she knew that as soon as her month of postpartum confinement was over there would be no opportunity for self-pity. She would have to return to her former royal grandeur – never faltering in the knowledge that she was the rightful queen of England.

Too many people wished for her downfall, and she would not let them defeat her. Katherine of Aragon would have another child, and this time it would be a boy.

It had to be.

1518
Greenwich Palace

At the age of only two years old, the little princess Mary became godmother to her cousin Frances Brandon, who was born to the king's friend and advisor, Charles Brandon and his wife the king's sister Mary Tudor. The occasion took place at the church of St. Etheldreda, and while Mary was only a toddler, she presented herself with grace and grandeur befitting her title.

20

Many that attended had remarked on the princess' gentle manner and stately behaviour, congratulating their king and queen on their beautiful daughter.

"Ah, our Mary! She is our pearl of the world!" king Henry called after the ceremony was complete and everyone was celebrating back at Greenwich Palace, "She is strong and fiery just like her father!"

Queen Katherine smiled and nodded in response, taking another sip of her wine.

Katherine had tried to love her daughter. But no matter how hard she tried, nothing the girl did held any meaning in Katherine's eyes.

The queen then spotted the little princess out of the corner of her eye as she toddled towards her parents through the crowd of people feasting and dancing, her governess following closely behind. As she approached, Henry's face beamed with delight for his only living child "Here's the most beautiful princess in all of Christendom! Princess Mary herself!"

Katherine watched as Henry tickled the girl under her chin and they both laughed heartily as he pretended to try to catch her as she tottered away from him, screeching with delight.

Henry then kissed Mary's chubby cheek and bid her goodnight before beckoning over her governess, who took the child by the hand and away from the celebrations.

The little princess then turned and waved a chubby hand at her father the king, a toothy smile brightening her face, and then she set her pale blue eyes on her mother and the innocent joy disappeared from her face and was replaced with a blank expression of uncertainty.

Katherine looked away quickly before the guilt could engulf her completely and turned her attention to her husband beside her.

She took his hand and spoke softly, "Husband?"

He turned his attention to her and jerked his chin, signalling for her to speak.

Instead, she sat back in her chair and placed a hand over her belly, and Henry knew instantly what his queen was alluding to.

He dropped the sweetmeats he had been eating eagerly and wiped his hands before placing them over his wife's belly. He looked up into her beautiful, tired face and smiled, and Katherine's heart fluttered briefly with hope.

But then he sighed heavily and removed his hands.

"It will be a boy this time, Katherine? A living boy?" his voice was low, and although his smile remained, his tone was threatening.

Katherine nodded quickly and sat up straight once more, "Yes Henry, I believe with all my heart he is a boy," she placed her hand over his, "And his movements inside me are strong. This boy will be your living heir Henry, I know it."

Henry looked at his queen and nodded once, then he ran his tongue over his yellowing teeth and stood up, his cup of wine in his hand, "A toast!" he roared and suddenly all eyes were on him, "To Charles Brandon, my most loyal and trusted friend, and to my dearest sister Mary, for the birth of their beautiful Frances," he held his cup to his lips and took a sip while everyone cheered and mirrored his actions, "And to the queen!" he continued, "Who has this moment informed me that she is with child once more!" he stopped while the crowd cheered loudly, raising their cups to their queen, "And this time" Henry went on, "… it will be a prince!" he took a long gulp, draining his cup and then slammed it down on the table with a loud *bang*, "May God grant me my heir, for He knows how long we have waited for him!" he stopped while shouts of agreement followed, "May He grant me my heir, so that we may all go on with peace in our hearts, knowing that England's future is secured! I beg you all to keep your king and queen in your prayers and to pray that the queen will bestow onto me a healthy, living son!"

As the crowd cheered heartily at the news, the king looked down at his queen sitting beside him, his face suddenly indifferent, and spoke in a voice so low only she could hear, "Last chance, wife. One last chance."

9th November 1518

Thunder cracked loudly outside, followed quickly by the flash of lightning as the queen was suddenly awakened by an all too familiar feeling. The room was dimly lit by the embers that remained in the fireplace, but as Katherine sat upright in bed, she could see the dark stain forming on her nightshift between her legs.

The thunder, as well as the queen's sudden jolt awake, had alerted her ladies and one by one they began to stir.

Elizabeth Blount, the youngest of Katherine's ladies-in-waiting, swiftly got out of bed and lit a candle, her concerned expression unmistakeable in the flickering candlelight "Your Grace?" she whispered.

Katherine stared at her, tears welling in her eyes, and she shook her head ever so slightly, "It's too soon..."

Bessie Blount looked down at the queens' swollen belly and the bloody sheets, fear welling up inside her, "I will fetch the midwives."

In moments the room was filled with noise and chaos as the midwives tried desperately to calm and tend to their queen as she sobbed, "It's too early, it's too early!"

But there was no stopping what was happening, and unlike her last birthing experience, this babe was too eager to be born.

It easily slipped out of her with only two contractions and Katherine fell back onto her pillows and sobbed quietly, her teeth chattering with terror while the midwife bundled the tiny baby up and wrapped it in blankets.

The room went deathly still, and as the storm outside began to ease, the storm within Katherine was building greater with every passing second of silence as she awaited her child's first cry.

The baby, wrapped in the old midwife's arms gave a little gurgle, then another, and Katherine felt the world fall out from underneath her. She knew the sound of death all too well, and having lost child after child she knew that this one was also born too soon to breathe on its own outside of her womb.

Nobody made a sound as they all watched the little child struggle to breathe, all feeling powerless, unable to do anything to help it. The midwife looked up at Katherine, her tired eyes bloodshot with grief for her queen, "Does your majesty wish to hold her?"

"Her?" Katherine whispered as she frowned, but she knew it did not matter. Boy or girl, the child was not meant for this world, her body having expelled the poor babe ahead of time, like so many of her brothers and sisters before her.

The midwife nodded, "Let her pass in her mothers' arms," and she gently handed Katherine her dying babe and took a step back, ashamed to be in such close proximity of her queen's pain.

Katherine held her baby and watched as its little chest shuddered with every inhale, each desperate gurgle more hopeless than the last. And then suddenly, all too soon, there was utter silence once more, and Katherine's last hope was gone from this world.

Chapter 2

Katherine emerged from her confinement knowing in her heart and soul that it would be her last time doing so, and with that knowledge came the realisation that God had taken all her children from her for a reason; to remind her that she was the daughter of Spain, and the daughter of a warrior queen.

Spain was a country of the future, where women were not only consorts to provide heirs, but queens in their own merit, who did not need a king by their side to rule.

Katherine would no longer wallow in self-pity and she stood tall in the knowledge that her children were taken from her not as a punishment for her sins, but to guide her into the realisation that her daughter had been her only surviving child for a great cause, and that it had been God's will all along that Mary would be Henry's heir.

But the king had had no such epiphany, and he spent his days avoiding the queen's presence. For many days in a row, he would saddle up his great warhorse and ride off with a company of men and spend the day hunting or hawking, and in the evenings, he would not send for her to share private dinners but instead busied himself with matters of parliament, or – as Katherine assumed was most likely – with his whores.

Though Katherine knew of her husband's deceptions, she tried not to let them affect her. A king's right to gallivant and whore was implied in the title, and the queen's personal dislike of it would do nothing to stop it, especially when she had done nothing to promote the king's appreciation.

And yet, Katherine could not help but wonder just who her husband was spending his time with, and whether she had finally lost him to someone else due to her endless failures to produce a male heir.

Katherine shook her head to ease her spiralling thoughts and focused her mind once more at the bible in her hands, since it no longer mattered if he shared her bed or another's. What mattered now was that he recognised that Mary would be England's future.

But after reading and re-reading the same passage without taking it in, she decided that she could wait no longer for the king to forgive her, and that she would need to convey her request to speak to him about their daughter through a messenger she could trust.

"Bessie," the queen called, and her lady approached.

"Yes, your majesty?" the girl replied, a pretty yet slightly plain-looking girl with light blond hair and piercing green eyes.

At only fourteen years old, Bessie Blount was Katherine's youngest lady-in-waiting, but despite her age, or perhaps because of it, Katherine believed her to be a loyal and faithful servant, being one of the only ladies at court that she could not imagine her husband being interested in.

How wrong she had been.

As she approached, the queen offered her a warm smile, "I need your help with regards to the king," she said, and Bessie looked back at her queen, her green eyes wide, "I wish to speak with him about our daughter. I believe it to be of great importance and urgency, but as he is much displeased with me still, he will not allow me in his presence. Would you go in my stead and ask my lord husband for a kindness to his queen?"

Bessie nodded at her mistress once, curtsied, and exited the queen's rooms before making her way through the dark corridors, the only light guiding her way coming from the distantly lit torches dotted along the walls, her shoes sounding eerily on the stone floor as she hurried towards the king's chambers.

"I am here to see the king," Bessie told the guards when she arrived, "Her majesty the queen has sent me."

The guards allowed her through and upon her entrance the king's usher announced her.

The king and his courtiers glanced in her direction, breaking off their conversation mid-sentence, the matter of the poor winter harvest suddenly forgotten at the sight of the pretty young visitor.

Bessie, feeling suddenly self-conscious, curtsied while keeping her eyes fixed on the ground before her.

"Your majesty, forgive me," she said, "but her majesty the queen wishes to speak with you about the princess Mary."

Bessie heard footsteps approaching and looked up to see the handsome king standing before her.

"The queen wants to speak with me about our daughter?" he asked, mockingly, "she has never cared about the girl until now," then he turned to his courtiers and continued aloud, "perhaps the queen's newfound interest in our only child has something to do with her inability to produce me a living male heir."

Silence befell the king's chambers, not even his fool Will Sommers daring to utter a single word. But then, much to everyone's relief, the king turned his attention back to Bessie.

"You may inform the queen that matters regarding our daughter are taken care of. She is to arrive within two days for her betrothal to the dauphin of France. As the queen surely knows."

"Yes, your majesty," Bessie replied, "But her grace means to speak with you in person about the princess. She says it is of great importance."

Henry furrowed his brows briefly but gestured for Bessie to come closer with a wave of his hand, "You may inform the queen that I am not opposed to speaking with her about our daughter. But it shall happen when I decide it, not because she

27

has summoned me," he said in a low voice, "Whatever sudden maternal instinct she may have developed for the girl does not interest me."

Bessie nodded as she looked up into the king's pale blue eyes and then, after a brief curtsy, she began to leave when the king suddenly held her by the arm, stopping her in her tracks.

"Visit my chambers again after you've tended to the queen tonight," he whispered hoarsely, his voice filled with desire.

The young girl flashed her king a hidden smile and left to tell the queen the good news that her husband had not entirely refused her request for a private audience, all the while burning up with lust at the prospect of entertaining the king of England once again that night.

December 1518

Princess Mary and her household arrived in London just a day before the French ships arrived on the shores of England, making it just in time to prepare for their meeting. At the age of just two years old, the little princess had no clear understanding of the situation at hand, knowing only that she would be promised in marriage to someone everyone kept calling "the dauphin of France".

But the little girl thought that, as long as she would get to see her lord father, she cared little for any other reasons for her to be summoned to court.

The following morning Mary awoke early in preparation for the grand occasion. Her governess, Margaret Pole the Countess of Salisbury, dressed her in a gown of cloth of gold and tucked her wispy auburn hair under a rich cap of black cloth. Around her neck and on her fingers, she placed half a dozen jewels and diamonds leaving Mary utterly mesmerized as they twinkled in the sunlight.

When they entered the great hall, the usher announced her to the court, his voice echoing through the high ceilings, and everyone turned to look at the little princess, the ladies curtsying and the gentlemen bowing, as she made her way through the throng of people.

As the sun shone through the stained-glass windows of the great hall, her mother and father appeared almost godlike as they sat upon their thrones.

Little Mary approached the king and queen quickly, her heart soaring at the sight of her father, and she offered him a cheery smile to which he replied with a little wink.

But then her heart sank as she carefully risked a peek at her mother, fully expecting to be met with her usual disdain, but was surprised to notice a warmth in her mother's eyes that she had not been prepared for.

Mary blinked with confusion as she climbed the steps to the thrones and curtsied elegantly to her mother and father in greeting, "Your majesties," she said prettily, and then she took her place beside her mother's throne, her governess close behind her as they awaited the arrival of the French.

Word came only moments later that their guests had arrived within the palace, and trumpets soon sounded to announce the noblemen's arrival.

The king's usher called out two gentlemen's names as they entered, and once they had approached, they took off their caps and bowed deeply at the waist.

"Your Majesties," said one of the bearded men in a heavy French accent, "I have come to ask for your consent to the marriage of our two nations."

King Henry rose from his throne, "I, King Henry VIII and my wife Queen Katherine of Aragon," he proclaimed, "do hereby give our consent to the betrothal of our daughter, the princess Mary, to the dauphin of France, and thereby joining our two great nations."

Mary watched in silence as her godfather, the Cardinal Wolsey, then approached the two men, his long red robes flowing with each step, and presented the one who had not yet spoken with a diamond ring.

The man then stepped closer to Mary, took her hand in his and placed the ring in the little palm of her chubby hand. Mary looked at the diamond ring in her palm, and then at the man's bearded face and frowned.

"Are you the dauphin of France?" she squeaked. The man smiled and opened his mouth to speak but before he was able to reply Mary continued, "I wish to kiss you," and she leaned forward and pecked the man on the cheek.

The courtiers all around gasped and laughed quietly as the princess smiled up at the two men before her, and then her father's booming laughter broke out from behind her, "That is not your new betrothed, Mary, it is the Lord Admiral of France. The dauphin of France is just an infant, and you won't be wed until you are both of age," the king roared with laughter again and tickled his daughter under her chin, "My beautiful Mary. What a splendid match we have made for you. One day you will be Queen of France! And with this marriage we will ensure that our Universal Peace Treaty be upheld."

Mary tried to understand what her father was saying but the words held no meaning for her, and so instead, she giggled as the king tickled her again.

"If she is to be queen of France we must prepare her," her mother suddenly said from behind her.

"Of course!" answered the king with a slight frown, and without another word to his queen, he announced, "To the main hall! Where we will continue this joyful celebration with a feast fit for the Queen of France herself!" and he roared with laughter at his own joke as he led the way out through the great archways, with his queen and daughter following closely behind.

March 1519

For a time, Mary felt as though she were the luckiest child in all of England. Upon her betrothal to the dauphin of France, she promptly began her studies of the French language and despite being only three years old, Mary was exceptionally quick to pick up the new vocabulary.

She would often receive praise from her lady mother, and on occasions when the weather permitted, they would take walks together in the gardens, where the early signs of Spring were becoming visible.

Mary did not know why her mother had suddenly started to take an interest in her, but she soaked in every kind word, every smile and every caress, in an effort to erase the past three years of disinterest and neglect. She even began to include a personal wish in her nightly prayers that soon there would come a time where she would no longer remembered how her lady mother used to look at her.

But sadly, Mary's stability was not meant to last, for the tidings of adult affairs continued even as children went on blissfully unaware.

June 1519

The scandal that befell England came to light in June when king Henry's mistress, the young Bessie Blount, gave birth to a strong and healthy baby boy.

The news spread all over London like wildfire, and it was not long before all of England had heard the news.

Though the princess Mary was but a young child she understood the significance of it – for this boy, despite being illegitimate, was a reminder that she was not one.

The king immediately laid his claim on the illegitimate child, naming the boy after himself, and therefore showing England – and the world – that despite being born a bastard, the boy would be acknowledged as Henry's own.

"This boy is proof, Wolsey," the king said to Cardinal Wolsey, hours before the child's christening, "He is proof that the fault never lay with me! I *can* bear sons!" the king sniffed excitedly and went on, "I am acknowledging him as mine. I must show the world that I, Henry VIII, am young and able to produce a male heir. This child is the proof, and I shall name him Henry Fitzroy."

The Cardinal bowed in agreement, "Fitzroy... *The son of the king*. It has a certain ring to it, your majesty. This undoubtedly implies there may be male heirs to follow."

Henry did not reply but simply stared out of the window for a time. After a long pause he inhaled deeply and turned to the Cardinal, "I am feeling rather triumphant, and I should like to officially announce my son's birth."

"Of course, your majesty," replied Cardinal Wolsey.

"See to it that arrangements are made for a lavish celebration. The queen is away at a banquet soon. Do it then."

The Cardinal bowed deeply in response and withdrew, leaving his king to ponder his newfound insight.

Henry returned to his place at the window and looked out over London, a self-satisfied grin spread across his pale face. He stood there for a long time, watching the world pass by, and never faltering as he repeated to himself under his breath, "I knew it wasn't my fault."

November 1519
Hatfield House, Hertfordshire

Since the birth of her father's bastard son, princess Mary had returned to her residence at Hatfield House in

Hertfordshire, just twenty-one miles north of the city of London, where she spent months without a word from either of her royal parents. The days in which she had been able to spend time with her lady mother were gone, and the usually easy affection her father had always shown her in forms of gifts or letters became less and less frequent.

While she knew that the illegitimate boy would never inherit the throne, she wondered if by simply being born male, that he meant more to her father than she did. Would her father so easily revoke the space in his heart he had always held for her, in place of this son, while completely disregarding his lack of rank and nobility?

Was she this easily forgotten?

Was a baseborn and illegitimate boy child all it took to replace her?

Mary felt more invisible and worthless with every passing day that went by without a word from either of them.

The glorious summer months went by in a repetitive blur. The leaves turned brown, and the days turned dark, and still Mary heard nothing from her mother or father.

And then, one day, as the snow fell thick and covered all the gardens outside with a smooth, white blanket, a messenger came.

"A letter from her majesty the queen," the messenger said as Mary's governess took it and peeled it open to read aloud to the little princess.

She cleared her throat, "It reads '*Dearest daughter, I heartily invite you to court for the Christmas celebrations. All my love, your lady mother, Katherine Regina.*'"

The messenger and her governess exchanged a quick, uneasy look at the briefness of the note, having had no mention of the months of solitude that Mary had endured, and certainly no question as to her well-being.

But Mary did not notice, for the words danced joyfully within her minds' eye.

All my love, your lady mother.

All my love.

All my love.

Her mother *did* love her, Mary had known it all along!

That night she went to bed and did not pray, for why would she need to?

Everything she had ever prayed for had this very day come true.

January 1520
Greenwich Palace, London

The king and queen shared very little conversation ever since Katherine's final pregnancy had ended in stillbirth, but what they shared much less of still was physical affection. As if Katherine's final confinement ending in tragedy had not been enough to force a wedge between her and her husband, her young lady, Bessie Blount, giving birth to a healthy son had been the final straw to break Henry's love for his wife.

Ever since the birth of Henry's baseborn son, Katherine felt that they had grown more distant than ever before. In fact, they had not shared a bed since the conception of their last child, and although it had been almost three years since, Katherine could not help but hope that her husband would one day return to her. But her childbearing days were behind her, and she knew in her heart that there was no going back to the marital bliss they had once shared in their earlier years.

These days, Katherine would content herself with what little attention she got from her husband, namely their once-weekly private supper together.

It was on one such occasion that Katherine saw a merriment in Henry that she knew would work in her favour, and she braved herself to broach a subject she had been eager to discuss for some time. "Henry, my love," she began, "I wish to discuss our daughter's education with you," and she offered him a gentle smile.

Henry wiped the back of his hand across his mouth and gestured with the other hand that she may continue.

Katherine went on, "Now that Mary is four years old, I would like to expand her education. I have consulted with Juan-Luis Vives to draw up an excellent programme on the education of girls. He calls it *De Institutione feminae Christianae,*" she reached for her cup and took a sip before continuing, "He is a humanist, as you are, my lord. And it is a remarkable programme, Henry, it includes all she may need to become a true model of feminine virtue."

Henry was quiet as he listened to his wife's request, for in all his years as king he had heard enough rambling to know that a point was yet to be made. He resumed eating as he watched his queen take another sip of wine, no doubt to steel herself for whatever reaction she thought he would have.

"It will include not only learning Latin and French," Katherine went on, "but also philosophy, music, history, as well as outdoor pursuits – hunting, falconry and archery."

Henry swallowed the greasy meat he had been chewing and grabbed his cup of wine, "Why would Mary need all these lessons?" Henry asked, "Archery?" he scoffed, "Whatever for!? It is not suitable for a girl."

Katherine watched as her husband looked down at his plate and picked at the sweetmeats, and she took a deep breath, "Henry, we must make her fit to rule. She is our only living heir," her voice had been barely above a whisper, but she knew Henry had heard.

She could see the colour rising up his neck as the rage inside him threatened to spill out, then he glanced around at the servants who stood nearby, still as statues but always listening.

Henry dropped the sweetmeats and laid his greasy hand out flat upon the table "Do you think me weak, wife?" he scowled.

"Henry," Katherine stammered as she looked up at him wide-eyed, "Why else would God have seen fit to take all our other babies from us?" she pleaded, "Lord knows I have given you many children, but don't you see? It is Mary. Our daughter was born to sit on the throne of England."

Katherine hoped he would understand and accept the truth as she had done, but the look on his face did nothing to suggest that he was willing to recognize what was right in front of him.

"This is not Spain, Katherine!" he snapped suddenly, "England expects a male heir! Princes and kings sit on the throne, not meek-minded women! I will not be the first King of England to pass his crown to a girl! What would the people think of me? I would be remembered forever as the Futile King!" he rubbed his hands over his red face, then ordered all the servants to leave.

"You forget your history, my lord," Katherine whispered bravely as the passion to defend herself and her daughter rose, "You would not be the first to leave his throne to a female heir. Henry I proclaimed his daughter Matilda as his inheritor."

"And she was overthrown," Henry replied swiftly with a wave of his hand, "By the very court that swore an oath of loyalty to her!" and he watched through narrowed eyes as the servants exited his chambers.

Katherine looked down at her untouched plate of food as she awaited his wrath, her heart beating loudly in her chest.

"Don't you understand?!" he hissed at her in a hoarse voice once they were alone, "The Tudor dynasty is but into its

36

second generation and already it fails? I am my father's only remaining heir! When Arthur died it all fell to me," and he reached for his cup of wine and swallowed its contents in one before wiping his hand over his mouth once more.

Then he leaned threateningly close into Katherine's face and whispered, "I will not be remembered for your failings, Katherine. I *have* a healthy boy. The deaths of our children were not *my* doing, and if you cannot provide me with a male heir then I shall find another way to ensure I leave England in the capable hands of a man. There will be no girl taking my throne!"

With that he stood up abruptly, his chair crashing backwards onto the ground. He cleared his throat and headed towards the door and as he yanked it open, he turned back to his wife, "You may commission this girls' programme from your Spanish humanist," he said loudly so that the servants waiting in the corridor could witness his generosity, "Mary may never rule England in her own right, but she will be the queen of France one day," and with that he sighed deeply and smiled, suddenly happy with his decision, "Yes, I like it. See to it that it's done."

Katherine exhaled the breath she had been holding and covered her face with her hands in shame. She had gained what she had hoped for her daughter's education, but at the expense of her own broken heart.

Chapter 3

May 1520
Greenwich Palace, London

"Will I get to meet my betrothed, the dauphin of France, lady mother?" Mary asked her mother while they were walking together in the palace gardens.

"No, Mary," the queen replies, "You are to stay here and look after England for us," she offered her daughter a bright smile, but the girl did not return it.

Instead, she sighed and said, "But I would so like to see France."

"Ah but this summit is to be held in Balinghem, my dear daughter," Katherine replied with a cheery smile, "which belongs to England. So, you are not missing a visit to France, because we too will not be in France."

While Mary was only four years old, she was aware that her mother was jesting with her, and that although Balinghem – a village located just southeast of Calais – belonged to England, it was still within the country of France.

But she knew that the decision had been made and no amount of pleading would change the king and queen's mind, and though Mary and her household were not to accompany them on this adventure, she would be left in nominal charge of the kingdom during their absence, which was by no means a small feat.

The royal procession of over five-thousand people departed England on the 31st of May and had been gone only two weeks when Mary received a letter from her mother the queen. Margaret Pole the Countess of Salisbury broke the royal seal and scanned the letter, her brows furrowing as she read it.

"What does it read, lady Pole?" Mary asked.

"Your grace, the queen writes that their arrival at Balighem has been a success but that the French king and his queen were not best please that your grace was not with them," Margaret Pole summarised, "Your lady mother writes that they may send envoys to check on your grace's health as they seemed concerned as to why you were not present. She urges you to maintain your composure and to entertain their concerns with the utmost care, for your betrothal may come in jeopardy if they fear you are feeble," the countess folded the letter and handed it to the princess, who merely stared at her mother's royal signature at the bottom.

"I shall be prepared for anyone that would visit me," Mary said, a cheerful smile brightening her pale face, "I know my duty."

The French ambassadors arrived at the English court without a word in advance, but the young princess received them cheerfully and with the utmost poise as she sat on her little makeshift throne in the great hall.

She welcomed them with such grace and obvious health that the French ambassadors were good enough to display their discomfort at their unannounced intrusions. They bowed apologetically as they began to retreat from the hall, but the little princess would not let the opportunity to impress pass her by.

"Please, *mon seigneurs,* do not trouble yourselves," princess Mary said chirpily in fluent French, "You did your duty to your king and queen. But now that you can see that I am in perfect health I ask that we put this behind us," and she waved her little hand before turning her attention to one of her ladies, "To celebrate this special visit I request strawberries to be served to my visitors," she said prettily, and her lady hurried out in pursuit of a kitchen maid.

"Now, gentlemen, let us be merry while you are here!" she declared happily as she rose from her little throne, "This visit need not be in vain," and she escorted them towards the virginal in the corner of the great hall. Then she took a seat at the great instrument and began to play a cheerful tune on the keyboard.

As her skilful performance went on, several servants entered carrying silver platters of strawberries which the French delegation eagerly enjoyed as they watched the little princess' proficient musical performance.

And so, when the French returned to their masters with nothing but cheerful news that the princess of England was not only well and full of life, but also as pretty and graceful as any princess of Europe, Mary took pride in knowing that she had done a great deed for her country by continuing to secure her betrothal to the dauphin of France and cementing the Peace Treaty that kept England safe.

May 1522

Two glorious years had passed since the Anglo-French summit at the Field of Cloth of Gold in Balinghem, where England and France had officially signed the Universal Peace Treaty and cemented their countries' friendship. Two steadfast years of certainty that Mary would one day be the queen of France and formally unite the two countries in peace.

In that time the little princess had perfected her grasp of the French language in preparation for that future, and though she had never visited the country or seen a portrait of her future husband, Mary would go to bed every night with the comforting knowledge that her future was secured.

But on a day like any other, while Mary was sitting by the window as her French tutor recited the day's lesson, there was a knock on the door and the queen entered the princess' chambers, bringing with her news that would alter Mary's entire life.

Mary stood up from her seat and smiled at her mother, "Good morning, lady mother," she offered her mother in faultless French.

The queen smiled, "Good morning, my darling daughter," she replied, her brown eyes shining with pride for her child, "I see your lessons are a success."

Mary's tutor bowed his head in thanks at the queen.

"To what do we owe this honour, mother?" Mary asked then, her eyebrows creased together with curiosity.

"It is nothing of concern, Mary," the queen replied, her Spanish accent suddenly more prominent, "I simply wished to see you now before our visitors arrive."

"Visitors?" Mary asked in confusion, "Are the French here again? Will I finally meet the boy who is to be my future husband, the dauphin of France?"

Katherine shook her head, "No, Mary," she said before looking over at the girl's French tutor and dismissing him with a small smile.

"I am sorry to tell you this, Mary," Katherine said once the tutor had exited the rooms, "but it seems you are never to meet the dauphin."

Mary, who had only recently turned six-years-old, furrowed her brow in confusion, "I do not understand."

Her mother sighed and sat down by the window, inviting her daughter to sit beside her.

"Your father the king is at war with France," she explained, "The Peace Treaty is broken, and with it your betrothal to the heir to the French throne."

Mary looked at her mother blankly. While she could not fully understand the whys or wherefores of these new circumstances, she knew that as the daughter of the king of

England, if her father and country were at war with France, then so would she be.

"If we are at war with France," she said in thought, "then I should not want to be betrothed to the dauphin," Mary simply said, her chin raised defiantly.

Her mother smiled encouragingly, "It was not to be, my darling daughter. But this is a valuable lesson for you, Mary. As a woman in this world, we do not make our own choices. We follow the rules of our king, and our God. And if our king declares the French prince is not to be your husband, then it must be God's will that you marry another."

Mary nodded enthusiastically at her mother's words, and she knew that she must be right.

"We shall make you a better match, Mary," Katherine said then as she stroked her cheek, and with that the queen stood and held her hand out to her daughter.

Mary took her mother's hand in hers and with her ladies following closely behind, they walked together out of the room.

"Am I not to continue my lessons today, lady mother?" the princess asked as they made their way through the corridor.

"No," Katherine replied, "today we have important visitors. My nephew, Charles V of Spain and Holy Roman Emperor, will arrive shortly."

Mary nodded once as though she understood, all the while having no idea who had arrived or why, but she was simply happy to be walking hand-in-hand with her mother. They made their way through the corridors and into the great hall where her mother and father would receive their guests, and as they entered, the courtiers bowed and curtsied in respect for their queen and princess. The crowd had gone silent as they cleared a path for them, and as Mary and Katherine climbed the steps to the thrones, Mary noticed that her father was not there to greet them; but the queen took her seat on her throne while Mary stood at her side, and they waited patiently.

The arrival of the two kings was heard before it was seen, and as they approached the throne room with great guffaw and merriment, Katherine rose from her throne, her usually anxious and heavy chest feeling slightly relieved by the joyful sounds of friendship between her husband and her nephew.

Though the war on France worried the queen immensely, Katherine had hope that Henry's newfound love for Spain, and what her country had to offer him, would aid him in his path back to her. For at this foul stage in her marriage, she would settle for any kind of reconciliation, even if only through political reconnection.

Mary watched from her place by her mother's throne as Katherine descended the steps and waited for the arrival of the two kings. The young princess stood elegantly as she waited, her head held high and her hands clasped together before her in a steady yet peaceful manner, the very image of her mother who stood before her in the exact same stance.

The two kings entered the great hall, their endless courtiers and ambassadors following closely behind, all seeming exceptionally merry, and Mary could hear her father's voice above all others, discussing the grandeur of his newly built warship, the Mary Rose. As the people of the court made a path for them to pass, the kings' attentions turned to Katherine who had begun slowly walking towards them.

The king of Spain approached his aunt with outstretched arms and a warm smile on his face, "My dear aunt!" he said and then kneeled before her, "I ask for your blessing."

Mary watched as her mother placed her hand gently on the Holy Roman Emperor's head, and when the Spanish king rose once again, she could not help but notice the man's misshapen jawline. She stared in wonder at the oversized chin as he and her mother spoke and was only made aware of her staring when her father flashed her a knowing grin and sneakily pushed out his own chin in mockery, making Mary giggle quietly.

Behind her, Margaret Pole cleared her throat, communicating to Mary to behave and the princess instantly regained her composure.

As soon as both the king and queen of England had taken their places upon their thrones, Henry cleared his throat.

"We welcome you, king Charles of Spain and Holy Roman Emperor, to England," he stated proudly, and the Spanish court all bowed their heads in thanks as the king continued, "we are honoured at your visit and welcome you to our court and country. We are also honoured to announce that England and Spain will be joining forces against the French in the hopes of regaining our rightful lands!" Henry paused and scanned the room, "To seal this treaty between our two countries, queen Katherine of Aragon and I offer you, king Charles V of Spain and Holy Roman Emperor, our daughter the princess Mary, in marriage."

Mary's eyes widened in shock at her father's announcement, feeling both bewildered and betrayed. But she had little time to ponder her emotions, for all eyes of the court were on her, smiling, clapping and bowing their head, and she could feel her governess' hand on her shoulder prompting her to approach the hideous king of Spain.

She took one uncertain step toward the Spanish king, a man she had never met before, and then quickly looked back at her parents, who were smiling at her as if this was the most natural thing in the world.

She must have looked aghast, for her mother offered her a reassuring look, which inevitably inspired Mary to remember who she was. She swallowed her horror and with a deep inhale she offered the king of Spain a glowing smile before curtsying as low as she could.

"It is my great joy to see you, princess Mary," said king Charles.

"The joy and honour is mine, my lord," Mary replied gracefully, while her mind reeled with dread.

At her reply, the king of Spain and his courtiers expressed their delight at her poise, murmuring approvingly amongst each other.

"How old are you, cousin?" the little girl then said as her curiosity overwhelmed her.

Immediately the king before her laughed, his black moustache dancing above his lip, "Oh Mary I know I must look like an old man to you but do not fret, we are not to wed until you are of age."

Mary curtsied again, "Then I shall be honoured to one day become queen of Spain," and she turned to resume her place beside her mother, her heart pounding uncontrollably in her chest.

Her governess squeezed her shoulder gently in reassurance as she stood behind her young ward, but Mary stood as still as a statue for fear she would reveal her true emotions before everyone and bring shame upon her house.

She was vaguely aware of her father giving another speech, but Mary could hear nothing but the rushing of her blood in her ears as it pumped rapidly through her body, urging her to pick up her skirts and flee. But she stood frozen in place and watched as her father spoke, spittle escaping his mouth with the passion of his words of war. She watched as the Spanish king nodded in agreement at her father's words, and Mary fixed her gaze at his overly proportioned chin, unable to peel her eyes away from it this time.

After what had felt like an age, her father finally announced the banquet, and her parents rose from their thrones.

During the festivities everyone was cheerful but Mary. She could not understand how her mother and father had not

45

prepared her for such a momentous occasion regarding her future, and how they could have ambushed her in such a manner. Their betrayal left her unable to eat, and while she knew her father was rash and spontaneous, it seemed almost uncouth to allow her to be made a spectacle of before the entire court – and as she sat at the high table beside her mother, her stomach began to turn with humiliation.

The evening continued merrily as everyone ate, drank, and danced, and then, as the servants began clearing away the empty plates, her moustached betrothed rose from his seat beside her father and clapped his hands together.

"I have an announcement to make!" he called, and the room fell silent, the musicians abruptly ending their song.

"I have a gift," he continued, "For the princess Mary on our engagement," and he turned in direction of the great hall's main entrance, where a little pony was being brought in by a stable boy.

Mary gasped, her pale blue eyes wide with excitement as she hopped off her seat and hurried towards the animal, the betrayal she felt towards her father quickly forgotten.

"Thank you, my lord!" she said as she looked back at her cousin.

She imagined herself as the future queen of Spain then and was relieved to realise that she would not be entirely opposed to it.

As the daughter of their very own princess of Aragon, and granddaughter of the mighty Isabella of Castille, Mary would surely be loved by the people of Spain.

Though she was still hesitant that her betrothed was so much older than her, she would do her duty.

And all she could do was pray that he would be kind.

Unbeknownst to the princess Mary, king Henry and his council were busy discussing the details of their newly attained peace treaty with Spain, and the upcoming war on France that would be made possible because of it.

"The republic of Venice and the Swiss have been sent invitations to enter our league," Henry said to his councillors as he sifted through the documents before him, "as agreed by myself and king Charles of Spain, we hope to have word from them soon to strengthen our alliance further."

"And what of the Pope, your majesty?" Cardinal Wolsey asked from his seat at the council table.

"Pope Adrian VI has always been a friend to us," Henry replied, "and we have sent ambassadors to him to ask if he will become the head of our league. It is all going to plan, gentlemen. Soon we will rage war on France!"

The councilmen banged their fists on the table as they cheered the king, but Henry noticed that one of his advisors did not join in the cries of admiration, "What do you say, Thomas?" he called across the table at his friend and advisor, Sir Thomas Moore.

Sir Thomas Moore was a man of many talents. As a lawyer, social philosopher, author and the king's lifelong friend, his opinion mattered a great deal to Henry. He and the king shared a liking of many things, and both were passionate about the stance on humanism: a belief that stood for the building of a more humane and democratic society, where ethics were judged by the consequences of human actions, and where the well-being of all life on Earth was priority. It was because of his strong stance on humanism, that Sir Thomas Moore did not join in the celebration of this war on France, and he could not fully understand Henry's need for it.

Moore raised his head and met his king's stare calmly, "I am your majesty's humble servant, as always," he said, his dark eyes blinking back at Henry, "But I am opposed to this war, Henry. I will not pretend to think otherwise."

The king pressed his finger and thumb into the corners of his eyes in irritation.

"How can you justify the thousands of deaths that will come from this, Henry?" Moore continued, "Land? Glory?"

"Exactly," Henry replied with a grin.

"It is not right," Sir Thomas Moore said bravely.

Cardinal Wolsey watched their back-and-forth gleefully, his sly face looking far too amused by the discussion for Moore's liking.

Henry stared back at him; the room having gone completely silent.

When the silence continued, and the members of the council began to shift uncomfortably in their seats, Thomas decided on another tactic, "What of the marriage between the princess Mary and king Charles?" he said, "Should we not at least wait until they are wed to ensure Spain's loyalty?"

Henry licked his lips and sighed, "Mary and he will not be wed for six years, Thomas!"

"It would give your majesty time to reconsider this needless war," Thomas Moore said as he scoffed.

Henry narrowed his eyes threateningly as he looked back at Sir Thomas, but once again he offered no reply, and the room went deathly still.

In an effort to push forward from the disagreement, Cardinal Wolsey raised his bushy grey eyebrows and interjected.

"If I may be so bold as to point out, your majesty," he said with a slight smirk, "that while I know Mr Moore is thinking of the people's best interests, we have no time to waste. King Charles is as adamant for this war as we are, and it would be dangerous for the sake of the treaty with Spain to ask him to wait until the princess is of age to wed before we invade."

"Wolsey is right, Thomas," Henry replied immediately, "Sometimes we must sacrifice the few to achieve eternal glory. English soldiers would gladly give their life for this."

48

Thomas Moore stared blankly ahead as the council moved on to the next matter of state. He had done what he could. He had spoken up for what he thought was right in an effort to open his king's eyes to the needlessness of this invasion, and only some years ago, Thomas could have said with absolute certainty that Henry would have agreed.

But Wolsey had dripped his poison in the king's ear for far too long, and no matter how reasonable anyone's argument may be, if Wolsey disagreed, then his word was final.

1525

The war on France had been a disaster.

Strategically, Henry had had much leaning to his advantage during the design of the invasion two years earlier, but their alliance with Spain had not been enough.

Their great supporter and head of their league, Pope Adrian VI had suddenly died and when his successor Clement VII did not agree to finance the supplies for the English troops, it left king Henry with no other choice but to withdraw his soldiers.

It had been a hopeless cause, one which caused much disappointment, leaving Henry feeling defeated and unaccomplished; and without a war to distract and fulfil him, Henry soon realised that if his goal to achieving eternal glory would not come from a great battle, then he would have to ensure his name lived on through his heir.

It was now undeniable that the queen's ability to bear fruit was well and truly behind her, and so Henry was left to determine which of his two surviving children he would choose to name as his successor.

Henry struggled to agree with what his Spanish wife had been trying to make him consider for years – that England was ready for a female ruler – and while he knew in his heart that the only acceptable answer for his heir to be his only

49

legitimate child, the princess Mary, he could not bring himself to accept that *she* was his only option.

Above all else, he could not begin to imagine the shame of being the first king in the history of England to leave the country in the protection of a feeble woman.

He battled within himself against what he knew would be the correct thing, and what he would prefer to do, and when he was unable to come to a conclusion by himself, Henry summoned his old friend Sir Thomas Moore.

Moore entered the king's chambers to find his friend sitting by the fire in such a pensive state that he had not noticed Thomas' arrival. The room was dimly lit, the only light being that of the flickering flames in the fireplace, which cast a wide shadow upon the opposite wall as the king sat hunched over before it.

Thomas cleared his throat, "Your majesty, you asked for me?"

Henry sat upright as he looked at him but did not stand up, "Ah, Thomas!" the king said, "pour yourself a cup of small ale and sit with me."

Thomas did as he was commanded and took a seat beside Henry by the fire, "To what do I owe the pleasure of my lord's private company?" he said with a small smile.

"Thomas," Henry said with a sigh, "I am in two minds about who I should name my successor. And I need your judgment."

Thomas' dark eyebrows creased together in confusion, "Your grace, who could you be choosing between? The princess Mary –"

"– don't you see, Thomas?" the king interrupted excitedly, "I *have* a son. Henry Fitzroy. He could be my heir."

Thomas let out a short, breathy laugh, so shocked he could not contain his bewilderment.

"Forgive me, Henry, but you cannot overlook a legitimate child for an illegitimate one. Son or no."

"But that's the thing," Henry replied as he shook his finger in the air, "I could have him legitimized. It is being done all over Europe."

Thomas fell silent for a moment in which he carefully chose his next words, "My lord, the people of England would not accept your son by Bessie Blount as the next king," he paused and swallowed, fearing his friend's temper, "There is too much love for the queen and the princess. To choose your illegitimate son by your mistress over your legitimate and royal daughter by the queen would cause uproar. It could even mean war with Spain at the insult."

Henry looked back into the flames and sniffed irritably and when he did not reply, Thomas continued.

"While your majesty could legitimize the boy," he said carefully, "it would not bring an end to what you seek. I know you've long yearned for a son by the queen, but perhaps this is the way of God."

Henry scoffed and shook his head before taking a long pull of his small ale.

They sat in silence for a long time in which Thomas hoped his words had been enough for his king to see reason. To name his bastard boy his heir would bring civil unrest as well as a potential war with Spain that England could not win. The queen would never accept the insult and for the years to come would potentially plot to overthrow the boy to place her daughter on her rightful throne.

While he understood the king's need to name his only living boy his heir, it would not be accepted.

The two men sat for some time in an awkward silence while the king considered Thomas' words. Then he rose from his seat and looked down at his friend

"Thank you, Thomas," he said, patting his friend on the shoulder, "You are a good friend, and I am grateful for your advice."

Thomas stood up and smiled, "I am glad to be of use to your majesty."

Sir Thomas Moore left the king's chambers feeling honoured to have aided the king in seeing the light on this matter, but while he believed that he had managed to play a part in avoiding chaos, he had a disturbing feeling that this would not be the end of Henry's need to bend the rules of God, in pursuit of a male heir.

Chapter 4

1525
Greenwich Palace, London

Six months later, on an afternoon much like any other, the nine-year-old princess Mary was busying herself with her needlework, surrounded by her ladies and her governess Margaret Pole, when the doors to her chambers were opened and the queen was announced.

They all rose and curtsied to Katherine as she swiftly approached and took her daughter by the hand, guiding her towards the window to speak with Mary in private.

"What is it, mother?" Mary said, her red eyebrows creased together in shock at the sudden interruption.

"*Hija,* there is news," said Katherine, her tone solemn as she whispered hoarsely.

Immediately, Mary feared for the worst, "Is it my lord father? Is he unwell?" her pale blue eyes wide with worry.

"No, Mary," her mother replied, shaking her head, "The king is well. He is with his council now, discussing your future as his heir."

Mary's eyebrows shot up in amazement and she fell silent while she pondered the enormity of the information, "But this is good news, is it not, mother?" the princess asked as she reflected on her mother's sombre tone, "is this not what you have always wanted for me?"

At that Katherine smiled and raised her hand to stroke her daughter's cheek, "My darling daughter," was all she said.

Mary reached up and took her mother's hand in hers, "Whatever is troubling you, mother, it will be alright."

Katherine simply gazed into her daughter's eyes as if she was scared to forget their colour, a sad smile pulling at the corners of her lips. But then she inhaled deeply, straightened up and regained her composure.

"You are to be sent to Ludlow, Mary," Katherine announced proudly.

"Ludlow, in Wales?" asked the princess.

Katherine nodded, "You are to preside over the Prince's Council. It is the custom for the Prince of Wales, and as his majesty has no prince, he has chosen you, Mary, to go instead."

Though Mary was only nine years old she understood the significance of such an honour. Never had a girl been sent where only previously princes of Wales had gone.

"But then why are you sad, mother?" Mary asked.

"Because I cannot go with you," Katherine replied, "Once you depart, I shall not see you for a long time, and it pains me to be away from you, *mi querida.*"

"Mother," Mary soothed as she embraced her mother, "I shall write you every day and visit you whenever I am permitted."

Mary squeezed her usually stoic mother, then offered her a reassuring smile.

Katherine looked down at her little daughter's face, "I am so proud of you, Mary," she said as she tucked a stray strand of Mary's hair back under her hood, "You were sent to me by God Himself. And one day you will rule over England. I have known it since you were a little girl, and it is now coming to pass. I just wished I had known it sooner. It would have spared us both so much pain."

There was a hubbub around the palace for days as preparations were being made for the princess' journey to Ludlow Castle in Wales.

Her ladies packed her dresses and all her silks and textiles, the Lady Margaret Pole organised for Mary's tutors to arrive at

Ludlow within a week of their own, and king Henry had sent servants to heat and clean the castle before his daughter's arrival.

On the day of Mary's departure, as her household were saddling their horses and preparing the wagons for travel, Katherine stood with Mary by the Palace gates, eager to spend every last moment together before their separation.

"Mary, you must remember to study your Latin each day," the queen said as they watched the servants lifting the travel trunks onto the wagons.

"Yes, lady mother," Mary replied.

"And write to me."

"Of course, lady mother. Every day," Mary promised.

Then the queen smiled and sighed, "But above all else," she said, "you must never forget who you are."

Mary merely nodded in reply, unable to understand her mother's remark, for while she was being blinded by the gift her father had lain before her, Mary was completely unaware that her parent's marriage was crumbling, and that Henry VIII had turned his beady eyed gaze to another lady at court.

Anne Boleyn.

May 1525
Ludlow, Wales

As the royal party made its slow ascent through the town of Ludlow and its bustling marketplace, curious onlookers began to gather.

By now, rumours had spread throughout the country that their king had not named his legitimate daughter to succeed him but had secretly legitimised his mistresses' bastard boy and sent him in the princess' stead to Ludlow Castle, to begin his princely duties. And so, when the royal company finally arrived, the people of Wales were curious to sneak a peek at who was truly riding in the royal carriage on their way to preside over the Prince's Council.

The princess Mary, equally as curious of her new surroundings as the people of Ludlow were of their arrival, looked out of the window of her wagon as dozens of curious faces searched the carriages for a sign of their beloved princess. As people caught sight of her and word spread through the crowd that it was in fact the royal princess who would take up residence in Ludlow Castle, and not the king's bastard boy, many cheered and waved with delight.

Mary smiled and waved at the crowd that had gathered, but then felt suddenly overwhelmed by the close proximity of so many people, all of which expected so much of her, and she shrank away from the open window and edged closer to her governess, who sat calmly in the centre of the carriage.

Margaret Pole smiled down at her young ward.

"Never fear, princess," she said, her soothing voice comforting Mary instantly, "The people are happy to see you. In fact, all this commotion reminds me of when I came here with your mother, over twenty years ago."

"With my mother?" asked the princess, suddenly extremely interested.

"When she and prince Arthur were wed," Margate Pole said casually. Mary furrowed her brow in confusion, but her governess went on, "Before your father married your mother, she was betrothed to your late uncle, prince Arthur, from a very young age. And shortly after he and your mother were married, they travelled up here to begin their royal tour as the next king and queen in line to the English throne."

Mary raised her eyebrows and blinked in surprise, "I did not know my lady mother was married before she wed my father," she said, "I have heard stories of my uncle Arthur, and that he died tragically of the Sweating sickness."

"That is correct," Margaret Pole nodded.

56

"But I do not understand," Mary went on, "How can my mother have married my father after she had been wed to Uncle Arthur? It goes against the laws of God to marry your brother's wife…"

"Ah," Margaret said as she waved her hand, as though she would clear the air of the insinuation, "It is nothing to concern yourself with, princess. I was merely thinking out loud."

Mary sat back in her seat in the carriage and frowned. If what her governess said was true, then according to the laws of God, her mother and father should never have married.

As her uncle's wife, Mary's mother could not have been promised to Henry, even after Arthur's death. So then why – and more importantly, *how* – had her parents been allowed to wed despite that?

But before Mary could breathe life into her uncertainties, a guard rode up beside their wagon and announced that they would be approaching Ludlow Castle very soon and the princess' curiosities about her parent's union dispersed into the wind.

As they approached the magnificent castle and made their way through the gatehouse, they emerged through to the vast outer bailey. The surroundings were considerable, containing stables, storehouses, and workshops, and Mary looked about herself in awe.

The princess' carriage came to a halt and as Mary and her governess gathered up their fur blankets, they could hear commotion all around them as orders were being barked at servants and the guards dismounted their horses, their heavy boots thumping loudly upon the ground.

When Mary emerged from her wagon, she breathed the fresh air deeply into her lungs and smiled as she took in her surroundings.

"Come now, Mary," said her governess as the servants began heaving their trunks off the carriages, "Plenty of time to

57

look around. Now we must get inside and warm up. Let me show you to your royal apartments."

They walked through a beautiful arched entrance and made their way through the great hall and up a spiral staircase to the uppermost storey where the royal apartments were.

"These are your chambers, princess," Margaret said as she threw open the heavy wooden doors and entered a warmly decorated and open room.

Mary entered and nodded approvingly as she took in the high ceilings and beautiful tapestries that hung on all the walls. On the far wall was a great, four-poster bed with an upholstered seat at the foot of it, and at the wall opposite was a magnificently stone carved fireplace, and Mary was relieved to see a roaring fire blazing within it.

She immediately took off her furs and made her way towards the fire, "Come, Lady Pole," Mary said to her governess, "Sit with me by the fire for a while."

They both sat before the fire for some time in silent companionship, rubbing their hands together or simply watching the flames flicker, but then Margaret sat back in her seat, took a look around the chambers and sighed.

"What is it?" the princess asked.

"It's nothing, Mary," she replied, "These chambers just remind me of prince Arthur. These were his royal apartments during his time here."

"When you were here with Uncle Arthur and my mother?" Mary asked, hoping to learn more.

"Yes," Margaret replied with a sad smile, "It feels like a whole other lifetime ago."

"Lady Pole," Mary then said as she tried to appear indifferent, "Could you tell me more about that time? I would love to know more of the recent history surrounding this place."

"Ah, Mary," Margaret Pole said, "We mustn't dwell on what was."

"But I am curious," Mary continued, desperate to understand, "how it came to be that my mother married my uncle and then my father," her eyes searched her governess' face for a reaction, "How did it come to be allowed by the Pope?"

The countess cleared her throat and dropped her gaze, focusing instead on the dancing flames in the hearth before her.

"It was a strange time after Arthur died, Mary" she said distantly, "It was so sudden, and the country was in great mourning. But none more so that your grandmother, queen Elizabeth. She was with child at the time of Arthur's death, and the sorrow brought on an early labour. But the poor babe was already dead before it had been born, and with the grief and distress of it all, the queen died that same day," Margaret looked back at the young princess and offered her a sad smile, "They were very sad times, Mary, and the king, your grandfather was left utterly heartbroken. He had lost his eldest son and heir, his beloved wife, and his unborn child all at once. But the country was in financial ruin, and the only thing that would keep it afloat was the money from the young infanta's dowry."

"My mother's marriage dowry," Mary said, "Did her father not send it as soon as she and Arthur had been wed?"

Margaret shook her head, "No," she said, raising an eyebrow, "Your mother's father, king Ferdinand of Spain, was not a trustworthy man," and she paused for a moment and cleared her throat, "But, with the king needing Spain's financial aid, as well as a new queen, the newly widowed king had a choice to make and he announced that he would wed the young infanta himself."

"What?" Mary gasped and shook her head, unable to wrap her head around what she was hearing.

Margaret raised her eyebrows and released one short, breathy laugh, "All you need to understand is that, when your grandfather announced his betrothal to the infanta of Spain, there were conflicting reactions, mainly that of the king's only remaining son, your father."

"My father wanted to marry the Spanish infanta…" Mary said dreamily, immersed in her parent's love story.

"Correct," Margaret said with a smile, her long nose crinkling with affection for the young princess, "Your father spoke up of his wish to marry your mother, but of course, as you yourself have pointed out, it would go against the laws of God."

"Then how?" Mary asked as she propped her hand under her chin as she listened intently.

Margaret raised her eyebrows and inhaled deeply, "According to your mother, her marriage to Arthur had never been a full one."

Mary frowned, "Not a full one?"

Margaret nodded, "She claimed that because she and your uncle had been so young and he so sickly, that their marriage had never been consummated. And therefore, she was never truly his wife."

"But they were married for months, were they not?" the young princess pointed out.

Margaret shrugged her slender shoulders, "It is what your mother claimed, and your father believed her," she said simply, "And with the Pope's dispensation to allow their union, your parents were married."

Mary sat back in her chair wide-eyed, "That is quite a love story."

The countess of Salisbury nodded slowly at Mary, "Quite," she agreed and they sat in silence one again, both in their own thoughts, "But," Margaret then said as she sat up and clapped her hands together, "let's not dwell on what was. These rooms remind me of a time long ago but now they are yours, Mary, and we shall make new and happier memories, yes?"

Mary smiled at her governess and felt a wave of excitement flood through her.

Although she had been uneasy parting from her mother, she took comfort in the knowledge that it had been here where her mother's journey to the throne of England had begun. And as Mary stood from her seat by the fire and soaked in her beautiful surroundings, she thanked God that she had been chosen to follow in her mother's footsteps.

June 1525

The first letter Mary would receive at Ludlow castle was one that carried disturbing news.

In her absence, her father had had his bastard boy elevated into Dukedom and given him the semi-regal title of Duke of Richmond and Somerset, as well as President of the council of the North.

As soon as Mary had finished reading the letter, her vision blurred with hot tears threatening to spill as she stared down at the parchment in her hands. But before anyone noticed her distress, she blinked them away using every ounce of her energy.

By now her ladies had crowded her as they wondered what news had come from London, but Mary scrunched up the paper and tossed it into the hearth.

"It is nothing of importance," Mary said icily as she raised her chin, "Only the futile ascension of Bessie Blount's bastard into Dukedom."

But later that day when Mary was alone with Margaret Pole, she was brave enough to voice her concerns.

"Why would my father do this just as I have left London?" she cried, "Does he mean to slowly replace me with that poorly educated nobody?"

"Of course not, princess," her governess soothed.

"Can my father not forget his need for a boy heir?" Mary continued, uneasily, "Am I not enough?"

Margaret *tsked* and took Mary's hand, "Hush now, child. Your father is a king," she said as way of explanation, "His want for a male heir will always be heavy on his conscience. But he has *you* instead, and that is better than any male heir," she smiled at her young ward, "He just needs more time to fully accept that, and in the meantime, he is showering this boy with titles. But it doesn't make him worthy to ascend the throne in your stead. You are the king's only legitimate child, never forget that, Mary."

Mary sniffed as she realised the tears she had been holding in all day had finally spilled over, and she wiped them away angrily.

Margaret went on, "The king sent *you* here. Not the boy. He and God have big plans for you, Mary. These titles and gifts are all that the king can give the child. But they mean nothing," she offered Mary a reassuring smile and squeezed her hand, "Now come. Your tutors await you."

The princess stood and breathed in deeply, swallowing the last of the tears, "You are right of course, Lady Pole," and she dabbed at her eyes with her handkerchief, "My father may lay titles before the bastard's feet and call him son, but I am his true heir. I am the daughter of England and Spain. And that is something no one can take away from me."

18th February 1526

It was the morning of Mary's tenth birthday, and as soon as she opened her eyes and saw daylight peeking over the sill of her windows, she threw off her covers and jumped out of bed.

There was no time to waste. Mary had only this one day of freedom from her daily lessons and duties, and she would not be spending it cooped up indoors.

"Wake up, Cecily!" Mary sang as she skipped across the room to her ladies' beds, "Frances! It is morning!"

"Barely," her twelve-year-old lady-in-waiting, Cecily, mumbled as she rubbed the sleep from her eyes and stretched, but Mary only laughed, for nothing would dampen her mood today.

The lady Cecily, while still in her nightshift, padded barefoot to the door, opened it a crack, and requested for a servant to bring a plate of food up for Mary, and to send a message to the stables to ready the horses.

Her ladies quickly readied themselves while Mary sat by the window eating her breakfast of dried fruit and cheese and watching the cold winter sun becoming brighter. Then, as the servants entered the princess' chambers to stoke the burnt-out fire, Cecily dressed Mary in her riding gear while Frances picked at her knotted plait and then pinned Mary's auburn hair under her riding hat.

As soon as she was dressed, Mary and her ladies hurried out of her chambers and down the spiral staircase to the great hall below.

"Your riding gloves, your highness," Frances then called as she hurried to catch up with the princess.

"Thank you, Frances," Mary replied, looking over her shoulder and turning to reach as she blindly continued ahead. And then suddenly, as she turned the corner towards the gated archway, she collided head on with one of the servants.

"Your grace, I'm so sorry," the servant boy yelped in horror as he saw the princess crumpled on the floor, "It was all me fault, I'm so sorry! Please let me 'elp you up," and he stretched out his hand.

"Remember your place!" Cecily hissed at him as she knelt down beside Mary, and the boy flinched and retracted his hand.

The boy took a step back to give her ladies space to help Mary to her feet before continuing on in his fearful babbling, "Forgive me, your grace, t'was an accident. I wasn't looking – "

"It is alright," Mary interrupted as she stood, her hand pressed over her eye and forehead.

"Should I get the physician, princess?" the boy asked as he watched the princess' ladies fretting over her.

"No, no," Mary said, waving her ladies away from her, "I'm alright. Please let me pass."

She sidestepped him awkwardly, her head banging in pain as she looked ahead and into the bright sunlight.

"I am alright too," she heard the boy's voice suddenly call from behind her and she turned around in shock, "Don't fret, ya grace, I am well," and the servant boy bowed theatrically as her ladies gasped in horror at his crassness. But then he flashed her a mischievous grin before disappearing back into the castle. Mary could do nothing but scoff in disbelief as she was left utterly speechless by the strange encounter.

Later that day, as the sun began its descent, Mary and her group returned through the castle gates, pulling behind them a wagon carrying a dead boar and six rabbits caught during their hunt – three of which Mary had dealt the killing shot to, thanks to the archery lessons her mother had insisted on.

The princess' court was merry that evening as the music played in continuum and the wine flowed freely, and yet all too soon, the hours had passed by in a jolly blur and her courtiers had one by one returned to their chambers for the night.

"It is late, your grace," the countess of Salisbury told the princess as they sat side by side at the high table of her little court, "Perhaps it is time to dismiss the musicians?"

Mary looked around and saw, as if for the first time, the vastness of the great hall of Ludlow castle. She looked around herself in amazement, the several cups of sweet wine she had had throughout the night enhancing the castle's beauty, "It's so magnificent here, isn't it Lady Pole?" Mary said dreamily.

"Yes," Margaret chuckled, "It is marvellous. Now come, your grace, the day is at an end," and she waved the princess' ladies over to help Mary up the spiral staircase to her chambers.

Mary stood and clapped her hands, signalling for the music to be stopped, "You are dismissed," she announced to the remaining servants and musicians, who all breathed a sigh of relief.

As Mary and her ladies arrived at her chambers, Cecily untied Mary's bodice and removed the pins and hood from the princess' head and Mary sighed with relief as her long hair tumbled freely over her shoulders. She ran her fingers through her hair and massaged her scalp, "The pins were so tight tonight," she mumbled, and Cecily offered her a sympathetic smile.

Then, as the exhaustion overcame Mary, she climbed into bed and watched as Frances stocked the fire that had burned down into embers, and as she watched she remembered the curious encounter she had had with the servant boy that morning, "Frances, do you know all the servants?"

Frances straightened up from her task and turned to face the princess.

"My lady there are hundreds of servants in the castle," she said with a small laugh, "I cannot know them all. Is there someone in particular you wish to enquire about?"

"The boy from this morning."

"The clumsy fool?" Cecily called from across the room, one eyebrow shooting up in disdain.

"Him," Mary said as she nodded her head at Cecily.

Frances shook her head, "I do not know him, your grace," she said.

Mary shrugged as she stifled a yawn, "It is of no importance," she said, but as she lay her head down on her pillow, she could not help but wonder about the impertinent young boy she had met, and how freeing it must feel to live each day without the heavy weight of the world on one's shoulders.

March 1526

The rain that fell over Ludlow came pouring down with a vengeance, and for two straight weeks it felt as though Mary would never again see the sunshine.

The dark and gloomy days seemed to stretch on into one continuous loop of methodical routine and unshakable boredom, and as Mary endured yet another long Latin lesson, she found herself beginning to daydream.

"Princess!" her tutor called as he clapped his hands together sharply, making Mary jolt in her seat, "It is not the time for ignorance. It is the time for learning!" he snapped, noticing her obvious lack of interest.

"Yes Dr Fetherstone," Mary replied shakily, as she returned her gaze to the work ahead.

But every minute that ticked by felt like an hour, and no matter how hard Mary tried, she could barely keep her eyes open; and fearing another explosive lambasting, she cleared her throat and looked up innocently at her ghastly tutor.

"Sir, you must forgive me," Mary said, her voice the sweetest tone she could muster, "But I am in need of my ladies' services."

"Whatever is the matter, your grace?" her tutor asked, baffled at her curious behaviour, "The queen will request your Latin work to be sent to her! What shall I tell her when there is no news of your improvement?"

"Dr Fetherstone," Mary said quietly as she stood and took a step towards the elderly tutor, hanging her head in mock shame, "this is a matter of feminine discretion but if you must know, I need aid with my bodice - it is too tight, and I am struggling to breathe."

At the mention of her royal highness' bodice, the elderly tutor visibly reddened in discomfort and took a step back from the young princess. Mary watched as he ran his slender fingers through his grey hair awkwardly and she pressed her lips together to avoid breaking out into laughter at the man's obvious embarrassment.

With a wave of his hand, Dr Fetherstone allowed her to leave as he muttered incoherently under his breath, and Mary grasped the opportunity, quickly fleeing from the room with her ladies following hastily behind her.

Once far enough down the dark corridor, Mary stopped to catch her breath at one of the lit torches that hung on the wall, turned to her ladies and laughed.

"Your highness," Cecily said as she caught up to Mary, "Let's retreat to your chambers so we may loosen your bodice."

Mary waved her hand in the air, "I am well, Cecily," she admitted and gave another little laugh.

"Can you not tell a farce when you see one, Cecily," Frances said beside her as she joined Mary in her giggles.

Cecily shook her head as she realised her naivete.

67

"Ladies," Mary then said, her face half-lit by the flickering torch, "You are dismissed for now. Return to my chambers and await either for my return or for when Dr Fetherstone comes looking for me. I wish to simply be free for a moment."

Frances nodded wide-eyed as Cecily raised one sharp eyebrow, but both did as Mary bid and walked away as Mary picked up her skirts and ran off down the spiral staircase, eager to get as far away from her duties as possible.

Mary snuck through the great hall unseen, rushing from one pillar to another as a handful of courtiers laughed and flirted in a corner, completely oblivious to their surroundings.

Then she turned down into a small stone staircase and frowned as she realised that she had never noticed it before.

As Mary slowly continued down the dark staircase, she noticed it getting colder with each step, and when she suddenly saw the flicker of a candle and heard the sound of footsteps approaching, her heart jolted inside her chest as she feared being caught and dragged back to her agonizing Latin lesson. Mary turned around and quickly picked up her skirts in the hopes of escaping unseen, but before she could reach the top of the stairs a voice called out from below, "Ya grace! Are you lost?"

At the sound of the servant boy's voice, Mary turned around, his unmistakable dialect being hard to forget, "You!" she said, her eyebrows crinkling.

Upon reaching Mary at the top of the stairwell the boy bowed deeply, but Mary was not entirely convinced that it was not in mockery.

"My lady," he said, and Mary crossed her arms defensively.

"You have some nerve addressing me as such," Mary said as she raised her chin arrogantly, "I am 'Your grace' or 'Princess' to you."

"Forgive me, your grace," the boy said as he grinned, "May I help you wi' anythin'?"

68

"No."

"Then may I ask why your grace was a-wanderin' down to the servants' quarters?" he asked, unable to contain his obvious entertainment at the princess' self-importance.

"It is none of your concern what a princess does or does not do," Mary replied, her cheeks blushing with embarrassment at being caught out.

"I am only lookin' out for your grace's safety," the boy said with an exaggerated bow at the waist.

Mary opened her mouth to scold him for his disrespectful nature when she suddenly heard her tutor calling for her in the distance.

"Quick!" she hissed instead, "I must hide!" and she began to turn when the servant boy suddenly grabbed her by the wrist and pulled her behind him into the darkened staircase they had just emerged from. The boy blew out the candle he had been holding and the darkness engulfed them. They remained there, unmoving, until Dr Fetherstone walked past, huffing discontentment under his breath.

As his footsteps dissipated into the distance the boy let go of Mary's wrist and whispered, "He would never look down this way when searchin' for ya. No royal lady would make their way down to the servant's quarters if she knew where she was goin'," and even in the complete darkness, Mary could hear the grin in his voice.

"Well of course not!" Mary whispered back huffily, "Whatever would a princess need in such places?"

The boy squeezed past Mary and made his way up the stairs once more, ignoring her question.

"How dare you turn your back on me?" Mary stormed, following him up the stairs as she stomped her little feet with every step, "I demand to know your name so that I may report your insolence to your master!"

"The name is Reginald, ya grace," he said, "But my friends call me Reggie."

"Well then, Mr Reginald," Mary said as she crossed her arms again, "You should expect a lashing for the way you have behaved towards me," and she turned on her heels and began to walk away when Reginald called after her.

"Another lashin' for troublin' you, ya grace," he called, "Nothin' I'm not already used to."

At that Mary stopped, "Another lashing?" she asked as she turned back around to face him, "Why another?"

"For bumpin' into you that day, ya grace," he replied, "Or for joking wi' you thereafter, I don't rightly know what it was for," he grinned at her then, which she could not understand.

"Why do you smile?" Mary asked.

Reginald shrugged his shoulders, "What else can a servant do when presented with another hardship in life? If we did not smile, we would weep, no?"

Mary stared back at the young boy before her and chewed the inside of her cheek in shame for her part in his punishment, unable to come up with the right words to acknowledge her guilt.

Just then, Margaret Pole came walking down the corridor, "Princess!" she called, her face disapproving, "I hear you ran off from your lessons! Dr Fetherstone has been up and down this castle looking for you! You get back to your lectures right this instant."

Mary turned to her red-faced governess and began to explain herself when she noticed that the boy had disappeared as if into thin air, and for the briefest of moments before she was dragged off back to her duties, the princess found herself wondering if perhaps she had entirely imagined her encounter with that mysterious servant boy.

Later that day as supper was brought to her chambers and Cecily poured her a cup of small ale, she crinkled her nose, "I would prefer a cup of sweet wine, Cecily."

"I shall have a kitchen maid bring some up for you," and she turned to leave.

"I should like to speak to the servant boy," Mary called after Cecily before she had reached the door, "The clumsy one."

Cecily frowned but did not dispute the princess' request, instead she bowed her head in acknowledgement and left the room.

Mary ate her supper of bread and cheese slowly as she watched the fire flickering in the hearth before her, and her mind began to wonder what made that boy – Reginald, was it? – so bold at the risk of receiving painful punishments. Did he have no fear? Or was the punishment not enough of a deterrent for him to dismiss his freedom to act as he pleased? She wondered what that sense of self and liberty felt like.

Lady Cecily returned to the princess' chambers, the servant boy wandered in behind her, scanning the room as his mouth hung open in awe at its vastness, "Woah," he said, to which Cecily turned to look at him disapprovingly.

"Reginald," Mary said with a smile, welcoming him.

"Your grace sent fo' me?" Reginald said, bowing his head briefly.

"I did," Mary replied and then turned to her ladies, "You may give us some privacy. Retire to the lounge and work on your embroidery."

Her ladies exchanged a shocked look but then they bobbed a quick curtsy and walked to the far end of the room, leaving Mary and the boy behind.

Reginald watched her ladies walk away as Mary watched him, curious to understand his behaviours.

When Reginald turned his attention back to the princess, she nodded her head at the chair opposite her, inviting him to sit.

He did as he was ordered, running his fingers over the fabric of the armchair as though he had never felt anything so soft.

They sat in silence for some time while Mary considered what to say, and the boy became increasingly uncomfortable.

He raised his eyebrows in anticipation and then let out a slow sigh, "So, me lady –" he began and stopped himself, realising his mistake, "I mean, your grace. To what do I owe this peculiar pleasure?"

Mary leaned forward, "You know, I am not quite sure," she admitted with a small laugh, "I am simply curious about you."

"About me?" Reginald exclaimed in shock as he jabbed a thumb at his chest, "What is there 'bout a common servant to be of interest to you, princess?"

Mary shrugged her shoulders, "Well that is it. I wish to find out."

Reginald pursed his lips and raised his eyebrows once more, unable to comprehend what was being asked of him, "Princess, I wanna help, but I dunno what you want."

Mary sighed, "Reginald, all my life I have been surrounded by servants. I have never known a day to go by without someone serving me, hand and foot, and I must confess, not once did it cross my mind that they were any more than that – servants."

Reginald sat back abruptly then and began picking at his teeth. Mary watched; her face crumpled in disgusted awe.

"Well, princess, may I be honest?"

"Yes."

"Am I supposed to simply sit 'ere and listen to you insultin' me? 'Cause I'd rather take another lashin'."

Mary furrowed her brow, but the boy went on, "You sit 'ere in your 'eated room that is bigger than the entire servants' quarters and tell me that in your whole life you never realised your servants 'ave a life away from your orders and commands?" he shook his head, "I say again, me lady, I don't know what it is I am doing 'ere. I clearly don't belong."

Mary frowned and looked up to see her lady Cecily had approached them, "Is everything alright, your grace?"

"Yes, Cecily, I am fine."

Cecily looked from her princess to the boy and with a quick look of disdain, made her way back to her seat in the far corner of the room. Mary watched her leave and then brought her attention back to Reginald who had resumed picking his teeth, and Mary was sure then that he must be doing it in disrespect.

She looked away and picked up the flagon of wine that had been brought up at her request. She poured herself a cup and then one for the boy who watched eagerly as the liquid flowed.

Mary raised his cup and offered it to him, "I apologise for the offence, it was not my intention," she said as he took the cup from her hand.

She watched him take a sip and then went on, "It is hard for me to explain, but all I want is to have a conversation. I shall ask questions and you shall answer. There is no offence and certainly no mockery. I wish to learn about a world I know nothing of."

Reginald frowned then, "But why from me? There are 'undreds of servants at your disposal, as well as your lovely ladies – I'm sure they know a thing or two," and he grinned in their direction to which they simultaneously cringed at his brazenness.

"True," Mary agreed as she took a sip from her cup, "But I have a feeling asking you about these matters will be more entertaining," and she grinned at him.

"Ah, now on that we can agree, your grace!" Reginald said as he laughed and stretched his legs out before him, getting comfortable in such a nonchalant way that Mary raised her eyebrows in shock. But she quickly shook the expression from her face as she remembered this was precisely what she wished to observe, his actions of own free will.

"Let us begin then with a simple question," Mary said, "How old are you?"

"Fourteen."

"And how is it that you are in my service here in Ludlow? Reginald took a sip of his wine, "Me father sold me, when I was seven."

"Sold you?"

"Yeah. How else do you think people acquire servants?" Mary shook her head, "Why did he sell you?"

"Ah for fun, your grace!" Reginald said as he sat upright and leaned forward, "You see, he 'ad nothing to do one day and decided to sell me to see 'ow much he'd get for me!" Reginald scoffed and picked up a piece of bread from the princess' plate before popping it into his mouth, "No," he then confessed as he chewed open-mouthed, to which Mary could not help but express her aversion.

He swallowed and went on, "Me mum died when I was six," he admitted, his voice suddenly solemn at the memory, "I'm the youngest of five. Me dad couldn't feed all of us, and I tried to 'elp but, in the end – me bein' the least able to contribute – he sold me," and he sipped his wine.

"I am so sorry," Mary said quietly, "About your mother and about… being sold," and she flinched as she spoke the words. She could not imagine what it must have felt like to be ripped from one's family in such circumstances.

Reginald shrugged, "It's some time ago now, it's ok. And I like it 'ere; when I'm not gettin' lashin's for mistreatin' the future queen of Spain," he chuckled then as he picked up a piece of cheese.

"Again – I am sorry for that too," Mary said, "I did not order it."

They sat in silence for a while and Reginald leaned his head onto the back of the chair, looking up at the high ceilings, "I am quite 'onoured to be in the royal apartments," he said, "My work in the kitchens or as cup bearer never did allow me entrance in 'ere before."

Mary did not know how to answer so she merely smiled and asked another question, "What is it that you do on a normal day? I would wager you have lots of time to be outside in the wilderness or for other activities you enjoy?"

The boy gave her a sideways look, thinking she must be teasing, but as he saw her naïvely eager expression, he knew the princess truly had no idea.

He rubbed a hand over his face, "I don't even know where t' begin. How can ya be so completely unaware?"

Mary flinched at his hostility, "Well I can only imagine!" Mary said, "Every day I am busy learning a new skill from one tutor or perfecting one I already acquired from another! I must learn Latin and French and Spanish, and how to ride and hunt, to lead an army one day but never be too hostile for, of course, I am a princess. I must learn all the new dances so as to be entertaining at events but learn how to remain composed and to never falter. It is strenuous. I would simply adore to have some free time, which I assumed you had. Am I wrong?"

"Yes!" Reginald exclaimed, "I'd give me left arm to be taught to ride and dance and speak languages. From the moment I wake up – which is afore the sun rises – I am guttin' rabbits. If I'm not needed in the kitchen, I am sent to empty all the chamber pots," he paused and forced a gag, "or to sweep the stairs. At the events where you get to sit and be merry and dance and sing, I stand in the cold shadows for hours, awaitin' for someone to wave their bejewelled 'and in me direction signallin' they want somethin'. At night I curl up in a ball underneath me 'oley blanket for some scrap of warmth - warmth which doesn't come from a roarin' fire in an 'earth like yours – but a warmth that comes from other peoples' breath and farts and dyin' embers from the kitchen pot –"

Reginald stopped abruptly then, as the expression on Mary's face was one of such utter disgust and horror that he could not help but burst out laughing. He laughed so hard that tears began to stream from his eyes and all the while Mary could do nothing but wonder which part of what he had just said was so funny.

"Your face!" Reginald said in between laughing, "Your grace, I am sorry but –" he wiped the tears from his face and breathed in deeply, "You do not need to know about 'ow I spend me days. They are not of interest and clearly, by your expression, you aren't prepared to 'ear of it," he chuckled once more and inhaled deeply to compose himself.

"That was rather a lot of vulgarity all at once. I admit I was not prepared," Mary said as she leaned back against her chair. They sat in silence for a long time as Mary stared down at the floor, deep in thought.

Reginald picked up his cup of wine and sipped it, all the while watching the princess as she absorbed the information he had just bestowed onto her and he wondered if perhaps her newfound knowledge into how the poor lived would help to shape her into a ruler that would take the people's needs into consideration.

He watched her young face contort and crinkle at the realisation that there were many that were so much less fortunate than she, and it gave him a sense of hope for the future. He smiled at the notion that this very conversation might one day mark the turn of the tide for many who struggle across all of England. Perhaps this insight would mould the future queen into a great monarch, one that would lead England into a brighter future.

Reginald and Mary were snapped out of their own thoughts as Margaret Pole approached them, "Your grace, it is getting late, perhaps it would be wise to retire?"

Mary inhaled deeply and rose from her chair, "Yes, lady Pole, it is getting rather late."

The countess nodded once to the princess, then turned her gaze at the servant who was still sitting, "Young man, the princess has stood up from her seat. I would advise you to do the same!"

Reginald scrambled up off his seat, "I apologise," he said as he bowed his head to the lady Pole, "These chairs are just so very comfortable."

Mary giggled from behind her hand and they both turned to look at her. She cleared her throat at her governess' disapproving expression and addressed the boy, "Thank you for speaking with me. I believe I learned a lot."

"No, princess," Reginald said as he bowed his head at her "I thank you for your invitation. It's been an 'onour to be in your company," he replied charmingly.

"It seems you do have some manners after all," Mary said, blissfully perplexed by his sudden change in conduct.

Reginald smiled, "I shall take my leave, your grace."

Mary watched as he and her governess walked towards the doors, "I bid you goodnight, Reginald," she said.

He turned and grinned, "Please your grace, didn't I say that me friends call me 'Reggie'," then he turned on his heels and he was gone.

April 1526

Mary was standing in her linen shift before the mirror while Cecily began dressing her, when suddenly her governess burst through the doors, unannounced and dishevelled.

"Your grace," she gasped breathlessly, "forgive the intrusion, but we must leave at once."

Behind her, Mary's ladies looked at one another and without a word began grabbing the princess' most treasured possessions and throwing them into travel chests.

"What is going on, lady Pole?" Mary asked as she was handed her riding gear and attempted to dress herself.

"We must get you dressed," Margaret said as she snatched Mary's clothes from her, "There is an outbreak in the city," she whispered.

Mary gasped in fear, "The plague!? How near?"

"In the very castle, your grace," Margaret whispered as she pulled Mary's bodice cords tightly, then crossed herself.

The lady Pole then turned and hurried from the room and returned in mere moments with the guards in tow, "We must leave," she said, her normally cheery face now ashen with fear.

"How could this happen?" Mary asked, her voice shaking as she stared wide eyed at her governess.

"We received a letter from Cardinal Wolsey," Margaret said as they made their way out the door, two guards walking ahead and two behind to ensure the princess' safety, "to remove you from the castle. They had news of the Black Death spreading across towns nearby and by now it has reached Ludlow," Margaret stopped to look behind them, and when she saw three more guards entering Mary's chambers to collect her belongings, she turned back and continued down the corridor, "We shall leave now for the nearby castle of Hartlebury. It is the only safe place to retreat that is suitable to house you, princess. But we must go now."

Mary nodded bravely, swallowing her panic and, while surrounded by their guards, they made their way down the spiral staircase.

As they walked through the great hall, careful to ensure they did not accidentally approach anyone that may be infected, Mary's entire body felt tense with dread.

Her guards cornered off any entrance between herself and the their escape route, and although the great hall remained empty but for them, Mary could hear the disruption and chaos that was escalating outside as people hurried to escape the castle grounds.

The guards went ahead as they reached the portcullis of the castle and called for the stable boy to bring the horses.

"I am frightened, lady Pole," Mary confessed to her governess.

The countess took the princess' hand and squeezed it tightly, "God will not forsake you, your grace. Stay strong."

Mary nodded, and as the stable boy brought the horses and the guards ordered him to step away, Mary and her ladies scurried through the archway and into the sunlight.

As the princess and her ladies got on their horses, Margaret Pole quickly ordered riders to scout ahead for a clear path to Hartlebury for the royal party to follow, and as guards shouted orders at one another and hurried past with their heavy-footed march, Mary looked around herself in fear as her mind tried to make sense of the devastation, and suddenly she caught a glimpse of a familiar face.

"The guards have gone ahead, your grace," her lady Cecily said beside her, "The path ahead is clear for us to go."

Mary nodded and pressed her heels into her pony's sides, spurring it ahead.

With one last look back, Mary saw, this time more clearly, that the familiar face she had spotted had been Reggie's. She watched him as he watched her and her royal party fleeing the plague-stricken castle, and a sad smile spread across his face.

Mary returned the smile and watched, as if in slow motion, as her unlikely friend raised his hand in goodbye, and she noticed in horror that his fingers were stained with the unmistakable blackness common in victims of the Black Death.

Hartlebury Castle, Worcestershire

The princess and her small household remained for some time at Hartlebury while the plague ran its course. Thrice each day the entire manor was cleansed with the fumigation torches which were filled with spices and herbs that physicians believed fought the spread of the disease; and all the hearths within the manor were lit and remained constantly roaring so as to burn the illness from the air.

Mary remained in her chambers whenever possible, receiving no one but her ladies and her governess.

It was on one such occasion, while Mary remained confined to her chamber, that the lady Margaret Pole entered, bringing with her a letter bearing the king's seal, which she held before her with a long metal tong. She walked towards a small pit which burned the concoction of herbs and spices that were used in the fumigation torches, and held the letter over its fumes, purging it of any residual infestation it may be carrying. She then passed it to Mary who carefully broke the seal and read the letter.

"Daughter,
It would seem your Spanish betrothed, King Charles V and Holy Roman Emperor, could no longer wait to begin producing his heirs, and has wed another. He has made a new alliance with Portugal by marrying the princess Isabela, and so you are once again without a future husband.
Our alliance with Spain has ended in betrayal once more and this time it shall be the last!

We have reports that the black death is dispersing, and you
will soon be safe to return home, and when you do, we shall
make you a new match with France.
Remain strong.
Your father,
King Henry VIII"

Mary dropped the letter as if it had suddenly become too heavy to hold.

"What news, your grace?" her governess asked as she bent down to pick up the discarded letter.

"It seems I shall not be queen of Spain after all," Mary muttered mournfully and then swiftly felt a pang of guilt at showing disappointed in her life's new outcome, when so many innocent people had died needlessly due to this mysterious and dreadful disease. Had it not been for her high rank and nobility, she may very well have been one of the bodies to be thrown dead upon a pile and burned to ash. But alas, she was the princess of England, and her life, above all others at Ludlow, had had to be saved.

She *tsked* angrily as she stood up from her seat and walked over to the window, her arms folded across her stomach as if to hold herself together as the tears pricked her eyes.

Later that same day Mary received another letter, this time from her mother which read:

"To my darling daughter,
By now I am sure you will have received word that our
alliance with Spain is dead. My nephew has betrayed us and
married Isabela of Portugal in your stead.
The king is furious. He is furious with King Charles V and he
is furious with me for he sees all of Spain's misdoings as
though they were my own. He does not wish to see me. I am

afraid he has lost all faith in my country, and I, of course, understand his disdain. But it hurts my heart, nonetheless.

The only joy I take from this is that you will soon be returned to me. I have missed you very much, hija, *and I cannot wait to see how beautiful you have grown.*

Until then, remember your studies and your prayers. We shall be reunited soon.

Katherine R."

Chapter 5

1527
Greenwich Palace, London

As king Henry walked towards the window and held a letter up into the sunlight, his councillors quietly discussed their views on the princess' newest betrothal among themselves.

Sir Thomas Moore watched in silence as the men bickered and debated about the young girl as though she were a prized piece of meat until he could take it no longer and stood from his seat at the council table, "Your majesty," he called to the king, who looked up from the letter before him, "can we put the matter to a vote?"

"There's no need, Thomas," Henry replied as he waved the letter in the air, "The French king writes that Mary shall not be betrothed to him, but to his second son Henri, Duke of Orleans, instead."

There was a sigh of relief from most of the men at the council, including Moore, as they learned of the king of Frances' decision.

"God be praised he saw reason," Moore said, "To have taken the young princess for himself at his age may not have been easily accepted by her, or indeed by the queen."

"The princess knows her duty," Henry replied as he sat down on his throne at the head of table, "She and the queen would have accepted what I as their master would have told them to."

Moore bowed and resumed his seat but did not reply, relieved enough by the outcome to allow his king his necessary boastful remark.

"The princess' third betrothal in her eleven short years," said Charles Brandon the Duke of Sussex then, a small smile playing on his lips, "Let's hope this one sticks."

"Wipe that smirk off your face, Charles," the king said threateningly, "Whatever may or may not come from this betrothal, the princess will do whatever is decided for her without complaint. She shall do her duty and be happy to broker an alliance for her country."

"Of course, your majesty," Charles Brandon replied hastily, "I only meant –"

"France is our ally now," Henry interrupted as he looked down at the letter in front of him, "Spain has caused us too much grief over the years, first through king Ferdinand and now king Charles. They have betrayed us too often. We can no longer trust them."

The men of the council nodded in agreement.

"At least there was one good thing to come from your Spanish alliance, your majesty," Thomas Moore chimed in, hoping to remind the king of his earlier marital years where he and the queen had been happy.

But Henry raised an eyebrow in contempt, "Really, Thomas?" he said, his pale blue eyes staring menacingly at his friend, "Because from where I'm sitting, it looks like Spain has brought me nothing but disappointments, betrayals and losses. England has gained nothing from our alliances with Spain, not the one Charles has broken and certainly not the one brokered over twenty years ago to attain queen Katherine."

Sir Thomas Moore shook his head in disbelief at the king's rage, "You disappoint me, Harry," he said.

"The time for 'Harry' is over!" the king exclaimed as he stood abruptly and banged his fist on the table, "I will no longer be taken for a fool – by anyone! That includes the *queen!* And it includes you!" and he pointed a finger at Moore as his face reddened with each word, and all the while

Cardinal Wolsey sat back in his seat, watching silently as the play unfolded.

The king's rooms were dimly lit, the only light coming from the fire that burned brightly in the hearth and a thin sliver of moonlight as it shone through the open window.

Henry and his most trusted advisor, the Cardinal Thomas Wolsey, sat in the darkness as the king indulged in his second helping of roasted pig, his chin and fingers wet with grease.

Wolsey watched from his seat adjacent to the young king as he ripped the meat from the bone and greedily stuffed it in his mouth. He sat there in silence, his dark, fox-like eyes observing the king's every move, studying him to ensure he always knew what the king's next step would be, or to at least not be surprised when he changed his fickle mind.

"I tell you, Wolsey," the king said then, breaking the silence, "I have long prayed on this matter," then he stopped to swallow and wiped his chin with the back of his hand, "And I believe" he went on, "that the death of my sons by Katherine to be the outcome of a terrible lapse in judgement. I was young and foolish and believed myself invincible," he looked down at his plate and picked up a handful of meat, "So – God has seen fit to show me the light. As the bible itself says: 'If a man shall take his brother's wife, it is an unclean thing; he hath uncovered his brother's nakedness; they shall be childless.'" And he stuffed the meat in his mouth.

"You need not quote the bible to me, your grace," Wolsey said, "But while I share your majesty's frustrations, you are not in fact *childless*."

Henry suddenly slammed his fist hard upon the table, "A girl is not the desired outcome to a *legitimate* marriage for a king!" he exclaimed through gritted teeth as he stared into his advisor's aged face, "My daughter renders me '*not childless*' as you say, but her useless gender implies it!"

"My lord," Wolsey said, his voice taking on a soothing tone he always made sure to use around the king, as if to calm a crying baby, "I must ask then, why did you send the girl to Ludlow for her kingly education if you were not prepared to name her your heir?" Wolsey knew he was treading on thin ice, but he believed his relationship with the king to be an unbreakable bond.

Henry sat back in his chair and licked his lips, "I must confess that when I sent her away, I had accepted that perhaps this was God's will," Henry said as he watched the fire burning in the hearth, "I saw no other options since the queen was past her child-bearing years."

He fell silent then, his face aglow with the flickering orange flames.

"But then I had an epiphany!" he suddenly announced, as he looked back at Wolsey, his temper having swiftly subsided, "God sent to me an angel. And I know now that all those years of the unknown and all the pain of loss was God's way of testing my resolve!"

Wolsey held his breath as he waited for the king to continue, completely terrified of what he may be alluding to.

"He sent me an angel, Wolsey," Henry repeated, his face bright with the unmistakeable glow of love "She shall be the one to give me what I want."

"But, my lord, I fail to see how –"

"That's why I called you in here today, Wolsey," the king interrupted and then cleared his throat, "My marriage to Katherine is unlawful and has been from the very first day. I now believe that her marriage to my brother was, in fact, consummated and that she was no maid when I wed her. God has taken all our sons to show me her betrayal and I have finally accepted the disturbing truth – Katherine of Aragon was never my true wife, and now it is up to *you* to get my marriage to her annulled!"

February 1528

It had been two years since the outbreak of the plague had caused havoc in Ludlow and its surrounding towns, and twelve-year-old Mary and her household had not remained in one place for too long, moving from one castle to another to ensure the princess' safety. Despite the constant disturbances, Mary had continued to show dutifully dedication to her studies, while continuing completely unaware of the crisis taking place back in London, which would turn her entire world upside down.

Almost three years had passed since she had left Greenwich Palace on her pursuit to learn how to become a strong and righteous monarch, and though she felt eternally grateful to God and to her father for the unbelievable honour of being chosen as England's heir, Mary could say with absolute certainty that she was very much looking forward to her return home.

When word finally came from London, inviting her to return, the young princess spent the slow ten-hour journey imagining what her new life as the unofficial 'Princess of Wales' would look like upon her return home. She dreamed of great masquerades in her honour, and of feasts with dancing and music. She imagined magnificent jousts where all the noble gentlemen would participate and ask for her favour. But above all else, Mary imagined how her mother and father would dote on her for the rest of their days, embracing her heartily as their only living heir, and with the knowledge that she, princess Mary, would be the one to continue the Tudor dynasty.

But when she finally made her entrance into the city of London, she was surprised to see very little celebration for her return. The amount of people that had gathered was far less than she had expected. Although they cheered and waved to her, it was a lot less spectacular than she had hoped for, and she wondered if perhaps her return had not been officially announced.

But her confusion was instantly forgotten upon her entrance into Greenwich castle when her carriage pulled up and she saw her mother awaiting her arrival, her hands clasped before her in that composed, queenly fashion Mary had always known, and with a bright smile on her face.

"Mother!" Mary called as she stepped out of her carriage, overcome with emotion. She hurried towards the queen and quickly curtsied to receive her blessing, then she threw her arms around her mother's neck and embraced her as the tears of joy pricked her eyes.

"Oh *hija*! Let me see you!" Katherine said as she pulled away from her daughter's embrace, and held her at arms' length to look into her face, "You have grown so beautiful, Mary," the queen said, and Mary realised that her mother too had changed, and she wondered just what could have caused such a deep sadness to be etched into her eyes, "And I am told you are an excellent student and very devout," Katherine continued, "I am so proud of you."

"Thank you, lady mother," Mary said with a smile, and they made their way inside, "Where is my lord father?" the princess asked, suddenly much more aware of her surroundings.

Katherine opened her mouth to reply but then paused momentarily before speaking, allowing herself time to keep her true thoughts hidden from her daughter, "I do not know, child," she said sadly, "Only that he is not in the palace."

"He is not here?" the princess asked, her brows furrowed in confusion, "But his heir has returned. Does that not inspire the need for his presence?" she said as that all too familiar knot of uncertainty tightened in her stomach.

Katherine linked her daughter's arm in hers, "Do not let this trouble you, my daughter. Your father will do as he pleases. He is king after all," and Katherine offered her a reassuring smile, which Mary noticed did not reach her eyes, "One day – God willing – " the queen continued, "you shall have that privilege too as head of the country. But for now, we must contend ourselves with however much time your father wishes to grant us."

"Has something happened?" Mary asked then as she turned to look at her mother beside her, and she noticed for the first time just how much she had aged. Though Mary had only been gone for three years, the queen appeared to have matured significantly during that time. Her once raven hair was now speckled with greys and the sadness in her eyes seemed almost to have drowned out all her remaining youth.

"No, Mary," Katherine replied as she looked away, "All is as it should be. God is with us, and we are beloved, never forget that."

But Mary was no fool, and she was painfully aware of the sorrow in her mother's voice, as well as the gloomy atmosphere that surrounded the usually merry English court.

Later that same day, as Mary sat by the window in her chambers reading her bible, she realised that her ladies had begun whispering in the next room as they unpacked Mary's trunks from their journey. Curious to know what had caused the miserable ambience on a day that she believed should have brought rejoicing, Mary placed the bible down on her lap and leaned slightly forward, hoping to catch what was being discussed; but to no avail.

In her frustration, Mary stood up from her seat in one fluid motion and was about to insist she be told what they knew, when suddenly Margaret Pole was announced.

"Mary," lady Pole said cheerfully, which the princess noticed instantly was too forced, "I trust you are finding everything to your liking? I see not much has changed," and she looked around at the rooms, a bright smile on her mousey face.

"All is well, thank you," Mary replied icily as she crossed her arms.

"Whatever is the matter, princess?" Margaret asked.

Mary raised her eyebrows and looked her governess straight in the eye, "I was hoping you would tell me, lady Pole."

Margaret breathed a short, nervous chuckle and swallowed before stammering a response, "I – I must confess I am not exactly sure what is happening," she admitted, "Only that your father has made some … unseemly accusations against the queen."

"What accusations?" Mary asked, her face twisted in confusion.

The countess of Salisbury cleared her throat and looked down at her hands, "I am not sure I am the person to ask."

"Who then? Who shall I ask?" Mary fired back in sudden anger, "Shall I find out through court gossip?" and then Mary called, "Frances, Cecily!" to which the two ladies joined the princess and her governess with their heads hanging in shame while Mary continued, "Perhaps they will tell me in glorious detail what the people are whispering behind their hands about their anointed queen!"

"Princess, please," Cecily mumbled as she kept her eyes firmly on the ground, humiliated.

"Well, lady Pole?" Mary exclaimed, her eyes blazing, "Will you tell me, or shall I hear the people's version?"

Margaret Pole wrung her hands together as she looked from Mary to her two ladies, all the while trying to find a way out of being the one to tell Mary the terrible news. But eventually she nodded her head.

"Do you remember when we spoke of your late uncle Arthur?" Margaret said quietly.

Mary frowned in confusion. How could her uncle, who had been dead over twenty years, have anything to do with what was happening today?

The countess continued, "And how I mentioned that the only reason your mother was able to wed your father after Arthur's death was because she had sworn that her marriage to Arthur had never been consummated?" to which Mary nodded once and Margaret sighed and went on, "The king is now seeking to annul the marriage to your mother, accusing her of having in fact, lain with his brother, your uncle – making your parents' marriage unlawful in the eyes of God."

The princess stood frozen in shock as her mind desperately tried to make sense of what she had heard. Then, as if she were waking from a trance, Mary moved slowly towards the window and plopped onto the seat she had moments ago vacated.

"Is it true?" she asked, her voice merely above a whisper as all the blood in her body rushed to her feet.

"Who is to say what is true and what is not?" her governess replied, her kind face crumpled with worry for her young ward.

"But if it is true," Mary mumbled as she stared at the ground before her, seeing nothing, "then their marriage was never a full one. Which would make me – a *bastard*."

No one replied and for a moment the room was deathly quiet.

Mary sat there unmoving, her ladies and governess watching helplessly as all the colour drained from her face, and then the princess doubled over and vomited violently onto the stone floor.

Frances jumped back and exclaimed in disgust, covering her own mouth with her hand while the princess retched uncontrollably, and Cecily pushed Frances out of the room in search of a servant, scolding her as they went. But the lady Pole, as a mother of five surviving children, was not fazed by the young girl's bodily reaction to the terrible news, and she crouched down beside her and gently rubbed her back as she hummed soothingly.

"Why would the king do this?" Mary mumbled when she had finally stopped heaving, "Am I not enough? Is his pursuit of a male heir the reason for this?"

The lady Pole fell silent as the two ladies returned with a servant in tow, and she took Mary gently by the arm and guided her away from the mess.

Her ladies helped her out of her sullied dress and tucked her into bed, her body having suddenly lost all its energy, "Am I not enough?" she repeated quietly as her vision began to blur with tears.

"It would seem," the lady Pole replied softly, "that he has set his sights on a certain lady of the court. It is said they are in love and that she is the cause of your mother's unhappiness."

Mary exhaled sharply as she fought with herself to keep her tears from falling, "I wish to see my mother," she said, "I must know the truth," to which her governess *tsked* her gently in disapproval and took the princess' hands in hers.

"You have every right to demand the truth, your grace," Margaret Pole said, "But it may not bring you peace. The *truth* is never a certain thing. It can be bended and moulded into any which way one wishes it to be, and though you feel a need to know it now, you may not like to know it once you do. And the moment it is spoken, it can never be untold."

March 1528

It had been over a month since Mary had learned of her father's grotesque undertaking, and though she desperately wished to know if his accusations held any truth to them, Mary could not shake her governess' words from her mind. Not only did she fear the outcome if she did confront the queen for the truth, but she could also not bear to cause her mother any more pain than she undoubtedly already felt at this ordeal.

Mary knew that her mother had endured the king's fair share of endless mistresses and ladies whose families hoped to gain prestige and lands through their short relationships with the king.

And while it was not uncommon for a king to take a mistress, especially during the times when his queen was with child; in this case, something was different.

From what Mary had learned through court gossip, this was not just some sordid affair, and if the endless whispers were to be believed, the lady who had stolen her father's heart, had – though Mary found it hard to believe – not yet given her virtue to him.

There was no escaping the incessant gossiping on the matter of her father's new love interest, and not a day would go by without her hearing new developments on the king's endeavours with his mistress.

One warm and dry spring day, Mary and her ladies were enjoying a leisurely stroll through the palace gardens in hopes of escaping the cold and gloomy mood that had befallen the English court, when they were suddenly approached by the Spanish ambassador.

"Don Inigo de Mendoza," the Ambassador said as he bowed at the waist, introducing himself to the young princess.

"Ambassador, what a pleasure," Mary replied sweetly though she had never met the man before due to her absence from court.

"Princess Mary," he said with a heavy Spanish accent, "it is an honour to finally meet you in person," and his thick moustache twitched as he offered her a smile, "May I offer my deepest apology for interrupting your stroll. I do not wish to impose, but I have an urgent matter I must discuss with you and the queen."

"An urgent matter?" Mary echoed, and her eyebrows shot up.

"Yes, your grace," he replied with a nod of his head, "Your mother has called for us to meet in her chambers."

When the princess and her ladies entered the queen's chambers only moments later, the ambassador following closely behind, Katherine rose from her seat at the window and, with a wave of her hand, dismissed Mary's ladies, "They need not be here, Mary. This is a private matter," the queen said, and Mary's ladies curtsied and exited the room, Cecily closing the door behind them.

"What is the meaning of this, lady mother?"

"Let the ambassador speak, Mary," the queen said monotonously, as though all the joy had been sucked from her very soul, "He shall tell us the news."

"*Gracias,* your grace," the Ambassador said once they were all seated, "I shall get right to the point, as it is a delicate matter," and he cleared his throat, "At your request, the king of Spain and Holy Roman Emperor, your nephew, has done all he could to influence the Pope in your favour on this sensitive matter."

"And?" Katherine prompted, visibly anxious to know the Pope's ruling.

"Pope Clement has given his answer to King Henry," and the Ambassador smiled, "He has rebuffed your husband's petition for the annulment."

Katherine crossed herself and whispered a small prayer, her hands clasped tightly around her rosary beads.

"It is said," Ambassador Mendoza continued slowly, "that your husband, the king, is rather displeased and is taking his rage out on his favourite."

"Wolsey," Katherine whispered, a slow smile spreading across her face at the news. Wolsey had been nothing but a thorn in the queen's side ever since the death of her first-born son. She fervently believed that it was Wolsey who was greatly to blame for the ever-expanding rift between herself and her husband, and so the news that the king was finally turning on his venomous favourite, brought great joy to Katherine during these uncertain times.

"Indeed," Mendoza replied, "It would seem his love for the man is dwindling now that he has failed him."

"I long to see the day that he is thrown from the palace," the queen said, her tone dripping with hatred.

"So, it is not true then?" Mary chimed in as a silence ensued. The ambassador and the queen looked at the princess, "What?" Katherine asked.

"Father's accusations," Mary said, her heart beating uncontrollably in her chest, "If the Pope has denied his petition for an annulment, then your marriage is legal in the eyes of God."

"Of course, Mary," Katherine replied, her dark eyebrows furrowed in frustration, as though the matter had never been under dispute, "But your father has been displeased with me for many years, Mary, through no fault of my own."

The young princess dropped her gaze in shame as she suddenly could not help but wonder: Why *had* God taken all her parent's sons if he had, in fact, blessed their marriage?

Was it punishment, as her father now believed?

Or was it as her mother said - that it was God's plan for England to have a female ruler on the throne?

Mary was ashamed to admit, she was no longer sure.

June 1528

Suddenly and without warning, the infamous Sweating sickness had once again returned to London, and within only days it had claimed hundreds of victims on its mysterious rampage through the south of the country.

Having experienced personal trauma due to the sudden death of his older brother Arthur to the unforgiving sickness, as well as his constant fear over the survival of the Tudor line, the king and those closest to him wasted no time in fleeing the densely populated city and its surrounding areas in favour of his countryside residence, Hampton Court Palace, to avoid the deadly disease.

It came as quite a pleasant surprise to Mary then when, in the king's haste, he did not think to protect his so-called beloved from the lethal disease and chose instead to leave her behind at her family estate in Kent, Hever Castle.

Mary took this unexpected piece of information as good news, trusting that it meant the beginning of the end of the king's infatuation with the lady, and though his neglect to consider her safety put her at risk of perishing, Mary believed that it may very well be in everyone's best interest if she did indeed succumb to the Sweat.

And so, when news came in the form of a secret messenger to the queen that Hever Castle had had reports of deaths due to the sickness, Mary and her mother breathed a sigh of relief at the supposed end to their ordeal.

The king, having received the same news from his own messengers, locked himself away in his chambers for days, refusing all food and all company, and though Mary's heart broke for her father's obvious distress at the likely death of the lady, she could not help but feel comforted in the knowledge that soon, things would return to normal.

July 1528
Hampton Court Palace

"She is the Devil!" Mary exclaimed through gritted teeth as she crumpled a note in her hand that brought the terrible news of the king's mistress' survival.

"It is not unheard of," Margaret Pole replied matter-of-factly as they sat on a stone bench in the Palace gardens, "People do recover from the sweating sickness, princess. The lady and her father must not have had direct contact with the infected maid that died – God rest her soul."

Mary shot a quick, disapproving glance at her governess for her casual tone at the critical issue, but then breathed in deeply to contain her fury, "It does not matter," she said as she stood up and began to pace, exhaling slowly through her nose, "Whatever happens, my lord father cannot divorce my mother, whether the harlot is alive or not."

"I must advise you not to use that language, Mary," the lady Pole chimed in as she picked up the embroidery she had momentarily discarded, "It is unseemly."

Mary sat back down beside her governess as a cramp slowly began to tighten in her belly, and she looked up at the clear blue sky, "I beg your pardon, lady Pole," she mumbled then as she rubbed a hand over her corseted belly and exhaled through her mouth.

"Is it the pains again?" Margaret asked as she noticed the young princess' discomfort from the corner of her eye.

Mary nodded, "Yes," she replied, "my courses have not been kind this month."

"Would you like me to fetch a physician?"

"No, no. Thank you Maggie," Mary said, waving her hand before her, dismissing her governess' concern, "But I think I shall retire; the sunshine is hurting my eyes." ·

The lady Pole watched as Mary rose from the bench beside her and walked out of the Palace gardens, her ladies following closely behind like two shadows she would never shake. Once they were out of sight the countess of Salisbury returned her attention to the embroidery before her and considered the young princess' sudden ailments.

It was a strange occurrence, one that would befall the princess often in the recent months since she had bloomed into womanhood and commenced her courses. It saddened the lady Pole that the poor girl suffered so extremely with her monthly courses and wondered if perhaps the distress over her parents' disconnect was somehow responsible for the girl's suffering. If only the king could abandon this reckless path he had set out on, so much grief could be avoided. But wishing death upon the lady that brought all this unhappiness was not the way, and Margaret made a mental note to remind the princess to trust in God, and to leave the ill-wishing and the anger in the past, for it surely could not be doing the princess' health any good.

1529

"Ambassador Mendoza has been arrested," the lady Frances told Mary as she laced up her corset one morning.

"Whatever for?" Mary asked bewildered, her arms stretched out before her, holding onto her bedpost as her lady pulled the corset strings tightly.

"I heard the kitchen maids gossiping," the lady continued, "The king is most displeased with him."

"Well, obviously, Frances!" Mary replied angrily as she turned her head to look at her lady, her long dark red hair whipping over her shoulder, "The man is in the tower!"

Frances dropped her gaze and fell silent, only fuelling the princess' anger further, "Well?" she demanded, "Tell me why he has been arrested!"

"It is said that he was working against the king on his great matter –"

"Ah, that," Mary interrupted as she straightened upright, immediately disinterested in the topic, "the king's 'great matter'…" she scoffed incredulously, and Frances turned to pick up the princess' dress, "The Pope has given his verdict on it," Mary continued as she stepped into the dress, "My parent's marriage is legal under the laws of God. He cannot simply divorce my mother," and she shrugged, "The matter is closed."

"Yes, your grace," Frances replied monotonously, while silently disagreeing entirely with the princess. From what she had heard, the king would not give up on this until he got exactly what he wanted, namely the one lady whose name was on everyone's lips – Anne Boleyn.

When Mary was dressed and sitting before her mirror while Cecily pinned her long wavy hair under her hood, a messenger brought a note.

"Open it for me, Frances," Mary ordered, and the girl tore the king's seal and unfolded the letter, then handed it to the princess.

Her ladies watched patiently as Mary scanned the parchment, her thin lips moving silently as she tried to make sense of the newest development in the scandalous ménage-a-trois.

Then Mary raised her head and sniffed sharply as she folded the note in half, "I must speak to my father."

The ladies looked at one another, wordlessly daring the other to voice what they both knew, "But your grace, the king will not see you," Cecily then braved, defeated by Frances' cowardly silence.

Mary met her lady's gaze through the looking glass, "I will address this issue," she said determinedly, "I am still the princess, whether he likes it or not!" and she rose from her seat, brushed down her skirts and exited her chambers in such a hurry that her ladies struggled to keep up.

She marched through the halls with her head held high, past curious courtiers who bowed and curtsied as she glided past them, until she reached the king's chambers.

His guards, upon noticing her approach, stiffened visibly and straightened their backs, and she could see in their faces that they were unsure on how to receive her.

"I demand to see the king," Mary said, her tone charming yet firm.

One of the guards cleared his throat, "The king wishes not to be disturbed," and Mary turned her attention onto him.

"Nonsense," Mary replied unbaffled, her expression never once giving away how irked she felt at his rebuttal, "This folly has gone on for far too long. I demand to be admitted."

The guards exchanged a glance but stood fast.

Mary raised her chin in defiance, "Very well," she said sweetly, "I shall speak to him another time. Good day to you," and she turned and walked away.

"Send for the countess of Salisbury," Mary ordered as she hurried past her ladies on her return to her chambers, "I will have my answer on this."

Once Margaret Pole arrived at the princess' apartments, Mary held up the note and said, "Have you heard?" and before she could reply, Mary bent her head and read the note aloud, "Daughter, your betrothal to Henri d'Orleans, second son of the king of France, has been revoked!" and she raised her head and jabbed a finger at the document, "Have you heard?" she repeated incredulously.

Her governess held out her hands in an attempt to calm the princess, "Yes, I have heard, your grace," she admitted, "I understand you must be in shock."

Mary began pacing up and down her rooms, one hand on her forehead as she breathed deeply in and out, "What am I to do? My very legitimacy is in doubt! No one shall have me now!"

Margaret Pole took a step towards the princess, "Mary, this is but one person's opinion."

"Not just one person! The king of France! And therefore, his entire country!" Mary wailed.

"Whatever some people think, doesn't make it so," Margaret soothed, but her wise words could do nothing to calm the princess.

"If my father gets his way it will be so," Mary mumbled as she plopped down heavily onto a seat by the window, "And this is just the beginning of it."

Mary dropped the note and held her hands over her face as the hot tears spilled out.

The countess simply let the girl sob for a moment and then patted her shoulder trying to comfort the princess, "The king of France may have revoked the marriage proposal to his son Henri, but there are other matches to be made, your grace," she said calmly, "Perhaps even a better one."

"It is not the *who* I shall marry," Mary said as she raised her head from her hands, "It is the *why* the betrothal has been rescinded that troubles me. Father's persistence that his marriage to my mother is invalid sullies my worth and *everything* that I am, and if I was never his legitimate daughter and heir to the English throne, then what value do I have?"

And suddenly a memory flashed into Mary's mind of the conversation she had had with Reggie, and what her life could be like if she were to be reduced to nothing – a lifetime of emptying chamber pots and gutting rabbits as Reggie had spent his days doing.

"But this is simply rumours and slander, princess. It will pass," Margaret said with a small smile, although she herself was no longer sure that that was entirely true.

Mary sniffed and looked at her governess, "Do you truly believe that?"

"Yes," the lady Pole lied, and her heart sank in her chest. The truth was - at the rate and force that the king was acting out his 'great matter' in his attempt to divorce the queen, Margaret feared for the princess' future. But until anything was absolutely certain, it aided no one to admit this to the young princess, "I have faith in God and his mysterious ways," Margaret added to ease Mary's mind.

"I was really hoping for a more solid answer," Mary said as she wiped the tears from her rosy cheeks.

"It is the only answer I can give you, Mary," her governess admitted, a sad smile on her face, "You must persist with your belief in God, and trust that He will guide your father back to his queen and to you."

Mary could do nothing but nod, her emotions bubbling inside her as her once perfectly planned out future now lay out before her as dark and unclear as Reggie's blackened fingers.

It had become rather a rare occasion for the king and queen to be seen together in the same room. Ever since the king's whore, Anne Boleyn, had – by some witchcraft – survived the Sweating Sickness, the king would go nowhere without the lady close by and showed her off all over court as though she were his most prized possession. As well as that, the king had given the order that neither the queen nor his daughter were to be allowed a private audience with him, regardless of the situation, and had by all means possible cut all ties with his family. He had made it abundantly clear that they were no longer of any use or interest to him, and that the only thing keeping their status within the monarchy intact was the Pope's judgment on his marriage to the queen. But in the eyes of the king, he believed he was no longer a married man.

Which was why, when Mary was called to be present at the introduction of the new Spanish Ambassador to the English court, she found it extremely strange to see her mother and father sitting side by side on their thrones in the great hall as they awaited the arrival of the new ambassador for Spain. It made the young princess wonder if perhaps there was some underlying meaning behind this announcement, one her young mind could not even begin to guess, and the thought made her stomach lurch with anxiety as she climbed the three steps to stand at her place beside her mother's throne.

Since Ambassador Mendoza's sudden arrest and confinement to the Tower, his health had rapidly deteriorated, leaving his mind and body weakened by the poor conditions of his surroundings. His sudden ill health had, however, given the king cause for his release, and had allowed the man to return to Spain to live out his final days.

But the morbid reality did not escape Mary. She saw the cause for her father's unexpected show of 'mercy' to have been anything but, for while the man had escaped execution at the hands of the axeman or the noose, he had been sent home to die a slower and more painful death by his own body's deterioration.

In Mendoza's place, a new Spanish Ambassador had been appointed; a man whom Mary hoped would not be intimidated by her father.

"*Senor* Eustace Chapuys," the usher called as the middle-aged man was presented to the king and queen, and he bowed deeply.

"Ambassador Chapuys," king Henry said in welcome, "I trust you shall serve us better than Mendoza," and Mary's head snapped to look at her father, his insensitivity leaving her completely humiliated.

"I shall do my best to facilitate the communications between our two countries, your majesty," Chapuys replied expertly, "But I must remind your grace that I serve my king, Charles V of Spain, before all others."

Henry waved his comment aside, ignoring it entirely, "Anyone would do better than that conniving snake who came before you," he declared loudly, and behind the new ambassador, the nobles of the court nodded and expressed their agreement with the king, "that fool is lucky I showed him mercy."

Ambassador Chapuys raised his eyebrows but bowed his head, "I am sure he thanks your majesty every day for your… generosity."

As the two men exchanged words, Mary looked at her mother beside her as she stared straight ahead, hardly even acknowledging her daughter's presence, and Mary regretfully noticed how tired she looked. Not only had her once shiny black hair gone almost completely grey, but her eyes drooped at the sides in a way Mary imagined could only have been caused by the extreme sadness and stress her father had been putting her through.

Mary raised her head and looked once again at the new ambassador, who met her gaze and offered her a warm smile. Mary blinked and smiled back, feeling strangely at ease.

She got the distinct impression that this new ambassador would be an honourable and loyal servant to his Spanish king, and by extension to her mother, the Spanish king's aunt; and though it may have been purely wishful thinking, Mary thought that perhaps he would be the one to finally repair the ever-growing rift between England and Spain.

Chapter 6

November 1530

Mary had been wrong.

It seemed nothing and no one would reforge her parent's reconciliation, and no amount of support from Spain or even from the Pope himself would help her mother win back her husband's love.

The king and his mistress seemed to spend every waking moment together, and though the rumour was that they had not yet shared a bed, Mary could not bring herself to believe it.

But ultimately, the young princess was very much left in the dark when it came to all things regarding the king and queen's marital status, and it was only on the very rarest of occasions that she would even be graced with either of her parents' presence.

It all came as a huge shock then, when Mary's governess entered her chambers unannounced one day, her face ashen with the news she carried with her.

"Princess," she said as she looked around the rooms to judge if those present were trustworthy, "I bring news."

Mary stood from her place by the fire, "Lady Pole, what is it?" she asked as she took her governess' shaky hands in hers.

"It's Cardinal Wolsey," she said quietly, as though she was unsure if it was safe to utter his name.

"What of him?" Mary asked bewildered.

"He's – he has been arrested."

"What?!" Mary exclaimed, her surprise forfeiting all manners of decorum.

"Under what grounds?" Mary's lady Cecily chimed in as she approached them, her cool head always seeing to reason quickly.

Margaret Pole shook her head slightly, "I am not sure," she said.

Mary let go of her governess' hands and walked towards the window, as though looking out into the city below would somehow bring her answers, "This does not make any sense," she said, "Wolsey is my father's favourite. He is his most trusted advisor, and his friend!" and she turned back to her ladies and lady Pole, "What could he have possibly done to warrant such harsh treatment from the king?"

Frances cleared her throat, "Treason, your grace," she muttered as she looked at Mary from below her dark eyelashes, fearing reprimanding, "That's what the servants are saying."

"How do you know of this?" Mary asked.

Frances looked at Cecily uncertainly, "I like to listen," she admitted, "court gossip is rife with interesting information," and she dropped her gaze shamefully, "Forgive me, princess, I know it is unseemly to pay attention to idle gossip but –"

"What else have you heard?" Mary interrupted as she took a step closer to her lady.

Frances looked at Cecily once more as if to draw strength from her, "Well, it – it dates back a little, your grace," she stammered, "What is it you wish to know?"

Mary took her lady by the arm and pulled her to the seats by the fireplace, "All of it."

Had it not been for her short, yet eye-opening friendship with Reggie, Mary may have very likely discredited everything Frances had conveyed to her about Wolsey's demise, simply due to the very source of her information. But if Reggie's bluntness had taught Mary

106

anything, it was that servants paid more attention to the nobles' goings on than they would like to believe, and that sometimes they held a great insight into the nobles' lives that they themselves lacked.

And in this very case it would seem absolutely accurate, for Mary had been completely unaware of everything Frances had revealed, "So you see the king tasked him with an impossible undertaking," Frances continued, "No doubt the Cardinal was in deep personal turmoil choosing to do right by his king or by his faith. But the king demanded an annulment."

"And when he failed to achieve it," Mary concluded, "He fell from grace."

"He did try, as you know," Frances added.

Mary nodded and raised an eyebrow, "Yes," she admitted, "I will not easily forget the trials my mother was called to like some sinner."

Frances sighed, "But parliament ruled in the queen's favour. It was decided by the Pope and by the king's own parliament that your mother be your father's true wife," Frances went on, "And Wolsey saw he was in a losing battle. I have no doubt that he feared for his life or at the very least for his reputation," Frances cleared her throat, "And so they say that he secretly changed sides in favour of the queen."

"But Wolsey always hated my mother," Mary pointed out, her face twisted in confusion, "Why would he have done that?"

"His dislike towards your mother was petulant at best," lady Pole chimed in, "He used the king's frustration with your mother to nestle deeper into the king's bosom. His dislike of the queen over the years was never personal but rather for his own advancement in the world."

"And now that the king would be displeased with him for failing to secure his much-desired annulment," Mary deduced, "He had no other choice but to seek protection from the next

107

most powerful person in the realm – the very woman he had been seeking to destroy for all these years."

"It is also said that Wolsey tried to amount foreign support for the queen, and against the king and his mistress," Frances added more quietly.

"That I cannot believe," Mary exclaimed then, "My mother would never have supported that. She would never do anything that might jeopardise the king's reign, not even for her own benefit," and she looked at her governess for assurance in her belief, which Margaret gave in the form of an eager nod.

Cecily exhaled suddenly as she sat back in her chair and shook her head, "I am baffled," she admitted, "Can this really all be true?"

Frances nodded, "That is what they say," and she sighed.

Mary rose from her seat and walked slowly up and down the length of the room, rubbing her hands together in thought, "But this is a good thing," she said after some time, "The king is no closer to achieving his blasphemous purpose in ridding himself of my mother, and one of my mother's greatest rivals is now locked up in the Tower for treason against the king."

Margaret Pole stood then, "While that is true," she admitted, "It does not mean the end of the king's determination."

Mary looked at the older lady, her eyes begging for even a scrap of hope, "Surely this new development must mean something positive, lady Pole?"

Her governess nodded and smiled sadly, "I pray that you are right, your grace," but she knew that praying would not deter the king from his ungodly quest for a son.

30th November 1530
Greenwich Palace, London

     Charles Brandon entered the king's chambers and found Henry pacing up and down with his fingers pressed against his temple as he muttered angrily to himself.

Charles cleared his throat and scratched at his bearded chin, "Your majesty," he said, "you sent for me."

Henry looked up and steered directly towards his friend, "That lecherous traitor!" he spat out in anger, just inches from Charles' face, "I should have his head cut off and put on a spike for all of London to see as it rots and leave it for the crows to peck out his evil eyes!"

Charles Brandon was silent for a moment as he watched the king resume his pacing, "I do not dispute your majesty's rage towards the man," he said carefully, "But to punish his body after death does not seem productive to me."

The news of Cardinal Wolsey's death had been a shock to all who had known him, and even to those who had hated him. While his arrest had been warranted with his own treasonous mistakes, it had been many people's belief that he would be released in due time, stripped of his titles, and banished from court. But when news broke that he had been found dead one morning by the servant who brought him his food, Charles Brandon, and indeed most of the nobility, had found themselves wondering exactly how that may have happened, for he had entered the Tower only days prior in perfectly good health.

But life being the mystery that it was, and Charles having had no love for the man, had dismissed the obscurity quickly, believing that it mattered very little in the grand scheme of things.

Failing to receive an answer from his old friend, Charles inhaled as he took a step further into the king's chambers,

"Henry, I don't believe it was the man's intent to die. I am certain he believed you may still forgive him."

Henry turned angrily, "No Charles! He did not believe that!" he said through gritted teeth, "Would a man who believed his release was fast approaching, *poison* himself?!"

Charles furrowed his brows in confusion, "Poison?"

"His heart was black from it, Charles. I know it as true as I know you are standing here before me," the king said, "That coward!"

"Indeed, your majesty," Charles Brandon agreed as he tried to make sense of the news, "What a coward, indeed. But nevertheless, the man is dead, which is what you aimed to achieve."

"Yes," Henry replied as he rubbed his hands over his face, exhausted from the fit of rage that had consumed him, and Charles suddenly noticed that the normally clean-shaven and well-presented king looked dishevelled and ungroomed. His chin and cheeks sported a red stubble which Charles had long ago learned took his old friend many days to achieve, having failed to inherit his father's dark features, and he wondered if perhaps the issue of his Great Matter to marry his mistress Anne Boleyn, was finally catching up with him.

Henry flopped down heavily into his seat by the fire and groaned, "I am getting weary of all this, Charles," the king mumbled as he stared at the flames, "Wolsey betrayed me in life, and even now in death."

Charles walked towards the hearth then and slowly sat down beside the king, all the while considering what purpose a Cardinal would have had to commit the ultimate sin and condemn his soul to hell.

"I do wonder –" he began but paused to judge the potential outcome of his words.

"What, Charles?"

Charles looked at his king, "Wolsey was a devout catholic. I do find it hard to believe he would kill himself and commit such a sin against God."

Henry sat up in his chair, having slumped down earlier in his exhaustion, "You believe," he said as he realised Charles' implication, "that he did not poison *himself*?"

"I do not know, your majesty," Charles said quickly, all too aware that he was treading on thin ice if he spoke the words of accusation against whom he believed may be at fault, "I simply find that the Cardinal's sudden demise by his own hand as your majesty seems to believe is... *odd.*"

"A man may do crazy things at desperate times," Henry concluded simply.

"Perhaps," Charles agreed, "yet I cannot believe that a man so pious would commit such a diabolical final act and condemn his soul."

Henry inhaled deeply as he considered what his old friend was implying, "Then who?"

Charles looked sideways at Henry then and shrugged, "I cannot begin to guess who, your majesty," he said, though he had, in fact, a very strong speculation who may have had the intent, "But perhaps," Charles suggested slyly, "someone who held the Cardinal in high regard? Perhaps as an act of mercy?" and Charles watched his friend, hoping he would dismiss the suggestion as folly and consider the opposite reason for why one would want the Cardinal dead: revenge.

Henry frowned and waved the assumption aside, just as Charles had hoped he would, "There is no one at court who did not want Wolsey to be publicly executed," and he rubbed his hand over his stubbly chin, "No, Charles. It is simple. Wolsey procured the poison – bribed a guard to get it for him – and as a final act against his king, he denied me my right to publicly execute him for a traitor."

Charles Brandon nodded his head in agreement to his king, all the while cursing him for a blind fool, for the true answer to this mystery lay right underneath the king's nose.

Poison was woman's weapon.

And while Charles hoped to believe that no woman could be that dangerous and sly, he could think of no other woman but one who not only had cause, but who would be cunning enough to achieve such a murder.

Charles had been watching the king's favourite lady in most recent months, to try to understand the nature of the king's obsession. While it was plain to see that the Boleyn girl was pretty, in Charles' humble opinion, she did not hold a candle to her younger sister, Mary. But then of course, the king had already had his fun with the prettier sister.

But then, what could have caused to king to have such a strong infatuation for the lesser of the two beauties? Anne was no doubt stunning, and after some observation Charles had quickly learned that she was also witty – which he knew Henry appreciated in a woman – and though she lacked obvious sex appeal, she exuded a more mysterious type of sexual attraction, namely through her extremely expressive eyes.

Charles could tell what had attracted the king in the very first moments. But he failed to understand what it was that kept the king from discarding her, like all others before her, and throw away everything he had built to attain her as his wife.

After months of reflexion, he was no closer to understanding it, and as the queen's power at court dwindled and the mistress' influence grew, he was beginning to see a darker and more unfavourable side of the pretty lady, as though her mask was beginning to slip the closer she got to the throne. And more recently, Charles had begun considering that perhaps the king's destructive obsession with the lady stemmed from a much more sinister place.

Perhaps the reason for all this insanity and destructive devotion was not due to the power of love, but rather through the powers of witchcraft.

But to imply Henry's most beloved to be the one behind such an act would not bode well for even the king's closest and dearest friend.

After all, had he not only days ago arrested his most trusted advisor and condemned him to death?

No, to point a finger at the king's favourite would not end well while his obsession with the lady Anne remained strong.

And so, Charles sat back in his chair in companionable silence as he and the king watched the fire dancing in the fireplace, and he concluded that it did not matter. Regardless as to who's assumption on Wolsey's death was the correct one, the result remained the same: Cardinal Thomas Wolsey, King Henry VIII's most trusted advisor, right-hand man, and second most powerful man in all of England, was dead.

And his death sparked the beginning of a long list of people king Henry would be willing to sacrifice on his journey to achieve his goal.

July 1531

It was summer, and the Palace gardens were in bloom. Though Mary and Katherine continued to have no direct contact with the king, and were no longer invited to attend banquets, jousts or dances, their lives continued much as before. Mary kept herself busy with her studies and spent many hours a day praying either at her private prie deux in her chambers, or at the chapel with her mother, and though it suited them both perfectly well to devote their time into Mary's studies and to God, it ached their hearts to hear the joyous laughter and music from the great hall below as the king's court celebrated and danced without their queen and princess present.

But they refused to let it affect their spirits, and on days such as this, where God granted them good weather and good health, Mary and her mother would forfeit studies and enjoy the great outdoors.

The princess Mary and her mother were leisurely strolling through the neatly trimmed hedges, the pebbled path crunching lightly underneath their feet as the warm sun shone down on them, warming their pale skin.

As her mother spoke quietly beside her, Mary looked up at the blue sky and closed her eyes to feel the full power of the summer sun on her face, completely overjoyed to finally be free of the cold confinements of her chambers after having been bedbound in agony for the past three weeks.

It had become unbearably common, ever since she had begun her monthly bleeds, for the princess to experience sharp headaches and painful stomach cramps which would often riddle her unable to even stand due to vertigo and fainting. On these occasions Mary would remain shut up in her rooms, with all the windows covered to block out the sunlight, which did nothing but aggravate her excruciating migraines. She would endure days of strong bleeding during her courses, and often be bloated and uncomfortable as her body twisted and cramped to expel whatever evil it harboured inside her, and yet the physicians could do nothing to help her overcome the symptoms.

The physicians diagnosed the princess with 'hysteria', also known as 'strangulation of the womb', and assured her that while the disease was incurable, it would not affect her ability to lead a normal life.

But they had been wrong, as men often were in matters of women.

It affected Mary in unpredictable waves, sometimes appearing only once a year and other times once a month with her courses, and she would sink into a deep depression, cursing the sunlight for its potency and wishing to see no one but her mother. But when the pains would finally cease -which could sometimes be only a couple of days, and other times several weeks – her mood would instantly improve, and it was on an occasion such as this, that she would wash, dress and hurry out of her chambers to enjoy all aspects of life she had missed out on while curled up in agony in her bed.

"How fares the king?" Mary asked then as she and her mother approached the fountain, "Have you heard any news on him?"

Katherine raised an eyebrow, "I am told he is well," she said in her thick Spanish accent, "although he continues to disallow me to see him."

"He must tire of the lady soon," Mary said, then exhaled through her nose in frustration and looked away into the distance.

Katherine smiled upon hearing her daughter's hopeful tone, "Do not trouble your mind, Mary," she soothed, "I have accepted that, while I will always be the king's true wife, I am only so now in name. It is being your mother that gives me joy every day. It is what gives me the strength to get up every morning, and it is what fuels me to fight this annulment until my last breath."

Mary turned to face her mother and felt her chest tighten as she looked into the queen's sad eyes, aged visibly by her ongoing grief.

Katherine took her daughter's face in her hands, closed her eyes, and pressed her forehead gently against hers, "It is God's will that you be England's queen," she said softly, "England is ready for a woman king. And I predict that when you shall finally take the throne, your reign shall be glorious."

Mary smiled back at her mother and opened her mouth to speak when suddenly a voice called out from behind them, interrupting their private moment.

"Your graces," the voice called, "Pardon the intrusion. But his majesty, the king, has this moment departed to Woodstock."

Katherine's face drained of colour, "I do not understand."

Sensing the queen's distress, the messenger bowed deeply in shame. Katherine regained her composure and cleared her throat, "Who remains at the palace?"

"The king has moved the whole court, your majesty," the messenger replied, "They will remain at Woodstock. He has allowed that your ladies remain with you, and the princess her governess and tutors. The kitchen servants are sparce, but some are left behind for your pleasure," replied the messenger.

"He cannot do this, can he mother?" Mary asked, her voice cracking in shock.

"He may do as he pleases, Mary," the queen replied calmly, "He is the king," and she straightened her back and raised her chin, addressing the messenger, "If it pleases the king that we stay behind it will be for a good cause."

The messenger bowed once more and scurried away quickly, eager to remove himself from the shameful situation he had been put in.

"Why do you defend the king, lady mother?" Mary asked hot-headedly, "He is going against God and treating you, and me, his heir, appallingly. You should write to the Pope --"

"The Pope cannot help us, Mary," Katherine interrupted, "the king no longer answers to Rome."

"But lady mother, he cannot –"

"Hush, child!" Katherine ordered, suddenly furious, "You shall never speak ill of your father. He is the king of England

116

and no matter what opinion you may have of him or his actions, you shall obey his every whim without question."

Mary stared wide-eyed as her mother spoke to her, her voice cracking like a whip.

"Though it aches my heart that he resorts to such cruelty," the queen went on, her eyes shining with heartache, "I shall never think ill of your father. He is my king! He is my husband, and my best friend. He may have strayed from our love, but it is my failures that pushed him away, and I shall not allow you to speak of your king in that manner."

Katherine sniffed and held back the tears that threatened to fall, "Now you must promise me, Mary, that no matter what your thoughts may be, if they go against your father's wishes then you *must* remain loyal, even in the face of the utmost cruelty. I know my husband, and his temper and his whims sway from one day to the next like a leaf in the wind. He is not a consistent man. And though his light shines away from us now, it shall shine upon us again. And on that glorious day, you will be thankful that you remained his loyal and humble subject."

Mary realised then that she had tears streaming down her face, and she wiped them away forcefully as she attempted to calm her thundering heart, "I promise you, lady mother," she said, "that I shall remain his true, constant and loyal subject. For you, I shall be strong and endure."

Katherine took her daughter's hand and smiled, "Come," she said, "Let us continue our walk and speak of other matters. There has been too much time spent suffering over things we cannot change. The path ahead is long but for today we shall be merry and enjoy each other's company."

The following day the same messenger returned, his face crumpled in shame as he handed his queen a letter, "From the king, your majesty," he said, his voice low.

Katherine took it slowly, her heart heavy with dread of what she would find inside. She steeled herself as she broke the seal and unfolded the paper:

Katherine,
Though I feel some shame for my unannounced departure, I must remind you that you gave me no other choice. I have tried to reason with you for too long and as you will not accept that our marriage was never a true one, I saw no other choice but to treat you as though you were not even there. You will never admit to it, but I know it to be true that you lay with my brother on your wedding night to him. I have my own opinions on the matter as well as enough proof to satisfy my belief. The death of all our sons is alone proof enough. But I have also the word of my own brother, which I wish I had heeded closely before deciding to marry you. He himself told me on the morning after your wedding that he 'had that night been in Spain'. My foolish younger self did not want to believe him for I held a lust for you myself, and when he died and you gave your word that your marriage had not been consummated, I chose to believe you. And even when God took my heirs one by one, still I stood by you - by us - because I believed we were the future of England. But I can no longer dismiss what has been so clearly before me all along – that I have been married to my brother's wife, and I have wasted my youth on this sinful life with you. And for all that I cannot forgive you.
Therefore, I hereby banish you from my court and from my life. You shall be removed at once and may remain at Kimbolton Castle, of which I have no use.
You are also forbidden from seeing our daughter Mary or having any contact with her from this day forward, as I cannot risk her humility and loyalty to be tarnished by the poisonous

words you may spew against me.

King Henry VIII of England

Chapter 7

1532

     King Henry VIII's patience had run out, and chaos had begun.

Since the shunning of the queen of England from her rightful place at court, king Henry had sparked a war on anyone who would deny him what he believed to be true in his heart – that Katherine of Aragon was not his wife.

It did not matter to the stubborn king that not the Pope nor his people would stand with him in this belief, and that what was in his heart mattered little against the laws of God.

But his devotion to his cause – to marry the lady Boleyn and to produce sons by her – would not be abandoned, and if the Vatican would not grant him his wish, then he would take it for himself.

It began with the dissolution of the monasteries and many other religious institutions when the king and his parliament passed a series of Acts which stripped the Pope of his power over England and transferred it instead to the king.

It was no secret that Henry's new righthand man, Thomas Cromwell, had a strong dislike of the papal supremacy, and he eagerly supported the king in his decision to withdraw England from the Vatican's clutches, favouring the claim of royal supremacy over the church.

As Chancellor of the Exchequer, Cromwell was able to manipulate the members of the House of Commons in finally presenting a petition to the king, describing him as "the only head, sovereign lord, protector and defender" of the Church – The Church of England. And though parliament had previously, under the laws of Rome, denied the king his annulment to the queen, as supreme head of the church of

120

England, he no longer needed approval from a higher power on the matter.

"I would like to resign," said Sir Thomas Moore as he stopped the king in his tracks in the great hall two days after Parliament put forth the bill renouncing papal supremacy in England, "I can no longer offer you my services as Lord Chancellor, your majesty, while I do not support the path you have chosen to take."

Henry stared back at his old friend and councilman and inhaled deeply before replying, "You will do no such thing," he said icily.

"I do not support your majesty's decisions," Moore replied bravely, raising his chin in defiance, "I stand firm in my belief in the Pope's higher authority, and I support the queen's cause. You cannot want me for Lord Chancellor of your council."

"You support the queen?" Henry said casually, though Moore knew his answer would not be forgotten.

He nodded once, "I do. Your marriage is sacred and lawful, and nothing but death can change that."

Henry looked over his shoulder to judge the distance of his guards and whether they had heard their conversation, then he cleared his throat, "I regret your decision," Henry said and then ran his tongue over his yellowing teeth in thought, "But I trust you will sign the oath of supremacy when it is drawn up in due course."

Thomas Moore did not reply but merely bowed deeply to his monarch and old friend, turning on his heels before he could change his mind about accepting Moore's resignation.

But it was not long before the king began installing new, fresh faces within the court, specifically those who showed great favour towards the king's new ideals and offered support for his reformation from Rome.

Thomas Cranmer was one such new addition. Having had only minor positions in the church in his time, as well as having been out of the country as a resident ambassador at the court of the Holy Roman Emperor, Charles V, for the better part of a year, it came as a great surprise when Cranmer was suddenly recalled to England and appointed Archbishop of Canterbury. And while it was not his achievements in his professional career that secured him the position, but rather his passionate take on the reformation, it was the Boleyn family who made sure to secure him the position above all others, though many other bishops had far more merit and experience for the role. And for the first time in history, England would have a Protestant Archbishop of Canterbury.

King Henry VIII's council was finally strong and united under one purpose.

Even the queen's supporters had all given up hope of their reconciliation, and before long it was clear that any such conversation would not be tolerated lightly.

And so, while most of the people abhorred the new developments at court, no one dared to utter a word against it, for fear of losing their own precious heads.

November 1532

"Is there any word?" Mary asked her ladies, as she did every morning since her mother's banishment from court.

"No, your grace," Cecily replied as she replaced the cold cloth on the princess' forehead, "Nothing from the queen."

Mary groaned in pain, rolled over in her bed and covered her face with her hands, "It is too bright!" she wailed, "I want my mother!"

The lady Cecily walked towards the window and stuffed a cloth in between the panels of the shutters in an attempt to block out the lazy winter sunlight.

Mary moaned in pain as she so often did, her belly cramping uncontrollably, "I need the physician," she begged as she gritted her teeth against the pain.

"Your grace, he will not come again," Cecily replied as she returned to Mary's side and wiped her sweaty brow, "Mary," she cooed, picking up a cup of small ale from the side and holding it to Mary's cracked lips, "you must try to drink something."

Mary pushed Cecily's hand away, "I do not want it!" she exclaimed and knocked the cup from her lady's hand.

Cecily immediately got down on all fours and dabbed at the liquid on the floor, indifferent to the princess' fits of rage.

Frances padded over quietly so as not to upset the princess with any loud or sudden movements and knelt down to help her friend clean up the mess. When they were done, they moved away from the princess' bed and through to the adjoining room, so that they could speak openly without being overheard.

"Should we summon the physician?" Frances asked, her voice barely audible over the wailing that came from the princess in the bed next door.

Cecily shook her head, "He has been five times this week," she replied knowingly, "He has already said she has the 'strangulation of the womb' and that she may suffer with this all her life. It is something we must become accustomed to."

Frances crossed herself, "It is hard when the only thing that will soothe the princess in this state is the queen, and she is not allowed to visit."

"Hush, Frances!" Cecily suddenly snapped, "It is by the order of the king, and we must obey his word."

"Of – of course," Frances stammered, her blue eyes widening in shock, "I only mean that the princess would recover quicker if her mind was at ease."

"While that is true," Cecily agreed, her stern face softening a little, "there is nothing we can do but tend to her and make sure she is as comfortable as possible. Another day or so and she should be recovered."

They nodded at one another in agreement and suddenly realised the silence that engulfed the princess' apartments, and they both moved closer to the open archway into Mary's room and peered in to see that she was finally fast asleep.

Cecily turned back to Frances, placed a finger to her lips and jerked her head towards the chairs by the far window.

"She is asleep," she whispered victoriously, the shadow of a smile twitching at the corners of her mouth, "Let us enjoy some quiet before she wakes to continue her wailing."

Frances pursed her lips in disdain at Cecily's mocking words but followed her to the window nonetheless, eager to sit down and relax for a moment before their duties to the princess began all over again, for Mary's rages were frequent and intense since her spontaneous parting from her mother.

But they did their duty uncomplainingly, and drew comfort from the belief that, surely, things could not get any worse.

May 1533

But things did get worse.

"Your grace, a messenger," the lady Frances said as the door to Mary's chambers was opened, and the messenger entered. He bowed his head briefly at Mary and handed her a note before exiting the chambers without being dismissed. Her ladies watched him leave in awe as they wondered what madness had befallen him to disrespect the princess in that way.

But Mary did not even notice for fear of what news the note may bring, and as she quickly pealed open the seal and read its contents, all the colour drained from her face.

124

"Oh God…" she whispered, covering her mouth with her hand, "No, no!"

"Your grace?" the lady Cecily asked as she dropped the linens she had been folding and hurried towards Mary.

Mary dropped the note as though it had burned her and held her hands over her eyes, howling uncontrollably.

Her ladies knelt beside her and tried to soothe her but to no avail.

While Cecily continued to try to calm the princess, Frances picked up the discarded note and scanned it, hoping to understand what news from court had distressed Mary so.

"Frances!" Cecily suddenly hissed over Mary's weeping when she saw Frances' breach in privacy, ready to scold the younger lady for her insubordination.

But when Frances looked up, her eyes wide in horror, Cecily's stern look melted away and her expression changed into a wordless question.

"Archbishop Cranmer," Frances read aloud, her voice shaking, "has declared the king's marriage to Katherine of Aragon as null and void. The king has already married the lady in secret… It says that the princess shall henceforth be styled 'the lady Mary' and has been deemed as illegitimate from this day forth."

Upon hearing the words spoken aloud, Mary suddenly doubled over in her seat and vomited, her body expelling her distress in any way it could.

She continued retching even after her stomach had nothing left to pass, and her body trembled, exhausted and in shock.

Cecily called for a servant to come and clean up the mess and then she took Mary by the arm, steering her away from the puddle of vomit, and wiped her face with her handkerchief as the princess' teeth chattered violently.

No one spoke for what seemed like an eternity as the servant cleaned the mess and her ladies undressed and washed her.

Once all was cleaned, the servant was dismissed and Mary, wrapped in a gown for comfort, walked towards the fireplace and watched in silence as the flames consumed the wood into ash.

Her ladies stood motionless behind her, uncertain of what to do, when suddenly Mary's voice broke the silence, "Where is the note?"

Frances took a step towards her and handed Mary the parchment, who without hesitation flung it into the hearth before her and stared emotionlessly as it curled at the edges and melted into nonexistence.

Frances moved closer to Mary as she continued to stare blankly ahead and placed a comforting hand on her mistress' shoulder, then jolted back in terror when, as if out of nowhere, Mary let out an excruciating, primal shriek, covered her face with her hands, and crumpled into a heap on the floor, utterly defeated.

June 1533

Despite the glorious sunshine and the elaborate occasion, the people of England had felt no joy on the day of Anne Boleyn's coronation.

"The streets were bare save for a few dozen people," Margaret Pole the Countess of Salisbury told Mary when she visited her to share the news, "And those that were there cheered with little to no enthusiasm."

Mary rose from her seat in one fluid motion, waved her governess' comment aside and walked through the archway to the adjacent room and away from the conversation.

"It is hard for her to hear anything at all about it," Frances mumbled.

"I understand," Margaret said sadly, as they both stood and listened as Mary began to rant and rave in the next room.

"But I heard," Frances said, turning back to face the lady Pole, eager to continue the topic, "that the few that were present, were in fact paid by Thomas Boleyn, the lady's father, to make an appearance."

"That I can absolutely believe to be true," Margaret replied, her eyebrows raised in disdain for the man.

Frances *tsked* then as she looked quickly over her shoulder, "I do hate to see the prin – I mean, the lady Mary, in such distress."

"There is nothing for it," Margaret replied, shaking her head, "Cecily is in there with her now. Mary does not need you both present while she rages and weeps."

Frances nodded in agreement, then added with a whisper, "Do you know what is to happen once the king's new baby is born?"

"I am not even certain that the king knows what shall happen," the older lady replied, "It will all depend on the babe's sex. Let us pray it is a boy so we can all regain some peace in this lifetime," and Margaret crossed herself, "I fear none of us shall be safe if this new wife of his does not provide him with a living son and heir."

"But if we pray for a boy then the pri – the lady Mary will be replaced in the line of succession," Frances said quietly, jolting in fright when she heard a crash in the next room suggesting Mary had begun throwing objects in her anger yet again.

"My dear girl," Margaret said as she raised an eyebrow at the commotion next door, "with the old queen's marriage to the king annulled, the lady Mary is a bastard, regardless of this new child's gender. It shall surpass Mary in rank just as she surpassed Henry Fitzroy, his bastard by Bessie Blount," Margaret stepped around Frances then and made her way towards the archway into the next room, "But if God grants the king a son, we can all rest easy again. And in time he may find it in his heart to reinstate Mary to her former title."

"Do you really believe that could happen?" Frances asked incredulously as she watched Mary's governess stepping bravely into the lion's den as Mary's screams continued, "After everything that the king has done?"

Margaret shrugged, "We can only pray," and then she stepped out of Frances' line of sight and called, "Now, that is enough, Mary!" her voice cracking like a whip, and Frances raised her eyebrows and turned away, glad to be safely away from Mary's latest outburst.

September 1533
Greenwich Palace, London

But it was not to be, and despite the king's prayers, his new queen gave birth to a daughter.

The child was strong, with hair as red as fire like her father's; but she was a girl, nonetheless.

"Cancel the celebratory joust," king Henry said over his shoulder as he angrily waved his messenger away, "I am in no mood to celebrate the occasion."

Henry was sitting with his back towards the fireplace, his feet propped up on the table as he stared into the distance, unseeing.

"What shall the princess be named, your majesty?" Charles Brandon asked, in an attempt to cheer his king. Though the king's closest and oldest friend had recently been dealing with his own personal sufferings, he knew not to burden Henry with such things. And while the death of Charles' wife meant also the death of the king's own sister, it came as no shock to Charles that Henry would not mourn her passing for long in the wake of his own turmoil. For nothing mattered more to

Henry than his own successes, and his younger sister's death meant little to him in the grand scheme of things.

Henry only shrugged in response.

Charles moved closer to Henry and sat down, "Your majesty…" he started, then thought better of the formality of his tone and took on his role as a friend, believing that the situation asked for a more familiar approach, "Henry," he said, then cleared his throat, "the next one will surely be a prince."

Henry scoffed, "That is what the queen has promised," he replied, raising an eyebrow, "But she also promised that *this one* would be a boy so…"

"Do not dwell on the matter," Charles said then, "A princess will secure an alliance for England one day to strengthen and safeguard our people."

Henry looked at his oldest friend then through narrowed eyes, "That is what you told me on the day of the lady Mary's birth."

"I did?" Charles replied, his eyes widening in memory of that day, over sixteen years ago.

So much had changed since then, things Charles never thought he would witness, things which still shocked him to consider even now. But he cleared his mind of it, focusing instead on the future ahead, "This time it is a legitimate princess," Charles said astutely, "Your marriage to your new queen is indisputable, and no one can deny your child's legitimacy when it comes to creating a match."

Henry grunted and nodded in agreement, both men thinking back on when the French king revoked the betrothal of his second son, Henri, to Mary some years ago.

Henry sighed pensively then as he stared blindly ahead, the embers glowing in the hearth, casting shadows on his face.

Having nothing left to say, the king waved his hand, dismissing his friend, and Charles bowed his head to the king, then rose slowly from his seat and exited the room, leaving the king to wallow in self-pity.

Hunsdon House, Hertfordshire

When the newly titled lady Mary heard news from court that the king's harlot had birthed a useless girl, she threw her head back and cackled so loudly that the ceilings echoed with her laughter. And yet the irony of her own laughter reverberating right back onto her did not escape the former princess, for her new replacement's worthless gender reminded her that she too was not what her father had wanted, and that it had been the sole cause of all her troubles.

It seemed that, once again, the prince that was promised was not to be, and though she found herself in her own grievous circumstances, Mary tried to see the light in her ever-darkening situation.

Following the harlot's coronation, Mary, like her mother, had been banished from court and sent to reside in Hertfordshire until further instructions for her future were decided. Much to her humiliation, her household was drastically reduced on the eve before her departure, a messenger notifying her rather informally and spontaneously that her servants were to be dismissed, as well as her governess, the lady Pole, and that she was to travel to Hunsdon House with only her two ladies-in-waiting.

Mary had watched the messenger leave her chambers, and though she could not even remember if she had ever seen him before, she wondered if indeed she would ever see him, or any of her personal servants, again.

Mary had been at Hunsdon House for a little over a week when she awoke shivering in her bed one morning.

"Someone light a fire!" she called from underneath her blankets and listened as her ladies hurried along the cold wooden floorboards and began breathing life into last night's embers. Mary lay there shivering, staring blankly ahead as she finally allowed herself to dwell on her new situation, and the realisation of the new baby's birth finally dawned on her. Girl or boy, the child was her replacement as heir apparent. Everything Mary had had just days ago was suddenly that little girl's, and she was simply discarded and left to rot, out of sight. Mary groaned and pulled the covers over her head and curled up into a ball, classing the day ahead as pointless to attend.

She spent the following days locked in her room, either in bed or wrapped in blankets near the fireplace. She dismissed her ladies as soon as the fire was lit in the mornings and refused any food, feeling no desire to nourish the worthless body that she had been born into.

The one thing Mary did draw comfort from in those gloomy days was her correspondence with her mother, who had begun writing her almost every day since her arrival at Hunsdon House, claiming that Mary's newly dissolved household meant their communications would remain safe from prying eyes.

Her mother wrote mainly of strength and persistence, sharing little of her own personal struggles, no doubt to remind Mary that earthly possessions and comforts mattered little when confronted with one's higher purpose. But Mary, never having known another way of life but that of a princess could not help but feel wronged, and she made that clear to her mother in her responding letters.

But Katherine's replies never strayed into vengeful slander, no matter how often Mary coaxed her to agree with her own feelings of betrayal, for Katherine did not need verbal recognition for what she believed with all her heart and soul to be true. Katherine believed herself to be Henry VIII's true and lawful wife. Everything else that came after that fact did not matter, for Katherine knew that her husband's rage towards her did not stem from a place of evil, but rather a place of hurt. And if he believed that he may find his happiness on this path, then Katherine would stand by her husband's decision, as her master and her king.

But though Katherine's letters to Mary had never been anything but loyal about the king, those too were quickly forbidden, no doubt at the venomous suggestion of the king's great whore.

Mary received the order to immediately stop all interaction with her mother gracefully – as a princess ought to react to an order from her father and king – but inside she began to spiral, and the fear and rage she felt within her grew unchecked.

She took herself to the private prie deux in the corner of her rooms at Hunsdon House and knelt before Jesus on the cross before pulling out her rosary beads and clasping her hands together tightly. She closed her eyes and opened her mind and soul to God.

Almighty Father in heaven, I pray to you for strength and guidance. I ask You humbly to watch over my poor mother while I cannot, for she needs You now more than ever. I pray also that You would open my bewitched father's eyes to the she-devil's witchcraft, for surely You cannot want such a fiend on the throne of England. But above all else, oh Lord – and I know I am asking for much – but above all else I pray that you grant me patience during these strange times. For I know the journey to the throne shall be a long one, and I only wish to stay true to the destiny that You have granted me.

Chapter 8

October 1533
Hunsdon House, Hertfordshire

After a month of wallowing and grieving the life she should have had, Mary unlocked the doors to her chambers and announced to her ladies that she would like to take a stroll to the stables.

"Shall we bring up some food first, my lady," Cecily asked, and Mary flinched, her new title still sounding so strange to her. It made her briefly think of Reggie, and how comical he would have likely found her downfall, and the memory of his easy-going nature made her smile.

"My lady?" Cecily said again when Mary did not reply.

"I shall eat when I return," Mary said, and her ladies shared a concerned look.

Mary understood their worries, for she too had been shocked at her appearance when she had caught a glimpse of herself in the looking glass that morning.

And though she was but seventeen-years-old, after a month of refusing most of her food for lack of appetite, her body had become withered and gaunt, and her skin had turned as pale as ash.

But upon seeing the worry in her ladies' eyes, Mary knew that the time for self-pity was over, and that she would have to sustain herself with more than just God's strength.

"On second thought," Mary said, "I will take something to eat now."

Cecily curtsied and quickly hurried to fetch her mistress some much-needed sustenance.

As Mary nibbled on a piece of bread and took small sips of her wine, she ordered Frances to open the shutters to let in the

Autumn breeze – for the air inside her chambers had become stagnant and in much need of fresh air – and she contemplated her days ahead.

With her tutors dismissed on the king's order that she need not study for subjects unbefitting her new station, Mary found that she had, for the first time in her life, all the time in the world to do exactly what she wanted. And yet for a moment she was left baffled at her inability to conjure up even one thing she enjoyed doing for leisure.

But once the plate of food was cleared and the wine drained, Mary stood from her seat by the fire in one fluid motion, eager to explore her new residence, when all of a sudden her vision began to blur as the blood rushed to her head and she fell back down into her seat, her body feeling unsteady and her head heavy.

"You must not exert yourself, my lady," Cecily said, suddenly beside her.

"I wish to go for a walk," Mary said as she once again tried to stand.

"Forgive me," Cecily said quietly, fearing she would fuel the fire that often raged within her mistress, "but it would not be wise to do too much, in your weakened state."

"I must agree with Cecily," Frances added in the background, her tone pleading.

Mary looked at them both and saw their concerned expressions once more, but this time it did nothing but anger her, "I have eaten as you suggested," she said defiantly, "And now I should like to take a walk to the stables. Princess or not, *you* are still *my* ladies, and I shall do as I please."

Cecily dropped her gaze and pursed her lips, "Shall we accompany you, at least?" she asked.

"No," Mary replied curtly, "I should like to be alone," and she rose steadily from her seat, straightened herself and exited her chambers for the first time in weeks.

Mary strolled slowly through the brightly lit corridors, down the wide staircase and through the landing which led to the main entrance. As she emerged through the large wooden doorway, she noticed that it was drizzling, but rather than turning back into the dryness and warmth of the manor, Mary walked out into the courtyard and let the light rain wash over her.

She lifted her face up to the sky and closed her eyes as she breathed in the cold, wet air, then she opened her arms wide and began to slowly twirl around in circles as an overwhelming wave of liberty flowed through her, and with a giggle she made her way towards the stables.

Upon entering the long wooden building, Mary was surprised to see much kerfuffle being made around the fifty working horses that were housed within, and she realised that she had never actually stepped foot into a stable before, having always had her master of horse groom and bring her pony to her without her needing to enter the horses' premises.

Immediately she noticed an overwhelming smell that undoubtedly came not only from the many horses confined under one roof, but also from the labouring boys and men working tirelessly to maintain and keep the animals. Mary was not deterred though, but was rather intrigued, for this place had never been acceptable for her to enter as a princess of England, but now as a mere lady she had been granted access, and the sight before her was eye-opening.

She made her way slowly down through the middle of the stables where stable boys groomed or shoed a horse, while another was busy shovelling the manure from its standing stalls, and Mary watched in awe as the stable hands went about their business, completely unaware of her presence, as though the only thing that mattered were the horses.

But despite having walked the length of the stable and peered into almost every stall, Mary had failed to spot her pony, and as she craned her neck to see through all the workers and their assigned mounts, she noticed one stable hand was not occupied.

"You," Mary called as she lifted her skirts and trudged over the heaps of straw that covered the dusty floor, making her way towards him.

The stable boy, who was not a boy at all but a young man, pushed himself off the wall that he had been leaning against and turned to face Mary.

"Where is my pony?" she asked, "I could not see her in her assigned stall."

The lad, who must have been about twenty years old, raised his eyebrows in thought, "Forgive me," he said, "but your pony is in her assigned stall," and he nudged his chin into the air, directing Mary's gaze to the least favourable stall in the far back of the stable.

Mary frowned and looked back at the stable hand, "That is not her assigned stall," she said with great certainty, "She is a pony of noble standing, a gift from king Charles V of Spain himself and she belongs to your royal –" Mary broke off and held her hand over her mouth upon hearing her own words aloud, realising that with her downfall, came the downfall of all associated with her, even, it seemed, her pony. And if the reality had not hurt so much, Mary may have laughed aloud at her sudden pity for the animal, for surely it cared little as to which stall it stood in for hours a day.

"… that – is that her new stall?" she asked then, after adjusting her attitude.

"Yes, princess," the young man answered politely, and he smiled, hoping to restore Mary's assurance.

Mary nodded and looked down at the ground, suddenly ashamed at her outburst, "You do not need to call me 'princess'," she said as convincingly as she could, though she had felt comforted in being called by the title she had always been known by.

But the young man ignored Mary's comment, "Did you wish to see her?" he asked instead and stretched his arm out before him.

Mary nodded and he led the way back through the men as they called to one another for another nail or mumbled sweet nothings to their steads as they brushed them gently, and when they reached Mary's pony's stall, he cleared his throat, "Did you need anything else from me, princess?"

"You do not have to call me 'princess'," she said again, "I am the Lady Mary now," and though Mary had tried to say the words as cheerfully as possible, she noticed her voice drop as she spoke, as though her sadness weighed down each word.

He bowed his head quickly and smiled, "To me you will always be the princess," he said, then he turned and walked away, whistling as he went.

A week went by in which Mary focused on regaining her strength. Though she still spent hours each morning at prayer to nourish her soul, she made sure to eat all the meals her ladies brought her to also nourish her body, and it was not long before she and others noticed the changes.

"You are looking well today, my lady," Frances pointed out one afternoon as the three of them sat together by the fire reading their bibles.

Mary raised her head and smiled, "I feel well," she replied cheerily, "I may even have my pony saddled and go for a ride if the weather permits it."

Cecily and Frances both turned their heads to look outside at the darkening clouds and then shared a look, "May this be to do with the young stable hand you have been speaking of lately?"

Mary's cheeks blushed, "Not at all," she said as she pretended to regain interest in her reading.

Though she knew nothing about the young man who had shown her to her pony last week, Mary had felt strangely drawn to his confident nature despite his low station.

Perhaps it had been his unwillingness to steer away from calling her by her rightful title of 'princess', or maybe even the deep blackness of his eyes? Something had peaked Mary's interests in the young man, and though she felt impure to even think it, she had been itching for an excuse to return to the stables to see him.

"I would have to advise against it, if it were the case," said Cecily – ever the voice of reason.

"It is not the case," Mary insisted casually, keeping her eyes on the bible on her lap.

Later that day, without announcing her departure, Mary left her apartments and made her way to the stables at the end of the property.

As she approached the building, her heart skipped a beat, and she stopped in her tracks to internally chastise herself for her foolishness.

She was here to see her pony and request it be saddled up for the afternoon. There was no more to it than that. And in fact, it did not matter if the lad was there or not, for it had nothing to do with her visit.

And with that she nodded her head at herself and stepped through the stable's entrance.

There were far fewer stable hands at work than last time when Mary entered the building. In fact, it was practically empty but for one young boy, and as she took a step inside, she could see that all the horses were in their assigned standing stalls, some munching on the freshly laid out straw, while others simply stood facing the wall blankly, and her stomach lurched at the realisation that she would not in fact accidentally bump into him.

She *tsked* at herself and shook her head, then made her way towards the young boy in the far corner of the stables near her pony, "Pardon me," she called as she approached, but the boy did not look up from his work, "Pardon me!" Mary repeated when she got closer, but the boy still ignored her.

She frowned at his insolence and walked around to face him, "I demand you answer me!" she said angrily and upon seeing her standing before him, the young boy jumped backwards, his eyes wide with shock and his hand on his chest.

Mary too jolted a step backwards at his abrupt movement when suddenly she heard laughter behind her.

She turned around, eyes wide from the fright, and felt instantly relieved to see the young man she had been thinking of all week standing just a few feet behind her.

"Why do you laugh?" she said as an embarrassed smile spread across her face.

He took a step towards her, "The boy is deaf," he said in way of explanation for the young boy's behaviour.

Mary opened her mouth in realisation and looked back at the boy who was still standing there with his hand over his chest, no doubt to try and calm his pounding heart, "Sorry," she said quietly hoping he would see from her expression that she had meant no harm.

The boy waved his hand in the air as he turned and walked away, shaking his head as he went, then Mary turned back to the young man and breathed a small laugh, "I did not know."

"Of course not," he said with a crooked smile which sent a shiver down Mary's spine, and she was left wondering if it had been the sudden cold breeze that swept through the stables or his smile which had caused it, "How could you have?"

Mary nodded and they fell silent for a moment, and though they both stood before each other with nothing to say, Mary was surprised to realise that the silence between them did not feel awkward.

"I was actually hoping to have my pony saddled for this afternoon," Mary said then when the silence had stretched on for a moment too long.

The young man turned in the direction of her pony's stall, "Of course, princess," he said as he began walking and Mary's stomach tightened at the title, but this time she did not correct him.

She followed him to the pony's stall and watched as he quickly brushed her little mare and gently placed the bridle over her head and the bit between her teeth. Then he turned to pick up the saddle when suddenly there was a great flash followed by a rumble in the sky and they both looked at each other.

"I think perhaps it is best not to ride out today," Mary said then with a little laugh.

"Wise choice, your grace," the stable hand replied as he heaved the heavy saddle back onto its rack.

Mary moved closer to her pony and tickled its soft lips, "Sorry, girl," she mumbled, "Maybe tomorrow."

"I wouldn't count on it," the lad said as he approached and carefully removed the pony's bit from its mouth, "But one can hope," and he flashed her another crooked smile.

Mary suddenly felt giddy at the sight of his lopsided grin, and she was embarrassed to realise her face was turning red by the thrill of his proximity.

She turned away from him and cleared her throat, "So," she said as she tried to compose herself, "what is it you are doing here when no one else is?"

The lad shrugged, "I have not much else to do with my time," he admitted, "And I enjoy the horses' company – they are unproblematic."

Mary nodded, "Well I am glad that you were here," she said, and her cheeks burned at her bluntness, "to ready my pony for me, I mean," she added then.

"And to rescue you from your encounter with Deaf John," he said with a chuckle.

Mary breathed a laugh, "Deaf John," she repeated, "I am embarrassed at my behaviour towards him. I should have been more patient."

The young man bent under the pony's stall tie, which kept it from roaming around freely, and straightened up before replying, "You couldn't have known," he said again and then cleared his throat, "Is there anything else I can help you with, your grace?"

"Oh, no," Mary said immediately, feeling weak in the knees at his closeness, and she took a step back before she crumpled into a pile of satin on the dusty floor before him, "I should get back inside."

The young man looked outside at the heavy downpour that had begun as if out of nowhere and then back at Mary, "You'll get wet," he pointed out.

"I – it is alright," Mary stammered, "I will hurry," and with that she bent her head and walked around him towards the great wooden door that led outside.

She did not look back as she walked hastily up the path towards the house, her dress and hood becoming soaked in the rain, but as she reached the courtyard, she could not bring herself to step inside without casting a look behind her in hopes of catching one last quick glimpse of him.

When her eyes adjusted through the thick curtain of rain and she caught sight of the dark entrance of the stables, she was surprised to see that he was standing outside it, watching her just as she was watching him. And when their eyes met, he offered her small smile before bowing at the waist, then he turned on his heel and disappeared out of sight.

141

The storm that had hit as if out of nowhere, disappeared just as spontaneously two days later and Mary awoke with only one thing in mind.

"Send word to the stables," Mary told Frances whom she thought would be less judgmental, "that I wish to speak with…" and she broke off.

"Yes, my lady?" Frances asked, "Who shall I send for?"

Mary shook her head, "No, don't send for him," she said, "I – I was going to invite him for a stroll in the gardens, but I do not know his name," and the reality of her foolish infatuation dawned on her, "Forget it," she said quickly, "It doesn't matter," and she sat down heavily at the chair before her looking glass.

Frances curtsied and began plaiting her auburn locks before twisting and pinning them elegantly underneath Mary's hood, then turned to pick up her bodice. Once Mary was dressed and sitting by the fire eating her breakfast, Frances snuck out of the chambers and quickly made her way down to the stables.

"Good morning," Frances said to the first stable hand she encountered, "I am looking for a young man. The lady Mary requests to see him."

"Who d'ya mean?" the man answered gruffly, jerking his bald head towards the dozens of men within the busy stables.

"That is the question, my good sir," Frances said, trying to sound appeasing, "all I know is that the lady Mary spoke to him briefly last week in regard to her pony?"

"Arthur," the man grunted without looking up from his work.

"Arthur?" Frances repeated and started looking around the stable as though his name would help her identify the mystery man.

The man beside her raised his meaty arm and pointed, "Him," and Frances thanked him with a pretty smile before hurrying towards the young man he had pointed out.

As she approached, Frances immediately understood Mary's strange behaviour in the last week, for in front of her stood a tall, handsome young man with eyes as dark as the night and hair as golden as the sun, "Are you Arthur?" she asked.

"Yes," he answered it like a question, unsure what could be wanted from him.

"The lady Mary requests an audience," Frances said with a knowing smile and then she turned and walked away.

"Now?" she heard Arthur call from behind her and she turned around to face him, as she continued to walk backwards.

"Now."

When the doors to Mary's chambers were opened and Frances walked through the door practically skipping, Mary raised her head and frowned at her lady, "What has cheered you?" she asked but then froze as she saw who was following behind.

"Arthur, my lady," Frances said giddily, "As requested," and she grabbed Cecily by the arm and pulled her to the far corner of the rooms, giving Mary and Arthur some privacy.

The young man took a careful step into the royal apartments as though he were uncertain whether the floor beneath him would accept his unworthy tread.

He stood there, looking around himself, his arms hanging awkwardly at his sides when suddenly Frances cleared her throat, breaking the silence that had ensued.

Mary shifted uncomfortably in her seat, "Please," she said, and pointed at a chair before her.

Arthur did as he was asked, never once stopping from looking around at the beautiful tapestries and intricately carved stone

143

fireplace, "Your lady said you requested an audience?" he said quietly.

Mary looked over her shoulder at her ladies and saw Cecily whispering frantically at Frances, who ignored her and gave Mary a reassuring nod.

Mary turned her attention back to the stable boy, "Y – yes," she stammered, "I'm sorry, I am a little lost for words. I had planned to invite you for a stroll in the gardens, but – well, I guess this is fine too."

Arthur nodded, "Forgive me, princess," he said as he leaned forward in his seat, "But what is it you wished to speak with me about?"

"Well, I –" Mary mumbled and she looked back at her ladies, "I was rather hoping for a private audience, hence the suggestion of the garden where we may have spoken more freely."

"What is it you wished to speak freely with me about?" he asked, "What could you have to say to someone like me?"

Someone like me. The words exploded in Mary's head like a firework, and her cheeks flushed with desire as she looked into his black eyes.

Mary felt suddenly flustered as her mind went into overdrive and she began to consider just *what* she could have to say to someone like him, for his question held some merit. *What could she have to say?* And she realised quite quickly that there was absolutely nothing to say, and that what she felt from the moment she had set eyes on him was nothing more than sinful lust.

She knew nothing about this young man, not his thoughts, not his likes or dislikes, or anything else of importance. Had it not been only moments ago that she had even learned his name?

But there was no denying the desire that she felt for this stranger. It was as undeniable as the stars in the sky, and before she could change her mind Mary turned to her whispering ladies in the corner of her room and ordered them to leave.

Frances rose immediately while Cecily gave Mary a stern look, but Mary paid her no attention and simply waited patiently until they left the rooms, closing the door behind them.

"I should say this is not very wise," the young man said, "For a princess to be alone without supervision to ensure her virtue?"

Mary shrugged, "I have already told you – I am no longer the princess."

"Nevertheless," he said as he stood up from his seat and walked around it before placing both hands on the back of the chair, "I would hate to be blamed for the question to your name."

Mary stood up from her seat then and sighed, "I appreciate your concern," she said, "But I have been assigned to a lesser life. One where I may be in charge of my own future. And while I know this may seem impulsive, there is something between us that I should like to explore."

"Do I get a say in this?" Arthur said then, his lopsided smile assuring her that he was jesting.

"I would never give myself to someone fully until I am wed," Mary said as she took a step closer to him.

"And we are not wed," he pointed out.

"Nor shall we ever be, in all honesty," Mary added, and for a moment she felt utterly devastated at the truth, and she realised what a weak organ the heart was.

Arthur took a step out from behind the chair he had moments ago occupied and took her hand in his, his workman's skin feeling rough against Mary's, and she breathed a laugh at how mismatched they were.

But despite their differing pasts and their even more incompatible futures, Mary decided that if her father saw no more use for her then she should be allowed to make some choices for herself, and in that moment, she chose to live.

Mary reached up on her tiptoes and closed her eyes before brushing her lips softly over his, so lightly it may have been the breeze that flowed through the open window. And in that instant, though it had lasted only a second, she had felt her entire body come alive, and she wondered just how she had ever even lived before that moment.

When she opened her eyes and pulled away, her mind ablaze with delight, she believed for one brief instant that all that she had endured – all the loss and pain that she had suffered – had all been worth it if it had led her to this. And if her fall from grace would mean she could choose whom she would wed, then it had not all been in vain.

As she took a step back and smiled up at the handsome stable boy before her, she thought that perhaps God's plan for her had never been one of glory and grandeur, but to find joy in the simplicities of life. And as he looked back at her with that worshipping look in his eyes, she thought that maybe, just maybe, she had found it.

December 1533

A month later, Cecily burst into Mary's chambers, "My lady," she called, "Half a dozen men have arrived on horseback just this moment. Most of them guards."

"Did you see who it was?" Mary asked as she stood from her seat at the window and peered outside.

Cecily shook her head, "They flew the king's standard, but I could not recognise who it was."

"Nevertheless, we must greet them," Mary said as she swallowed her nervousness, "If my father has sent them, it must be important."

Mary brushed down her skirts in anticipation of her visitors while Cecily straightened her hood upon her head. Princess or not, she was still the daughter of the king, and presence was key.

"Find Frances and meet me at the top of the stairs," Mary ordered as they exited her rooms, and Cecily hurried away in search of Frances.

Once all together, Mary and her ladies descended the staircase to the hall, and the servants who had been passing scurried away.

The guards opened the doors to the hall and the usher announced them, "Sir Thomas Cromwell and the Imperial ambassador Eustace Chapuys."

The two men entered, Sir Thomas Cromwell first – his black velvet cloak suggesting to Mary he had recently had yet another promotion – followed closely by the ambassador to Spain and their guards. Mary watched them nervously, unaware of what brought them there that day.

She noticed with indignation that Sir Thomas Cromwell, Chancellor of the Exchequer, had barely looked at her and had completely failed to show any sign of respect, while *senor* Chapuys had removed his hat, revealing a full head of grey hair, and bowed deeply.

She smiled at him and nodded her head in gratitude for his respect, "Gentlemen, I welcome you both," she said gracefully, "What, may I ask, is the reason for your unannounced visit?"

"Lady Mary," Cromwell said without looking at her as a guard handed him a document, "I bring news from London," and he cleared his throat, his Adam's apple jumping up and down, "By order of the king, your entire household is hereby dissolved from this day forward –"

"What?!" Mary interrupted, unable to contain her surprise.

But Cromwell simply ignored her interjection and continued, "… dissolved from this day forward, and you are to be transferred from Hunsdon House into the princess Elizabeth's newly formed nursery at Hatfield, where you shall be placed under the guardianship of the Lady Anne Shelton, the aunt of Queen Anne."

Mary stared wide-eyed and frozen in shock, fumbling with her rosary beads that she had tucked inside her sleeve for comfort, as Sir Thomas Cromwell handed the document to the Imperial ambassador, who perused it swiftly and then looked up at Mary, a burdened expression on this kind face, "It is so," *senor* Chapuys simply said in confirmation.

Mary inhaled deeply and raised her chin, her hands clasped before her, "Very well," she said nonchalantly, though she was screaming inside, "if the king commands it."

She turned to her ladies who stood behind her, their faces contorted in confusion and grief, "By order of the king, I must relieve you of your duties to me," Mary said, her voice cracking with emotion.

She stopped for a moment and cleared her throat, trying to compose herself for she would not give Cromwell, her father's lap dog, the satisfaction of seeing her cry.

She took a step towards her friends, opened her arms and held them in an embrace, "I will miss you both," Mary whispered as they cried silently.

Behind them, Mary could hear the guards climbing the staircase to her chambers, where they would no doubt sift through her possessions and take anything of value back to her father's court, leaving her with only the bare essentials necessary for her new life as the baby princess' servant.

Mary released her ladies and turned to face Mr Cromwell, "When do we depart for Hatfield?" she asked.

"The horses are being made ready as we speak. Your belongings will follow," he said, his tone indifferent, almost bored.

Mary nodded, "Then I shall take a walk until our departure," she announced, "As my final moment of freedom I should like to be alone."

Eustace Chapuys bowed grandly as she walked by, "Your highness," he said quietly, and Mary offered him a small smile before hurrying outside.

Once outside she picked up her skirts and ran as fast as she could past the guards and the onlookers, and made her way to the stables, her sobs escaping her as she ran, too cruel was this latest act of her father's.

Was it not enough that she be stripped of her titles and nobility, that she be forbidden any contact with her mother and forced to live away from all that she knew?

Could he not have left her to live a simple life and forgotten about her existence?

As soon as Mary reached the stables, she craned her neck to find Arthur over the commotion that had ensued. All the horses were out of their stables and being brushed and saddled for her departure. But through the throng of stable hands, she saw him as he led her pony into its standing stall, and she called to him. He looked up and towards her and she signalled for him to follow, then she turned and ran towards the gardens at the back of the house.

Once Mary reached the gardens and stopped to catch her breath behind the tall hedgerows, she heard his fast approach, "In here," she called quietly.

When he found her hiding behind the hedges, she was breathing heavily – from exertion as well as distress – and though her skin shone with a thin layer of perspiration and several strands of hair had fallen free from underneath her hood, Arthur thought that she had never looked so beautiful.

In one quick motion he crushed Mary to him and bent his head down to kiss her hungrily as her tears streamed down her face. His rough hands caressed her gently as he held her close and their kiss grew frantic in the knowledge that, in any second, they would be parted forever.

"I do not want to leave you," Mary sobbed as they pulled apart.

"An end to this surprising encounter was inevitable, your grace," Arthur replied calmly.

Mary reached up to touch his face, "Was it foolish of me to imagine no end at all?"

"Perhaps a little," he said and breathed a small laugh, "You are a princess and I a stable boy, a servant."

Mary shook her head, "Why do you insist that I am a princess?" she asked, "When all of England would swear that I am not? It has been proclaimed: I'm a bastard – a no one."

The young man smiled that crooked smile, and Mary tried to memorise it, "Do you really believe all of England swears by it?" he answered rhetorically, "We, the little people, know what is true. The king's meddling in matters of God and Law does not extinguish what we have all witnessed! My parents saw your father and mother married, they lived through it all – Henry VII trying to marry the Spanish Infanta for himself after his son died, then his younger son fighting for her hand. It was all very romantic, apparently – a love story for the ages. The pope granted them their papal dispensation and they were allowed to wed. *That* is all that matters to us as Catholics. The Pope granted them the right to marry, and he later denied your father his annulment. There is no more to it than that, and if the new 'queen' truly believed you to be illegitimate," he said, his voice no more than a whisper, "this day would never have come."

Mary frowned, her expression a question, and Arthur continued.

"Your very existence haunts her," he said passionately, "You being proclaimed illegitimate may have been enough if she had borne the king a son. But this new princess has no greater claim to the throne than you yourself have had all your life. What better way to show to the world the new hierarchy of things than by proclaiming you not only a bastard, but also placing you in the princess' household as her nursemaid? She demeans your worth in actions because she *knows* that you are the true heir to the throne, the daughter of the king and *true* queen of England."

"But I am the lady Mary now, I'm just Mary."

He stroked her face and sighed, his rough hand scratching at her skin slightly, "Don't you see? You've never been *just* Mary," he said, "You are the princess of England. No one can take that from you. Not even the king himself."

She stared up at him, her chest heavy with the ache of loss, "I'd give it all up for you."

He chuckled, "And I wouldn't let you."

In the distance, they heard orders being shouted to find Mary then, and they knew they should not be found together.

"I must go," Mary said as she pulled away, suddenly frightened.

Arthur nodded, then he let go of her, "Your grace," he said in farewell.

And then Mary turned and walked away from him, fate taking her in yet another unknown direction.

Chapter 9

December 1533
Hatfield House, Hertfordshire

"What are we to do?" asked a small and mousy looking young girl, "She has been locked in her room for days! Sometimes I even hear her crying in there."

"Leave her," the lady Anne Shelton said, "the lady Mary will come out soon enough when she is hungry," and she returned to the needlework before her as she gently rocked the royal princess in her cradle with her foot.

"I heard she went weeks without eating when she was proclaimed illegitimate," the girl said then with a sly smile.

"Quiet, stupid girl!" the lady Shelton said harshly, her round face creased in anger, "I care nothing for gossip, nor do I care if the girl chooses to die of starvation in there. Now go about your duties and leave me to mine."

The young girl curtsied, "Yes, my lady," and hurried away.

The lady Anne Shelton sighed deeply and looked down at the new princess as she slept peacefully in her cradle. In truth, lady Shelton did not particularly wish for Mary to come out of her room.

As the aunt to the new queen of England, and great-aunt to the new princess, she believed that the safety of the royal baby was paramount above all else, and as the lady Mary's easily enraged temper was well known throughout court, it gave her no cause to wish for a swift exit from her room.

When Mary did emerge a few days later with her chin raised, and her jaw clenched in defiance, the lady Shelton knew from the expression on the young woman's face that she would have her work cut out for her.

"Lady Mary," she said, as if Mary had just that moment arrived at Hatfield House, rather than six days prior, "May I introduce to you the princess Elizabeth," and she stood aside for Mary to see the little red-headed babe.

Mary peered into the cradle warily, her upper lip curled up slightly in contempt, but upon glimpsing the baby's plump little cheeks, she had to admit to herself that she was no doubt a sweet little thing.

And if the circumstances of her birth had been different, Mary may even have liked to hold her.

"The queen has requested specific instructions that you are not to touch the princess Elizabeth," the lady Shelton said, almost as though she had read Mary's mind, "You shall be solely in charge of washing her swaddling and linens."

When Mary continued to simply look down at the bundle in its cradle, and gave no sign that she had even heard what had been said, lady Shelton asked, "Do you understand her majesty the queen's instructions?"

Anne Shelton's question made Mary consider her new circumstances, and how much humiliation they entailed.

She had been proclaimed a bastard – even though the laws of God clearly stated otherwise – and had been demoted as lesser than the child of the great whore. She had been banished from court and her household dissolved, and then been denied communication with her mother.

And yet, despite all that, Mary had found it in herself to push forward and to accept the new life she had been forced to lead. She had happily established herself as the lady Mary, without issue or complaint, and she had found joy in the simple things in life.

But this new insult had been a step too far, and to demote her to nothing more than a bastard baby's nursemaid, when she had been born the daughter of the king and queen of England, would not be taken lightly.

Arthur had been right. Mary *was* and always would be the rightful heir to the English throne, and she would no longer allow her father's harlot to take control over her future.

Mary blinked and turned her gaze slowly towards the older lady beside her, her face hard as stone as she looked her dead in the eyes, "Lady Shelton," Mary said casually, as though they had been discussing the weather, "While I hear the words you speak, I must admit I do not understand," and she presented her with an innocent smile, "For I recognise no other queen but my mother."

March 1534

When news came from court that parliament had passed an Act that secured the succession of king Henry's children with Anne Boleyn above all others, Mary abandoned her duties and hurried to Hatfield House's great chapel. The news arose such an uncontrollable rage that when Mary finally arrived within the beautiful chapel and saw that it was empty, she stomped up past all the pews and sank onto her knees before the altar in a flustered heap, for now that her father's new laws were beginning to set in, her new life and title was no longer simply hearsay; and while she knew deep down that the only laws that mattered were those of God, she suddenly needed to be near Him, and to ask if He was still watching over her.

She clasped her hands together tightly, her rosary beads hanging from between them, and briefly looked up at the intricately stained-glass windows before squeezing her eyes shut and begging God for enlightenment.

I beg You, oh Lord. I beg You, please – show me a sign that You wish for me to continue strong upon my path to the throne. Show me a sign – anything – so that I may know that You wish for me to one day be the queen of England, for I cannot help but feel lost. Or perhaps this is Your true plan for me? To be replaced and forgotten? I need to know, oh Lord. I need to know. If this is another test to assess my commitment, then I shall prevail... but I need a sign. Please – please, send me a sign.

Mary remained kneeling before the altar for hours until her knees tingled and numbed in pain, but she did not waiver, for in that moment there was no amount of earthly pain she would not endure if it brought her enlightenment to God's will.

"Fetch me the lady Mary," lady Shelton said impatiently, her thick brown eyebrows furrowed together.

"She is at prayer, my lady," replied the mousy lady-in-waiting as she handed the princess Elizabeth to her wet nurse.

Lady Shelton grumbled frustratedly as she pulled the linens off the cradle and balled them up before dropping them in a heap at her feet, "See to it that you tell her that her duties to the princess are awaiting."

"Yes, my lady," the girl said as she left the room to find Mary.

When she reached the chapel and saw the lady rocking back and forth on her knees at the altar, she sighed and rubbed her hand over her forehead, "My lady," she said as she approached, "Lady Shelton has requested your presence."

At the interruption Mary abruptly stopped her rocking but did not move to stand, and long moments went by before either of them made a movement or a sound.

"Lady Shelton asks that y – you remember your duties to the princess," the young girl stammered, and Mary breathed a short laugh at her fear, then she slowly rose to her feet and brushed down her skirts before turning to face the girl.

"The bastard will have to learn to wait," Mary replied icily, "until I have fulfilled my thrice daily prayers," and she glided past her, ignoring the girl's wide-eyed expression of shock.

155

But before Mary could even exit the chapel, the girl flew past her and through the courtyard towards the staircase that led to the princess' royal nursery, leaving Mary to calm her racing heart before following her back to where lady Shelton awaited her impatiently.

As Mary entered the nursery, she saw the girl whispering frantically to lady Shelton, whose face was turning redder with each passing second, "Lady Mary!" she screeched incredulously as she stood from her chair abruptly, "You should be careful of the words you utter regarding the princess! They may be misconstrued as treason."

Mary simply raised one eyebrow disdainfully, ignoring her anger and her threat, and instead of replying she picked up the pile of linens that had been bundled onto the floor and exited the nursery as though nothing had happened and no one had spoken, and she made her way to wash the precious princess' precious linens.

April 1534
Greenwich Palace, London

"With the new Act of Succession," said the recently promoted Principal Secretary and Chief Minister, Thomas Cromwell, "comes the swearing of the oath of Supremacy!" he shouted as he banged his hairy hand down hard on the council table, "To reject the oath is treason!"

"Then I shall have to commit treason!" Thomas Moore replied hotly, "For there is no amount of threat and pressure you or anyone may force upon me which would make me condemn my soul for the love of an earthly king! No king is supreme head of a church above the Pope!"

The room went still, and all heads turned to look at king Henry who had been sitting quietly at the head of the council table, his stare becoming more sinister with each passing second.

Henry did not take his eyes off his dear friend, Sir Thomas Moore, and he in return did the same, and it was as though there was an internal conversation taking place between the two men in mere looks, one the other members of the council could not understand.

Finally, Henry looked away from his advisor and friend and grumbled underneath his breath.

Then he rose from his seat and, without so much as a second glance, he said, "Arrest him."

Henry's entire council looked at him aghast as the guards entered and looked about themselves, uncertain of which of the king's great advisors he wished to relegate.

"Arrest him!" Henry repeated, his face red with anger as he pointed towards Moore, and suddenly the room broke out in a frenzy as the three guards stormed towards Moore and forced his arms behind his back.

"You are lost, Henry," Thomas Moore said with a sad smile as the guards marched him towards the door, "None of this will end as you hope it will! And I am but the first to stand up to you against this, but there isn't a soul in England that indeed accepts your separation from your *true* wife or your separation from Rome!"

"Get him out of here!" Thomas Cromwell shouted above the commotion, and then Moore was gone, and the door closed behind him.

Henry sank back down onto his throne and exhaled deeply. No one moved or made a sound, and not even Charles Brandon dared to look in the king's direction.

"Let this be a warning to all of you!" the king said quietly, the menace in his voice speaking volumes, "and to all of England. That no matter your rank or station, if you defy me on this, you will suffer the consequences!"

157

1535
Hatfield House, Hertfordshire

By now, almost all of England had signed the oath of Supremacy and the Act of Succession which legally removed Mary from the line of succession and placed Anne Boleyn's daughter in her stead.

The arrest of Sir Thomas Moore, as well as the swift execution of Elizabeth Barton – a nun of Kent, who had been preaching against the king's new marriage – frightened the people of England enough to sign regardless of their own personal opinions.

But when the oath was presented to Mary she blatantly refused to sign it, having previously prepared herself for an immediate arrest as the consequence. But days went by, and no arrest warrant ever came.

She later heard, through the baby Elizabeth's ladies' gossip, that her mother too had refused to sign the oath, and that she had been stripped of all her luxuries as punishment, as well as having her household drastically diminished at her banished residence in Kimbolton Castle. And though she had once been a queen of England, and then been demoted to the Dowager Princess of Wales, she now lived as pennilessly as a pauper.

"She has not been charged with treason then?" one lady whispered to another one morning as Mary bundled the baby's swaddling into a pile.

"Not *yet,*" the mousey-looking girl replied, purposefully loud enough for Mary to hear, "I hear Queen Anne is pushing the king to reconsider his punishment to Katherine though."

The other girl did not reply, and Mary wondered if she was, perhaps, secretly against the oath too.

"I dare say the king will yet change his mind and arrest *anyone* who defies him," the mousey girl said again, clearly directing her words at Mary.

"Hush," the other girl said then, "It is enough."

Mary collected the linens and left the nursery without looking back, hoping that they would believe that she had not overheard; but the words sent a shiver down her spine nevertheless, and she wondered just how long it would be before she would lose her head, just as the nun of Kent had lost hers.

Some days later, Mary heard that two more people had been arrested and shortly thereafter, hung, drawn, and quartered at Tyburn in London, for refusing to sign the oath of Supremacy, and every morning since she had awoken soaked in her own sweat, for fear that today would be the day that she would meet her own violent end.

Mary spoke to no one during the next few weeks other than to God.

She kept her head down and did her duties to her half-sister without complaint so that no one could utter a single negative word against her to the king, and after a while she thought that perhaps he had forgotten about her existence all together, and that she may indeed be allowed to live.

One morning, as Mary was busy hanging the baby's freshly washed linens on the line in the courtyard outside, a messenger arrived from court with a letter for the lady Shelton.

While this was not uncommon, Mary did however look up from her work, her stomach in a tight knot, fearing that it would bring bad news, and she was left staring wide-eyed when, strangely, the young messenger walked straight towards her, quickly looking over his shoulder as he approached.

In her fear that he had been sent to arrest her she dropped the swaddling she was holding and quickly bent to pick it up when the boy's face was suddenly just inches from hers, "My deepest apologies," he whispered as he pretended to help her pick up the dropped swaddling, "For you," he said quietly as he quickly glanced down at their hands and Mary saw that he had slipped something in between the cloths.

Then, without even another look in her direction, he straightened himself and headed inside to bring lady Shelton the news from court.

Mary stood up slowly, fumbling with the cloths in an attempt to retrieve the note before anyone would notice her acting suspiciously, then she tucked it up her sleeve and continued with her chores.

Later, when she was finally alone in her tiny, dark room, she quietly removed the note from her sleeve and peeled it open, her heart racing in her chest, dreading that she would be caught.

Though the note had had no seal or signature to identify who it was from, Mary instantly knew from the handwriting that it had been sent to her by her mother, and her heart leapt with surprise. She covered her mouth with her hand as a gasp escaped her and tears of joy began to well in her eyes.

Mary quickly lit a candle and sat on the edge of her hard, wooden bed, holding the note up to the candle's dim illumination, and as she read through the letter, it was as if she could hear her mother's voice as clearly as though she was sitting right there beside her:

Daughter,
I heard reports today that the Almighty God put onto you His biggest test, and I beseech you to continue to stand with God and know that if you do, He will not allow you to suffer. I pray you, good daughter, to offer yourself to Him completely, take

Him into your heart completely and then you will be armed against anything that may befall you. And if you receive a letter from the king commanding you to obey him before God, you must answer with few words. While I know you have already denied signing his oath of supremacy – for which I am so proud of you – I must remind you that you must obey the king, your father, in everything, except *for what would offend God and risk your own soul. God will be your shield. And you must remind your father that the choice you made was only to protect your soul, and not to offend him.*

Another thing I especially ask of you, is that you keep your heart and mind chaste, and your body and company pure, not thinking of or desiring a husband until this troublesome time is past.

I will make sure that you will see a very good end, for all that I do is to ensure your future as the next reigning monarch of England, as is your birth right above all others.

I do pray that you know how much love I have for you, my darling daughter.

Mary read and re-read the note until it was smudged with her tears, and her body shook as she tried to contain the sounds of her sobs. This was the sign from God that she had so ardently prayed for, the sign that would give her a clear understanding of what He wished for her to do.

She wiped the tears from her face, then reluctantly held the note up to the candle and watched it burn.

After so many weeks of worrying and fearing for her life, her mother's wise words made Mary realise that as long as she stayed true to God, she had nothing to fear, for her soul would be safe.

She sat upon the edge of her hard bed for a long time as she watched the candle flicker back and forth, and she thought back on her time in Hunsdon House, and the handful of innocent kisses and caresses she had shared with Arthur.

While she would not regret what had happened, her mother's note reminded her that her honour must remain intact, for whenever God decided to remedy her father's wrongdoings, her virtue must never be able to come into question.

Mary sighed and began to undress while the candle still offered some light, then she lay down under her thin covers and watched as the flame sank lower into the end of its waxy lifespan, and she decided that come morning Mary would dedicate her prayers to asking God for forgiveness for her lustful sins.

Mary would pray day and night if she had to, to gain His forgiveness and to wipe her slate clean of sin. She would keep her heart and mind chaste, and her body and company pure, just as her mother had asked her to.

Mary gave Arthur, and the joy he had brought her, one last thought, for he had loved her at her worst, while knowing that she could offer him nothing in return, and had faithfully believed in her and who she was even when she had doubted it herself – and for all that Mary would be forever grateful.

But now she would have to lock his crooked smile and the sound of his laugh away into the deepest chasm of her mind, and though her heart ached at the prospect, with one deep exhale of breath she banished Arthur from her mind; and that night Mary slept a peaceful and dreamless sleep, her mother's comforting words and her trust in God warming her like a blanket.

July 1535

Sir Thomas Moore had been executed by beheading with one blow of the axe on Tower Hill.

There was no denying that, while it was an awful tragedy, Moore's death had been an act of martyrdom. He had willingly and knowingly walked towards that fate and had never strayed from his course once his mind had been made up, and Mary could say with complete certainty that she respected and empathised with his cause, for she shared his higher understanding that one must conserve one's soul over one's earthly body when it came to the laws of God. And that afternoon Mary devoted a prayer for his soul and thanked him for his service to God and to her mother, whom he had stood up for throughout the course of all this blasphemy.

Mary had learned of the dreadful news when she had overheard her half-sister's ladies gossiping about it openly in front of the little Elizabeth one morning as she sat playing with her wooden toys by the window.

"The king was merciful after all," one said to the other as they sat by the window stitching.

"He was one of his favourites," the other replied, "To have had him beheaded rather than hung, drawn and quartered as was promised, is of course merciful, but to have gone through it at all... I must admit I am a little shocked."

At nearly two years old, Elizabeth did not talk much, but Mary had observed from the shadows that she had been shunned into, that the toddler understood a lot more than people would give her credit for – this moment being one such instance. In fact, Mary had found herself observing the little girl more and more frequently over the past few months, and as the initial disdain for the child had slowly started to melt away, the realisation that she was an innocent in this merciless game began to dawn on Mary. Much like herself, Elizabeth was simply a pawn caught up in the middle of a war, a war which held no prisoners and where the only victors were male heirs. And with that newfound perspective Mary had learned to put her immature jealousy for the toddler behind her, and focused instead on what they could mean to one another.

Mary shot a heated look in the ladies' direction as they continued to talk frivolously about the execution, as though it were no more than a play for their personal entertainment, and paying no mind to the little Elizabeth who could hear every word they were saying.

In an effort to distract her little half-sister from the gruesome details of death, Mary bent down and smiled at the little redheaded child as she sat on the floor.

"This is a pretty horse," Mary announced as she picked up one of the wooden toys, feigning excitement for it, and the child offered her a toothy smile as she babbled back at her.

As she continued to play on the floor with her half-sister, lady Shelton entered the room and immediately stormed towards them.

"Lady Mary!" she shrieked, pulling the toddler away from her, "need I remind you of the queen's specific instructions that you are not to interact with the princess?!"

Mary rose and straightened her back, her eyes blazing at the implication that *she* was the one subjecting the child to unpleasantness, "Perhaps you would do well to remind Elizabeth's ladies that they ought not to speak of inappropriate things around her."

Lady Shelton snapped her head around to the two ladies behind her, who quickly dropped their gaze and abandoned their stitching, scurrying off into different directions.

Then she looked back at Mary, "It is no concern of yours what goes on in this household," she said, her wide nostrils flaring in anger, "You are to attend to your duties to the princess, and that is all."

Mary raised her chin and did not reply, but simply looked down at her little half-sister, offered her a little smile and then walked out of the nursery, shunned into the background once more.

December 1535
Greenwich Palace, London

King Henry and his wife, Anne Boleyn, sat side by side upon their gold thrones in the great hall as they received their guests and gifts for the Christmastide.

The court was alive with merriment and festivities, candles were lit all around and a delicious, spiced aroma hung about in the air.

The king and his queen welcomed the lords and ladies of the court, then the ambassadors of France, who bowed deeply to queen Anne, and the Imperial Ambassador, Eustace Chapuys.

Chapuys entered through the large wooden doors of the great hall looking troubled and bleak, and as he stood before the royal couple, he merely bowed his head to the king in greeting while utterly ignoring the queen's presence altogether.

"Your majesty," he said, looking directly at the king, "I bring grave news that Katherine of Aragon is grievously ill."

Henry sat forward in his seat, unable to hide his immediate concern, then shifted slightly as he felt Anne's eyes on him, "Ill?" he simply said.

Queen Anne leered at her husband with piercingly blue eyes – the kind of eyes that could bewitch a man with their beauty – and squinted them at Henry in suspicion for his obvious interest for the old queen's wellbeing.

"Yes, your highness," said Eustace Chapuys, "I also bring you a letter from the Prin— from the lady Mary," he stepped forward and handed the king the letter, "She begs your majesty to allow her to visit her mother on her deathbed."

The king bent his head to read his daughter's letter, skimming the documents' contents.

"I must ask your forgiveness, majesty," the ambassador said as a silence had ensued, "but it is of vital importance that a decision be made in haste, so that the lady Mary may travel to Cambridgeshire in time."

"It is that concerning then, this illness?" the king asked suddenly without looking up from the letter. Though his tone was indifferent, the young queen beside him never tore her suspicious eyes away from Henry, warning him to choose his words carefully.

The Imperial ambassador nodded in response to the king, then turned to observe the harlot's face as she watched the king beside her, and Chapuys thought that it seemed almost as though she were baiting the king to misstep, perhaps so that she may go off on one of her many tempers.

Henry rubbed a hand over his handsome, yet aging, face while he contemplated his decision, and Chapuys noticed that as he considered he risked a quick glance in the concubine's direction, as if to assess her opinion on the matter.

"I cannot allow it," he finally said as he sat back in his throne, "Katherine, the Dowager Princess of Wales, cannot be suddenly so mortally ill that it be necessary to uproot the lady Mary from her duties to the princess Elizabeth," and with that he simply waved the ambassador away.

Chapuys stared wide-eyed and shocked for a brief moment but then blinked and bowed curtly, his face showing clearly that he disagreed with the king's decision, but the stare he received from the king's concubine when he looked up made him realise that there would be no further discussion on the matter.

January 1536
Kimbolton Castle, Cambridgeshire

"Your visit has cheered her majesty," said Maria de Salinas, one of Katherine's former ladies-in-waiting, "She hadn't eaten in days, and now she sits up and has eaten well."

Maria de Salinas, as well as Maud Green, had been the only two ladies-in-waiting remaining in Katherine's service upon her banishment from court. They had stayed on to serve their queen, despite the very meagre pay, due to their undying loyalty to the great lady, and wanting nothing more than to accompany her through this difficult time of her life.

It had come as a great shock then, when shortly after Katherine's denial to sign the king's Act of Succession and the oath, her only two remaining ladies had too been dismissed by the king, leaving her utterly abandoned.

But when news had spread that the former wife of the king had become deathly ill, Maria de Salinas had mounted her horse and ridden tirelessly to return to her queen's side, despite the fact that the king had denied her permission to do so.

"It is not only my presence that has brought her joy," Imperial Ambassador Eustace Chapuys replied with a kind smile, "I was glad to hear the queen laughing with you yesterday. It brings me great peace to know she is getting better."

"Yes," said Maria, looking over her shoulder at the pale queen sitting before the fireplace, "But now you must return to London?" she asked, turning back to the gentleman before her.

"Indeed," he replied, hanging his head, "The king has summoned me back, as the queen is feeling better."

"Perhaps the king will yet change his mind about allowing the princess Mary to visit her mother," the lady said, her tone lacking any hope, "With the poor conditions and the damp of this castle, the next time she is to become ill, we may not be so lucky to see her recover."

The ambassador crossed himself, "Pray God the king will soon rescind his whore and return to his true and lawful wife."

The lady exhaled deeply and raised her eyebrows, nodding in agreement.

That night, as Maria slept uncomfortably in the chair beside Katherine's bed, the former queen of England was haunted by dreams of innocent men and women being put to death by bloody and violent beheadings, Sir Thomas Moore among them.

She dreamed of the division and hatred of the people of England towards each other, as Catholics and Reformers fought violently in the streets, blood and mud flowing through the streets of London like a river; and a giant axe falling from the sky, slicing England from the loving embrace of Rome.

As she dreamt these dark dreams, she jerked and whimpered in her sleep, her lucid mind trying to rouse her from the deep chasms of her imagination.

Maria, upon hearing her queen's distressed sobs, sat up in her chair and gently shook Katherine awake.

As soon as she opened her eyes, breathing heavily as her mind recovered from her visions, Katherine demanded that she take communion, for she knew that her time on this earth was quickly coming to an end.

Greenwich Palace, London

"Poisoned?" king Henry said in disbelief.

"Yes, your majesty," his physician replied, "That is how it would seem."

"How can you be sure?"

"The heart was black," the physicians replied with a shrug, as though it were obvious, "a common sign of poisoning, my lord."

"Black?" Henry whispered to himself as he turned away from the old man and rubbed his hand over his chin, recalling the suspicions he had had at Cardinal Wolsey's sudden death, for his heart too had been black upon examination.

"All other organs seem unaffected and healthy –"

Henry raised his hand suddenly, silencing and dismissing the physician simultaneously. The man bowed and left the king's chambers.

Henry sighed and walked over to the fireplace where Charles Brandon the Duke of Suffolk stood. "They say she may have been poisoned, did you hear, Charles?" Henry said heavily as he approached.

"I did, your majesty," the duke replied as he turned to face the king.

Henry was staring into the flames in thought, "If word of this gets out," he whispered, "I will be blamed."

Charles Brandon watched the king closely, his dark eyes narrowed as he considered the king's involvement in this, or if he was indeed as shocked and abhorred at this fresh news as he alleged. "You did not order this," Charles said matter-of-factly, and he watched Henry's face closely for his reaction.

"Of course not!" Henry replied, his eyes shining with tears that threatened to spill, his emotion suggesting that he was indeed innocent of the crime, "As much grief as the woman gave me, I would not have ordered her death and certainly not by poison – such a woman's weapon!"

At the outburst, Charles nodded his head slowly, glad to finally see that Henry's eyes were beginning to open to the possibility that someone may have been involved in the strange and sudden demises of two people a certain lady wished dead.

"A woman's weapon of choice indeed," Charles said, hoping to spur the king on in his new realisation.

Henry raised his head slowly and searched his friend's face for any sign that he was going mad, unable to believe that the woman he had given everything up for and changed the course of history for would be capable of such an act. But Charles' face was like a statue of stone, giving away nothing and yet simultaneously holding a secret in his eyes.

"You are not suggesting the queen had anything to do with this?" Henry said quietly, half his face flickering orange and red as the fire in the hearth roared beside him.

"I would not dare to ever put forward such a vicious implication," Charles said expertly, choosing his words with the utmost care, "I was merely agreeing with your majesty that poison is not the choosing of a king."

Henry nodded once as he stared at his friend, "You would do well to put your opinions of the queen aside," he said, having become increasingly aware of the tension between his friend and his wife, "She is innocent of this, and so am I!"

"Of course, Henry," Charles said as he bowed.

But while he could say that he fully believed the king's hands to be clean from sin regarding this matter, he could not shake the feeling that if he were to look into things a little closer, he would find that the queen's hands might very well be stained with blood.

Hatfield House, Hertfordshire

Since news of her mother's passing had reached Mary's ears, she had been inconsolable and unable to rise out of bed for days.

When the messenger had delivered the wretched news, Mary had fallen to her knees and wailed like a small child, her face contorted with a grief she had never known before.

The heartache she had felt in that moment had made her chest feel both heavy and hollow all at once, and though she had inhaled deeply as she howled, it had felt as though her lungs could take in no air at all.

No one had come to comfort her as she lay crumpled on the great hall's floor where Elizabeth's household had received the messenger, and she had been left a twisted mess, sobbing uncontrollably until the guards had taken pity on her and helped her back to her room, where she was left to weep until exhaustion overcame her.

Following her mind and body's shock over her great loss, Mary had once again begun suffering from her unusual bouts of cramps and migraines, leaving her unable to keep down even a morsel of the stale bread and mouldy cheese she was given for her meals. And while the lady Shelton and the rest of the princess Elizabeth's household had grown accustomed to Mary's regular need to lock herself away to overcome her unusual ailment, even they began to worry for her wellbeing when she did not eat anything in nearly ten days. And so, to avoid another death in the royal family, the lady Shelton reluctantly sent a letter to London, informing the king of his daughter's ill health after the loss of her beloved mother.

To everyone's great surprise – none more so than queen Anne herself – the king immediately sent his best physician to attend the lady Mary at Hatfield House. The physician arrived the very next day without delay and began treating her that very evening.

"We will bleed you with leeches, my lady," he said to her as she lay shivering in her wooden bed.

Mary merely nodded and turned her head to face the wall so that she would not have to observe the procedure whereby those disgusting creatures were placed upon a freshly sliced cut on her body. She flinched slightly when the physician nicked the skin of her upper arm and then felt his cold hands place one of the leeches. He repeated this on two more places on her arm.

"These will suck out any impure fluids in your blood, my lady," he said softly, noticing her distress, "which is what I believe has been causing your suffering."

"Mm-hmm," Mary mumbled, although she was not really listening.

"We shall leave the leeches to do their work," he continued as he turned around and opened his bag, "while I mix up a remedy for you to take."

Mary continued facing the wall and simply listened as the man mumbled to himself as he prepared the remedy. She heard *clinking* as he stirred the contents of the glass bottles, and then placed them all on her narrow windowsill before turning to her and clearing his throat.

"Let's remove these little pests now," he said, more to himself than to Mary, she thought, and Mary closed her eyes so as not to see the slimy creatures, no doubt swollen with her blood.

"Those bottles," the physician said once Mary turned to look at him, her eyes two wet and bloodshot orbs blinking up at him, "They are a concoction of lavender, sage, and rue. They will help ease your pain."

"Thank you," Mary mumbled, her lips dry from dehydration, and the physicians smiled at her kindly, his pity for the poor child evident in his eyes. Then he nodded his head before taking the two small steps he needed to reach the door of Mary's tiny room and left.

Mary sat up in bed, reached for one of the small glass vials and held it to her lips, sipping it carefully for fear that it would taste terrible. But to her surprise it was not offensive, and she swallowed the contents in one.

That night, thanks to the physician's remedy, she finally slept a dreamless sleep for the first time in days, her pain having almost completely subsided, and when she awoke the following morning, she considered just how glorious it would be if there were a simple concoction, she could take that would heal her broken heart.

The king's physician had remained all night and only returned to London the following day when Mary had visibly recovered and had been able to take some broth.

But that night Mary's cramps returned and as she tried and failed to fall asleep, she reached for the bottles to ease her pain.

As she picked up one of the vials something caught her eye, and as she looked closer, she realised that the physician had secretly hidden a letter underneath them. She slowly moved the six small glass bottles to one side so she could reach the folded document, then she held it up to the candlelight and was instantly shocked at the words that jumped out at her.

The concubine has had a miscarriage. It appeared to have been a boy. The physicians say that it was caused due to the stress and worry she felt for the king's wellbeing when he suffered an accident during a joust where the king was thrown from his horse, which had left him unconscious for over two hours.

Do not be alarmed, princess, for this was several days ago, and the king has since awoken and is well.

But I must admit, I do not believe the cause of the harlot's miscarriage to have been due to worry over the king's fall, for when she was informed about it, it was worded in such a way as to not cause any distress, for fear of harming the unborn child.

I believe the true cause for her personal anguish, and loss of the baby, is due to the king's sudden public interest in a new lady at court. He has been sending this lady gifts and openly showing her favour – much like he did with the lady Anne herself when your mother was queen – and this, no doubt, has made the harlot fear for her position. You may have heard of this new lady? Her name is Jane Seymour.

The hurriedly scribbled letter left Mary feeling utterly numb, for it had carried too much information for her weakened mind to process.

While she knew that she should revel at the prospect that the whore's power over her father was finally dwindling, she was unable to feel the extreme joy that she long assumed she would feel at such news. The fact that her mother had not lived to see this day sent a wave of guilt through her and her vision blurred with a sudden onset of hot tears.

Her grief overcame her once again and she sat there for a long time sobbing quietly into her lap, and even when her tears ran out and the note's contents re-emerged into her thoughts, Mary's grief developed into dread. Not for herself but rather for her innocent little half-sister, for she knew perhaps better than anyone the consequences that might ensue for the child due to the king's fickle devotion to his wife.

She dreaded to think what Elizabeth's future would hold if the contents of this letter were in fact true, and Mary suddenly feared that the little girl she had grown to care for would too grow up feeling worthless and constantly uncertain of the path that lay before her.

Mary decided that, to properly mull over the multitude of information that the letter had conveyed, she would have to be fully recovered, and so she folded the paper into a small square and hid it under her pillow. Then she swallowed the sage and lavender concoction, laid her heavy head down on her lumpy pillow, and slept the night through.

The following morning Mary awoke to find that her stomach had settled, and her headache had eased, and so she sluggishly stood and began to dress herself. She opened the door and walked slowly through the corridors, in search of a kitchen servant to bring her some breakfast.

Upon her return Mary's stomach dropped with the sudden realisation that someone had been in her room when she noticed her pillow and bedsheet had been pulled off her bed. She bent down and grabbed the discarded items and shook them out, hoping the letter would fall out from in between them. When it did not, she searched under the bed and lifted her mattress, but to her utter disbelief, the letter was gone.

Mary sat down on the edge of her bed and held her head in her hands as she awaited the consequences that she knew would follow, and it was not long before she heard angry footsteps approaching.

She raised her head and stood up slowly, preparing herself for whatever was to come. Though she stood as tall as she could, with her hands clasped before her, and her chin raised – the very picture of strength – inside she as felt weak and helpless as a small child.

Lady Shelton burst into her room unannounced, slamming the door against the wall behind it, holding Mary's letter in her hand before her.

"Lady Mary," she said, her voice like acid, "I must inform you, though I am sure you already know, that this letter is riddled with vile lies, as well as treason. I shall be sending it back to court for the king to read for himself so that he may decide how to punish you and whoever wrote this ungodly letter."

Mary stood perfectly still, not looking at nor responding to the red-faced lady, for Mary had faith that the king would not stoop so low as to arrest and put to death his own daughter, regardless of his resentment and their estrangement in recent years. The swift arrival of his very best physician had shown Mary that much at least, that though he may have lost his love for her – and this ached Mary's heart deeply – he had not completely abandoned her. And for now, she would have to believe that that would be enough to save her from whatever wrath might follow the discovery of the secret letter.

Several days went by with no word from court. But with each day that passed, Mary's certainty that her father's affection for her would keep her from the Tower and the scaffold, began to dwindle bit by bit and she found herself trembling in panic at the slightest noise, always fearing that it would be the moment that she would be arrested.

To distract herself from the niggling thoughts of death and destruction, Mary kept herself busy at prayer and with her daily chores to the little princess, both of which left little time for anything else.

But at night the terror would set in, and not only would her thoughts of impending doom overcome her, but the grief over her mother's loss would sneak into her chest and squeeze her heart.

The fact that her father had not permitted Mary to visit her mother on her deathbed still played heavily on her mind, and she was not sure she could ever truly forgive her father for that.

But then the sun would rise, and she would head to the chapel for her morning prayers and ask for forgiveness from God from thinking ill of her lord father and king.

She would pray for hours at a time most days, in hopes of regaining strength after having suffered so much loss, and most days God would grant her it. But there were times when prayer did little to ease her grieving soul and Mary would rise from the cold chapel floor and be strangely drawn to her little half-sister.

Mary found that the little red-headed girl's company and her giggles nourished Mary's soul in a way that she had not been prepared for, and though she felt a twinge of guilt about it, she knew that she loved the child.

After all, none of what had happened to Mary was Elizabeth's fault, for she was as much an innocent caught in this tumultuous tragedy, as Mary was. And if Chapuys' secret letter to Mary held any truth to it, then it may not be long before Elizabeth too would be cast out and rejected just as Mary herself had been.

February 1536

On a damp and cold day in February, twenty-year-old Mary was rocking back and forth on her knees, her eyes closed in prayer, when she heard horses approaching.

Immediately she stood and ran to peer outside the corridor's windows but when she saw nothing she hurried to the nursery where she would no doubt learn more.

"I am come to see my daughter," Mary heard her father's voice boom in the princess' nursery, and she swiftly hid behind a pillar in the corridor outside.

The time had come. She would finally be made to answer for her disobedience.

Mary had long awaited this day and had thought herself ready for whatever fate had in store for her, but in that moment, she was ashamed to feel utterly terrified, and her stomach lurched with fear over what was to come.

Had he personally come to pass her sentence? Would he drag her back to London with him and throw her into the Tower for her insolence and refusal to accept his mistress as the new queen?

She swallowed hard in an attempt to quash the rapid beating of her heart, and then she heard Elizabeth's happy laugh at the sight of her father and Mary realised: the king had not come to see her at all. He had come to see his *other* daughter. The daughter that he counted as legitimate and true. He had come to see the princess of England.

Though relief washed over her that she would perhaps be spared this day, she also felt that familiar and intense bout of jealousy bubbling within her. A jealousy that she had almost completely forgotten, as her love for her half-sister had grown.

Mary stood perfectly still behind the pillar outside the child's nursery and listened as the king spoke quietly to Elizabeth and her giggling in return, and Mary imagined him holding her in his arms as he had done when she was a little girl, and suddenly her eyes stung as the tears threatened to spill.

She could watch for no longer, and her aching heart could sustain no more hurt, and so Mary sniffed quietly and turned away slowly so as not to be heard.

She hurried along the candlelit corridors and emerged out onto the nearest balcony where she breathed the cold, crisp air deeply into her lungs and blinked the tears away, refusing to let them fall.

Enough tears had been shed over her own ill-fated situation, and she felt sick at the thought of shedding even one more over it.

As she continued to breathe in the refreshing air, she looked over the balcony and saw the king's guards outside. They were still mounted upon their great warhorses and all of them appeared ready to depart at any moment, and suddenly Mary wondered why they had not followed their king inside. She understood then, as her father suddenly emerged from the gates of Hatfield House and walked towards his horse, that he had planned only a short visit.

Upon seeing her father in the sunlight, she realised with a pang that it had been years since she had set eyes on her beloved father, and though he had personally put her through Hell, Mary's heart still soared at the sight of him.

His normally trimmed auburn hair was now longer, almost touching his shoulders, and he had grown a moustache and goatee – which she instantly thought her mother would have disliked – and she thought that his eyes looked tired – and dare she think it – sad?

Mary watched as the king approached his horse and grabbed the reins off the stable boy beside it, and as he raised his head to mount his steed, he caught sight of her on the balcony above and did a double take as though he had forgotten that she too resided there.

He and Mary locked eyes and, for a brief moment, they simply stared at one another, taking in each other's changed faces as though they had met in a former life.

Then the king took a step towards her and bowed deeply, before lifting himself up onto his horse and commanding the guards ahead. He gifted her one last smile and a nod of his head, then he turned his horse around and galloped away.

Mary watched as he rode out of the gate, her heart swelling with hope that perhaps her father did hold some love for her after all, and that maybe, just maybe, all was not lost.

Chapter 10

May 1536
Hatfield House, Hertfordshire

It was over.

The news Mary had long been praying for had finally come.

The harlot had been arrested and tried for high treason against the king, for acts of adultery – supposedly in pursuit of conception since the king had abandoned his marital bed – as well as performing witchcraft to entice and enthral the king – all of which Mary could absolutely believe to be true.

And so, it would seem, did Parliament, for she and her loathsome family were either arrested or executed within just two days, the witch herself having been made a head shorter, never to spew her evil venom again.

No one at court, or indeed in the country, had then been surprised to receive news of the king's betrothal to the lady Jane Seymour just one day later, having already witnessed for the greater part of a year how he had fawned over her.

And only nine days after that, their wedding took place, and all the while Mary was still a part of the little Elizabeth's household. Though the servants were slowly being dismissed and the tapestries and valuables removed, she went on with her duties to the little girl, unable to believe their father's heartlessness.

Mary, despite her own joy over the harlot's beheading, felt utterly devastated for her half-sister, who was just three years old and completely unable to understand what had happened and what the future would hold for her. All she knew was that her father had ordered the death of her mother – a truth no child should ever know – and Mary's heart broke for the little Elizabeth.

No matter the hatred Mary had personally felt for the witch, she would never dispute that she had loved and adored her little daughter and had indeed done all that she could to protect her from this fate, much like Mary's own mother had done.

But it would seem there was no stopping their father on his mission for a son, and Mary wondered just how many more lives he would destroy in the pursuit of a male heir, before he realised that all he needed had been right before him all along.

Just eight days after his marriage to the lady Jane Seymour had taken place, parliament passed an act declaring the king's marriage to Elizabeth's mother to have been invalid, and Elizabeth's little world and all that she knew was ripped out from underneath her, and she was left as motherless, and deemed as worthless to inherit the throne, as Mary.

June 1536
Kenninghall, Norfolk

The now-illegitimate Elizabeth's household was disbanded and Mary's duties to the little girl were no more, and though the poor little child was allowed to remain at Hatfield House with a small entourage, this did not include Mary.

The two unlikely companions were separated, the little girl losing not only her mother but also her sister whom she had surprisingly bonded with above all others, being undoubtedly drawn towards the genuine affection Mary had for her.

It had been a heart-breaking scene, one Mary would remember for the rest of her days as the small child screamed and cried red-faced in her governess' arms trying to keep Mary from leaving her behind, no doubt utterly bewildered at all the recent losses she was experiencing.

Mary's heart ached for her half-sister, for she could feel all the pain the little girl was suffering through, and as she slowly rode out of the girl's sight, completely helpless to stop the toddler's pain, Mary trembled in anguish, and she wondered just how much suffering one person could endure before simply dying of sorrow.

Mary was sent to reside at Kenninghall Palace, owned, but not inhabited by Thomas Howard the duke of Norfolk, where she was once again tucked out of the way to live as the lady Mary. She arrived with her assigned guards at the magnificent building with two fronts and was left awestruck at the grandness of it. For a palace which did not belong to the crown it certainly was exceptional.

They entered through the gates and were greeted by the housekeeper as they dismounted their horses. She was a short and plump woman with rosy cheeks and thinning hair, and though her smile was almost completely toothless it held a warmth to it that drew Mary to her.

"Welcome, my lady," she said, with a broad Norfolk accent. Mary nodded her head and smiled.

"You travelled lightly," she pointed out when she looked over Mary's shoulder at the three guards that had followed and the few bags that hung from their horses.

"Yes," Mary replied simply, remembering the trunks of belongings she used to have before she was sent to Hatfield House as a nursemaid and servant.

"Well," the housekeeper said as she turned and waved her hand for Mary to follow, "this way to your rooms."

They made their way through the courtyard and the large wooden doors of the Palace, then headed straight up a windy staircase and headed towards the first door ahead, "Here you are," she said, and Mary entered the warmly lit room.

It was bigger than her accommodation at Hatfield House but still smaller than any rooms she had inhabited as a princess, but she was glad for the roaring fire in the hearth which warmed the room nicely. She noticed a single bed tucked into the corner, noting gladly that it was of better quality than her previous one and her shoulders visibly relaxed as she realised that she would no doubt sleep well in the coming nights.

The guards entered and dropped her bags on the ground by a small wooden table and chair, then bowed their heads and left, their armour clunking as they walked back downstairs.

"I shall bring some food up for you once you have had time to settle in," the housekeeper said before closing the door behind her.

Once she was alone Mary sighed, walked over to the bed in the corner and gingerly sat down upon it, fearing that her first glance at it had been misleading, but she was glad to find the mattress soft and the pillow lump-free.

Mary swiftly removed her riding boots, cloak and gloves and lay down in the bed, eager to rest her head after the disturbing morning she had had.

Hours had gone by though Mary felt as though she had only just closed her eyes, when suddenly she was awoken by a rapping on the door, and the plump housekeeper came in.

"My apologies, my lady," she said, and Mary sat up and noticed that the fire had been reduced to embers and a bowl of broth had been placed on her table.

"What is it?" Mary said, her eyes wide with fear.

"I did not wish to wake you," the housekeeper said, "but my lord the duke of Norfolk has arrived."

Mary hopped out of bed and fumbled with her hood which had become loose in her sleep. She removed the pins from her head and tried to re-adjust it, quivering as she went, utterly unprepared for the lord's arrival.

Once she was marginally suitable to receive the proprietor of her new residence, the housekeeper led her downstairs and into the great hall, where she found a group of lords awaiting her.

She immediately recognised the duke of Norfolk, Sir Thomas Howard and as he turned at the sound of her entrance, Mary bobbed him a quick curtsy, "My lord," she said in greeting, "You have my thanks for allowing me to reside in your beautiful home."

No one replied and Mary looked from one man to the next, recognising some as members of the king's council, and she suddenly knew that this was not a welcoming committee.

Her heart began to beat faster then, having learned long ago that an unannounced visit from the council was never for a good reason.

"May I enquire as to the purpose of your visit?" she asked.

The duke of Norfolk cleared his throat and smiled, but it did not put Mary at ease.

"Lady Mary," he said, "we have come by order of the king to demand once and for all that you accept that the marriage of your late mother, the Dowager Princess of Wales, Katherine of Aragon, to King Henry VIII, was never valid, and that you are therefore illegitimate," he paused and looked Mary straight in the eyes before continuing, "Moreover, he demands that you must also declare that you accept the king's position as Supreme Head of the Church of England."

Mary looked from one man to another and inhaled a shaky breath before replying.

"No," she said, "I cannot."

The men stared back in silence, the only sound being that of the birdsong outside.

Mary shifted her weight from one foot to another, becoming increasingly uncomfortable in the situation, and when no one spoke, she felt compelled to elaborate, and her mother's final words to her in her secret letter came to mind, "While I shall always obey the king in everything, I cannot in good conscience offend Almighty God. I cannot risk the damnation of my soul."

The duke of Norfolk glanced down at his hands and then at the men beside him.

One of them, a bishop, took a step towards Mary, "Lady Mary," he said, looking slightly uncomfortable, "I am the Bishop or Chester, Roland Lee, and I am here today to ensure you that your soul is safe," he offered her a half smile, "Agreeing to the king's supremacy is not a damnable offence, but rather the will of God Himself."

Mary scoffed, "While I thank you for your assurance," she said, "I must stand firm in my beliefs," and she raised her chin, hoping that that would be the end of it.

The bishop of Chester turned back around and shook his head at the others, resuming his place amongst the group.

"I shall ask you again," the duke of Norfolk said, almost growling with anger, "Do you accept your mother and father's marriage to have been invalid, and the king as supreme head of the church of England?"

His dark eyes were boring into Mary's face, his nostrils flared in anger, but Mary remained strong as she fingered her prayer beads which were tucked safely in her sleeve. She inhaled deeply to compose herself, then raised her chin and replied, "No."

The duke of Norfolk raised his hands up and exclaimed impatiently, his outraged shout echoing through the great hall. Then he stepped back as if to turn away from Mary, and at a sudden change of mind he spun back around and pressed his face just inches away from hers, "You are such an unnatural child as to disobey the king's rulings, I can hardly believe that you are the king's own bastard daughter! Were you mine or *any* other man's daughter I would beat you to death for such insolence. I should strike your head against the wall until it is as soft as a boiled apple!" then he pointed his finger in her face, "You are a traitor to the king, and it is only for his love for you that you are still alive this day."

Mary stared wide-eyed in shock and in terror as the duke turned and walked away from her, no doubt to compose his temper and to avoid doing just as he threatened.

Beneath her dress she could feel her knees shaking and she was for once thankful to have been born a woman and to have the luxury of hiding her fear beneath her fashions.

But despite her body trembling in terror and her knees almost giving way, on the surface she remained stoic. With her hands clasped firmly before her and her jaw pressed together tightly, she stared them all down as they continued their relentless and repetitive questions.

And never once did she respond.

When they eventually gave up and announced their departure, Mary nodded to them in farewell and silently thanked God for watching over her; but as soon as the guards closed the doors behind them and she heard their horses galloping away, she fell into a crumpled heap on the floor and sobbed.

The following day, after a fitful night's sleep haunted with nightmares brought on by the duke's threats, Mary was surprised to receive another visit – this time a happy one.

"The imperial ambassador, Eustace Chapuys," her guard announced as he opened the door to her room, and Mary welcomed him warmly inside.

"Ambassador," she said with a smile.

He took her hand and kissed it before bowing, "Lady Mary," he said, "I heard about what happened," and he shook his head in disdain.

Mary's cheeks blushed and she dropped her gaze, "I am sure the whole court has heard," and she sat down at the small table and waved her hand at the seat beside her, inviting him to join her.

Senor Chapuys accepted the offer of the seat and sighed sadly, "Perhaps it is time," he said with a small smile, his eyes conveying the worry he had for Mary's safety.

Mary met his gaze, "What? Never!" she declared, but her heart dropped at the prospect of what would happen if she did not. Despite her strong catholic beliefs and the importance for the security of her soul, Mary realised that she did in fact fear death. The realisation came with a pang of guilt as she remembered Sir Thomas Moore's sacrifice and his unbreakable certainty for what was right, even at the cost of his own survival.

Tears welled in her eyes as she began to understand that though she knew that her father was acting against God's laws, she did not have the courage to continue standing up to him if it would indeed cost her her life.

"Mary," the Spanish ambassador whispered as he reached his hand across the table, but Mary snatched her hand away, too proud to accept his sympathy.

"I could never denounce my faith," she said hotly, "Not to mention betray my mother and damn my own soul to Hell!"

Eustace Chapuys looked at the young lady before him with sadness in his eyes and he observed that, though she was but twenty years old, her appearance betrayed her greatly, the years of fear and torment having taken its toll on her youth.

His heart ached for the young lady before him, and he thought how wretched it was for someone so young to have experienced so much suffering and misery.

In his opinion, her courage was to be congratulated, for never had he known a young lady quite so constant in her faith. But after all that she had endured, now was the time to allow some lax, for he feared that if she were to continue on this crusade, that her life would be forfeit, whether she be the king's daughter or not.

"You must listen to this old man," he said slowly and calmly, his eyes crinkling as he offered her another smile, "Your mother would not have wanted you to live your life in fear, or to give up your life. She stood firm to the very end that her marriage to the king was valid, and most of the world will agree with her – as would God. But right now, it is a dangerous world. And if you want to live, you must agree to the terms."

Mary's tears slid down her face, "But why does it matter now that my mother is no longer with us?" she asked, confused as to why he would remain on this path when her mother was no longer an obstacle to his new marriage to Jane Seymour, "In the eyes of the law, he is a widower. And his new wife is said to be of the catholic faith," Mary pointed out, "Why then must he continue on this path towards reformation?"

"While it is true that the new queen is of the catholic faith," Chapuys replied, "it does not help your cause. He has had a taste of ultimate power, Mary. Without Rome telling him what he can and cannot do, as well as the riches of the church going directly to the crown, the king would not give up on the reformation now, and I doubt he ever will," the ambassador shook his head, "Now more than ever the king must be seen to clamp down on those that would oppose him as supreme head of the church, no matter who they are. His marriage to a catholic must not be viewed by the people as a step backwards. He is making that very clear."

Mary sat in silence for a long time, unable to think of any more to say in her defence.

"You must agree on paper," Eustace whispered, "And you may continue to disagree in your heart. I urge you to consider this."

Mary looked away from the ambassador's kind eyes. She knew now, and had known for a long time, that this moment had been inevitable if she wished to keep her head, but her heart ached at the thought of bowing down to such tyranny when her mother had died to protect her claim to the throne.

But the ambassador was right. Her mother would have wanted her to live.

And to do just that, Mary had to submit.

In return for Mary's obedience – relinquishing her legitimacy and accepting her father as Supreme Head of the Church of England – Mary was restored into his favour.

She received word from court not two weeks after she had taken up residence at Kenninghall that she was to return to court with immediate effect, and to take up residence at Greenwich Palace with her father and new stepmother.

While she looked forward to spending time with her father again after five long years apart, her mind felt perturbed at the thought of the price she had had to pay for his love, for almost as soon as she had signed the Act of Supremacy, she had felt a heaviness bearing down upon her shoulders, as though the guilt of her betrayal weighed more than she could carry.

She had signed away her legitimacy, her birth right and her future as queen of England – something her mother had fought and died for trying to protect – and within just a few months since her death, Mary had failed to keep hold of it. And she knew, from the moment her quill had touched the parchment, that she would regret her submission for the rest of her life.

July 1536
Greenwich Palace, London

Within a mere few days, Mary arrived back at court.

Upon her arrival at the king's court in London, her father welcomed her back with open arms and gifted her jewels and new dresses, indicating to the world that he was a generous king, and that if you accepted his higher authority, you would be greatly rewarded. But somehow, though she had long prayed for this day, none of it brought Mary any real joy, for it was as though she were seeing herself going through the motions from a great height, never actually experiencing any moments through her own eyes. And it would not be for several years before she would begin to forgive herself for her acquiescence.

Mary was also offered her choice of servants to re-form her household. She instantly and without delay reinstated her former ladies-in-waiting Cecily and Frances, whom she personally wrote to that very evening to inform them of the happy news, and as she sat down before her writing desk, she wondered just how much her two friends had changed over the years that they had been parted.

Mary's life returned to very much the same as it had been before her banishment, and she was once again a valued member of the king's court. The royal apartments she had inhabited years prior, were hers once again, despite her lack of royal status. People bowed and curtsied to her as she glided past them in the corridors, and she sat beside the king at dinners and feasts.

Though she was legally declared a bastard and held no formal ranking other than her standing as the king's daughter, Mary now took precedence over any other lady at court excluding only the new queen herself, and her father offered her everything befitting to a princess – except for, of course, the promise of the crown.

But despite all those niceties, Mary still could not shake the feeling that, while her life was once again perfect on the outside, on the inside her soul was slowly but surely rotting away.

July 1536

"Am I cursed?" the king asked Charles Brandon as he held his head in his hands, "Must all my children die?"

Charles had found Henry alone in the great hall, slumped and dishevelled as he sat upon his gold throne at the end of the vast, open room. His footsteps had echoed as he had made his approach towards the king, and the empty hall suddenly felt cold and dreary, its usually merry atmosphere having died along with the king's happiness.

The king's only surviving son, his bastard boy by his former mistress Bessie Blount, had suddenly and without warning, died in the night to a fever.

While the teenaged Henry Fitzroy had been an illegitimate son and unable to ever succeed the king to the throne, Fitzroy had been his only son to have surpassed the dangerous years of infancy and had been living proof that king Henry VIII could in fact produce a healthy male heir.

"I feel as though there is no more hope, Charles," the king admitted as he wiped his dripping nose with the back of his hand.

"Of course there is hope, your majesty," Charles Brandon replied tactfully and he took a step closer to his grieving friend, "Henry, you have a new, young wife," he said, "She will bear you many more sons, God willing!"

But even as Charles spoke the words, he was not entirely certain if he believed them anymore, for Henry had spent over two decades on his pursuit for a male successor, and after three wives and countless mistresses, it was becoming increasingly clear that perhaps a surviving son was not in God's plan for England's king.

Henry only nodded and then mumbled, "Yes, God willing," then he sniffed loudly and dabbed at his eyes with his sleeve before rising from his throne and walking out of the great hall without another word, leaving the confused Charles Brandon behind.

Later that day, Henry and his new queen, Jane Seymour, were alone in the king's chambers, naked underneath his silk sheets.

They were wrapped in each other's arms, staring at the high ceiling above them, exhausted from their lovemaking; and in the intimate darkness, Henry opened up about the boy he had lost.

"He was a good boy," Henry said dreamily, "He had been the proof I had needed all those years ago."

Queen Jane listened as her husband spoke about what his late son had meant to him for nearly an hour and was surprised at the lack of detail he could provide about the boy himself.

But for his shortage of knowledge on the child, Henry made up for it with enthusiasm for the future he had imagined for him.

Despite his illegitimacy, it seemed the king had always held a candle of hope for the boy's acceptance by the people if he were to one day have been declared his heir. Jane knew the people of England would never have accepted a low-born bastard boy, but she let her husband voice his secret hopes – hopes that were now utterly shattered – as she knew that they stemmed from a deep-rooted fear that he would never have the heir he had long dreamed of.

As Henry spoke without pause, his words flowing freely in the darkness, Jane's mind wandered and she began to contemplate what her own future as queen of England would hold, and the pressures that came with the new title.

Two queens had previously failed to give the king a son and heir, two queens that he had shunned or killed... and while she knew that the king loved her intensely, his son's death gave Jane a new perspective on his desperation for a male heir.

Jane shifted, suddenly uncomfortable in the king's embrace, and hoped that he would not notice her sudden need for him to leave so that she may kneel at her private prie-deux and pray to God for a swift conception of a healthy son.

And then, on second thought – realising that the only way to a swift conception being the one presented to her this very moment – Jane licked her lips and turned back into her husband's arms, running her finger over his chest suggestively.

He stopped talking mid-sentence and glanced down at his wife, and with only the look in her eyes she incited a stirring in the king. She craned her neck up and kissed him firmly, wasting no time on frivolities as she pressed her naked body up against his and felt his erection against her thigh.

With a satisfied smile, Jane opened her legs as the king pushed her back against the pillows, and closed her eyes as he entered her, a gasp escaping her as he thrusted over and over again.

But when his thrusts grew weaker before he had cried out in pleasure, she rolled him over with one push of her leg against the mattress and then she was straddling him in a way that she knew was not befitting of a queen, but Jane knew she could not falter until he had filled her with his essence.

She took his hands and placed them upon her bare breasts as she moved on top of him, her stomach muscles beginning to ache from it, but she only allowed herself to stop when he finally threw his head back and shuddered beneath her as he cried out in pleasure.

Then she gingerly climbed off him as he lay there spent and fell back onto the feather pillows. Within moments she heard her husband snoring beside her, and she turned to look at him, wondering if she should wake him in a few moments to increase her chances of conception threefold.

But then she thought better of it, her stomach aching from the unusual exercise and instead she covered herself with the cotton sheets until she had regained a steady breath.

Then she sat up and wrapped a robe around herself before padding over to the prie-deux in the corner of her room and knelt before it. She crossed herself quickly and closed her eyes, and there she remained, praying to the Lord Almighty that she may be pregnant with a son that very moment, to fill her husband's aching heart.

She prayed until the sun began to rise in the East, unable to confidently leave her conception simply to chance, for she knew– given the king's track record with surviving sons – that she would be praying for a miracle.

During her prayers, queen Jane had had a moment of clarity in which God had steered her mind away from her immediate need for her own child and directed it towards the one other thing she believed could alleviate the king's troubled nature.

As a devout catholic Jane had – and always would – believe that the king's marriage to his first wife, Katherine of Aragon, to have been lawful, and that the child that had been produced from it to be legitimate and true.

While she was not foolish enough to voice her beliefs aloud to her husband, Jane did however believe that it was her duty – as well as her own salvation while her womb remained empty – that she carefully attempt to persuade the king into readmitting Mary within the line of succession.

One evening over a private supper in the king's chambers, after queen Jane had disappointingly commenced her courses, signifying that another month would pass without the hope of an heir, she decided to broach the subject of the lady Mary's value to her lord husband.

"My love," she said, as she glanced up at him from beneath her lashes, her voice smooth like melted butter, "Forgive my boldness but I must ask you to consider something."

Henry looked up from his plate of food before him, "What is it?" he said as he chewed loudly, and for a moment Jane wondered how a man so handsome could simultaneously be so unappealing.

But she reached a delicate hand across the table and touched his forearm, stroking it lovingly as she spoke.

"I know the loss of your son weighs heavily on your heart, and on your mind," she smiled at him sympathetically, "his death leaves you without a son, and though he was illegitimate, I am sure the people would have accepted him as king if it had been your wish," she watched as Henry sat back heavily in his chair and took a large gulp of wine, blinking away tears as he drank, and she went on, "But perhaps, now that he is gone, we should look to your other children to succeed you?"

Her voice had been sweet, her demeanour alluring, and yet, as soon as she uttered the last syllable, she regretted every word.

Henry's glare turned quickly from despair into disbelief and Jane, feeling suddenly flustered at his change in temperament, muttered on in an effort to explain herself.

"I suggest this only to keep your throne secure until I have borne you sons," she said hurriedly as fear overcame her, "The lady Mary is loved by many, and if you reinstate her as heir apparent, it would keep your majesty from –"

He held up his hand, his eyes blazing with anger in a way she had never seen before, and she felt a sudden and intense panic that she imagined both his previous wives had known all too well.

She swallowed slowly as she awaited his response.

"Jane," he said as he continued to chew loudly, then he sighed deeply and stuffed some more sweetmeats in his mouth, "don't ever speak to me of matters such as these again."

"But –" she started.

"Are you mad, woman!?" he shouted suddenly, his eyes wild, "I said: do not *ever* speak of this again. Do you understand?"

Jane stared back at her husband, her beautiful face completely drained of colour, and she nodded, "Yes, your majesty," she mumbled and resumed eating, the meat and bread tasting like dust in her mouth.

"In any case," the king said then, his rage gone in an instant, "you should be focusing on the continuation of *our* line, not that of dead women's bastard children."

Jane felt sick. His sudden aggression had utterly horrified her, and for the first time since he had begun courting her over a year ago, Jane gave the former queens a sympathetic thought.

His response had also left her stunned, for she had never imagined it possible for someone so desperate for a successor to hold such contempt for one's own children. At this very moment, at the age of forty-five, and after over two decades of attempting to sire a son, Jane would have thought that Henry himself must know that their chance of conception was low.

But perhaps Jane had been fooled.

Perhaps he was not the loving and rational man she had thought him to be, and her chest felt hollow with the realisation that she had been misled by his charm and that, in reality, she did not really know her husband at all.

July 1537

"The king still dotes on the lady Mary," Cecily pointed out quietly one morning as she and Frances walked side by side on their way to wake Mary for the day, "It has been a year since her return. Perhaps it will last."

Frances raised an eyebrow, "I pray you are right. Mary has been through enough. But I would say it will depend on the sex of the queen's baby."

Queen Jane was finally with child. It had taken over half a year for the king and his new wife to conceive, and while the king had noticeably become edgy and impatient, upon her announcement he was once again the loving and attentive man she had married, and suddenly a blanket of calm had fallen over the king and country as they awaited the day of the babe's arrival.

Some might have thought that the king's affection towards the lady Mary would not have lasted past the announcement of his queen's pregnancy, and so it came as a happy surprise to everyone when he openly continued to dance with her at feasts and invited her out on hunting expeditions.

But Mary herself had changed. Her ladies had noticed it as soon as they had arrived back at court a year prior, and while they had hoped that her contentment for life would return, it would seem that something inside her had broken during their time apart.

"She has not yet recovered from her mother's loss," Frances continued as they stopped before the door to Mary's apartments.

Cecily *tsked* her, "The circumstances were horrific," she whispered, "Would you be over the death of your mother if your father had forbidden you to see or write to her for four years, then denied you to visit her on her death bed?"

Frances shook her head slightly.

"And do not forget," Cecily continued, "The vile threats made to her life soon afterwards. And the signing of the oath," Cecily sighed, "It was too much for one soul to suffer through."

Frances placed one hand onto the doorhandle but stopped before she pushed it open, "Do you think she will ever fully return to her former self?"

Cecily raised her eyebrows in thought, "Truthfully," she said, "I think the Mary we know is dead."

Frances' mouth twitched in sadness at Cecily's words, but then she nodded and pushed the door to Mary's rooms open, a bright smile on her face as she entered.

Cecily wandered over to the fireplace and poked at the ashes, revealing a handful of glowing embers which she left to warm the room a little before the summer sun rose in the sky, and Frances opened the wooden shutters in Mary's bedroom.

"Good morning, my lady," Frances chirped happily, and Cecily shook her head at her exaggerated glee.

When Mary was up, the two ladies brushed her waist-length auburn hair and twisted it up before pinning her hood upon her head while a servant brought a bowl of water with orange slices and rose petals for Mary to wash her face, and another brought in a plate of breakfast.

"How is the queen this morning?" Mary asked her ladies as she picked up a grape and popped it into her mouth while they fetched her clothes.

"I hear she is better today," Frances said, "Her stomach is settled, and she has taken some bread this morning without feeling sick."

"That is a relief," Mary said as she stepped into the skirts Cecily held ready for her.

Mary and her new stepmother had become close since her readmittance at court, their shared devotion to Catholicism having been the steppingstone towards a great friendship.

At first, they had begun praying together at the Palace's chapel, where they had bonded over their favourite passages from the Bible and which psalms gave them inner peace. Soon after they had taken to walking together in the Palace gardens whenever the weather allowed, and there they would talk for hours about their childhoods, their mothers, and their God.

Mary had decided long before Jane had announced her pregnancy, that she would treasure her as a friend for all her life, simply by the delightful aura Jane emitted. Unlike her previous stepmother, who would have quite clearly preferred Mary dead than alive, Jane did not exude any superiority, vanity, or maliciousness.

Instead, she was quite simply and openly someone who truly cared for Mary's wellbeing – something Mary had not felt in a long time – and she admitted regularly that she would always do her best to keep her in her father's favour.

"You are his true and legitimate daughter," queen Jane had said to her one day as they had wandered leisurely through the gardens, "I will always believe his marriage to your mother was lawful, and so do many others. And while I am queen, I will continue to try to get the king to change his mind about your legitimacy. Perhaps one day when I have given him a son, he may reconsider your future."

Mary had cried tears of joy at the whispered revelation, and while she prayed that her new stepmother would be successful in her pledge, she could not allow herself to invest wholeheartedly into that possibility.

For she knew that her father's love was fickle and unreliable, and Mary feared that it would only be a matter of time before his adoration for this new wife would one day turn to dust in his hands.

12th October 1537

It had been three full days and nights since the queen's tightenings had begun.

Three days in which the midwives could do nothing but soothe her with hopeful words, but when the queen could push no longer for fatigue and weakness, the physicians were called to cut the babe out.

Everyone knew that this would surely mean the loss of the mother for the sake of the child...

It was a miracle then, when the babe was ripped from the mother's womb, that it turned out to be the long-awaited son and heir that the king and country had long held their breath for.

Immediately, the country celebrated. Church bells rang in celebration all over London, and parish churches around the country sang Te Deum. Bonfires were lit and merchants gave out fruit, wine, and beer to nobles and the poor alike. The country was united in their shared joy for their king and, by extension, for themselves as they hoped that this joy would bring a calm to their monarch that they knew he had not felt in years.

It had been over a quarter of a century since a prince had been christened in England, when queen Katherine's firstborn son, Henry, had been born.

And though Mary had only ever heard stories of the poor babe that had suddenly perished just fifty-two days after its birth, she imagined his christening had been much as grand as this one.

As Mary was assigned the role of godmother to little prince Edward, she briefly contemplated just how differently her life would have turned out, had that firstborn son of her mother's lived.

But life being what it is and not what it ought to have been, she took her role as godmother to the prince very seriously. Mary saw it as a sign that though her father had deemed her unfit to rule or to bear the royal title she had been born with, she was fit, however, to present the new heir – her replacement – to the world and to God.

Though Mary accepted her duty gracefully and with immense gratitude, she could not quash the little voice in her head that wished this day had never come.

For years she had had the title of the oldest living child of the king of England, whether she be deemed illegitimate one day or reinstated princess another was of little consequence to Mary.

For she knew that if her father had never had this *precious son*, that she would have inevitably been the one to whom the crown would have fallen to.

But she felt no jealousy towards the little prince, for he, just as Elizabeth and Mary herself, were innocents in this deadly race to the throne.

A week had gone by since the prince's christening and Mary decided that she would visit her friend and stepmother to bring her sugared grapes as a treat during her confinement.

When Mary entered the chambers, she was greeted by the queen's ladies who curtsied briefly and led her to the queen in a gloomy silence. Mary frowned at the ominous atmosphere within the chambers, but when she pulled back the curtain to the queen's room, Mary instantly recoiled at the stench of death that she encountered.

She looked aghast at the queen as she lay awkwardly on the dozens of cushions on her bed, her skin as pale as her sheets, and though her eyes were closed, she did not seem to be at ease.

When Mary slowly moved closer, unsure if she should announce her presence, she noticed that while Jane seemed to be shaking with cold, her skin was shining with perspiration, and it was clear that she was suffering from complications.

Mary turned on her heel and marched towards the queen's ladies, closing the heavy curtain behind her, "Why is the physician not here?" she asked, "The queen is clearly in distress."

The lady's eyes went wide with fear, "The physician was here this morning and gave the queen a physic to help her sleep," she said.

"The physician was allowed in?" Mary asked, confused.

The lady shook her head, "No, my lady. A midwife requested it from the physician upon examining the queen this morning."

"And what of the smell?"

The lady dropped her gaze, "It is the wound. It will not heal," she whispered.

Mary, and all of England, had known that the prince's violent birth had meant the inevitable demise of the mother. But when the lucky queen had emerged from it alive, all had assumed the worst was over.

But queen Jane's difficult birth had left her weak and pale, and due to the continuous presence of birthing blood – which deemed the queen as unclean and not suitable to receive male visitors, including the king himself – it left her unable to receive treatment until she was properly churched by a priest.

"It won't heal?" Mary echoed, dumbfounded.

The lady shook her head.

"Well then a physician needs to see her," Mary declared logically.

"But she has not been churched, my lady."

"And how is she to be churched if the bleeding does not cease?" Mary said over her shoulder angrily as she exited the room.

She stormed off towards the king's chambers, which were opposite the queen's, and entered without waiting for permission.

"Your majesty," she said as she gave a quick curtsy, "Your queen is in distress. She needs urgent assistance from the physicians."

Henry looked up at her, his eyes bloodshot with grief "I know," he simply replied, his voice faint, "It is a tragedy!" and he buried his face in his hands.

"My lord, what can we do?" Mary asked bewildered, unable to believe that men's logic would defy the obvious course of action. For surely the presence of blood, whether it be caused by battle or by birth, should not deny someone their need for medical attention.

"Nothing," the king answered, "She is in God's hands now. We must pray that she recovers enough to be churched so that the physicians can tend to her."

"But…" Mary scoffed, completely astonished by her father's response, "Did my lady mother not have a physician attend her at my birth?" she suddenly pointed out bravely, remembering some such story being mentioned to her years ago.

Henry's head snapped up, *"That!"* he spat out in sudden anger, "That man was lucky I did not execute him! It goes against God for a man to attend a lady during childbed and the recuperation of it."

"But had it not been for Dr Vittoria, mother and I might have perished!" Mary countered.

Henry stared back at his daughter, and his expression sent a shiver down Mary's spine.

She had said too much, and yet she had answered her own question: the king knew what *could* be done. But for some reason unknown to her, he would not.

She had no words.

His queen, whom Mary and the country had believed he had loved, had just delivered onto him the son he had been praying for, for decades. She had done her duty by her king and by her

203

God, and yet it did not stir enough emotion in her father to bend the rules so that her life may be spared.

He had turned the country on its head so that he could marry the harlot Anne Boleyn, but he would not bring himself to order a physician to tend to the angel Jane Seymour.

Mary watched wide-eyed and deflated as her father, the king of England, sat upon his throne, feigning powerlessness to aid his dying wife. She could feel her face growing hot with anger, and while she still had control over her rage, she turned and left the king behind and made her way to the chapel to try to help in the only way she knew how.

By praying to the good Lord for her stepmother's salvation.

But it was to no avail, and only two days later, the country was in mourning for the tragic death of their queen.

Mary, who had grown to love and respect her stepmother, was inconsolable, and she locked herself away in her chambers. She wept for days, not only for herself, but also for her baby brother who would grow up never to know his own mother.

Queen Jane's loss would be felt all over the country for her purity and kind-heartedness had become common knowledge among the people. And the fact that the gentle queen had given her life to deliver the king his long-awaited son only made her death so much more tragic.

In place of her father, who traditionally could not attend any funeral, Mary was appointed Chief Mourner at the queen's interment in his stead, and while she acted dutifully and in honour of her father, Mary could not bring herself to fully believe that his mourning was genuine due to his lack of intervention to aid her healing.

But it was a mystery she would never uncover, her father's mind being an ever-changing labyrinth that likely no one would ever decipher.

And so, while Jane's coffin was being transported to Windsor on a hearse drawn by a horse draped in black, and the country mourned her passing, Mary found herself wondering if her father would ever take another wife. And would marriage even be on the forefront of his mind now that he had his precious male heir?

As the coffin was being lifted off the horse-drawn hearse and brought into St. George's Chapel, she could not stop the tears from falling and her mind fell to her brand-new baby brother, and the emptiness with which his life had begun. She imagined how his heart would forever be searching for someone he had never even known, and as the misery of it all dawned on Mary, in her mind she began to tumble into a dark and endless abyss of sorrow.

Chapter 11

England was weak.

Though the king finally had his long-awaited son and heir thriving in the nursery, he was once again unwed and therefore without the prospect of potentially producing any spares, which – as the second born son to his own royal parents – he knew first hand to be critical for the security of the Tudor line.

However, even with that in mind, Henry could not bring himself to consider another lady, whether for personal or political gain, for the guilt over Jane's loss was still too much to bear.

He could not even bring himself to visit his precious son for more than a few moments without Jane's face flashing before his mind's eye and bringing about a new onslaught of remorse.

And so, visitations fell to Mary who obeyed without complaint or disparity, for at the age of twenty-two with no marriage prospects in sight and no children of her own, Mary took the opportunity to pour all her motherly love and affection towards her little baby brother.

She would often bring him little gifts, silver rattles or wooden horses, which he would grab in his chubby little fists and bang about enthusiastically.

Prince Edward's household resided at Richmond Palace which was located upstream on the river Thames in London and was therefore close enough to warrant Mary many regular visits.

It had been only six months since his mother's passing and little Edward was already sitting up and babbling away, which was considered rather advanced, and this brought the king much pride when Mary conveyed the princes' developments to him after her weekly visits.

Mary enjoyed nothing more than to get down on the floor with the little blonde prince and make silly noises and faces to make him laugh. His loud and carefree gurgle filled her heart with such joy that she sometimes forgot he was not in fact her child, and she tried to spend as much time with him as she could, knowing in her heart that she may very well never have a child of her own if her father would not arrange a suitable marriage for her. And even then, who would have her as a disgraced former princess? No one of worth, she imagined.

Unbeknownst to her, however, king Henry had begun negotiations with Europe in an attempt to secure an alliance to strengthen England in a way which would allow the king some time to overcome his dear Jane's loss.

He and his council had put together several proposals for marital prospects to the lady Mary, including a proposal to Mary's former betrothed Henri of Orleans, the king of France's second son, as well as one to Dom Luis of Portugal.

But weeks had gone by since their messengers' departures and with each day that passed without a word, Henry became increasingly agitated, for his health had taken a turn for the worse in the months since Jane's death.

An old wound from a past jousting accident had suddenly become inflamed and painful before bursting open one night as he slept. An extraordinary amount of infected fluid and blood had seeped from the wound, rendering Henry's bedsheets sullied beyond repair.

The king's physicians had cleaned the wound and given him a remedy for the pain, but after several weeks the wound had not yet begun to heal and as a result Henry's irritation was never far behind even the mildest of inconveniences.

"There is no respect!" he shouted, his unshaven face red with anger, "Regardless of status, she is still the daughter of the king of England. That should count for something."

Charles Brandon merely blinked at his friend as he sat opposite him and casually shuffled a deck of cards in his hands, no longer affected by the king's constant mood swings, "Yes, but you deemed her illegitimate, Henry," he pointed out, "You cannot expect to receive many responses from legitimate sons of kings who are in line to their thrones. While they may choose to wed a lady or a princess, whoever they choose would no doubt have to, at least, be legitimate, don't you think?"

Henry grunted as he watched Charles deal out the cards for their game of Piquet, "What am I to do then?" he asked, "I am not ready to re-marry, and England needs new alliances to keep us strong."

Charles did not reply and simply picked up the cards before him, organizing them tactfully so that he could easily feign defeat, having learned long ago that it was never a good idea to beat the king at even a simple game of cards. The two of them remained in a comfortable silence as they played hand after hand, both knowing but not voicing what Henry *could* do to arrange a marriage of worth for his eldest daughter – namely by re-legitimizing her.

But Charles knew it did not even warrant mentioning, for Henry would never accept it as an option, even though Charles – and potentially all of England – would stand firm in the knowledge that it was the *right* option.

Mary entered the great hall, curtsied elegantly before her father the king and smiled as he greeted her warmly from upon his throne, "Ah Mary, my beautiful daughter."

"Your majesty, I hope you are well?" she replied charmingly, though she could tell almost immediately that her father was no longer the fit young man he used to be.

Henry stood up awkwardly from his throne, his left leg stretched out before him, and slowly walked towards his daughter, "I am very well, Mary," he said before embracing her, "You are looking well," he pointed out kindly.

But while Mary smiled in response, she could not bring herself to reply, for a pungent stench suddenly struck her, and Mary realised that the old wound on his leg must have burst once again, the rotting wound no doubt oozing its infected fluid into the tightly wrapped bandage.

But then the king turned and slowly hobbled back up the three steps to his throne, and Mary inhaled deeply after realising she had subconsciously held her breath at the vile aroma that her father emitted of late. Then she steeled herself in preparation for the uncharted topic of discussion she knew would likely cause, at the very least, a heated dialogue from the king.

"Your majesty," she finally said after having waited patiently for him to carefully sit back down on his throne, "I am come to speak on behalf of your other daughter, the Lady Elizabeth."

Instantly his expression changed into one of disdain, but Mary continued bravely.

"She has outgrown her dresses and I am here to beg your grace to have mercy on the poor child."

Henry rubbed his hand over his face and groaned, "Why should I concern myself with the girl when she is likely not even my own?"

Mary was not surprised at her father's words, but she was nonetheless taken aback at the acidity in his tone towards the innocent child.

"The lady Elizabeth may have been born illegitimate," Mary replied tactfully, "but there is no denying that she is your daughter, father. She is such a clever and witty young girl, with many interests beyond her age. Not to mention her fiery red hair. All characteristics she has undoubtedly received from you."

Mary knew her father well enough to know that he would not only accept the logic in her words, but he would also no doubt fall for the blatant compliments she had laid upon him, especially now that he was struggling to accept his lost youth.

Henry watched her carefully as he contemplated her words, running his tongue over his yellow teeth in thought, "She is clever and wise beyond her years, that I can admit she has from me. However, her wit she got from her mother, that *whore*!"

Mary did not argue. Instead, she remained silent while Henry's temper faded, and he contemplated her request.

There was absolutely no doubt in Mary's mind that Elizabeth was her father's daughter. If not only for her similarities to the king but also for the fact that, regardless of her utter hatred for the woman, Mary knew that the lady Anne Boleyn had not been foolish. She would have conceived the king's child if it had been the last thing she would do. It had been her ultimate quest to conceive an heir for England and to keep the title of queen. Whatever she may or may not have done after Elizabeth's birth in an attempt to continue her reign was beyond Mary's realm of imagination. But while they were happy, the harlot would have certainly only lain with the king in the hopes of giving him a son.

Mary was snapped out of her thoughts when the king broke the silence, "I admire your kindness towards the child, Mary," he said, "Though you saw her as your replacement for a time, I see that you have grown fond of her. And as you say, she is a clever thing. Or so I am told. It is a shame that her mother was such a deceitful wench. Perhaps if she had been more like your mother, she would still be here."

Mary held her breath for fear of saying the wrong thing and she decided that to stay silent would be the best course of action, but the sudden mention of her mother sent a shiver down Mary's spine, and she felt the back of her eyes sting at the thought of her.

It was a strange feeling, to stand before her mother's gaoler, knowing him to have been the cause of all her problems, while simultaneously wishing him no harm. And she realised yet again what a weak organ the heart was.

"Your mother was loyal at least," the king continued in thought as Mary stared back at him warily, "Until the very end."

He sighed deeply and then smiled, "I grant you your request, Mary. I shall have bolts of cloth sent to the girl's household. The servants can make of it what they will."

Mary smiled and curtsied, "I thank your majesty for your generosity," she said and then swiftly turned and hurried out of the great hall before her father could change his mind.

Although Mary had hoped that he would also offer to send a purse of monies to the little Elizabeth to treat her to a proper meal and to pay her servants on her behalf, Mary knew that she should be glad he listened to her request at all.

She decided that she would have one of her own gold plates sent to Hatfield as a form of payment for the girl's few servants so that they would remain in her service and continue to care for her, since no one else wished to do it for free.

August 1539

"Damn Francois and the Emperor!" Henry shouted as he threw the documents before him to the ground, "This reconciliation between their two countries leaves England completely without allies. With the constant threat from Scotland above us and now France and Spain's new alliance…" Henry shook his head, "We need to make a new ally. And soon."

The king of France and the Holy Roman Emperor, King Charles V of Spain, had reconciled their decades long hatred for one another and turned their mutual attention towards England, which they knew to be weakened due the king's ill health and his only successor to be an easily overthrowable baby.

Though Henry's spies informed him that there were no preparations being made for an immediate invasion, he knew that if a war did ensue and England stood alone against two of Europe's most powerful countries, it would end tragically for him.

And so, after Mary's marriage proposals were all rejected, Henry finally let go of his internal turmoil over Jane's demise and braved himself to allow another lady into his bruised heart – marital union with a powerful ally being the only thing that would ensure England's safety.

"Your majesty," Mr Cromwell said as he stood from his seat at the council table, his black hair showing signs of greying at the temples, likely due to the stressors of his ever-growing responsibilities, "Might I suggest we consider a partnership with Germany?"

"What of the duchess of Milan, or Mary of Hungary?" Henry asked, having heard far and wide of their beauty, "Has either of them accepted?"

Cromwell looked down, uncomfortable with having to be the bearer of bad news, "It appears neither is in favour of a match with your majesty," he said.

Henry's face went red with humiliation and anger, and Cromwell continued quickly, "But I have a proposition for your majesty, if you would permit me to continue?"

Henry clenched his jaw but sat down and waved his hand for Cromwell to continue.

"I would like to suggest a match with Germany," Cromwell announced, "Specifically, the princess Anne of Cleves. It would strengthen England against the new alliance between France and Spain, and I hear the princess Anne is very well spoken and considered a beauty."

The men of the council watched as their king rubbed his chin slowly in thought.

Sensing a lack of enthusiasm over the matter, Cromwell added, "Perhaps there could even be a match for the Lady Mary with this union? The princess' brother Wilhelm I, the Duke of Julich-Cleves-Berg himself is in need of a wife. This match would safeguard England doubly against the threat of invasion."

While Cromwell knew this proposition would indeed help to strengthen the country, his suggestion of the princess of Cleves as a wife for the king stemmed mainly from a personal gain, for a union with a devout Protestant princess from a deeply Lutheran family would, in Cromwell's mind, give England the push it needed to fully reform from the catholic faith, which he abhorred above all else.

Henry met Cromwell's gaze; his lips pursed in thought.

"Have them bring me a portrait of the lady," he simply said, his voice low and emotionless.

"Your majesty," Cromwell bowed and resumed his seat, eager to move on before the king changed his mind and perhaps considered another catholic lady for his next queen instead.

October 1539

"What is all the commotion about?" Mary asked her ladies as they walked through the crowd of gossiping courtiers on their way to the chapel.

"It is said that the king is to wed again," her lady Cecily said.

"Not that Lutheran I hope?!" Mary exclaimed, causing a small group of ladies to look in her direction at the outburst.

"I heard that is what Mr Cromwell has arranged," Cecily replied quietly after having noticed people beginning to look at Mary to gauge her reaction to the news.

Mary ignored the onlookers and eavesdroppers and crossed herself in disgust, "I cannot believe it. He will stop at nothing!"

Lady Cecily and lady Frances exchanged a look but said nothing. Though the king finally had a healthy son and heir to the throne, it was a widely known fact that having only one son in the nursery was not enough to guarantee the kingdom's safety. As the only surviving child to come from her parent's twenty-four year marriage, Mary herself was proof that the likelihood of a child reaching adulthood was slim.

"What of your match, Mary?" Frances asked then, an impish grin brightening her pretty face.

"If I have anything to say about it, then there will not be one," Mary said as she clasped her prayer beads tightly, "I would rather die than be made to marry a Lutheran!" and she stormed off ahead with her head held high in defiance.

Though Mary had often dreamt of her wedding day and prayed daily that her father would reinstate her as princess, she knew that she too had her boundaries. No matter how charming or powerful this Wilhelm I may be, Mary knew that she would not agree to a marriage to a Protestant.

Mary dreaded the thought of having another stepmother with the same beliefs as the first, after so much had changed for the worst throughout England.

And so, as she knelt at the altar with her prayer beads clasped tightly in her hands, she dedicated her morning prayers to the failure of this unity, and that her father would change his mind about marrying yet another heretic.

It seemed that, at least in part, Mary's prayers had been answered.

Though the king formally announced his betrothal to the princess Anne of Cleves, to Mary's great relief, he made no mention of her betrothal to Wilhelm I.

"Oh, thank God," Mary breathed silently from among the crowd at her father's announcement, and though it felt strange to have yet another betrothal fall through, Mary revelled at this one, for she knew that a union with a protestant would not be one she could live with.

Her lady Cecily who stood beside her shot her a knowing glance and offered her a small smile at the small victory and Mary nodded her head in reply.

She and her ladies had stayed up late the night before, playing cards before the roaring fire in Mary's chambers and discussing the life she would have led had her marriage to the German Duke been accepted.

"Your father was happily married to Jane," Frances had said at one point in the conversation, "And she was a Catholic while he favours reform."

"Yes, but Jane married for love," Mary pointed out sadly as she arranged the cards in her hands, the memory of her beloved stepmother causing a jolt of sorrow in her chest.

The three young women were silent for a while, then Cecily said, "If this betrothal goes ahead, then you too may grow to love Wilhelm."

Mary looked up from her fanned out cards, "I doubt it," she said petulantly.

Cecily shrugged, "It could happen."

At that Mary had sighed irritably, "I should rather die an old maid than be made to marry some Lutheran heretic I have never met," she said, "love or no love – it is irrelevant."

Her ladies had raised their eyebrows but did not reply as they continued to play on in silence, all three of them knowing that it mattered very little what Mary wanted, for in a world where men made the rules, women could do nothing but endure.

November 1539

All of Mary's strong will and determination was swept away just days later, when the princess Anne of Cleves and her household arrived in London.

As they made their entrance into the great hall and were announced by the usher, Mary was surprised to notice that her supposed betrothed, Wilhelm I of Cleves, had not been announced and was therefore absent from the party.

"Will the duke not even come?" Mary asked her ladies over her shoulder incredulously.

"It is said that another suitor has come in his stead, my lady," Frances whispered, "The princess Anne's cousin," her face bright with the excitement of the new information she had learned just minutes earlier from one of the guards that had escorted Anne of Cleves' household to Greenwich Palace.

Mary gave her a stern look, "Surely if I cared little for the match with one heretic, I shouldn't care much for one with another!" she said firmly, eager to hold on to the notion that she had any say in it whatsoever.

Frances shrugged lightly and just smiled, eager to have new faces at court.

Mary stood still beside her late mother's empty throne, her ladies on either side behind her, as everyone was announced and presented to the king.

Many names were stated, and after a while Mary began to pay little attention, her mind wandering at the prospect of a forced marriage with a heretic, and how utterly terrible it would be.

Suddenly Mary was brought out from her daze as she felt Frances tugging at her sleeve, "That's him, that's him!" she whispered excitedly.

Mary looked up at who was standing before the king and was startled to find the strangers' face not only handsome but undeniably captivating, and she felt ashamed to realise that her heart had skipped a beat at the sight of his crooked smile, so much like Arthur's, and though the two bore no other resemblance, that smile was enough to send a tingling sensation down the length of Mary's spine.

"Duke Phillip of Palatine-Neuburg," Charles Brandon introduced aloud to the king.

The duke removed his feathered hat from his head, revealing a full head of wavy dark hair, and bowed deeply, "Your majesty, it is an honour to be before you," he said, his voice somehow gruff yet smooth all at once, and with a hint of an accent which did nothing but impede Mary from regaining her composure.

She watched as he straightened himself and spoke with the king, but as her blood rushed within her body and her heart beat loudly inside her ears, she was rendered completely deaf to their conversation.

Suddenly all eyes were on her, and she felt her cheeks burning with humiliation. She forced herself to regain her composure and cleared her throat, and yet somehow her mind could not communicate to her body what she ought to do next.

Then Mary felt a light push from behind her and she took a step towards the handsome duke.

She offered him a quick curtsy, "Your grace," she said quietly.

"It is an honour to meet you, lady Mary," he said with a nod, and their eyes met before Mary resumed her place beside the empty throne.

The duke of Palatine-Neuburg was ushered along, and the remaining nobles of Anne of Cleves' household were presented before finally the princess herself approached.

She wore a plain dress of black damask and a dark veil which covered her face as well as her hood.

Mary frowned slightly at the sight of her, confused at the need for discretion, and noticed that her father beside her sat straight-backed and sour faced upon the princess' entrance.

If rumours were to be believed, the king had spontaneously paid the princess a visit upon their arrival at Rochester Castle a few days prior, as she and her household made their way towards London and had found the lady awfully uglier than had been depicted in her portrait.

But Mary had no sympathy for her father, whom she thought was playing a dangerous hand in marrying the German Lutheran. But she hoped that if past record held any merit, then surely this next marriage would be as short lived as the others; especially if it were to begin with such obvious unwillingness from the king.

When Anne of Cleves had her veil removed and was formally presented to the king, Mary noticed that though she was not extremely beautiful, she was also not as ugly as rumours would have made her believe. She was plain, yes, but not unattractive.

Her face was round like the moon, which Mary had to admit was not preferable, but she noted that her awfully styled hood did not help the matter either. Despite her round face, Mary noticed that her eyes were a beautiful pale green, and her nose was small and straight, features which she believed were not undesirable in a woman.

She wondered, as the princess Anne curtsied elegantly, what exactly had happened during the king's brief visit at Kent to warrant such a cold reception from the king, for by looking at the princess herself, Mary could not say with certainty that her appearance would have been the problem.

She looked away from the round-faced princess and glanced quickly at her father as he welcomed her cooly to his court – his expression one of utter disappointment – and she suddenly felt extremely sorry for the poor woman standing awkwardly before them.

Though they may have nothing in common as far as language or religion, Mary knew first-hand how crushing and demeaning rejection could be.

And so, when the princess and Mary's eyes met, she offered her a reassuring smile.

Anne of Cleves smiled back briefly and then looked down at the ground before her, and Mary thought for a moment that she saw something else in her eyes, something besides the shame of rejection. Something Mary had seen far too often in her own eyes throughout the years: Fear.

Over the following weeks, while preparations were being made for the royal wedding, Mary would receive daily invitations from the duke of Palatine-Neuburg to accompany him on walks in the palace gardens or for a game of cards, but Mary would send them all back without a reply.

"How can you be so cruel?" Frances pouted as she handed yet another invitation back to the messenger and turned back to Mary, "He is so good-looking!"

Mary rolled her eyes, "Good looks will aid me naught when we are both old and grey and I am left tethered to a heretic for life."

Frances raised her eyebrows, "He simply wishes to get to know you," she said as she sat down opposite her and picked up her discarded embroidery, "You might even like to get to know him."

"Doubtful," Mary replied snidely as she stuck her nose back into the bible in her hands, but while she could continue to fool her ladies, she could not fool herself, for every time that she had received one of his invitations, her heart had begun to pound in her chest.

The following day, however, when no invitation came, Mary became suddenly agitated at the notion that he had given up his pursuit of her, and that evening she realised that she did in fact wish for his attention. And though she had no intention of even considering a protestant for a husband, she thought that to give him a little of her time could not hurt either.

"Fetch my furs, Frances," she said casually then as she stood up from her seat by the fire.

"My lady?" Frances asked, wondering where Mary would be planning to go at this hour in the cold winter's night.

Mary met her curious gaze, "I wish to stroll the gardens."

"Now?" Frances blurted, forgetting herself for a moment.

Mary chuckled at her bluntness, "Yes, now," she replied, "And you may send a message to the duke that I wish to see him there."

Frances' eyes widened and she looked at Cecily who had been quietly folding linens behind them. Cecily raised her eyebrows and shook her head slightly, but a small smile twitched at the corners of her mouth in approval.

The Palace gardens were dark and misty on this December night, but the pebbled grounds were dry enough to take a leisurely walk without catching cold. And as Mary and Cecily slowly crunched their way along the hedgerows, they heard two other sets of footsteps approaching, and Mary's stomach dropped with sudden apprehension as Frances approached with the duke closely behind.

"Lady Mary," the duke said as he bowed before her, his voice as appealing as it had been in her memory from the weeks before.

"My lord," she replied as he straightened up.

"I had begun to think perhaps you would not see me," he said with a smile.

"I had not intended to," Mary admitted as she resumed her slow walk in the moonlit gardens.

The duke did not reply for a moment and instead looked up at the moon as if to gauge the amount of light they had to continue their walk, "What changed your mind?" he asked then.

Mary inhaled and then breathed a little laugh, "Truthfully, the lack of your invitation today made me reconsider."

He raised his eyebrows, appearing entertained.

"Do I amuse you?" Mary asked, noticing his expression in the moonlight.

"Not at all, my lady," he said with a chuckle.

Mary furrowed her brows and looked away.

They walked for a while, her ladies some paces behind them to give them privacy, and the only sound around them was that of their feet crunching on the pebbles as they went.

"May I be blunt?" Mary said then, breaking their silence.

"Of course," the duke replied.

"What gave you cause to come all this way?"

"What gave me cause?" he echoed as she turned to look at her.

"Yes," she said, stopping in her tracks.

The duke chuckled, and Mary noticed a twinkle in his blue eyes, "Are you always this straightforward?" he asked.

Mary blinked, surprised at his response, but did not reply.

The duke cocked his head to one side then as he looked at her, "You intrigue me, my lady," he said, and Mary's cheeks blushed.

She looked away and continued walking once again, "Nevertheless," she said, "That does not explain why you have come."

"I heard of your grace," he admitted as he fell back into step beside her, "and of your strength throughout your endeavours," he risked a quick glance in her direction which she met briefly, then both looked away, neither of them wanting to give voice to her struggles, "But no one prepared me for your beauty."

She was shocked.

No one had ever described her as a beauty. Pretty perhaps, inoffensive no doubt, but beauty? She did not know how to respond.

Instead, she let the word hang between them, and she cleared her throat awkwardly.

They had walked the length of the garden and it had suddenly become darker; their only source of light having become hidden behind a cloud.

"We should head back," Mary said, sounding reluctant.

The duke nodded and looked down at his shoes, "Perhaps now that we have officially met, you would allow me to court you?"

Mary sighed, "I do not see that there is much point," she said cuttingly.

"Because of my faith," he pointed out.

Mary did not need to reply.

"You know," he said then, "I always admired your mother."

"What?" Mary said, shocked at the change in topic.

"She was a formidable leader," he continued as though Mary had not spoken, "I regarded her highly. She was a good queen."

Mary could do nothing but stare back at him, her mind unable to understand what he was trying to say.

"You remind me of her," he said then, "Your courage to fight for your beliefs – it is a trait you no doubt inherited from her."

Mary's eyes had filled with tears at the mention of her mother in such a way, something she had not experienced in many years. She was taken aback at the emotion in his words, and she realised that she wanted to hear more.

"We should go back," she said again as she sniffed her tears away and began to walk towards the Palace.

The duke nodded once and followed closely behind, and they walked through the open gates and the courtyard in silence.

When they finally reached the corridor that led in different directions to their chambers Mary turned to the duke, "If you were to send me another invitation on the morrow," she said, unable to look him in the eyes, "I shall consider another meeting," and with that she hurried down the candle lit corridors, her ladies following closely behind, and out of the besotted duke's sight.

The English court was alive with merriment for the Christmastide and for the royal wedding, which was soon to follow it, though preparations for it went slowly due to the king's unwillingness for it.

The days had grown short and cold, but the palace was set alight almost all day with candles and roaring fires in all the hearths. The people of the court danced and played cards in the great hall while the musicians played festive music, and the atmosphere was a joyous one.

It was on one such afternoon that Mary invited the duke for a game of dominoes in the great hall, and as she sat at a games table she offered the duke the seat opposite her, "Will you join me for a game?" she said with a playful smile.

Since their night-time walk in the garden the week before, Mary and Phillip had spent a lot more time together, and despite her initial inner reluctance to continue the courtship, it had become quite clear to Mary – as well as the entire court – that they were falling in love with one another; and according to Frances there were whispers of a marriage agreement being drawn up for them by the king.

"You honour me, my lady," he said as he sat down, their eyes never straying from each other.

"Do you enjoy playing dominoes, Phillip?" Mary asked as she began setting up the game.

"I must confess I am not very familiar with this game," he replied, "But I look forward to you teaching me," he grinned a crooked smile at her, and Mary felt her heart jump out of sync, her stomach flipping simultaneously as her subconscious reprimanded her for the thrill she felt to be near him, her soul not yet being completely convinced that she ought to love a Protestant.

They played for a long time, and after several failed attempts to beat Mary at the game, Phillip sat back heavily in his chair and laughed, "I yield, my lady. You are undefeated!"

"Alas, my father taught me well," Mary grinned back at him. As a tune ended and the musicians began another, Phillip looked over his shoulder at the dancing couples behind him, "Would you care to dance?" he asked as he looked back at Mary, and she puckered her lips as if in thought before pushing her seat back and eagerly taking his outstretched hand.

They hurried to take their places beside the other courtiers and fell into step with them just in time before moving and twirling in tempo with the music.

The musicians increased their rhythm then and all the ladies exclaimed gleefully as their feet tried to keep up with the song, and Mary's face was bright with a joy she had not felt in years, her sides hurting from laughter.

It seemed to go on forever, and as they danced Mary noticed a desire in Phillip's expression when their eyes would meet from across the dancefloor and then, with one final note, the music faded and the room filled with applause for the musicians, who stood and bowed in thanks.

"Come walk with me," Phillip said suddenly from behind her, his deep voice low and demanding, and she could not help but let him lead the way out of the great hall and away from prying eyes.

They had barely exited the great hall and turned the corner when Phillip suddenly pushed Mary against the wall and kissed her with a passion that she had never known.

His lips pressed hard against hers and his hands caressed her face and neck, his fingers leaving her skin tingling with desire. As they kissed, she could feel, like the licking of a flame, as his hands moved slowly over her corseted waist and softly brushed the tops of her breasts, and though her body was responding eagerly, her conscience was raging a war within her.

Suddenly and all too soon, Phillip tore away from her and gasped for air, "Forgive me, Mary," he whispered hoarsely, "I could wait no longer."

Mary swallowed, trying to contain her erratic breathing, and she pressed her fingers to her lips, "There is nothing to forgive" she whispered back and with one quick look around, she took him by his hand and led him through the candlelit corridors and up the stairwell towards her chambers.

Once inside Mary stood with her back pressed against the locked door, "Am I being foolish?" she asked, her eyes searching his face for a hint of unwillingness.

"No," Phillip replied as he stood stock still just a few paced away, and yet Mary could feel an electric current pulsating between them, "I have asked your father for your hand," he said as he took one small step towards her.

Mary's heart leapt, and for a moment she was not sure if it was due to excitement or dread, but she pushed the thought aside, "But he has not yet given an answer," Mary said matter-of-factly.

He shook his head and his eyebrows twitched together as he took another step towards her, closing the space between them.

Mary looked up into his eyes as he ever so slowly leaned in to kiss her, and she noticed that he was being deliberately steady, as if to ensure that she had given her permission.

It was in that tiny moment – that one deliberate act of chivalry – that Mary dismissed all her doubts about their differing faiths and the battle that had been raging within her mind was finally silenced for good.

When their lips touched once more, this time much gentler than the last, Mary felt her entire body come alive as his fingertips skimmed the length of her neck.

As they kissed, Mary reached up to remove the pins from her hood and then slowly took it off, and her long auburn hair spilled out over her pale shoulders.

Phillip pulled away to look at her then and she became suddenly self-conscious, a ladies' loose hair being reserved only for one's husband, and though she remained fully clothed, Mary felt unexpectedly naked.

He watched her cheeks grow rosy as she stood before him, the very picture of a virginal bride, and he took a lock of her red hair between his thumb and forefinger before tucking it behind her ear.

"Are you sure we should do this?" he asked then, and Mary could have melted in his arms.

But then her mother's words flashed before her mind's eye, that she *must keep her body and company pure, and to not think of or desire a husband until this troublesome time had passed.*

But for how many years would Mary have to dedicate her life to waiting? How long would it be before her life had completely passed her by without having lived?

She pushed her mother's words aside and looked up into his blue eyes.

Mary was ready, and she wanted this. As well as that, he wanted her. He saw beyond her disgraced name and her tarnished past and saw only the person she was within – and Mary could hardly believe her luck to have found him when only a few weeks ago, no one in all of Europe had deemed her even worthy enough to meet.

As a reply she slowly turned her back towards him and drew all her long hair over her shoulder, revealing the laces of her bodice; and then she looked back at him from over her shoulder and nodded, giving her permission for him to undo them.

The following morning Mary and her ladies were strolling lazily through the snow-covered palace gardens, wrapped up in furs and giddy conversation about the upcoming festivities.

"Do you think the king will gift his new bride something?" Frances asked excitedly.

"Ever the romantic, Frances," Cecily remarked as she rolled her eyes, "don't you know? He is not as besotted with this one and he is still trying to find a way out of it."

"He cannot go back on his word," Mary interrupted abruptly, "the new alliance would crumble, and England is without allies right now. My father is desperate."

"He may yet grow to love her," Frances chimed in, "just as you have grown to love your unlikely suitor," and she poked Mary's side beneath her furs.

Mary squealed and jerked away from her, "What do you mean?" she asked, and though she smiled, inside she was weak with fear that some gossiping servant had seen them entering her chambers together the night before.

Frances raised an eyebrow and shrugged but said nothing.

Mary laughed once – a short, breathy laugh – and Cecily looked at her, aware of her mistress' sudden distress. She nudged Frances with her elbow, "What have you heard, Frances?"

"Well Mary and the duke have been seen together a lot," she blabbed, "and yesterday when she invited the duke to the great hall and dismissed us, well… people talk."

"But there were others," Mary said, "We were never alone," and she felt her stomach drop with shame at the lie.

She and Phillip had shared an evening she would likely never forget. An evening in which she had finally been able to imagine a future where she would not constantly feel like a worthless disappointment. And it had been heaven.

But as the music from the great hall had begun to cease and their time together had run out, they had dressed in haste and Mary had bundled him out of her rooms as though he had the plague, the guilt over what she had done suddenly becoming too much to bear; and she had sunk down, shivering on the ground as she sat with her back pressed against the door.

Her ladies had entered her chambers only moments later to find Mary kneeling before her private prie-deux with her eyes closed tightly as her lips moved in silent prayer and with her hands clasped together before her.

Frances and Cecily had shared a look but taken themselves to bed, only to wake the following morning to see Mary still kneeling fervently before the cross. But neither of them had dared to ask what had deemed such vehement prayer necessary, assuming only that she had needed divine counsel for the love she bore her Protestant beloved.

When a silence befell them that seemed to stretch on forever, Mary looked from one of her ladies to the other, "What is it?" she asked, and her face drained of colour.

"There are rumours of your wedding to the duke," Frances said then, "It is whispered all over court that you are to be wed," and she beamed at Mary.

Immediately Mary felt uneasy, "Rumours? Why – What are people whispering?"

Frances and Cecily shared a look but said nothing. Mary's heart began to race at the possibility that their secret encounter had been anything but. Did the whole court know about what had happened? Were people talking about her as they would a common harlot? Was her reputation and her virtue in question?

"Well," Frances said slowly, "The ladies of the court are gossiping. Saying that you and he… that you shared a kiss."

Mary inhaled deeply to try to steady her churning stomach as her worst fears were being confirmed. Someone had seen them, and the whole court was already gossiping about what a thoughtless and wanton whore she was.

Her reputation was destroyed.

She may as well be dead.

Mary stared bewilderedly at Frances, willing her to say more, but when her lady said nothing further, she realised that there was nothing more to follow.

Relief washed over her like a tidal wave, and she doubled over as her vision went blurry at the edges, her mind unable to contain the concoction of emotions she felt all at once. For while Mary knew that she would have to pray for forgiveness for the rest of her life for what she had done, at that moment she was intensely thankful to know that her sinful evening was not a matter of public knowledge.

"Nothing is confirmed," Mary said then once she had regained her composure, "Phillip has asked for my hand. But it is up to the king now," and she wrapped the furs more tightly around herself as they continued their slow stroll through the snow.

Though it had been impulsive and thoughtless, Mary believe that their actions had not been entirely without honour.

In their hearts, as well as in promise, she and Phillip had pledged themselves to one another, and once her father completed their marriage agreement and announced their engagement officially, God would forgive her this sin. After all, had she not consistently maintained her dedication to Him throughout every terrifying obstacle that life had thrown her way, even sometimes at the risk of her own life? Surely, God would grant her this one lapse in judgement?

Mary nodded to herself in thought as her ladies walked beside her in silence.

Yes, God would forgive her this. He had to.

Chapter 12

"There will be no marriage!" king Henry exclaimed as he banged his fist hard upon the table.

"You – your majesty," Cromwell stammered in fear much the same as he remembered Cardinal Wolsey had done near his end, "You cannot go back on your word now. The – the alliance with the House of Cleves is detrimental to the security of England against the Spanish and French alliance."

"Don't spout the facts to me, Thomas!" Henry shouted, spittle flying from his angry mouth, "I know well what I *must* do for my country!"

His anger filled the room and the men of his Privy Council sat motionless, desperate to avoid eye contact as he seethed over his obvious dislike for the duty that lay before him.

"Marry the lady, Henry," Charles Brandon braved then when Cromwell had ceased his pitiful grovelling, "Marry her, put a child in her belly and then take a mistress," and he shrugged his broad shoulders, "It is not unheard of. And as I recall, you are no novice to the matter of mistresses,"

Charles' bold banter with the king suggested that the king's anger was beyond its peak, and some of the members of the council dared a careful chuckle.

Henry fell into, rather than sat down, his throne, his face contorted in pain as the festering wound on his leg touched the fabric of his hose, "I care no longer for this discussion," he said then as he inhaled sharply at the pain, "I know what I must do."

He clicked his fingers to his page, who stood motionless in the corner of the room, "Culpeper," and the young man approached at his king's command, bowing once at the waist, "Fetch the physician to me for when I am done here."

"Majesty," Culpeper replied and exited the room.

Henry cleared his throat once his page had gone, "I have another matter that needs urgent attention," the king announced, "the matter of Reginald Pole and his embargo against us!"

Reginald Pole was one of Mary's former governess' – Margaret Pole the Countess of Salisbury – sons.

Cardinal Reginald Pole had decisively broken from his king some years earlier in a dispute over his marriage to Anne Boleyn, having left England in favour of Padua, Italy, shortly thereafter. Since then, Cardinal Pole had been made a papal legate to England, whereupon he received Holy Orders from the Pope to represent the Catholic Church in the matters that were occurring in his home country. Though he had not dared to return to England for fear or immediate arrest for his rejection of the king's Act of Supremacy, Pole orchestrated many efforts to denounce the king's policies, one such effort being that of a published pamphlet which clearly denied king Henry's annulment of his marriage to his rightful wife, Katherine of Aragon.

It had also then come to light that Pole had recently urged the princes of Europe to overthrow Henry, and to replace him with the king's own catholic cousin, Henry Courtenay 1st Marquess of Exeter – this no doubt being one of the reasons for Spain and France's recent union against England.

And yet, with Reginald Pole out of the country and the king's grasp, king Henry had little choice but to consider other options for punishment.

"He is unattainable, your majesty," said a black-bearded member of the council, "He is still hiding out in Rome, the coward!" and the others murmured in agreement at his insult.

"There is nothing more for it," Henry said, his tone pensive yet firm, "I have made the decision on how to deal with him."

"Majesty?" Charles Brandon asked, shifting uncomfortably in his seat at the menacing tone in his old friend's voice.

"If the coward cannot admit the allegations made against me of his own accord, then I shall have to *make* him face me," and he stood up slowly, wincing in pain as his wounded leg stretched out awkwardly before him, "Arrest Pole's family," he ordered, "Henry Courtenay 1st Marquess of Exeter, and Henry Pole Baron of Montagu. Their connection with Reginald is treasonous and will not be ignored."

Thomas Cromwell stood abruptly and bowed, eager to do the king's bidding "Right away, your majesty," he said.

"That is not all!" Henry boomed, "To worm out such a deceitful and evil traitor, one must use all methods at their disposal."

Charles Brandon watched his king and his stomach suddenly dropped with dread at the words he knew were to come.

"Arrest the lady Margaret Pole, the Countess of Salisbury, his mother," Henry declared, his face emotionless as he proclaimed the arrest of his own cousin and former governess to his daughter, "That should bring the traitor to his knees."

Some days later, Mary and her ladies were sitting silently by the fireplace in her chambers reading their bibles when there was a knock at the door, and the Imperial ambassador, Eustace Chapuys, was announced.

Upon his entrance, Mary immediately stood from her seat and hurried towards him, grabbing him by the sleeve and steering him towards the window, away from her guard and her ladies.

"Is it true?" Mary asked shortly, unable to control her racing heart, "My father has had the entire Pole family arrested?"

Eustace Chapuys bowed his head briefly and replied, "Indeed it is true, my lady."

Mary's brows furrowed together in fear for her former governess and friend, knowing all too well what the king was capable of doing to those that were close to him, "On what grounds?" she asked, and then whispered, "Will they at least have a fair trial?"

Chapuys raised his eyebrows and shook his head, "The grounds are treason," he replied, his voice dropping in volume to match Mary's, "for conspiring with her son, Cardinal Pole, and for plotting against the king," then he sighed deeply, "As you must have already guessed, my lady, there is likely to be no trial at all."

Mary shook her head in disbelief, her eyes wide with terror, "How could he do this?" she breathed, "My father will not rest until everyone is either desolate or dead!"

Chapuys looked over his shoulder at her ladies and the guards by Mary's door and then gently touched her elbow, leading her further into privacy, "My lady," he whispered hoarsely, "though I know you trust your ladies, it would be wise not to speak about the king in such a manner."

"Of course," she agreed immediately, "you are right. But the countess was my governess! She has been a loyal and loving member of the court for years."

"You must heed your words about the king, Mary," Chapuys said again as he looked pleadingly into her eyes, "You may be restored into his favour now, but you must never give your father cause to doubt *your* loyalty."

"*Senor* Chapuys," Mary said as she rubbed her hands over her forehead in dismay, "I must do something to help the poor lady Pole. I should plead her case to the king and remind him of her loyalty and the care that she has always showed me."

Chapuys took Mary's hand in his in an effort to calm her, as a father would to his child, "You are a good and kind young woman, Mary", he said, "But you must not put yourself in the direct line of fire. His child or no, if you show the king your defiance on this, I cannot guess what he may do. You are finally back in his good graces; you cannot throw that away in a futile attempt to speak for the countess."

Mary looked up into his kind eyes, and she wondered for a moment how much easier life would have been if he had been her father, for he had always put her welfare at the forefront of his mind, "You believe my efforts would be futile?" she asked then, considering his wisdom while being torn between her need to save her former governess, and knowing that she would be putting herself at risk if she were to interfere.

"On this matter, my lady," Chapuys said as he shook his head sadly, "no one will change the king's mind."

January 1540

There was no postponing it any longer.

The day had come in which the king of England took a new wife, and though the alliance between their two countries meant for a safer England and a new hope for a spare heir, the king did not conceal his immense distaste for the entire occasion.

The princess of Cleves looked fair and beautiful in her white gown, her long blond hair falling loosely over her shoulders, the very image of the virginal bride.

But the expression on her round face gave away her true emotions, that she too did not wish to partake in the union of their souls.

Though the princess had attempted to hide her fear and resistance with small smiles as she walked up the aisle, Mary could tell from her place among the crowd, that this was not the most joyful day of Anne's life, as she had no doubt been promised all her life it would be. And when Mary saw her father's glum face as the new couple turned towards the crowd as man and wife, she felt a wave of pity for the poor new queen.

What a truly awful thing it must be to be forced to marry someone who had such obvious dislike for their new spouse, and Mary, despite their religious differences, felt suddenly compelled to try to make the new queen's life at court a little brighter, even if only through friendly conversation.

As wedding festivities went on, and the lords and ladies drank and were merry, Mary found herself imagining what her own wedding day might be like.

She imagined that she would undoubtedly be a much happier bride, and that Phillip would be a much more eager groom. She envisioned a beautiful day filled with God, love and laughter; and the wedding night would be a delightful repeat of their previous secret encounter.

Mary watched from her seat beside her father at the high table as the wedding guests danced and twirled before them on the dancefloor, and as wine and the music flowed, she began to visualize just how her life as Phillip's wife would unfold.

She pictured the intense happiness in Phillip's face when she would reveal that she had missed her monthly courses, and the overwhelming rush of love that she would feel upon holding their baby in her arms.

Mary looked at the newlyweds to her left. Neither of them looked happy or even willing, and Mary said a little prayer to herself that the new queen may be fruitful and strong-willed, for she had a bad feeling that without those qualities, the king would find no joy in this new union.

And without a joyful king, no one in England was safe to live their life as they pleased.

Mary was living on a high she had never felt. She spent every moment she could with Phillip and only rarely felt hungry or tired, as though his love was all the nourishment she needed to sustain herself.

They would meet in the mornings and spend almost all day together, caring little for the fact that the weather permitted minimal outdoor activities, simply enjoying the thrill of each other's company.

But one morning, as Mary sat before her mirror and Cecily stood behind her twisting her locks and pinning them underneath her hood, Mary received a message from Phillip that he would not be able to meet her that day, and Mary's stomach dropped with anticipation that – finally – they would receive news of their wedding preparations.

"Frances!" Mary called as she turned in her seat. Her lady approached quickly, discarding the firewood she had been placing carefully in the hearth.

"My lady?" she said.

"Have you heard anything?" Mary said animatedly, in a way that Frances had never seen her react to the possibility of court gossip, "Are there new rumours about my wedding?"

Frances opened her mouth to speak but then looked at Cecily, and Mary followed her gaze, her joyful expression dropping at Cecily's uneasy look, "Wh – What have you heard?" Mary asked warily.

"I – " Frances stammered, "I have heard reports that ships were being made ready for departure in the early hours of the morning from the fishing village of Deptford."

"Departure to where?" Mary asked, her face draining of colour at the news.

Frances looked down at the ground, unable to meet Mary's eyes, "I hear they are to set sail to Germany, my lady. To return the duke and his household to his homeland."

Mary stared, pale faced and thin lipped, as Frances' words began to make sense, and then she stood up in a flash, nearly knocking Frances over in her hurry.

"I must go see my father," she said, her stomach threatening to expel its contents as her mind foresaw the misery that was to come, and she stormed past her ladies and out of her chambers before Cecily and Frances even rose from their curtseys.

As she hurriedly made her way through the stone corridors and up the stairwell to the king's chambers, she could hardly contain her emotions for fear of yet again losing everything that she held dear. And with the realisation that Phillip's proposal might have been rejected by the king, came the unbearable knowledge that she may very well have damned her soul for all eternity by placing her trust on her fickle father's word that she and Phillip would be wed.

She had willingly given away her virtue to a man before they were married before God – an act she felt ashamed of and asked for forgiveness for daily – but only under the pretext that he would be her husband.

Mary shook her head at her own foolishness. Love had blinded her from seeing what had been clearly before her all her life: that her father's word was not to be trusted. And now, if Frances' information was to be believed, Mary's soul would be damned to hell for committing a mortal sin.

"Father!" she exclaimed as she entered the throne room where the king was deep in conversation with the imperial ambassador. Her intrusion interrupted the ambassador mid-sentence and both he and the king looked in Mary's direction, stunned.

But Mary had no patience left for formalities, her anxiety bubbling within her.

She approached the two men and acknowledged the ambassador with a nod of her head before turning her attention to her father who, she noticed, was becoming more repugnant with each day that passed.

"Might I know what is to become of me?" Mary said without hesitation as she stood before him, her hands clasped tightly before her, the very image of her stoic mother.

The king raised his eyebrows at his daughter's candour, a trait he had not known that she possessed, and he was torn between feeling offended or proud.

"What is to become of you?" he repeated, still slightly stunned by her lack of decorum.

"Am I to be formally betrothed, and soon to be wed, to the duke of Palatine-Neuburg?" Mary asked, her voice clear and concise, "He has asked for my hand. He and I are both willing and merely awaiting your approval. Now that your own royal wedding is passed, I was hoping to know where I stand regarding my own wedded future."

When she finished, she felt, rather than saw, the imperial ambassador's discomfort as he stood beside her, and the all too familiar feeling of dread began to creep into the pit of her stomach.

But nevertheless, she inhaled deeply and stared her father down, desperately clinging to the hope that Frances had been wrong.

The king cleared his throat and shook his head briefly, "My darling daughter, the matter is closed," he said casually, as if he had not just stabbed her in the heart, "There will be no wedding for you until I myself arrange it. The duke asked for your hand, that is true, but I, as your father and your king, did not consent. He left on a ship back to Germany this morning, and I dare say, I have no knowledge of his intention to return."

At the words, Mary's heart felt as though it had been ripped from her chest and her entire body visibly slumped in defeat. She had been played for a fool.

Mary dropped her gaze from her father's aged face to the ground before her, her head feeling suddenly heavy, and she scoffed, "I had bent my entire life's beliefs," she said as she took a daring step towards her father, "to accommodate the notion that I was to wed the Lutheran duke, as you had apparently arranged."

Henry remained silent, his shock rendering him speechless, and Mary met his stunned gaze, her own eyes blazing with indignation.

"He and I had formed a bond," she continued brazenly, throwing all caution to the wind in her effort to convey the intense hurt her father had caused her, all the while knowing deep down that he would not care, "And I had hoped of finally knowing what it felt like to be loved for who I am, rather than for what I represent."

King Henry frowned and narrowed her eyes but did not respond, no doubt utterly unwilling to accept that he had been the cause of her heartache.

Mary breathed a tiny, exhausted chuckle at the silence that ensued, the disbelief at her misfortune becoming suddenly comical in her tormented mind, and she briefly considered that perhaps she was going mad.

Eustace Chapuys looked from Mary to the king, troubled by the cruelty he had just witnessed first-hand, for he, as well as the whole court, knew how Mary and the duke had become committed of late.

He took a step towards the young lady and offered her his arm, "I shall escort the lady back to her chambers," he said without looking at the king, his hatred for him too dangerous to display, "with your majesty's permission?"

Henry waved his hand irritably, giving his permission for their withdrawal, and he shook his head as he watched them leave, unable to understand his daughter's grief.

Chapuys led the speechless Mary gently back to her chambers and, with the help of her ladies, he tucked her into bed and closed the windows shutters of her bedroom. Then he squeezed her hand softly and offered her a sympathetic smile, as a loving father would do to a distraught daughter, before leaving her to mend her broken heart.

March 1540

With the distress that followed Phillip's sudden departure, it did not take long before Mary was suffering yet again from her ill-fated symptoms caused by her inexplicable ailment the physicians continued to call 'strangulation of the womb'.

She requested the sage and lavender remedies from the king's physician, but even they did little to ease the pain in her head and the cramps in her belly, and she wondered if perhaps her blackened soul was poisoning her from within.

As she lay in her bed in the darkened chambers Mary considered that perhaps the return of her agony was God's punishments for her having acted like a wanton whore, and if this was to be her penance then Mary would accept it willingly and without complaint.

During Mary's confinement to her dark chambers, Cecily would check on her every evening to be certain Mary had eaten, for she did not want a repeat of what had happened during their time at Hunsdon House where Mary had practically wasted away before their very eyes. Then would leave her to sleep and in the mornings two servant girls would enter Mary's rooms to bring her breakfast and to stoke the fire.

On one such morning, after eight days of bedrest, the taller of the two girls set down the plate of dried fruit and cheese beside Mary's bed and when she peeked through her bed curtains to find that Mary was still asleep, she picked a piece of fruit from her plate and popped it into her mouth before turning back to the other girl.

"Margery!" the smaller girl hissed, spotting her friend stealing from the king's daughter's plate.

The tall girl shrugged as she chewed, "She'll never know," she whispered and then they both giggled.

Mary awoke then to the sound of their sniggering and immediately placed a hand over her swollen belly as a cramp pierced through it and she lay there breathing deeply, unable to move until the pain subsided.

"-- but do you believe it to be true?" Mary heard one of the girls whisper as they went about their duties, "I can't imagine the shame!"

"I believe it to be true," she heard the other reply, "But I dunno how much of it is 'er fault."

Mary frowned as she listened, immediately curious to know who and what was being discussed, and as the cramp in her belly disappeared as quickly as it had come, she slowly sat up in bed, eager to hear the servant's gossip.

"What d'you mean?" she heard the other reply.

"Well, 'e is getting old! Perhaps 'e can no longer –"

"Don't say it!" she interrupted, "I don't want to speak of it. Rather we speak ill of the new queen. But never the king."

"I isn't speaking ill," she heard the other reply, "It's only what I 'eard myself! Everyone in the servant's quarters is sayin' it."

"So you think 'e's sayin' it is because she's ugly. But it's not?"

"I know nothin'. I ain't in the rooms with them," and the other girl laughed, "All's I know is what the kitchen servants

242

are whisperin': That it won't be long before 'e's rid of this one too."

For a moment there was silence and Mary leaned further forward in her bed, causing it to creak slightly and she froze as her heart beat in her chest.

"Let's get outta 'ere," she heard one of them say then, "before the lady wakes up. I don't wanna be mis'eard sayin' nothin' about this."

Mary listened until she heard the door to her chambers click closed behind them, and then she let out the breath she had been holding.

The following day, though she was still suffering with terrible pains and her corset was cutting into her swollen belly, Mary invited the imperial ambassador for a walk in the gardens, in hopes of learning more about the court gossip that she had overheard.

"*Senor* Chapuys," Mary said as they walked leisurely through the lower path of the gardens with her ladies walking behind, "forgive my bluntness but I must enquire as to the king and his new marriage," and she paused to observe his expression, "Is it fair to assume they are happier now that they are wed?"

The ambassador looked away for a moment, visibly uncomfortable, "I am hopeful that they will find happiness soon," he replied tactfully, and then he looked over his shoulder to judge the distance between them and her ladies so as not to be overheard, "But between you and me: If she does not manage to conquer the king's interest and produce a son, then it is likely she will be replaced."

Mary leaned closed and whispered, "What is it you mean, ambassador?"

"I mean," he replied quietly, his eyes darting to all sides to ensure their privacy, "the king and his queen are said to not yet have consummated their marriage."

"But they have been married for three months!" Mary exclaimed in horror as she finally realised what the two servant girls had been whispering about the day before, and that according to them, the whole of the servants' quarters were discussing the king's sexual abilities – or in this case, lack thereof.

"Nobody can know for certain at this point," Chapuys replied, his grey eyebrows darting upwards, "But the queen has supposedly confessed to her lady that she 'wished to produce an heir but is uncertain as to *how* without a miracle.'"

Mary shook her head in disbelief and suddenly felt a pang of guilt as she remembered her fervent prayers to God that her father's union to the Lutheran Anne of Cleves would not be successful.

"Is there anything to be done?" she asked, though she knew the answer.

The ambassador shrugged his shoulders casually, as though England's peace did not hang in the balance, "What can be done, my lady?" he replied rhetorically, "The king will do as he pleases, as he always has done."

"Yes," Mary simply replied.

They continued their stroll in silence as Mary contemplated the irony of it all: that she, an unmarried and illegitimate princess had acted sinfully and lustfully while out of wedlock because of the power that love had had over her; while the king, who was married before God and eager to produce a spare heir, was actively avoiding the act of reproduction.

If she did not feel so utterly heartbroken and convinced that her soul was irreversibly sullied, Mary would undoubtedly see the humour in it, "What an absolute debacle," Mary muttered then, shaking her head.

"Indeed," the imperial ambassador agreed, "Whatever next?"

Chapter 13

June 1540
Greenwich Palace, London

When news broke that the French and Spanish alliance had suddenly collapsed and that England was once again safe from foreign invasion, king Henry did not hesitate even a moment before calling a meeting of his Privy Council.

Sitting straight-backed and eagle-eyed upon his throne, he watched his advisors entering the room one by one and take their seat at the council table.

"Gentlemen," he said once they were all present, "it is with great relief that I can confirm the alliance between France and the Empire is no more, and with that we have avoided not only an invasion from the south, but also an invasion from the north as our troops can now concentrate solely on keeping the Scots off our borders!"

The councilmen nodded or mumbled their approval of the news.

Henry shifted in his seat to stretch his leg out awkwardly before him and winced at the pain as the inside of his hose touched his festering wound, "Groom!" he called, and the young man appeared as if out of nowhere.

The king grabbed a fistful of his jacket and pulled him towards him, "Bring my physician to me as soon as I am done here," he ordered quietly through gritted teeth, as though the young man were to blame for the king's pain.

"Yes, your majesty," the groom replied and bowed.

"Enough of that, Culpeper!" Henry growled as he waved the groom away, "just fetch me the damn physician!" and the young man was on his way.

After another failed attempt to readjust his trouser leg to alleviate his pain, the king continued, "Scotland has no chance against our armies on their own, and without the southern threat they will never dare to attack us. England is safe on all fronts once more!"

"Hear, hear!" some of the men exclaimed as they pumped their fists in the air.

"Cromwell," the king suddenly called out as he snapped his head in the chief minister's direction, his blue eyes piercing, "Without the threat from France and the Empire," he said, "I believe we have no more need for our alliance with Cleves."

Cromwell nodded once as he blinked in confusion, "Your majesty, I –"

"I have not asked for a response!" the king roared suddenly, slamming his closed fist hard on the arm of his throne, "You will speak when I require you to and not before!"

The room went deathly still as Henry breathed in deeply, his greying eyebrows furrowed together in anger, "Since it was you who arranged the marriage to the princess Anne," he continued, "it is now your charge to arrange its dissolution."

No one within the council was shocked at the king's announcement that he wished to end yet another marriage, since it was widely known that he had never warmed to the German princess. Though many did not understand the king's issue with his most recent queen – for while she was not beautiful, she appeared to be obedient and eager to please – they were simply glad that it was Cromwell, and not any of them, that had suggested the match.

"You should find it easy enough to get me my annulment," Henry said then as he stared down his former favourite, "under the grounds that she was pre-contracted to marry to the Duke of Lorraine's son and was therefore never mine to wed. Because of that I could not bring myself to touch her, and I now confess that the marriage remains unconsummated."

The men at the council table cleared their throats and looked around at each other, all of them eager to move on from the matter at hand as the king's ruddy face became brighter with each moment that passed.

Thomas Cromwell licked his thin lips anxiously and took a step towards his king before offering him a great bow, knowing all the while that if he did not get back into the king's good graces, that he would no doubt suffer terribly at his hands, "I will do all that is in my power to right my wrongs, your majesty," he said, as repentantly as he could.

The disgust the king felt towards his chief minister was palpable as he glared at him, his top lip curled up disdainfully, as if he had tasted something bitter, "Yes," Henry replied slowly, "I suggest that you do."

July 1540

It did not take long.

The king's claim that his marriage to the princess Anne of Cleves remained unconsummated was supported by the lady herself and parliament soon came to the conclusion that the king of England and Anne of Cleves never were husband and wife.

"It is done," the German ambassador said softly to the princess Anne as she sat by the window in the queen's chambers, which she would soon have to vacate, "the king's Archbishop, Mr Cranmer, has declared your marriage to the king of England as null and void."

Anne of Cleves sighed as though she had been holding her breath for the past six months and the elderly German ambassador noticed quite clearly that it was a sigh of relief.

She raised a small hand to her forehead, "I am very pleased to hear it," she replied quietly in German, "but, if I may ask, under what grounds?" and she looked up at the ambassador, her green eyes curious.

"Under the grounds that you are still pre-contracted to the Duke of Lorraine's son, Francis," and he watched as the princess' eyebrows twitched slightly, "as well as your marriage to the king being… erm, shall we say inconclusive."

He dropped his gaze and Anne saw his wrinkled face blush at the topic, but she felt no shame about it.

Anne knew that she had done her duty within the marriage. She had been, and still remained, inexperienced in the acts that went on within the marriage bed, but she could say with certainty that their marriage did not remain unconsummated because of anything that she had or had not done.

Anne nodded, "Yes that is true," she said in agreement, as they continued to speak openly in German, "For the first week after our union before God, the king would lay on top of me and awkwardly flail his hand over his manhood. I do not know what he was attempting to gain from it, but after a few minutes he would climb off of me, angry that I had not evoked something within him," she shook her head slightly, "After that first week, he would come to my chambers every night, lie down in bed beside me and say 'Goodnight, wife,' and the following morning he would wake and say, 'Good morning, wife'," she looked up at the ambassador's face, "Though I remain a virgin I am not a simple woman. I know that there must be a physical act of passion for a child to be produced."

"Indeed," the German ambassador agreed as he raised his eyebrows, mortified at what he had just heard.

"And his leg," the princess continued to the ambassador's surprise, her face twisting in disgust, "it stinks! He was not a joy to sleep next to. I am not at all displeased at this news that our marriage shall be dissolved," and she beamed a smile at him, her cheeks like two plump apples upon her round face.

248

The German ambassador grasped the moment of silence to remove himself from the potentially damning conversation and smiled back at the princess before she could continue on her overjoyed rant. Then he offered her a bow before excusing himself, leaving the delighted princess to revel at the notion that she was no longer Henry VIII's queen.

"Already another wife?" Mary drawled tediously at the news that, after just one week since the marriage to Anne of Cleves had been annulled, king Henry was to take yet another victim into his clutches, "He has only just ended his contractual obligation to the last one!"

As he stood before Mary, the imperial ambassador's kind face reflected her own boredom back at her as neither of them could quite bring themselves to show surprise, much less comprehend, the news that was spreading throughout the court.

"While that is true," Eustace Chapuys replied, "it is believed that part of the reason for his sudden need for an annulment was due to his infatuation with this new lady."

"Who is she?" Mary asked as she imagined some high-born noblewoman, or perhaps one of the ladies the king had had his eye on before the suggestion for Anne of Cleves was made, "Has the Duchess of Milan had a change of heart?"

Chapuys cocked his head to one side and pressed his lips together in a way that told Mary that her guess was far from the reality, "She was a lady of the former queen," he replied slowly, "A lady Kathryn Howard."

Mary's face crinkled in horror, "Kathryn Howard?" she repeated, "But that girl is just fifteen years old! And he a man of forty-nine!"

The imperial ambassador shrugged, "The king will do as he pleases," he said casually, but Mary saw in his expression that he too was abhorred at the prospect, "If I do recall correctly, his former mistress Bessie Blount was but fourteen when she bore him his bastard son, Henry Fitzroy."

Mary looked away at the mention of the king's former mistress, "His need to regain his youth is becoming ludicrous!" she hissed as she turned away from the ambassador and stared unseeingly out the window, "What more do we know of her?" she asked then, realising that if it were to become reality, she should know what to expect.

Chapuys cleared his throat, "The lady is indeed young," he said as he took a step towards Mary and looked out the window at the gardens below where the king was practicing his archery while courtiers observed, clapping and cheering with each shot no matter of its accuracy, "and, a cousin to his second wife, the concubine, Anne Boleyn."

Mary could hardly believe her ears, "What else?" she asked, knowing there would be more.

"It is not all bad news, my lady," Chapuys said, a small smile pulling at the corners of his lips, "I hear she is of the catholic faith."

Mary sighed, "Well, perhaps there is hope yet," and she looked out the window once more as the king's groom, Thomas Culpeper, retrieved her father's arrows from the mark and ran to bring them back to his king.

Chapuys cleared his throat, "I am afraid I bring other reports, my lady."

Mary turned to look at him.

"The chief minister, Mr Cromwell, has this morning been arrested," he said, his voice heavy with the magnitude the news, Thomas Cromwell having been an enemy to Mary and her mother ever since his arrival at court.

Mary stared back at her most trusted friend through narrowed eyes, unable to believe the words that had come out of his mouth, "Arrested?" she echoed in disbelief.

"*Si*, my lady," he replied with a nod of his head.

"On what grounds?" she asked, still unable to fully believe the information, Thomas Cromwell being the most powerful man in all of England, after only the king himself.

The ambassador gave a short chuckle, "On what grounds?" he repeated, finding the irony of Cromwell's sentencing amusing, "Thomas Cromwell, the king's most trusted advisor, has been locked in the tower, awaiting the scaffold for treason and heresy."

Mary's eyebrows shot up, "Heresy?!" she exclaimed, "In the eyes of God and to any Catholic he is of course a heretic. But my father himself raised Cromwell so high based on his protestant beliefs. And by his separation from Rome and the dissolution of the monasteries, my father cannot in good conscience say that even *he* is a Catholic!"

Chapuys shrugged, "It would seem the king himself is struggling to separate the two religions," he said, "and his newest testaments have received mixed reactions from his council. I believe that in his heart he remains a catholic, but he does not wish to be told by anyone – whether it be the Pope or his best advisor – what he can and cannot do."

"But Cromwell got my father his annulment from the princess Anne," Mary pointed out naively.

"Yes," Chapuys replied, "But he was also the one who arranged the union to begin with. And we all known how making such a mistake can be dangerous."

Mary nodded sadly, remembering all those that had fallen to the king's ever-changing temper, all of whom had been close to him – whether in friendship or in blood relation – and some even that he had loved.

Mary's mouth twitched, unsure if it was safe or even wise to reply, her mind spiralling as she tried to keep up with all the political goings on that she had failed to see due to her own personal anguish.

Sensing Mary's distress, the imperial ambassador bowed and muttered a soft, "My lady," before quietly leaving Mary alone with her thoughts.

July 1540

On the same day that the king secretly married his teenaged bride at Oatlands Palace in Surrey, his most loyal and trusted advisor, Sir Thomas Cromwell, was savagely beheaded at Tower Hill, after having been condemned as a traitor against the crown.

Though Mary was certainly not sympathetic towards the manipulative and ruthless man who had personally seen to the dissolution of her parent's marriage, she nonetheless found herself feeling no joy at the news of his death. For though he, much like Anne Boleyn herself, had been at the very root of all her problems, their deaths came as a haunting reminder that to be in favour with the king meant putting their life on the line.

"It's awful, Frances!" she declared as her lady conveyed the details of the man's execution to her the next morning, "Must you go into such detail?"

Her lady-in-waiting blinked at her, "It was a mess, my lady," she continued unapologetically, "I'm only telling you what I saw – it was utterly botched."

"Urgh," Mary exclaimed, unable to contain her disgust as she walked away from the conversation.

Frances turned to Cecily and the kitchen maid who had brought up Mary's breakfast and continued, "After the second blow to Cromwell's back and shoulder, the guard that had brought him to the scaffold, ripped the axe from the executioner's hands and delivered the fatal blow himself, finally putting the man out of his misery. Can you believe it?"

she asked, her hands on either side of her face in horror and awe.

"Any idea why it went so horribly wrong?" Cecily asked curiously.

Frances shrugged, "I couldn't tell from the distance whether the axeman was drunk or inexperienced, but Mr Cromwell had many enemies."

Cecily *tsked* and dismissed the kitchen maid before replying quietly, "Who would do such a thing? If the executioner was inexperienced then why choose him? The man was already sentenced to death – and without a trial! Why punish him further with an excruciating execution?"

Frances raised her eyebrows and shrugged, "I only know what I know," she replied causally, "And I know that the man was hated by most at court. *Anyone* could have paid for a botched execution. Perhaps the axeman even did it without pay... or it may have even been by the king's command."

Cecily pinched Frances' arm, "You mustn't say such things in front of the lady Mary!" she said in a harsh whisper, "To say the king would do all that to someone who he himself had raised so high, only reminds Mary that even she is not safe," Cecily quickly glanced over her shoulder to be sure they would not be overheard by Mary who had retreated to the other room.

"You are right," Frances said in agreement when Cecily faced her once more, "Sometimes I forget that beneath her strong façade she is but a scared little girl."

Cecily raised one eyebrow and then turned around at the sound of Mary's hurried pacing within the next room, "Trust me, Frances," she said sadly as the two of them watched their mistress pace to-and-fro nervously, "You too would be scared if your father was king Henry VIII."

August 1540

The king was in love. It was so plain to see.

Henry waltzed around court as a completely new man, gliding effortlessly and without limping, his ulcerous leg seemingly healed as if by the magic of love. His laugh was suddenly louder and his appearance younger, and many commented gladly that it was as though his new queen had breathed life back into him at their union.

Though the young queen quite clearly expressed her joy as the king flaunted her around as if she were a prized trophy, and gifted her new dresses and jewels every day, she did however seem to find her new life as the centre of attention to be somewhat daunting.

The young Kathryn Howard had been thrust into a world she had had very little personal experience in, having only arrived at court to serve the former queen six months prior. And then quite suddenly and without guidance she had been inserted into a rank that she had had no training in, where she was expected to conduct herself in a way that she had not been brought up to ever be.

But the king took great joy in her little mishaps, roaring loudly with laughter whenever Kathryn greeted nobles in the incorrect order befitting their station, or forgetting that she no longer had to curtsy to anyone at all, except to the king himself. He would tenderly justify her mistakes by point out her innocence and youth, as one would to explain away a child's unintentional mess, and the young girl would smile shyly and avert her gaze, clearly uncomfortable in the high-ranking position she had been forced into.

In an effort to facilitate the transition into her new life, the king arranged for all her ladies-in-waiting to be of a similar age to the queen – whom she quickly formed close friendships with – and it did not take long for it to become a common jest among the courtiers that the young queen and her flock were heard before they were seen, their constant giggling and gossiping echoing through the hallways wherever they went.

"It is absurd," Mary grumbled one afternoon as she and her ladies made their way to the Palace chapel, the queen and her new ladies having passed Mary only moments before, giggling incessantly as they went.

"My lady?" Cecily asked, having heard Mary muttering under her breath.

"How can my father expect me to act towards her?" she hissed rhetorically, "She is but a babe and I a lady of twenty-four, yet I must address her as stepmother? It is insulting!"
Cecily did not reply but shot a look at Frances beside her, conveying silently not to fuel the flames with a nonsense remark, as Frances so often did for lack of intuition.

"And that gaggle of geese of hers are utterly shameful!" she continued sourly, "Such behaviour from a queen and her ladies is simply unheard of! I can only imagine what people will be thinking."

"I believe they will simply think that the king is finally happy," Frances piped up then, and Cecily covered her face with her hands incredulously before shaking her head at Frances.
Frances shrugged back in response, "After such a long time grieving the death of queen Jane," she continued, "he deserves to be happy once more."

"But why with her!?" Mary exclaimed angrily, throwing her arms up in the air, and Cecily pinched Frances' arm for aggravating Mary further.

"Ow!" Frances exclaimed as she rubbed a hand over her arm, causing Mary to stop in her tracks and turn to face them, frowning in both confusion as well as annoyance.

"I find the new queen sweet," Frances continued shamelessly, "Forgive me, my lady, but I do not understand your hatred of her," she said as she shrugged.

Cecily scoffed and shook her head in disbelief at Frances' boldness.

Mary, who suddenly had nothing more to say in her own defence, fell silent, and she realised that her hatred toward the young queen stemmed from nothing more than jealousy that at only fifteen years old she had achieved wedlock, station, and glory while Mary continued to stagnate in the swamp that was her uneventful existence.

But in response, Mary grumbled childishly before turning on her heels and stomping off towards the chapel, eager to take her mind off the young and successful Kathryn Howard.

October 1540

As time went on and Kathryn became slowly accustomed to the life of a queen, she would receive new guests at the English court completely without the king by her side – which had recently become more frequent when the ulcer in his leg had once again burst, leaving him bedbound for several days.

On one such occasion, as the young and beautiful queen sat merrily upon her throne, a young lady entered the great hall without announcement, her low station granting no such presentation, and yet it had been obvious that Kathryn had recognised her in an instant.

Mary, who had been sitting with her ladies at a games table by the window, watching the queen flaunt her newfound power thoughtlessly, noticed a sudden change in the queen at the arrival of this young lady, leaving Mary to wonder who this girl could be to evoke such unease in the most powerful woman in all of England.

"Joan," queen Kathryn had said, her face having drained of colour.

"Kathryn!" the girl exclaimed, a broad smile across her face, "I mean, your majesty," she corrected herself, and yet her tone was mocking.

Mary continued to watch as queen Kathryn looked about herself nervously and then forced out an unsure smile before rising from her throne and taking the girl gently by the arm and walking away, whispering as they existed the great hall.

"Who was that?" Mary asked her fountain of information, Frances.

"Hm?" Frances replied, looking up from her dominoes, "Who?"

Mary sat forward, "I want to know who that is," Mary said, "Her name was Joan. The queen clearly knew her."

Frances looked around herself, "Which one?" she asked, unable to spot who Mary meant.

"They have left," Mary pointed out, "I want you to find out who she is."

Frances nodded and cleared her throat before rising from her chair, "My lady," she said before turning to one of the servants – whom Mary had not even noticed – and jerked her head for her to join Frances before hurrying out of the great hall, their heads bent closely together as they whispered inaudibly.

That evening, as Mary sat by the fire, Frances entered her chambers.

Mary looked up from the bible in her hands and raised her eyebrows questioningly, but Frances shook her head as she approached her mistress.

"Nothing," she simply said.

"Nothing?" Mary echoed, frowning in disbelief, "How can you have found out nothing?"

Frances shrugged, "They aren't like other nobles, my lady," she said as she took a seat opposite Mary, "They were always aware of someone listening. Not even the kitchen maids have heard anything. You forget she has only been queen for a few months, and she is still very much aware of the servants listening in the shadows."

Mary nodded.

"But," Frances continued, "the queen has made the girl one of her ladies-in-waiting."

Mary scoffed, "As if she needs more of them," and she bent her head to resume reading the passage in the bible she had abandoned.

"Do you not find it odd?" Frances asked.

"Odd?" Mary replied without looking up.

"That the queen showed no joy at the lady's arrival at court," Frances contemplated aloud, "And yet she is now part of the queen's household?"

"They must be old friends," Mary said.

Frances shrugged one shoulder, "I only know that I got a strange feeling while I watched them interacting today."

"How so?" Mary said, once again dropping her bible into her lap.

"The queen seemed uncomfortable," Frances said, "As though she would prefer the lady not to remain at court."

"Then why –" Mary began but then stopped herself, suddenly understanding, "Do you think this Joan has some sort of hold over the queen? Something from her past?"

Frances chewed on her lip, "Perhaps," she said.

Mary nodded and smiled, "Huh," she said gleefully.

"I do hope she does not cause disturbance between the king and queen," Frances said then, her eyebrows creased together.

Mary shot her a look, "Why do you care for Kathryn's well-being?"

258

Frances picked at a ragged nail then, unable to look Mary in the eyes, "She is innocent in all this, Mary," she mumbled, "Whatever has she done that would deserve you to wish her harm?"

"I do not wish her harm!" Mary exclaimed, "I simply cannot endure her self-importance."

"She is the queen of England, my lady," Frances pointed out, "I believe it comes with the territory," and she breathed a little laugh at her own joke.

Mary sighed as she sat back in her seat and observed her friend as she continued to pick at her nail, "Since when have you become so insightful?" she asked then.

Frances looked up and met Mary's gaze, "Who says I have not always been?"

The young Kathryn Howard and her half a dozen ladies-in-waiting were sitting on a large blanket on the lusciously green laws on the edge of the palace gardens as the king and a handful of his advisors took turns shooting arrows at a target. The king's groom, Culpeper, running to-and-fro to retrieve and deliver the different coloured arrows to their assigned archers.

The king, having almost completely recovered from the most recent pain in his rotting leg, looked over his shoulder and winked at his new wife before turning to face the target and releasing an exceptionally aimed shot.

Queen Kathryn *whooped* and clapped her hands together in appreciation for her husband's achievement.

"Lady Bulmer," the queen said then, turning her attention towards the newest addition to her household.

Joan Bulmer raised her hand as she continued to gossip and giggle with another lady beside her, suggesting to the queen that while she had heard her, she was not prepared to abandon her conversation over the call of her old friend.

Kathryn looked at the faces of her other ladies as her cheeks blushed in shame at Joan's disrespect, "Lady Bulmer!" she said again, her musical voice attempting to sound irate.

Joan turned to look at her queen and, noticing her anger, she offered her a smile, "Yes, your majesty?" she said, the mockery in her tone painfully obvious.

"Joan," Kathryn said as she raised her chin, "Shall we walk?" and then she stood, brushed down her skirts, and began strolling away from her ladies and towards the hedgerows of the gardens.

Once Bulmer had caught up to her old friend and Kathryn gauged there was enough distance between them and her other ladies, she linked her arm with Joan's and held it tightly, "What is the matter with you?" she hissed at the girl beside her while continuing to walk away from the crowd, "I have given you a place among my ladies. I have done as you asked. Now you must keep your end of the bargain and *stop* oversharing with everyone!"

Joan smiled at Kathryn, but it did not reach her eyes, "I only speak of our past when people ask."

"Nonsense," Kathryn replied angrily, "How can anyone know to ask about such things that I have heard you speaking of?"

The question was rhetorical, and yet Bulmer shrugged her shoulders in response.

"I beg you," Kathryn continued then, her voice having mellowed from angry to pleading, "you must stop speaking so blatantly of our past! You put us both in danger."

Joan ripped her arm free from Kathryn's grasp then, her smile vanished from her dull face, "It is hard for me to not speak of it," Bulmer snapped back, and Kathryn was glad to be away from the courtiers for fear of being misheard, yet she attempted to *shush* the girl gently.

260

"Don't you *shush* me, Kathryn!" she snapped, slapping Kathryn's hand away from her, "my heart aches still over what you did to me. And to think you never even apologised – but now you need not apologise to anyone, isn't that right? Because as queen you may do as you will."

"How can I apologise when I have done nothing wrong?" Kathryn whispered back angrily.

"You stole Francis Derenham from me, admit it!" Joan accused, "I heard the sounds of pleasure coming from your bed in the dark that night."

"For heaven's sake, Joan," Kathryn pleaded as she looked around herself in fear, "I did not *steal* Francis away from you!"

Joan crossed her arms defiantly, "Francis never came back to my bed after that night!" she whispered hoarsely, her face red with resentment, "What else am I to believe?"

Kathryn took a step towards her old friend and took her hand, "You must believe me this, sweet Joan," she said quietly, "I *never* invited him to my bed that night! And I did not consent to what he did to me."

Joan pulled her hand away and rolled her eyes, to which Kathryn's chest ached that her friend would not believe her.

After Kathryn's mother had died when Kathryn was just three years old, she had been sent to live with her father's stepmother, the Dowager Duchess of Norfolk, who housed dozens of wards. These wards were usually the children of the Howards' noble relatives that could not afford to keep their children and were therefore sent to reside at one of the Dowager Duchess' many households.

Kathryn had met and befriended Joan at the residence in Lambeth, and it was there that they met a young man named Francis Derenham. At the age of just twelve years old, Joan and he would sneak off together and commit acts of which Kathryn had little interest in. Yet Joan would share the goings-on of their trysts nonetheless, leaving the young Kathryn blushing with embarrassment, for she did not share her friend's interest in the acts of sex, finding the need for its nakedness nothing but mortifying.

One night, as Joan lay snoring in her small bed beside Kathryn's, Kathryn was woken by the sound of someone stumbling, and she sat up in her bed in fright only to find Francis Derenham standing in the dark at the foot of Joan's bed.

"Ah," he had said with a sigh, "She's already asleep?"

Kathryn had looked from Francis to Joan wide-eyed but did not reply. And then Francis had turned his gaze towards her, and in his eyes she had seen a hunger which had made the hairs on the back of her neck stand up in fear. What happened next remained a blur in Kathryn's mind, though she remembers – and perhaps always will – how his hand smelt like sweat as he covered her mouth, and how his face contorted like a monster's as he jerked his hand repeatedly within his trousers.

And Kathryn had thought that if those were the acts of passion that she had been missing out on, then she would be glad to never marry at all.

But then she had married. She had married the most powerful man in all of England. And though she had not pursued him by choice, she was happier now than she had ever been. And her happiness had not stemmed from the gifts and glory Henry had bestowed onto her, but rather from the way that he treated her, and despite the fact that he was older than her own father, Kathryn felt safe and comfortable around him. He taught her things she had never known she could do, and he showed her what true acts of passion were meant to feel like.

And now Joan Bulmer was threatening to take all that away over some silly and disgusting little boy who deserved neither of their attention or even their thoughts.

Kathryn could not allow that to happen.

"Lady Bulmer," the young queen said then with her chin raised regally, "you will listen to me on this," she said as she straightened her back, "I command you never to speak of that night again, or anything that may suggest something happened when I am telling you the truth now: that I was a virgin on the day that I wed the king! Your Francis Dereham did indeed force his way into my bed, but there was no act other than his hand upon himself, and I had not enticed him! Whatever you believe to know is not the case. I am telling you the truth, so help me God!"

Joan stared at her queen through narrowed eyes, her lips pursed tightly in disbelief as she looked away, "Will that be all, your majesty?"

Kathryn could tell that her old friend would not believe her, though she had finally been brave enough to give voice to the worst night of her life, and her heart sank at the prospect that it was likely no one would ever believe her on this, and that if Joan continued to gossip and besmirch her name, she may lose the king's love. The king, who had been nothing but gentlemanly to her, and had risen her from nothing and given her everything. The king, who, despite his older age and rotting leg, was the best man she had ever known. She loved the king with her whole heart and soul, and she believed that if there ever came a day when he did not look at her with love and desire, that she would surely die.

December 1540

"The imperial ambassador, Eustace Chapuys," Mary's guard announced as he opened the door, and the ambassador entered her chambers.

"Lady Mary," he said with a bow before approaching her by the fire, "May I?" he asked, pointing to the empty chair opposite her.

She put down the embroidery she was stitching and nodded, "Please," she said and then watched as he sat down heavily and sighed, "Are you not well, sir?" she asked, noticing his discomfort.

"Oh, it is nothing," he said, waving his hand, "The physicians say I have a touch of gout."

Mary sat forward, expressing concern through the look in her eyes but not knowing how to respond.

Chapuys chuckled, "I am fine, my lady," he said, noticing her expression of worry, "It is but my big toe. I am sure I shall survive this. I am told it is an ailment many suffer in old age," and then he chuckled, "But I have not come to discuss my sufferings, my lady. I have come to bring you something," and he sat forward in his seat as he dug in the pocket of his jacket, then he looked over his shoulder at her ladies who were talking amongst themselves in the next room, and subtly handed Mary a note.

"It was sent to the princess of Cleves," Chapuys explained quietly, "at her residence in Kent, Hever Castle. She sent for me to collect it, not daring to have a messenger bring it to you."

Mary flipped the note around and saw the unbroken seal of Palatine-Neuburg and gasped.

"It remains unopened," Chapuys said knowingly, "As I am sure whatever it contains is for your eyes only, my lady."

Mary looked up and met his kind gaze, "Thank you," she said and then watched as he carefully stood up and bowed his head. Then he turned and slowly walked out of the door, leaving Mary to do as she wished with her love letter.

Mary held the note in her hands and stared down at it for a long moment, considering whether she had the strength to reopen old wounds when they had just begun to heal. She stood up from her seat then and walked over to the fire, her mind telling her that whatever the letter contained was not worth the fresh heartache, and she held out her hand, ready to drop it into the flames.

Frances' laugh in the next room jolted Mary as if out a trance and she realised that no matter what pain it may cause her, Mary had to know if what she had felt had been true or if she had been played for a fool, and so she tore open the wax seal and read the note by the firelight.

Lady Mary,
I write to you with a heavy heart, to inform you that I did not leave England of my own free will. I would have gladly waited forever for the king's permission to wed you, but alas I was sent away by his majesty himself – an order I could have refused, but under pain of imprisonment.

Dearest Mary, I wish you only to know that, though the fates did not grant us the future we had hoped for, it does not dismiss my true and honourable feelings for you.

For I believe you are the most beautiful and enchanting creature that has ever walked the face of this earth.

I want you to understand, truly in your heart and soul, that what happened between us was with the complete intention and understanding that we would be married. If I had known of your father's intentions to banish me, I would have never allowed it to happen. I hate myself for having taken your honour, but I want you to know that after this letter, I shall never speak of it again. Though I do not regret anything, for the love I bear you is true, I would keep this secret and take it to the grave.

To me you are the purest and most noble lady that has ever lived, and you deserve to have everything. I pray that your father will allow a good match for you soon, and that you may

265

begin to live a life of love and laughter. And though it may not be with me, I pray that you will find happiness in this lifetime.

Yours forever,
Phillip, duke of Palatine-Neuburg.

Ps – burn this.

Her eyes welled with tears until the words blurred upon the paper and then she threw the parchment into the fireplace and watched as the embers consumed it at the edges and then disappeared in a sudden *woosh* of flame.

Though her eyes stung with tears of sadness at the memory of a life she could have had, Phillip's letter did not open old wounds. Instead, it confirmed what Mary had already known to be true: that at the root of all her heartache and loss was none other than her dearly beloved father.

Chapter 14

March 1541
Greenwich Palace, London

The court was rejoicing, for the queen had publicly announced that she was finally with child, and no one was more overjoyed than the old king himself.

"We shall name him Henry after myself!" he exclaimed cheerfully as he paced the queen's rooms excitedly, "Just as my father named me, his own second son, after him," and he grabbed her face with both hands and planted a wet kiss upon her lips.

The young queen laughed, "I should like that very much," she said as she watched him begin pacing again, and she realised that his usual limp was much less noticeable when he was happy.

The following day Henry departed on a celebratory hunt with a handful of his advisors and his groom Thomas Culpeper, leaving Kathryn to amuse herself in the company of her ladies.

It was a rare Spring day without rain, and though the light wind held a chill, Kathryn ordered for her luncheon to be served to her in the form of a picnic on the laws.

Wrapped in furs against the breeze, Kathryn and her ladies were making their way through the courtyard and towards the gardens when, upon turning a corner, Kathryn unexpectedly bumped into her stepdaughter, Mary.

"Oh!" Mary exclaimed as the two ladies collided and then when she noticed who it was, "Your majesty," she said sourly, "You ought to watch where you are going while carrying such precious cargo."

Kathryn's lady, Joan, croaked out a chuckle behind her, to which Mary peered at her over Kathryn's shoulder and stared her down disapprovingly, for though Mary cared little whether the lady disliked the queen or not, while married to the king, Kathryn merited her inferiors' respect.

In her flustered state, Kathryn quickly curtsied and then realised her mistake, for as queen she need not curtsy to anyone, "Actually," she said then as she straightened her back, "You should curtsy to me, should you not?"

But Mary did not consider *herself* an inferior to her father's child bride, and so her cheeks blushed in irritation, and she clenched her jaw so as not to reply in a way which would surely come back to haunt her. Instead, she ever so slightly bobbed up and down, then turned and walked around the queen's horde of mindless ladies and left without being dismissed.

As Kathryn watched her stepdaughter walk away, she heard a snort escaping from Joan behind her, and all the disdainful looks Mary had given Kathryn over the last few months came suddenly flashing back into her memory, and her usually accepting demeanour became overthrown by a rush of anger, Mary's snub being the final straw to break her patience.

She was the queen of England, and even her own lady showed her absolutely no respect.

"Ladies," Kathryn said as she lifted her skirts and turned back around, continuing her way through the courtyard.

She decided that from that moment forward she would no longer lay back and simply accept the way certain people treated her. She had had enough of those that would seek to belittle her. First Francis Derenham, then Joan, and now the lady Mary.

But it was enough. As queen of England, no one should feel comfortable enough to undermine her, and while she knew that Joan held damaging information over her head, she would have to do something to evoke some fear into her while also revealing her power among the court.

Kathryn decided that once she had gathered her thoughts and filled her belly, that she would pay her stepdaughter a visit.

Later that same day, Kathryn entered the lady Mary's chambers upon being announced by her guard and was immediately greeted with curtsies from her two ladies and a servant girl that was stoking the fire.

Kathryn smiled at them all in thanks for their courtesy and then extended her gaze to Mary who had merely stood from her seat by the fireplace.

Kathryn chose to begin pleasantly, "Lady Mary," she said sweetly, "I thought we might enjoy a moment to get to know each other better."

Mary stared back at the queen, her hands clasped before her and the cross at her neck bobbing up and down as she breathed erratically, clearly pestered by the unannounced visit.

Kathryn's gaze went from Mary's cross at her neck, to her face, and then to her ladies, who had moved to either side of their mistress as though in battle formation.

All remained silent as Mary did not reply, and after what felt like an eternity, Kathryn took a step towards her stepdaughter, "Lady Mary," she began again, this time more bluntly, "I am sorry that you do not like me. Truly, it causes me much discomfort to think of it. But I make your father happy, and he makes me happy. It is a shame therefore that we cannot all get along in a civilised manner. After all, as queen," and she cleared her throat, "I am entitled to your respect."

Mary stared; her eyes boring into the young queen's face.

Then, after a long moment, she looked down at her hands clasped before her and licked her lips.

"We are not friends," Mary said plainly, "nor would we ever be. But I will of course show you the respect you so poignantly explained you deserve," then she bowed her head and gave an exaggerated curtsy, all the way to the ground, her skirts ballooning at the sides.

Kathryn watched the mockery and felt a wave of anger bubbling inside her, "Perhaps it is jealousy that drives you to insult me thusly," the queen said.

"Jealousy?" Mary repeated as she stood from her deep curtsy, her forehead creased with a frown, "What would give *me* cause to be jealous of *you*... your majesty?"

Kathryn's face grew red with emotion, "Perhaps because I am married, in love and with child while you are none of those things and yet you are twice my age."

Mary's eyes went wide at the insult, her unmarried status at the age of twenty-five being a painful jibe made worse still by the insinuation that Mary was in fact much older, and she stared in disbelief that Kathryn would give voice to such opinions – opinions which stung so deeply because, despite the inaccurate age, they were in fact true.

But Mary could not admit defeat, and in her humiliation, she bit back, "Marriage, love and fruitfulness are not achievements one should brag about when none were achieved by themselves," she spat out angrily, "For clearly the king did not choose you for your intellect if you cannot even do simple addition."

The queen's ladies gasped in horror at the insult, but Mary continued, "If all those things I lack would cost me my intelligence, I would gladly die an old maid before I endured a moment in your majesty's empty head."

There was no other sound, and the two women glared at each other, Kathryn having covered her agape mouth with her hand.

Then Kathryn blinked in shock and breathed a stunned laugh, "I came here today," she said calmly, "to try and make amends. But you insist on hating me though you have no reason for it."

Mary raised her eyebrows and crossed her arms in defiance, caring nothing for what her teenaged stepmother had to say.

"As a punishment for your disrespect," the queen said then as she inhaled deeply, "I am removing two of your servants from your household, effective immediately. You," Kathryn pointed at Cecily, "and you," and at the girl by the fireplace, "You are both dismissed."

"You cannot dismiss my lady or my servants," Mary said without flinching as she watched Kathryn turn to leave.

Kathryn swung her head back and gave Mary a look from over her shoulder, "I think you will find that as queen of England, I can do whatever I like," and then she nodded at the guards, and they took the two ladies gently by their arms and led them out of Mary's chambers.

Later that same day, when king Henry returned from his celebratory hunt, a messenger came running up to his horse bringing an urgent note from the queen that she was awaiting him in his chambers.

Sweating and covered in mud, the king stormed through the castle to his chambers and burst through the door to find his queen sitting on the edge of his bed.

She turned her head towards him as he entered and he could instantly see that she had been crying, "What is it, my love? Is it the baby?" Henry asked in fear, pressing a hand over her flat belly.

Kathryn shook her head, "No Henry," she said as she sobbed, "I am so sorry. I am sorry. I didn't know."

"Shhh," the king said calmly, stroking her back as she embraced him, "What didn't you know?"

"I am so sorry, Henry," Kathryn said as she looked up into his concerned face, "I – it seems that," she sniffed once, "I don't believe that I was ever expecting after all," she admitted through blubbering sobs.

271

Henry's expression changed in an instant and he took a step back, "I don't understand," he said quietly, "How could you have gotten it wrong?"

The young queen shook her head and shrugged, "I didn't know" she said again, "I – I missed my courses for a few days, and I thought – I just thought that I had to be. Because it's never happened to me before, so I – I just believed I was with child."

"But you're not?" Henry asked, his greying eyebrows furrowed in confusion.

Kathryn shook her head, "No," she admitted, "My courses came this afternoon. The physician said it is not a miscarriage, but simply a late bloom this month –"

Henry raised his hand, cutting her off, and closed his eyes, his young wife's incessant whimpering causing him a headache, "I do not wish to hear the details, Kathryn," and he sighed heavily as he rubbed his hands over his face in disappointment.

He was silent for a moment while his wife stood before him, hunched over in grief, crying for the loss of something she had never had, while the ghosts of all Henry's own lost babies danced before him in his mind's eye. Then he abruptly turned on his heel and exited the room, unwilling to deal with his distraught young wife, and unable to face the unhealing wounds of his past.

May 1541

"She is not with child," king Henry said monotonously to his oldest friend Charles Brandon as they privately played cards in the king's rooms.

Charles raised his head, "Not with child?" he frowned.

"Apparently not," Henry said with a sigh as he shuffled the deck.

Charles shook his head, his thick hair flopping over his eyes which he subconsciously swept aside, "Why would she say she was if she was not?"

"Because she is a fool?" Henry offered casually.

"She is young," Charles said in the queen's defence, "We were young once too. The young are foolish and make mistakes."

Henry grabbed his cup of wine and drank its contents in one, "She should know better than to announce such a thing to me, her king, unless she were certain of it."

"While I agree with your majesty," he said as he picked up the cards before him, "I must remind you that though it did not happen this time, she may yet conceive and bear you a son."

Henry waved his hand, "I do not wish to speak of it," then he snapped his fingers, "Groom!" he called, and the young man appeared from the shadows holding a silver jug, "Culpeper, fill our wine cups," and then to Charles, "We have much to discuss for our journey tomorrow."

"Indeed, your majesty," Charles agreed, glad to have another matter of discussion to hopefully take the king's mind off of his disappointment with the Howard girl, "This journey shall be remembered in the history books!"

Henry raised his cup to that, "As well it should!" he agreed, "Never have I travelled further north than to Lincolnshire, and now the king of England travels to York to meet his nephew the king of Scotland."

"Not only that," Charles prompted his old friend, "but along the journey we shall also remind the north where their loyalties should lie," and he took a gulp of his wine in an attempt to banish the dark memories of the Northern rebellion where he himself had put hundreds of people to death for their uprising against the king not four years prior. The popular revolt had been dubbed the Pilgrimage of Grace and had been a massive protest against the king's break from the Catholic Church, the dissolution of the monasteries, as well as the rise of food prices across the country. In the end, the only way to put a stop to the ever-growing masses of this rebellion, Charles Brandon had been sent to the north with a small army and demanded the people return to their lands. Those that had refused, including some of their leaders, as well as women and children, were hung by order of Charles Brandon, for their treasonous acts against the king.

"Yes," Henry said quietly, remembering the terrible times where his reign had been so closely overthrown by peasants.

Henry shook his head, giving not a second thought to the innocent lives they had taken over an easily rectifiable dispute. But Charles stared ahead unseeingly, the many faces of the innocents he had killed for the sake of the king's favour having been etched into his mind's eye.

Then Henry slapped his old friend on the shoulder and Charles blinked as though he had awoken from a daze, and the two men raised their cups and took a sip before picking up their playing cards, neither of them mentioning how they resented the other for how the Northern Rebellion had affected them.

Mary watched from the window of her chambers as the king and queen mounted their horses and, along with nearly five-thousand members of their household, began their journey to York.

As soon as all horses and carriages were out of sight, she turned from the window to assess her surroundings and watched for a moment while Frances continued to pack her dresses and other belongings into chests. Mary walked over to her lady and began to help, eager to begin her own journey out of London during the hot and dangerous summer months.

"My lady, you need not do this," Frances said as Mary packed her own bible and books.

"If we wish to leave today I must," Mary answered, "Without Cecily there is too much for you to do."

"The servants can help me with the rest," Frances pointed out.

"They are busy enough closing up the palace," Mary said, "It will not take long, and soon we shall be on our way to Hunsdon House."

Frances and Mary remained quiet for a moment while they continued to pack.

"How do you feel about returning to Hunsdon House, my lady?" Frances asked coyly as she folded linens.

Mary knew what her lady was insinuating, but she gave herself a moment to consider the question before she answered, "I do not feel nervous or excited," Mary said slowly, "I am not sure I feel much at all about it, truthfully."

"Not even about seeing your stable boy?" Frances whispered, a smile on her lips.

"He is not *my* stable boy, Frances," Mary whispered back, "But no, I do not feel anything about it. Arthur is in the past. And something that should never had happened," then she paused, "I dare say he won't even remember me, if he is still there at all."

"Where else would he be?" Frances asked casually, shrugging one shoulder.

"Who knows," Mary said trying to sound nonchalant as she considered it, "Perhaps married and moved away. Perhaps taken on by some noble lord and travelling the world as his personal steward."

Frances looked at her mistress and smiled, "It seems you have put some thought into it, my lady."

Mary waved her hand, dismissing the notion, "Perhaps he's dead, Frances," she added then, "That is the most likely of outcomes."

"How morbid," her lady replied as she shivered.

Picking up her hoods, Mary walked over to the chest, "But likely all the same," she said, and she flung the hoods angrily into the chest as she realised that she deeply hoped that she would be wrong – and she hated herself for even caring.

July 1541
Hunsdon House, Hertfordshire

Mary had been at Hunsdon House a week before she allowed herself a walk in the gardens, fearful that it would awaken old emotions that she did not wish to revisit.

But she was, however, glad to see that it had not changed much, and the beautiful roses and hedges were much the same as the last time she had been there.

In fact, Mary felt oddly at peace and comforted by the memories it brought her. This was the place where she had admitted defeat, and where a humble stable boy had reminded her of who she was, and who she was born to be. Even before her mother's secret letter had fuelled the fire within her to fight on, Arthur had built the pyre, and for that she should at least thank him, if he was indeed still in service at Hunsdon House.

She entered the dusty stables and looked from one beautiful steed to the next as the stable hands brushed them down or lay fresh hay in their stalls, and Mary walked slowly past each horse, raising her hand to their soft muzzles as they lapped at her empty palm in search of an apple.

And then she saw him. He was darker skinned than she remembered, and his face unshaven, a light stubble having grown on his chin and cheeks. There were creases at his eyes, though he must only be around twenty-eight years old, and Mary hoped they developed from years of laughter rather than pain. But it was her Arthur, there was no doubt about it.

She cleared her throat to announce her presence, and he looked up from his work.

His eyes widened in recognition immediately, and his face broke into a great smile. He dropped his pitchfork and bowed, bending at the waist before her as though she were already the queen of England. Mary chuckled at the way he continued to respect and admire her so openly. It was something Mary would never forget.

"Princess Mary!" he said as he straightened up, "I never thought I'd see you again."

Mary shrugged, "Hunsdon House is my favourite residence," she confessed.

Then they simply looked into each other's faces, both completely aware of how much time had passed since the last time they had seen each other.

"How have you been?" Mary asked once the silence became too uncomfortable.

Arthur smiled that crooked smile she had loved.

"I have been well, your grace," he said easily, as though they had never been apart, "A lot has changed."

"For you perhaps," Mary said, fully aware that her comment could lead to so many questions. She looked over her shoulder then, aware of potential eavesdroppers, "Shall we take a stroll?"

Arthur looked around him, "Err..." he said as he considered his workload, "I could take a minute away," he said, and they both exited the stables.

Their feet took them automatically towards the gardens.

"I must be honest," Mary said as they walked side by side, "I wasn't sure if you would still be here."

"Where would I have gone?" Arthur asked with a slight chuckle.

Mary shook her head, "I imagined many different things."

"Such as?"

"Well," Mary said and then smiled, "It has been many years."

"Yes," Arthur replied as he looked up into the distance.

They walked silently for a while, and Mary was relieved to feel nothing but comfortable. Though the years had been kind to him, his handsome looks having aged well despite his manual work and endless days in the sun, Mary's heart did not leap uncontrollably at his close proximity as it had done but eight years ago. And as she looked into his face, a face she had loved long ago, she was pleased to feel nothing more than a strong desire for his happiness. Even one which would not include her.

"I had hoped to see you," Mary admitted, "But I had my concerns."

"Concerns?" he asked as they entered the gardens' hedgerows and took a right along the pebbled path.

"About how I would feel," Mary admitted.

Arthur nodded.

"I wasn't sure what I wanted to find on my return," Mary continued, "But I am glad to have been able to see you again. Simply to see that you are well and happy."

"I am happy," Arthur replied.

Mary smiled, "And I am glad for it."

Then he stopped abruptly, his feet crunching loudly on the pebbles as he turned to face her, "May I ask you something, your grace?" he asked.

Mary nodded, "Yes?"

"Why do you concern yourself with my happiness?"

"Why?" Mary echoed, confused at his question.

"Yes," he replied, "Why not focus on your own?" he asked.

Mary chuckled, "What is there to focus on for myself?"

Arthur took her hand then and she noticed its roughness had increased since the last time she had held it, "I will be blunt with you, Mary," he said, his words heavy, "I am married,"

278

and he stopped to smile, "I have five children, four girls and a boy. My wife – she is unwell – ever since our boy was born, she hasn't been herself. But I believe she will be again. We are happy," he said again, "God had granted us that much at least."

Mary smiled as she listened; it was the life she had hoped he would have had.

"Forgive my bluntness, your grace," Arthur whispered then when she did not respond, "But in all these years, I would have hoped for a similar life for you, albeit much grander. But I fear that has not been the case?"

Mary's chest felt heavy in her own defence, "I must admit," she said as she tore her hand free of his, "I have achieved nothing in comparison to you."

Arthur nodded once and his expression was one she had never seen in him before.

He was pitying her.

Mary frowned at him, "Do not feel sad or sorry for me, Arthur," she said defensively, "I may have achieved much less than you in terms of joy. But, while life has granted me wealth and a high rank, I have faced many other obstacles you could perhaps not imagine. I may have achieved nothing as joyous as you, and I may have experienced much less of life than most. But I have maintained my survival," Mary chuckled then at the realisation that followed, "Of all the women in my father's life, I have survived him the longest. And that alone is a great achievement!"

She looked up into his sad eyes, "I may have forsaken my soul, my past and my future for it, but one day God will repay me. I have faith I will achieve some of the happiness you speak of."

Arthur smiled but it did not reach his almost-black eyes, "I pray that you do."

"Thank you," Mary replied, her face hard as stone.

279

Arthur simply stood and observed as Mary clenched her jaw and looked down at her feet, and while she was a much icier and harder version of the girl he had once known, he was glad to see a fragment of her former self still remained alive within her, and that all the years of heartache and loneliness had not completely eradicated her kind and hopeful spirit. He only wished that the years had been kinder to her, for he knew first-hand what a gracious and caring princess she had been, and what a compassionate and kind-hearted queen she would one day – God willing – become.

Perhaps he would yet live to see her claim her destiny, one he had always so strongly wished for her to achieve.

"I am sorry," he said then, breaking the silence that had engulfed them, "that your path has not yet led you to greener pastures. But I am not sorry for pushing you to remember what you were born to become. Even if it meant that I lost you to it. I do not regret it," and he smiled that crooked smile at her, "You are meant to rule England one day, my princess. And you will need a man of noble birth beside you when the time comes. Not a lowly stable worker like me."

"I believe that you are right," Mary agreed, "God has a bigger plan for me, but you played your part in it very well."

They both chuckled and fell silent once more.

"Well," Mary said as she looked up into his face one last time, and he was suddenly taken aback at how striking she looked, even now, after all those years, "I believe there is nothing more to say," she said, and he was saddened by how much truth the words carried.

There was nothing more for them to discuss.

He raised his rough, workman's hand to her cheek and stroked it gently. Then he took a step back and bowed, before turning on his heel and walking out of the garden that they had shared, and back to his inconsequential little life, one which brought him so much happiness, without her.

September 1541

"My lady," Frances said as she placed Mary's breakfast before her and then handed her two letters.
Mary turned them over in her hand and ripped one of them open as soon as she saw the imperial ambassador's seal, her heart racing with fear for the news it would contain.

Lady Mary,
I write with a heavy heart, to inform you that the Countess of Salisbury, your former governess, and aunt to your father the king, has been executed under the charges of conspiring with her son, Reginald Pole. After a long time of imprisonment, she is now with God.
I am sorry to say that, though her suffering is now at an end, that she did not encounter a swift death. Her executioner was a young and inexperienced fool, and she suffered an end rather similar to that of the late Mr. Cromwell.
I tell you this not to distress you, my lady, but simply to remind you that even the sentence of death is sometimes not enough punishment for some people.

Eustace Chapuys

"My lady?" Frances' whispered, and Mary realised that she was crying.
She raised her head and angrily wiped her tears, "It is the lady Margaret Pole."
"The countess?"
Mary nodded, "She is with God," she said sadly, "Executed."
Frances covered her mouth in shock, the poor countess having endured imprisonment for two-and-a-half years over her son's crimes bringing a tear to her eyes.

"She was innocent," Frances pointed out quietly.

Mary shook her head and sniffed, "It no longer matters," she said, "We must pray for her soul and thank God that He has put an end to her suffering."

Frances nodded sadly and inhaled deeply to steady her nerves, then she looked down at the other letter on Mary's lap, "This one is dated one day after the other one," she noticed, "Whatever else could have happened?"

Mary looked down at the letter and felt her heart drop with anxiety and she wondered if she should open it at all, "Here," Mary said as she handed the letter to Frances, "Read it to me."

Frances turned it over, "It is the same seal," she announced, "from ambassador Chapuys."

Mary stood and walked towards the window and fumbled with the cross at her neck, bracing herself for more terrible news.

Frances unfolded the letter, "It reads: 'The Scottish King did not come. King Henry arrived at York on the 16th September only to be left to wait over ten days before news came from his nephew that they would not meet. The very next day the procession of over five thousand departed on their return to London. The king is furious, as you can imagine, and with the queen's lack of an heir, rumours are amounting that he wishes to take back his former bride the princess Anne of Cleves.'"

Frances gasped and looked up at Mary in shock, who waved her on, dismissing the rumours she knew to be completely fabricated. Frances cleared her throat and continued, "It goes on: 'The king has been said to be spending a lot less time with his young queen. It would seem their honeymoon is officially over, ever since her false pregnancy announcement. And with yet no heir in her womb, there seems to be no hope for a change in his foul mood. Remain at Hunsdon House for as long as you can. Perhaps even until he personally summons you for the Christmastide. For now, it is safer out of his immediate sight'."

When Frances stopped reading, Mary jerked her chin in the direction of the fireplace and watched as her lady balled up the letter and flung it into the flames. Any discussion about the king, whether it be fabricated or factual, was dangerous to keep in one's possession, and Mary didn't survive her tyrant father for all her twenty-five years by being reckless.

Frances turned back to her mistress, "What about the letter of the countess of Salisbury?" she asked carefully, "Shall we burn it too?"

"No," Mary replied as they both looked down at it, laying open on the table, "No, that one I shall keep as a reminder."

"A reminder of the lady Margaret?"

"Not *of* her," Mary admitted, "I do not need a piece of parchment depicting her violent death as a reminder of that gentle lady. She will live eternally in my heart," and she sighed, "No, I wish to keep it as a reminder that not even the king's own family is safe from a demise such as that."

Frances looked at her friend with sadness in her eyes and wished, not for the first time since her dismissal by the queen, that Cecily was here to help her manage Mary's increasingly icy persona.

October 1541
Hampton Court Palace, Surrey

"Lady Bulmer!" Queen Kathryn called as she entered her chambers at Hampton Court Palace, one of king Henry's favourite residences which he had procured from his former Lord Chancellor, Thomas Wolsey, who had invested a decade of his life as well as large sums of money into transforming it from an ordinary country house to a magnificent palace.

Joan Bulmer emerged from an adjoining room, her face conveying how indisposed she felt at being summoned, "Yes, your majesty?" she said.

Kathryn turned to the other ladies and servants in the room, "Leave us!" she commanded and then turned to Joan, staring at her as everyone else left. Once she heard the door click shut behind them, Kathryn grabbed her old friend by the wrists, "Who did you speak to?!" she demanded furiously.

"Kathryn, you're hurting me!" Joan whined as Kathryn's grip tightened.

"It's 'your majesty' to you, lady Bulmer!" Kathryn hissed as she let her go sharply, "Who have you been speaking to?" she repeated, "The Archbishop Cranmer is snooping and asking questions, obviously at the command of the king! So 'why' I ask myself! Why – of course because *someone* has been gossiping! So, I ask again: who have you been speaking to and what have you said!?"

Joan stared wide-eyed at her friend; her mouth agape but speechless as she rubbed her hand over her wrist.

"Kath – your majesty…" she said, then cleared her throat, "I have not said anything –"

"Ha!" Kathryn exclaimed incredulously, "You mean to tell me," she said as she approached her lady-in-waiting and stuck her face just inches from hers, "that you have spoken to no one about what you *think* you know about our time at the Dowager Duchess' house?"

Joan looked down at the ground but did not answer.

Kathryn moaned quietly, a mixture of fear and anger, and she turned away from her lady, her hands pressed against her temple, "You've ruined me," she said.

Suddenly Joan scoffed, "I ruined you?" she countered then, her own naïve discontent overshadowing Kathryn's fear for her life, "Look at where we both stand. You are the queen of England, and I? I am nothing and no one. When you are around, I matter to nobody, as always," and she crossed her arms like the petulant and immature child that she was.

"Who have you spoken to, Joan?" Kathryn asked again, her voice low, as though she had no more life left within her.

"I needed someone to speak to about my pain," Joan said defensively, "and the lady Rochford cared enough to listen." Kathryn blinked at the girl before her, someone she had once considered to be like a sister, but whom she no longer recognised. As the words sunk in that it had indeed been Joan's gossiping which had undoubtedly led to the king's sudden distrust in her, Kathryn squeezed her eyes closed and pressed her fingers into her temples.

"You *threatened* me," she said quietly, "to give you a place in my household. You *asked* to be here, as my lady in waiting!" and then she opened her eyes and looked at Joan, who raised an eyebrow and crossed her arms in response. Kathryn breathed a small chuckle then as she realised her lady's petulant vendetta, and she shook her head in disbelief, "Your silly resentment has destroyed me," she said again, unable to explain it any clearer to the stupid girl before her, "You think I *stole* Francis Dereham from you still, even when I have confided to you the truth of it – that he forced himself upon me and terrified me to fulfil his disgusting desires. I was a child!"

"Your grace –" Joan said mockingly as she rolled her eyes, and Kathryn's anger boiled over.

"Your disgusting lover," she suddenly screamed as she pointed her finger in Joan's face, "chose to molest me that night, Joan. He enjoyed my fear so much that, by the grace of God, he left me intact. I never invited him to my bed, and I have never lain with another man other than my husband. I swear this on my immortal soul!" Kathryn said, her eyes boring into Joan's.

Joan dropped her gaze then and Kathryn could tell that she wanted to say something.

"What is it?" Kathryn demanded.

285

Joan opened her mouth but then closed it again. She took a step back and then looked up at her queen, "I do not believe that if the archbishop is asking questions, that it would be entirely about your past," she said, her tone icy.

"What do you mean, Joan?" the young queen asked, her brows furrowed in confusion.

Joan raised her chin, a small smile dancing on her lips, "Haven't you heard?" she said sarcastically, "The court is ablaze with rumours."

"What rumours?" Kathryn demanded, taking a step towards her threateningly.

Joan did not move back, standing her ground against her old friend's attempt to intimidate her, "Why, your private meetings with the king's groom, Mr. Culpeper, of course," she said in mock certainty.

"My private meetings?" Kathryn echoed, "With Mr. Culpeper?" Kathryn asked, unable to understand.

Joan gave a small laugh, "You may say what you will about Francis - that he hurt you, that he forced you," she shrugged, "I do not believe it. He *loved* me."

Kathryn's face paled as the blood drained from her face, "What have you done, Joan?"

Joan walked around her queen and headed towards the door, "You are not fit to be queen, Kathryn," she said spitefully, "and I have seen to it that everyone knows what a wanton whore you really are."

Kathryn felt sick, and her vision blurred as she realised the extent of her demise.

She covered her mouth with her hand, but it did nothing to stop the vomit from arising, and as her fear engulfed her, she doubled over and vomited down the front of her exquisite dress and shoes. She retched until her stomach had nothing more to expel, then she wiped her chin with the back of her hand and breathed in deeply to steady herself, "I should have left you to rot in the Dowager Duchess' keeping," Kathryn cried out as the tears streamed down her rosy cheeks.

Joan shrugged casually and smiled, having enjoyed Kathryn's distress immensely, "Yes, Kathryn," she said as she opened the door, "You should have."

November 1541
Hunsdon House, Hertfordshire

Mary had taken to dismissing Frances more often than usual since the news of the Countess of Salisbury's death had reached her.

She had begun to believe that attachments were weaknesses, and that solitude would surely strengthen her over time, leaving her with no one she feared to lose.

She was surprised then, as she knelt at her prie-deux for her morning prayers, when she heard urgent footsteps approaching from behind her closed door, followed by the loud creaking as it was swung open.

She turned around with a frown etched upon her face at the disturbance, but when she saw that it was Frances – whom she had just that morning dismissed – Mary knew that something terrible had happened.

"What is it?" Mary asked immediately as she rose to her feet midway through her prayers, tucking her rosary beads into her sleeve.

"A letter from ambassador Chapuys," Frances said, her face pale as snow, "I fear I already know its contents. The messenger was bursting to speak of it as soon as he arrived."

Rather than listen to servants' gossip, Mary ripped open the letter from the imperial ambassador and walked over to a nearby candle to help her read its contents.

Lady Mary,

I am glad that you chose to stay away from the vipers' nest that is the English court, for it is rife with deceit and hatred. The young Kathryn Howard has been stripped of her title of queen after allegations of her past sexual relationships have come to light. The king was willing to forgive her those indiscretions for the love he bore her, but shortly thereafter she was accused of conducting private meetings in her chambers with the king's groom, a Mr. Culpeper. The young man proclaims his innocence but has nonetheless been arrested and tortured. The king left Hampton Court earlier this month, and in his rage left his wife behind to be interrogated.

It is not a safe time to return. I urge you to remain as invisible as possible and remain at Hunsdon House until the king's disposition has improved.

Immediately after reading the letter, Mary raised it to the candle and set it alight, then tossed it into the hearth.

"What does it say?" Frances asked quietly as they watched the parchment burn.

Mary looked from the burning letter to her friend, "That it is not safe to return," she said quietly, "The queen has been confined to Hampton Court and is being investigated. Her lover has been arrested and tortured."

Frances covered her mouth in shock, "So the messenger *was* telling the truth," she mumbled to herself.

"Who is to know what is true?" Mary said emotionlessly as she watched Frances' shocked expression, "But he has been displeased with her since her false pregnancy."

Frances swallowed and nodded, "Though, I did not think she would be as stupid as to go behind the king's back."

Mary shrugged, "She is in God's hands now," she said, "Perhaps the king will show mercy and find a pre-contract between herself and one of her past lovers, as he did with the princess Anne of Cleves."

Frances nodded, "The king does love her," she said as she recalled the way he treated his young queen, "May he show her mercy," she mumbled as she crossed herself.

"Don't be too hopeful," Mary added as she walked over to her prie-deux, "If there is one thing my father does not tolerate, it is being humiliated," she paused to pull her rosary beads from her sleeve, eager to return to her inner peace, "And if there is any truth to the secret affair with this Culpeper, then little Kathryn is headed straight for the block."

February 1542
Hampton Court Palace, Surrey

In his anger and humiliation, the king of England put forth a bill of attainder, which was swiftly passed by Parliament, that declared it treason for a queen consort to fail to disclose her sexual history to the king within twenty days of their marriage.

It was with this bill that seventeen-year-old Kathryn Howard was sentenced to death on all grounds, regardless as to whether she had in fact committed adultery or not, since she had failed to disclose her past sexual relationships within the allotted time frame. It was the king's way of ensuring that this humiliation would not go unpunished, and it made it clear to the world that, in one way or another, Kathryn Howard was a whore.

The former queen was kept imprisoned without a formal trial, to await her untimely death and as her final royal wish she requested that the block be brought up to her cell, so that she may practice how to lay her head upon it in her final moment.

Kathryn, though she had been born and raised of low birth, remained graceful and regal throughout her imprisonment, and on the morning of the 13th of February she went to the scaffold as composed as any queen could be as she faced her death.

Kathryn faced the crowd of people who watched eagerly from below, then she inhaled deeply to regain her composure, as the executioner waited behind her.

"Good people of England!" she called to the crowd before her, her voice never breaking, "Though I have never been a particularly devout person, I ask you all to pray for my soul today, for I have offended God, and his majesty the king, who has always treated me with grace and kindness. I wholeheartedly ask you all to pray for his majesty and to pray that he remains in good health and has a long life. It is all I wished for him then, and it is all I wish for him still," and she paused to place a trembling hand over her pounding heart. Then she closed her eyes and exhaled slowly, "Though I have been condemned to die today I do not begrudge anyone for this decision," she continued, "for I have been a sinner all my life. But I ask you to remember that I was always a loyal servant to his majesty, and that I loved him truly and gave my heart, body and soul *only* to him," at that she searched the faces of the strangers before her and was deeply troubled by some of their snickering, knowing that their disbelief of the truth would be what would be remembered throughout the ages, "Thus, I take my leave of this world," she said in conclusion, and as she spoke her final words, she was ashamed to feel urine pouring down her legs, and hot tears streaming down her face.

She was then blindfolded from behind as she mumbled for God to have mercy on her soul, and she knelt down slowly, feeling for the block before her with trembling hands. Then, just as she had practiced for many hours the night before, she lay her head down gracefully onto the block, and uncomplainingly awaited the swift blow of the axe.

Chapter 15

November 1542
Greenwich Castle, London

Soon after Kathryn Howard's execution, Mary was bid to return to court by the king himself to attend the Christmastide and to show the country that the Tudors were strong and united.

Almost immediately upon her arrival at court, the king had her lady in waiting Cecily reinstated as head of Mary's household, as well as returning all servants the former queen had had dismissed, as though little Kathryn Howard had never even existed.

Then, shortly after her return, news broke that the Scottish king had died, leaving only a single living heir to succeed him – a tiny, new-born daughter – who was proclaimed Scotland's new monarch at only six days old.

Not only did this leave Scotland weakened and a much lesser threat to England, but it also suggested to her own father, that female children *could* succeed as rulers – just as her mother had always believed.

Mary relished in this new age and secretly admired the Scots for staying true to their late king and for openly suggesting to the world that the people of England, Ireland and Scotland would be ready for female rulers.

Without a queen beside king Henry during the Christmastide, Mary took precedence over any other – except for the king himself – and though she continued to be proclaimed a bastard, as the king's own daughter she was the highest-ranking lady at English court.

She acted as hostess to the nobles of the land and sat at the high table beside her father at feasts, sending out plates of food to her favourites. Her father doted on her once more and treated her as though he had never revoked her legitimacy at all.

He gifted her jewels and dresses and even presented her with a new lady-in-waiting to join her household, a lady Catherine Parr.

"May I present you the lady Parr," Henry had said from his throne as the lady curtsied before Mary, "She is the daughter of the late Maud Green," he said, and Mary raised her eyebrows.

"Your mother was my mother's lady-in-waiting," Mary pointed out as she smiled.

"And I believe," Catherine Parr said, "they were very close friends."

"So I have been told," Mary replied and she nodded her head in acceptance of the lady into her household.

February 1543

After the Christmastide, there was talk circulating at court that the king was once again in negotiations with the Holy Roman Emperor, Mary's cousin, to form a new treaty against the French. And shortly thereafter a treaty was signed for an Anglo-Imperial invasion of France to occur within the following two years.

Though Mary remained nonchalant about their new alliance in public, she thanked God every night in her prayers for returning England to its former relationship with Spain. Between England's return to its friendship with Spain and the way her father had begun to treat her once more, it seemed that the wheel of fortune was finally turning in Mary's favour, and she relished every moment of it.

But Mary's good fortune did not last long when, without warning, she fell ill once again to the mysterious ailment that haunted her.

Mary was bedbound for several weeks in which she could neither sit nor stand, the pains in her head being so severe that she had to remain in complete darkness with her windows boarded up to block out every sliver of sunlight.

While her stomach churned and swelled, the rest of her became gaunt and pale, the nausea making her unable to keep down any food.

Though none of the symptoms were uncommon to Mary, they were undeniably more severe than ever before, and she would often dream of her quiet life at Hunsdon House where she had not been plagued by her illness. And in her lucid moments she finally admitted to herself that perhaps the hectic and chaotic lifestyle of the English court would one day be the death of her.

After two weeks of torture, the pains in her head and belly had begun to subside, and Mary was able to sit upright and swallow some broth and small ale. The colour in her cheeks returned and the king's physicians were positive that the worst was behind her.

But within a day Mary developed a strange fever, leaving her weak and suffering from heart palpitations, and the king was warned that she would likely not survive.

But rather than become fearful for his own daughter's survival, Mary's ill health resurfaced the king's chilling fears for his own impending end.

Her likely death opened the king's eyes to the fact that the children he had – namely one young son and two illegitimate daughters – were not a strong enough dynasty to leave behind to ensure the survival of the Tudor line.

And so, while his daughter lay dying in her dark and lonely chambers, he began his search for his sixth bride.

March 1543

By some miracle the physicians could not understand, Mary's strange fever broke and after three weeks of knocking at death's door, she mysteriously regained her strength once again.

The shutters were removed from the windows one by one and when Mary felt no aversion to the lazy Spring sunlight that streamed in, she invited her ladies to take breakfast with her in the gardens below. Her body was frail and gaunt as she got dressed with the help of her new lady Catherine Parr, and she needed assistance to walk through the long halls and down the stairs to the little table in the gardens.

Once she sat down in her seat, the warm sunshine washing over her pale face, she inhaled deeply, as though she had never smelt air so crisp, "I cannot tell you how very glad I am," she admitted, "to be out of my chambers, lady Catherine."

"As are all of us, my lady!" Catherine replied, her blue eyes crinkling as she smiled, "You gave us quite a fright for a moment!"

Mary nodded, her smile gone, "I must admit it was frightening," Mary said, "I felt as though I was already dead."

Catherine waved her hand and shook her head, her pale blond eyebrows creasing together, "Let us not speak of it," she said, troubled by the ordeal they had all endured at the near loss of England's beloved Mary Tudor, "Today is about your health! And what a beautiful day it is to eat breakfast outside."

Just then, Cecily and Frances came walking towards them with two kitchen maids in tow who carried plates of food and cups of small ale with them on silver trays.

Mary smiled and invited her ladies to sit down while the servants lay the table.

"Thank God you are recovered, my lady," Frances said as she sat down, "We prayed for you every day, didn't we Cecily?"

Cecily nodded, "God smiled upon you," Cecily agreed.

"But you have missed much," Frances said then as she inched her seat closer to Mary's, her face beaming with excitement.

Cecily rolled her eyes and poured Mary a glass of small ale.

"I should hope it is good news?" Mary remarked as she took a sip from her cup.

"There is a rumour," Frances began, and Mary breathed a laugh – there was *always* a rumour – "that the king has been courting a new lady."

Mary frowned at that and narrowed her eyes at Frances, not noticing the lady Catherine stiffening slightly in her seat beside her.

"The king has been sending several letters in secret," Frances continued, "And it is said that this lady is still in her first year of widowhood."

Mary shook her head as she nibbled on a piece of bread, "I cannot imagine that he would pursue a widow," she said thoughtfully.

Cecily shrugged, "Perhaps he has learned a valuable lesson with his last queen," she said as she spooned dried fruits onto Mary's plate, "that loyalty is more important than youth. And having been married before, her virtue will have been taken by another and there is nothing further to disclose."

Mary raised her eyebrows at Cecily, "That is true," then she turned to Catherine, "What do you think of this, being a widow yourself?"

Catherine set down her cup of small ale slowly and said, "Well," she said while looking down at the plate before her, "I was very young when my first husband died and that was quite a shock, to be widowed at such a young age. Then I was betrothed to Lord Latimer shortly after my year of mourning came to an end, and we were happily married for nine years until his death – God rest his soul –" then she cleared her throat, taking a moment to reflect on the right words, "It is hard to say what a lady might do when the king of England himself has shown interest in her. Normal rules may not apply if the king wishes to marry her before her year of mourning is complete," and she shrugged lightly before taking a piece of cheese and popping it into her mouth.

"So," Frances chimed in, "you would not insist on waiting to become betrothed if the king asked you for your hand?" she asked.

"Would I," Catherine countered, "or any other lady for that matter, have a choice on the subject if the king asked?" she replied.

"No, I would assume not," Mary mumbled quietly as she nibbled on some dried fruit.

Silence befell the ladies for a moment as they all mulled over their own thoughts on the matter, and Mary breathed the fresh Spring air into her lungs once again.

Then Frances cleared her throat, "There is more news, my lady," she said, "Archbishop Cranmer has been accused of heresy."

Mary sat up in her seat immediately and blinked, "Heresy?" she parroted, the news shocking her to her core, "Accused by the king?"

"Yes," Frances replied, her eyes wide.

Mary's head whipped from side to side as she examined the faces of her other two ladies, "I do not understand," she said, "How can he accuse his Archbishop of heresy, whom the king chose himself for his protestant faith?" Mary frowned then and shook her head in disbelief as her ladies watched her silently, none of them daring to speak on the matter.

Mary scoffed, "First Cromwell and now Cranmer," she said, "two men he specifically chose for their aversion to Catholicism... one dead and now another accused of heresy," and she shook her head, "I ask you this: what does the king believe in? Can anyone tell me? Is he for or against Catholicism?"

When no one replied she pressed her fingers against her temples and closed her eyes in frustration.

Eventually, when the silence had stretched on to its limit, Catherine braved an answer.

"I imagine the king has always been a catholic at heart," she surmised, "but likes to make his own rules, and not be tied to Rome," she said quietly before clearing her throat and picking up a piece of bread, hoping that would be the end of their dangerous conversation.

Mary nodded, "That is what I have been told in the past, yes," she replied, as she remembered *senor* Chapuys' own explanation on the topic some years ago.

"But," Mary continued, ignoring her ladies' obvious discomfort at the subject, "it leaves his people without knowing what they can or cannot do. They need a clear ruler to guide them on the right path without fearing that they may be burned as heretics the next day when he changes his mind." Cecily and Frances shared a look of agreement that they knew would be too dangerous to voice, even in their own company.

Mary sat forward then, continuing quietly, "I promise you this, ladies," she whispered, "when I am Queen, my people will know exactly which religion is the right one. I will steer the people of England back to the path of righteousness. Heretics will know what is coming for them, and all who follow the true faith can rest easy knowing that I will not waver from it. There will be no more to-and-fro as there has been for so many years, and all that are of the true faith, will have nothing to fear from me."

The four ladies resumed their breakfast in silence, all of them glad to see the conversation at an end. They enjoyed the beautiful setting and the warm sun above them for a moment when Frances abruptly broke the silence, unable to contain the rest of her information.

"Cranmer has not yet been convicted," she said as she chewed on a piece of cheese.

"What?" Mary said and she frowned in frustration at the continuous interruptions to her peace of mind.

Frances pressed her lips together and glanced at Cecily who replied wordlessly for her to go on with a wave of her hand.

"He has been forgiven," Frances explained, "He has been accepted back into the king's confidence after he was made to acknowledge the changes proposed to revise the Bishop's Book – now to be called The King's Book."

"The King's Book?" Mary replied.

Frances nodded but it was Cecily who replied, "The king has essentially rewritten the Bishop's Book and renamed it."

"Is that all?" Mary asked as she looked from one lady to another.

"You'll be glad to know," Cecily continued, "that the king has re-established most of the earlier Roman Catholic doctrines which the earlier published version, the Bishop's Book, had denied."

Mary raised her eyebrows as she finally understood, "That is why my father accused Archbishop Cranmer of heresy!" she said, "For not accepting the king's reinstated Roman Catholic dogmas."

Cecily smiled at Mary as she finally realised that things were looking positive for her future as a Catholic yet again.

"He is returning to the catholic ways?" Mary whispered then, fearful that to say it aloud might curse it from becoming true.

"To reunite with Rome is unlikely," Cecily said, "But it is a step in the right direction."

Mary nodded but remained silent as she tried to absorb all this new information. And while her mind could not fully comprehend the whys and wherefores of these new changes, she was nonetheless overjoyed.

Between this news, the king's new alliance with Spain and talks of England's Peace Treaty with Scotland, Mary was suddenly extremely hopeful for the future.

July 1543

Mary stared wide-eyed at the lady-turned-queen that stood before her, "It was you?" she asked incredulously, "You who my father had been secretly courting during your period of mourning?"

Catherine Parr took a step towards her, "He asked me not to speak of it," she said in her own defence.

Though the revelation came as a shock to Mary, she did not resent her newest lady, for just like their mothers before them, Mary and Catherine had formed a strong friendship and Mary believed that of all her stepmothers, this one would finally be worthy of the title.

The ceremony was a small one for a royal wedding, but it being the king's sixth and Catherine's third, they felt there was no need for a grand occasion.

Henry's children were all present and that alone gave Catherine so much joy, that she cared for little else.

Having had no children of her own from her previous marriages, she secretly held little hope for the creation of any more royal heirs from her womb. And so, she decided that to make up for her assumed inabilities, she would do her best as their assigned stepmother to remind the king of *all* his children's worths, and that every one of them was as special as the other, male or female.

The new queen wasted no time in requesting that her new stepchildren be more present at court, and that they be shown the love and affection they so desperately craved.

Henry, newlywed and besotted, took no offence to the suggestion that they had not received such love from him in the past, and took only from it that his new wife cared for his children as though they were her own, making her all the more attractive to him.

Soon after, the lady Elizabeth and Prince Edward were invited to attend court during the Christmastide, and Catherine could not wait to get to know her youngest stepchildren better.

December 1543

Without warning, Scottish parliament rejected the Greenwich Peace Treaty with England, which had stipulated that neither king shall make or procure war upon the other or his confederates. The Treaty has also sanctioned the terms for a marriage alliance between Prince Edward to the new-born Mary of Scots, which too was denied with the rejection of the Treaty.

King Henry reeled over the humiliation of the Scots' denial and his anger soon doubled when word came that Scotland had reinstated their old alliance with France.

But the bliss from his latest marriage quickly mellowed his temper and Henry did not linger in his anger for long, for his new wife gave him great reason to be happy.

"It is different this time, Charles," Henry admitted as the two men walked slowly through the courtyard, Henry's large frame unable to walk at any other speed, "My attraction for her is not only of the body as it had been for Anne Boleyn and Kathryn Howard," and his lips curled with hatred at the mention of the two women who he believed had scorned him so deeply, "Her ability to worship me – I must admit I had missed the spiritual side of marriage," and the rotund king allowed a quick thought of his first wife, Katherine of Aragon, whom had loved him faithfully until the end.

Charles nodded as they continued walking along the path and towards the target which was being set up by the servants for their target practice.

"But unlike my first wife," Henry said abruptly, as though Charles could read his mind, "Catherine does not question my supreme acumen. But she challenges it in ways I have never expected from a mere woman," he raised his grey eyebrows, which creased his forehead with several wrinkles, "and I am pleased to admit it is making me a better man."

Charles smiled at his old friend and slapped him warmly on his fat shoulder, "I am happy for you, your majesty," he said.

The aged men picked up their bows and colour-tipped arrows to begin their leisurely game.

As they took their turns shooting arrows at the target, Charles considered Henry's size and ill-health, and he wondered if perhaps the king had finally embraced the spiritual side of marriage due to his increasing inability to copulate with his wife.

When the king's younger children arrived at court for the Christmastide and he saw how his queen's face beamed with joy to see them all, his chest visibly filled with pride for what he had created. Though he had experienced much disappointment in his former marriages, he could admit to one thing: that the children he had produced from them, were children to be proud of, and for that at least he would remain grateful to the three wives that had borne them.

The Christmas festivities were much the same as every year. The king and queen welcomed their guests, nobles and

301

courtiers as well as their families, and received and gave gifts as they sat upon their thrones. The atmosphere was light and jolly, with the scent of spiced oranges circling throughout the castle, and once it was time for the feast, the musicians played cheerful songs, and everyone was merry.

The king and queen sat with all his children beside them at the high table, sending plates of food out to their favourites as the servants kept their wine cups full all day.

When the plates were cleared away and people began filling up the dancefloor, queen Catherine bid her stepchildren to dance, and they each took turns while the others remained at their father's side.

It was while prince Edward was dancing with his new stepmother, and the lady Elizabeth was being twirled around by Sir Thomas Seymour – one of the late queen Jane's brothers – that Henry turned to Mary beside him with a warm smile on his aged face.

"I have one last gift for you, my daughter," he said.

Mary, who had been watching the ten-year-old Elizabeth laugh and dance as she spun around the room, turned to face her father, "Another gift?"

The king nodded once, "I am restoring you and your sister, to the line of succession," he said as he looked over the crowd of courtiers before him, and Mary's face froze in shock.

She could do nothing but stare as her mouth hung agape in complete surprise, and when the king turned back to gauge her response he laughed aloud at her expression, "You mustn't be so surprised," he said, as though Mary was foolish, "Surely you always knew that this day would one day come."

Mary shook her head and swallowed her shock, "I – I did not dare to hope," she stammered, her heart soaring at the prospect that her father *did* love her after all.

"Well, it does not mean much," he suddenly said as he waved his hand, as though to clear the air of some

302

misunderstanding, "Edward will still be king after me, and his children will succeed him and so on. You and Elizabeth are still bastards after all. It is merely a precaution."

And just like that Mary's heart dropped and her throat tightened, "Of course," she croaked.

"Parliament has already passed it," Henry continued matter-of-factly, "but it will come into effect in the year to come."

Mary was only able to nod in response, but then she said, "Does Elizabeth know?"

"Not yet," the king shrugged, "You may tell her if you wish. As I said, it does not mean much since it does not deny either of your illegitimacies. But as it will come to pass, it is only right that you know."

Mary smiled, "Thank you, lord father," she said, and she pecked his fat cheek as she knew he would have expected, "It is the greatest gift. And I am sure Elizabeth will think so too."

Henry nodded once and shifted uncomfortably in his seat, the movement wafting the rotten stench of his putrid leg into the air around him, "You can thank the queen too," he said as he frowned through the pain in his leg, "She has been yours and Elizabeth's biggest advocate and has recently convinced me that daughters can be of use after all."

The snide remark pierced her heart, but Mary smiled and nodded, "I shall be sure to thank her majesty," she said, and she looked over at the queen as she danced with prince Edward.

Mary sat beside her father in silence as they watched everyone around them dancing, flirting, and laughing, and it dawned on Mary that, though she had finally heard the words she had so longed to hear, it did not fill the void in her heart in the way she had imagined it would.

Despite her restoration to the line of succession she still felt empty inside and all of a sudden, after years of playing the perfect daughter, she could no longer contain herself and she turned sharply to face the king.

"Did you ever love me, father?" she asked, her heart pumping uncontrollably inside her chest, "Or was I just always a pawn for you to use for your political advances?"

The king stared at her, his bloodshot eyes searching her face for the slightest hint that she might be jesting, but Mary only stared back, her mouth drawn in a tight line and her back as straight as an arrow.

"Mary," he said slowly as he put down his cup of wine, "The moment you were born was just another disappointment in a long line of disappointments that I had to endure while married to your mother," he said emotionlessly, "But as you grew healthy and strong and overcame your first year, I did grow to love you, yes."

It was not the exact answer Mary had hoped for, but she was not altogether shocked, "Then why have you treated me as you have, if you had any love for me?"

The king shrugged his broad shoulders, "Daughter, you will never understand the burdens of a king," he said, "The Tudor line that I inherited was *weak* and your mother promised me the strength of Spain and the safety of a nursery full of boys! When all our children died and I was left with only you – a *girl* – what was I to do with that but act logically?" he stuffed a handful of sweetmeats in his mouth and continued, "Princesses are betrothed to secure alliances, that is how it is in this world."

Mary scoffed and shook her head, "But that is not what I am referring to," she replied bravely.

Her father looked at her sideways, "Careful now, Mary," he warned, "You may be restored today but I can change my mind tomorrow."

They both fell silent as the musicians finished one song and began another.

Then, to Mary's surprise, the king continued quietly, "You were the only light during a dark time in my life, Mary" he admitted quietly, his voice softened with sentiment, "and I loved you for what you represented. Your survival meant that I was able to have healthy children…but you were still only a girl," he said, and he picked up his cup and took a gulp. Then he licked his lips and belched, the tender moment over in an instant, "And a man will always love his sons more than his daughters, it is nothing personal."

Mary blinked – she finally had her answer; and to her surprise, she did not feel as heartbroken and lost as she had always assumed she would, for deep down in her subconscious Mary had always known the truth.

Hearing the words spoken aloud did not leave her feeling desolate, but rather, they filled her with relief. Mary would no longer need to search for something within her father that he could not give; and though it ached her heart, she could finally let her father go.

Just then little Edward bowed to the queen mid-song and excused himself from the dancefloor, and Mary took it as an opportunity to escape her father's presence.

She excused herself abruptly and hurried to the floor, grabbed her stepmother's hands and squeezed them once in greeting as they fell into step with the others, "The king has just told me about mine and Elizabeth's restoration," Mary said above the loud music.

Catherine smiled warmly at her friend and stepdaughter, "It is the least I could do," she said.

"Why?" Mary asked, "Why would you risk yourself for Elizabeth and I?" Mary asked as they hopped side by side in step with the other courtiers.

"Mary, I merely voiced what the king already knew himself," Catherine replied, "I did very little, in fact. The king wished for it regardless."

305

Mary looked over at the fat king as he sat on his throne, "I don't understand why you would do this before you had your own child with the king."

Catherine smiled sadly and lowered her voice, "Mary, I have been married twice before and have never produced a child," she stopped as they stepped away from one another in step with the dance until they joined hands again, "I am not sure I am even able to have children," she whispered.

"Shh!" Mary whispered back sharply, "You must never say such a thing again if you wish to keep your head," and they both looked at the king at the same time, who nodded and raised his cup at them. Catherine smiled at him sweetly while Mary blinked and looked away.

"I am grateful," Mary said then, "More than you could imagine. It has been my greatest wish that this day would eventually come."

As the musicians played their final note, and the courtiers bowed and curtsied to one another, Mary curtsied as low as she was able, her dress ballooning at the sides as she bent her knees, and bowed her head at her queen, "Thank you, your majesty," she said once she had straightened up, "I am in your debt."

March 1544

The Third Act of Succession gained Royal Assent at the close of Parliament at the end of February, and officially re-established Mary and her half-sister Elizabeth to the line of succession.

Mary cried tears of joy as she heard the news and immediately commissioned for a portrait of herself to be painted by the excellent Master John, as a gift for her father.

She knew it was a small thing compared to the enormous gift he had bestowed onto her, and though the king had himself admitted it had been done merely for precautionary measures, and that she and Elizabeth were still proclaimed bastards, Mary took it as a firm step in the right direction which would one day see her on the throne of England.

Chapter 16

May 1544
Greenwich Palace, London

"Men are such strange creatures," Queen Catherine said with a laugh as she and Mary walked leisurely through the palace gardens, "I mean, how does the king and the Earl of Hertford expect the Scots to react to this invasion?"

Prince Edward's uncle and eldest brother to the late queen Jane Seymour, had, with the king's permission, sent a small army to rage war on Scotland in an attempt to force the Scots to reconsider their alliance through the betrothal of six-year-old Edward and the infant Mary, Queen of Scots. A political move Mary and her stepmother, the queen, could not understand.

Mary giggled and raised her eyebrows, "The Earl's pride has been bruised," she said, "As prince Edward's uncle he took it as a personal attack that they reneged the Greenwich Peace Treaty. Although, I must admit," she added, "The engagement of Edward to their Mary, Queen of Scots, would have been a great match."

Catherine shook her head, "I am surprised that the king would be onboard with it," she said quietly, "With his planned invasion of France on the horizon, we need all the men we can muster."

They walked in silence for a while, appreciating the beautiful flower beds.

"I fear for your father," Catherine said then, breaking their comfortable silence, "He is not a young man, but he is acting as though he is," Mary did not reply for fear of saying the wrong thing, but the queen continued despite receiving no reply, "I am not ready to lose him."

Mary looked at her stepmother then, surprised to hear genuine concern in her voice, "You do care for him then?"

"I do," Catherine admitted with a smile and then took Mary's arm before linking it with hers as they walked together side by side.

"The men of this world will do as they wish," she said in conclusion, "and we as women must accept their reasons, even though we may not agree or even understand them."

Mary nodded but could not help but disagree in secret – she believed women were just as able to understand the likes of war as any man and that, unlike men, women would not be tempted by the egotistical reasons for war.

But, at the same time, Mary understood her father's need for this invasion of Scotland and France at this stage of his life. He wished to be remembered for more than just beheading and divorcing, and he no doubt believed that this French war would be his final hurrah; his final attempt at being remembered in the history books.

For to be known throughout the ages for a great deed during their reign was a monarch's greatest achievement.

And *that* Mary could absolutely understand!

July 1544

The war on France had begun and shortly thereafter England's troops would siege the city of Boulogne under the command of Charles Brandon, the duke of Suffolk.

It was a great success for such an early stage of the invasion, and it filled the English troops with hope for a swift return home. Cunning methods were implemented to approach the central castle of Boulogne, the English troops digging tunnels and invading from underneath, and the French surrendered it in September.

King Henry rode back to England, leaving the dukes of Norfolk and Suffolk to defend it.

But Spain, being led by the untrustworthy Holy Roman Emperor Charles V, soon broke their alliance with England when they made a separate peace treaty with France; and in October – with the help of Spain's army – France attempted to retake Boulogne in king Henry's absence.

"It is an outrage!" Henry bellowed as he banged his fat fist down on the table in his chambers, "Suffolk and Norfolk should not have allowed this to happen!"

The handful of councilmen who were present did not respond, all of them clerks, and not men of war, who knew little about how to defend a sieged city.

Henry's bloodshot and angry eyes searched the room for something to eat, and as he saw a bowl of sugared grapes, he grabbed a handful and stuffed them into his mouth, "We should send more men to strengthen our hold on Boulogne," he said through his full mouth.

The king's secretary, Sir Ralph Sadler, then raised his head, "We don't have many more men to spare, your majesty," he said as he held documents before him, "The troops we sent from Scotland were all we had available. If we send any more, we will have none left to defend us here in London."

"Argh!" Henry exclaimed as he threw his hands in the air, "Just get out! All of you!" he commanded and watched as they one by one stood and fled the room.

Just then, as the king sat down heavily on his chair and covered his face with his hands, his queen emerged from the shadows, "You were victorious, my love," she said as she stroked his great back with her small hand, "Boulogne is ours."

Henry shook his head, "Boulogne is a great success, but the troops are depleted," and he turned to look at her, "We won't be able to gain more territory without more men."

310

Catherine exhaled and sat down, "What can be done?" she asked as she frowned.

"Nothing, woman, don't you see!" the king exploded, "Norfolk and Suffolk have left Boulogne in the care of some four-thousand men to defend the city, and have withdrawn the rest of the English army to Calais – our only English territory within France. Now they are trapped! Which leaves Boulogne easy pickings for the French to retake."

Catherine sat in silence, trying to understand the situation as well as trying to stay calm in the face of the king's anger.

Henry steepled his fingers and closed his eyes, "If this siege fails, what will I be remembered for?" he whispered.

Catherine swallowed, "You will be remembered as a mighty king," she said carefully, "who did his best for his country, and shepherded his people away from the darkness of Rome and allowed them to think for themselves. You will be remembered as the greatest king to ever have lived – the golden prince of Christendom."

The king knew flattery when he heard it, but he was not one to pass up an opportunity when it was presented to him, "Come wife," he said as he stood and grabbed his queen by the arm, "If I cannot take France as intended, I shall take you instead."

Catherine giggled, as she knew he would have hoped, "But Henry, it is broad daylight!" she said in mock refusal.

But his temper suddenly returned, "Be quiet, Catherine," he growled, the playfulness in his tone abruptly replaced with menace.

Catherine stared at him and swallowed, her eyes wide with fear at his tone, "My lord?" she said as she watched him lay down on his bed and fumbled with the tie of his breeches.

"Straddle me, woman," he commanded icily, and Catherine forced herself not to show her disgust as he lay on the bed, his belly protruded and his ulcerous leg oozing into the tightly wrapped bandage.

"I shall have a son from you yet," he said as he awkwardly removed his breeches and began tugging on his limp manhood to evoke an erection, "After all, that is what you are here for."

February 1545

The Earl of Hertford Edward Seymour, and the English army that was posted in Scotland, were the only remaining resources Henry had to make sure the French invasion would not be for nought.

And so, when the English troops in France had begun to deplete, Seymour and his army were finally told to abandon their position in Scotland and make their way to France.

It was this decision that made all the difference, for when France sent in their counterattack, the English army, reinforced with new men, was strong enough to defeat them.

It was another small victory for England in their fight against the French.

It did, however, cost England greatly in Scotland, for the small remaining English army that was left behind to defend the borders, was easily defeated by the Scots in Ancrum.

The king was in a foul mood.

No one and nothing could make him smile and Catherine was suddenly on high alert, careful to walk softly and to never speak unless spoken to. She knew all too well that the king's bad mood led to the people around him meeting terrible ends, and she would do anything to avoid such a fate as his previous queens had encountered.

She and Mary spent a lot of time together, both avoiding the king's presence whenever possible, and they would both visit Catherine's younger stepchildren at their residences.

Queen Catherine – having been correct as to her inability to conceive – invested all her love and attention into her husband's children, and over the years she had made sure to

312

have a strong connection with each of them, showering them with gifts and love, as well as taking a keen interest in their education.

And though the king was often angry and restless, Catherine did all that was expected of her.

She was a truly regal queen: courteous and loved by many, and she did her duty as graciously as possible while the king spiralled further and further into the darkest depths of his aging mind.

August 1545
Guildford, Surrey

"What is wrong, my love?" Charles Brandon's fourth wife, Catherine, asked as he sat down heavily by the window in their chambers at their residence in Guildford.

"Nothing," he replied, "I am well."

"You are not," she insisted as she placed the back of her hand over her sixty-one-year-old husband's forehead.

"I shall lie down," he said, "If it will cease your worrying," and he stood from his seat with difficulty, his legs quivering beneath him as he tried to stand.

"Hold my arm," his wife offered, which he willingly accepted as his head felt suddenly heavy.

Catherine led him to their bed and gently lay his head on the feather pillows, then she covered him with the blankets and left to fetch a cold cloth to mop his sweaty brow.

When she returned Catherine gently dabbed at his clammy forehead and when she noticed he did not stir, she left, assuming that he had fallen asleep.

Greenwich Palace, London

"A message for his majesty," a young man said as he handed a note to the queen, and she could tell from his face that it was not good news.

Catherine Parr took the note and dismissed her ladies, having learned that the king received bad news better in private.

"For you, my lord," she said carefully as she handed him the letter.

Henry took it without looking up from the documents before him, and tore open the seal, "Who from?" he asked, still not looking up.

"I –" Catherine began but then the king's face dropped as he read the words upon the page.

"Charles," he whispered as the blood drained from his face.

Catherine stood frozen as her husband read the news that his life-long friend and confidant had unexpectedly died that afternoon.

And though she had seen him through wars and childless disappointments, Catherine knew that this would be the thing that would sink her husband into a deep misery, one from which he would likely never recover.

February 1547

The king never did recover from the deeply saddening loss of his oldest and dearest friend, and over the following years he did little else but eat and sleep. Occasionally he would summon his queen in a fruitless attempt to put a baby inside her, but even he knew that it was all in vain – his final wife being as useless to produce male heirs as four others before her had been.

During the winter months king Henry, at the age of fifty-five, became increasingly unwell, the years of over-indulgence of rich foods in large quantities having finally caught up with him, and between his increasing weight and his festering leg, his body and mind had begun to deteriorate.

He decided to retire to his beloved residence at Whitehall Palace until he was fully recovered and left his wife behind at Greenwich Palace to host and entertain the court in his absence.

The king had not been gone long when Mary had awoken one morning feeling strangely serene – a feeling which she could not justify – but she had shrugged it off as nothing and had gone about her day as usual, mentioning it to no one.

It was only later that afternoon when Mary and queen Catherine sat before the roaring fire in the queen's chambers while reading their bibles in companiable silence, that Mary would get her answer.

They heard the horse hooves first and registered by their speed that something urgent had happened. The two ladies looked up from their bibles and searched the faces of their ladies-in-waiting for an answer, but all shook their heads or shrugged, as clueless as their mistresses.

Suddenly there was a commotion from behind the door, and they heard several pairs of footsteps hurrying through the stone hallways towards the queen's chambers.

Mary and Catherine looked at each other, then rose to receive their unannounced visitors.

Mary brushed down her skirts and cleared her throat before raising her head high, and she realised yet again that even now, as heavy footsteps raced towards them, she felt simply at ease.

The guards opened the doors to the queen's chambers and three messengers entered breathing heavily, all of them covered in dirt and sweat from riding their horses as quickly as they could.

Immediately upon entering, they all took off their hats and bent at the knee before Mary and Catherine.

"Forgive the intrusion, your majesty," the messenger at the head said, "But we bring urgent news."

"What has happened?" Catherine asked with a hint of hysteria, "Is it the king?"

"The king is dead," the same messenger replied heavily, "Died in his sleep last night."

Suddenly Mary felt her knees give way and she grabbed the back of her chair to steady herself.

She looked over at her stepmother who had covered her mouth with her hand and as she looked back at the messengers she felt as though everything was moving in slow motion.

"The Earl of Hertford," the messenger continued as all three of them remained on bended knee, "has ridden off to fetch Prince Edward to London. He is to be crowned as soon as possible," he said swiftly, but to Mary it felt as though his words stretched on and on.

She saw her vision blur as her heart raced within her chest, and she gripped the back of the chair tightly with her hands, her knuckles whitening under the strain.

But despite her body's shock at the news, her mind was as clear as the skies on a summer's day, and she finally understood that the inner peace she had felt all day had been her soul breaking free of the lifetime of tyranny it had been put under by her father's existence.

Somehow, deep within her subconscious, Mary had known that her father had finally departed this earth.

After all, Mary had awaited this moment eagerly for two decades, ever since he had disowned her most regal and gracious mother; and though she knew that a part of her would grieve the loss of the father she had once known when she was but a little girl, the woman she had become knew that it would be a short-lived period of mourning.

And now, though her younger brother was yet to be crowned king, she had the distinct feeling that a crown was being gently placed upon her head.

Upon king Henry VIII's death, his only son, prince Edward, was crowned the next king of England at the tender age of only nine-years-old.

Being but a child, he would rule under the regency of his council, which was largely dominated by Protestants, and it did not take long for Mary, a devout Catholic, to once again feel unwelcome at court.

She decided, for her safety as well as her sanity, to move herself and her household into her newly inherited estate left to her by the late king, Hunsdon House, and it was there that she would enjoy her newfound tranquillity, away from the prying eyes that wondered why she did not mourn her father's passing.

At the late king's grand funeral, Mary had worn the traditional black gown and veil, she had shed one genuine tear of sadness for the father she had wished he had been, and she had maintained a solemn attitude throughout the entirety of her time at court. But as soon as her brother had been crowned and she was able to leave London, Mary no longer pretended to grieve this new chapter in her life.

The time for solemnity was over, for until the young king married and produced an heir, she would be the highest-ranking lady in all of England once more.

And after all the years of waiting, Mary was right back to where she belonged: as next in line to the throne.

May 1547
Chelsea Palace, London

It felt like a totally different world since the late king's passing, as England and its people began to readjust to the new order of things.

After so many years of uncertainty whether Protestantism was legal practice or not, it came as a breath of fresh air to the reformers when King Edward VI assented the throne as the first king to have been raised a Protestant.

Catherine Parr, now the Dowager Queen, was one of those reformers that was finally able to openly acknowledge her beliefs without the fear of divorce or worse, and she openly supported the new king, her stepson, in this.

But England's new path did not sit right with Mary, and she feared for the people as more and more betrayed the catholic practices and chose to forsake their soul. It filled her with such contempt that, when she was invited to Catherine's newly inherited residence at Chelsea Palace for supper, she could not help but rage about it.

"It is an atrocity," Mary voiced openly, "what the king's council are allowing in his name," she said as Catherine's servants placed plates of food along the dining table.

Catherine, who had invited both Mary and Elizabeth to dine with her, cleared her throat and turned away from Mary, "Shall we eat?" she said, hoping to avoid Mary's obvious resentment on the matter.

Elizabeth, now thirteen-years-old, smiled at her stepmother, "I am pleased to be here, Catherine," she said sweetly, her light red eyebrows raised, "Thank you for the invitation."

"You are always welcome, Elizabeth," Catherine replied as they each took their seats.

But Mary's expression was still twisted in anger and as her cup was filled with wine, she snatched it and took a large gulp.

Catherine took some samples from the plates of food before her and proceeded to offer them to her stepdaughters, "Please eat," she said, and they both filled their plates.

"I hope you do not find me impolite," Elizabeth said after a short silence, "But I have noticed that you are no longer in your black mourning dress," and the young girl looked up from her plate, her doe eyes questioning, "Ought it not be a year before a widow proceeds to wearing her normal attire?"

Catherine slowly placed her fork down and wiped her mouth with a handkerchief as Mary too looked up from her food and frowned in confusion, not having noticed the Dowager Queen's lack of mourning gown until now, and she was suddenly utterly perplexed by what she was seeing.

"Catherine?" Mary asked, "What is going on?"

Catherine took a deep breath, "Well," she said slowly, "This is the reason why I invited you both here today. I am no longer wearing my mourning dress because I am no longer in mourning."

"But you are in your widowhood," Mary pointed out as she looked from her stepmother to her young sister. Elizabeth met her gaze with a sideways glance which suddenly reminded Mary of Elizabeth's mother, and she looked away quickly, "You are to mourn for a year."

Catherine nodded, "While that is true, I came out of mourning early once before if you remember? To marry the king."

Mary raised an eyebrow but said nothing.

Catherine looked at Elizabeth who quickly averted her gaze and continued eating slowly.

"I have news I wish to share with you," Catherine said after a sigh, "And I hope with all my heart that you can be happy for me, for I have re-married, and I have never been as happy as this in all my life."

Mary dropped her fork and her mouth fell open in shock as Elizabeth jumped up from her seat and embraced Catherine, a wide smile spread across her pale face.

As Mary watched her half-sister and her former stepmother embrace each other, she felt her stomach churn, "How could you?" she said incredulously.

Catherine looked over at her friend, "Mary," she said, "I know this won't be easy to hear but I am in love, and I have been for years. I did my duty by marrying the king and I was a good wife to him and a good queen to the country. But I am getting older, and I could not wait another year before I began living the life I wanted. I believe I deserve this time now, to be happy."

"You were queen of England," Mary pointed out acidly, "What more could you have wanted?"

"Being queen was not my choice," Catherine explained, "It was never what I would have wanted for myself. But I accepted your father's proposal, as was expected of me, and I devoted my life to him while he was with us, God rest his soul. But he is gone. And it is my time to be selfish."

Mary scoffed, "You are right," she said as she stood up abruptly, her chair scratching at the wooden floorboards, "It is selfish. But above that, it is disrespectful. I cannot believe that Edward would have given his permission for this union!"

Catherine looked away, "We did not ask..." she admitted, and Mary shook her head.

"How could you?" she raged, "Not only is it against the law to marry without the king's consent, but to marry so soon after our father's passing is a besmirchment of his memory! As a former queen of England how could you undermine the crown's authority like this?"

Catherine closed her eyes and raised her hand, "I knew you would see it that way," she said calmly, "but I wanted you both to find out from me before you heard it as gossip. You deserve to know the truth. And the truth is that I married for love, and I have no remorse."

Mary could do nothing more but stare in disbelief.

"Who is it?" Elizabeth then said as she turned to face Catherine once again, her pretty face beaming with excitement, "Who is it that you love more than any other?"

Catherine smiled and breathed in deeply, "It is Thomas Seymour," she said, and Mary watched as her face beamed with joy and her cheeks reddened with passion, "He is my husband, and we are happy."

The young king's own uncle, Mary thought.

"It is so romantic," Elizabeth sighed as she resumed her seat beside Catherine.

Mary stood there, watching the newly married Lady Seymour and her half-sister as they smiled at each other idiotically, and she shook her head at them, "You are a fool, Catherine."

"Mary!" Elizabeth exclaimed in shock then.

"She is, Elizabeth!" Mary replied hotly, "Married for love? The king and his council will not take this news well no matter what reason she married for!" then she turned to Catherine, "I will be the first to admit that my father was not a kind father and as we can all attest, he was not a good husband."

Elizabeth dropped her gaze as she thought of her mother, but Mary continued, "But this betrayal to his memory – it is a distinct lack of respect for our late king and the monarchy, and I will not stand for it," and with that, Mary turned on her heel and left her former stepmother and friend, whom she had so greatly admired, behind, never to see her again.

As Mary had predicted, king Edward and his council were most displeased with the former queen of England for marrying not only without the king's consent but also to have married so soon after the late king's passing.

The little king himself, though young and naïve in matters of the world, could clearly understand that his stepmother's actions directly undermined the monarchy's authority. And with it already being at its most vulnerable this early on in his reign, it came as a shock to him that his stepmother would be the one to deal such a blow.

The fact that her chosen husband was the king's very own uncle, was of little consequence and the newlyweds were reprimanded and shunned from court life.

January 1548
Hunsdon House, Hertfordshire

"She's gone to live with Catherine and Thomas Seymour?" Mary exclaimed as she looked up from the letter in her hands.

Cecily, who had been embroidering beside her, looked up from her work, "Who, my lady?"

"Elizabeth!" Mary snapped, "Catherine has taken guardianship of her, and she is residing with them at her estate at Chelsea Palace."

"Perhaps it is for the best?" Cecily offered as she shrugged her shoulders, "The lady Elizabeth needs a parent to look after her in her final years of girlhood."

"But that woman has proven herself to be completely rotten at the core," Mary said, "She has allowed her bodily wants to sully her good name. Elizabeth should not be made to surround herself with such people."

Mary stomach dropped then as she heard her own hypocrisy aloud, having given herself to a man who was not her husband for the sake of love. But she pushed the damning thought aside and swallowed the bile that had begun to rise in her throat.

"From what I have heard they are all rather happy with the arrangement," Frances piped up from behind them as she approached.

"What do you mean?" Mary asked as Frances took a seat.

Her lady raised an eyebrow, "Only that Thomas Seymour seems to be enjoying the power he now holds," she remarked knowingly, "with the second in line to the throne living under his roof."

Mary frowned, "Whatever could he be planning?" she asked, her forehead creasing in thought, "He is not clever enough to be a threat to my brother."

Frances shrugged, "I do not suggest he is hatching an elaborate plan, my lady," she said as she picked up a needle and threat, "It is much simpler than that."

"What?" Mary snapped, and Cecily sighed deeply beside her, clearly vexed by Frances' gossip-mongering.

Frances leaned forward, "Rumour has it," she whispered dramatically, though no one else was present, "that Sir Thomas Seymour is madly in love with the young lady."

Mary's face drained of colour, but she shook her head, "With Elizabeth?!" she exclaimed, "That is preposterous. Of course he is not. He is in love with Catherine. They have only just married!"

Frances leaned back in her seat and shrugged, "I only repeat what I have heard."

"What gives you the idea that rumour is even worth repeating?" Cecily interjected; her expression completely bored.

Frances looked from Cecily to Mary, "Maybe not all that I hear is truthful, but I can assure you some things are," then she dropped her gaze, suddenly uncomfortable.

323

Mary watched as her friend casually picked at a loose threat on her skirts, and she knew that whatever Frances was trying to hold back would be news worth hearing.

"What is it, Frances?" Mary prompted.

Frances looked up, her eyes wide, and she inhaled deeply, "I am not sure I should be the one to share this news with you, my lady," she admitted, "It should come from the lady Catherine herself."

"The lady Catherine has not told me yet and somehow you know," Mary pointed out, her auburn eyebrows shooting up in annoyance, "So perhaps you should just tell me."

Frances looked at Cecily, who nodded once in silent reply that she should go on.

"Catherine is with child," Frances said.

"Oh," Mary simply said as she remembered what Catherine had shared with her on the dancefloor some years ago, and her belief that she may never have children of her own; and yet, in her fourth marriage and on her thirty-sixth year of life, she had succeeded. And though their friendship had died, Mary could not help but feel happy for her former stepmother.

"You are not upset, my lady?" Frances asked.

"Upset?" Mary replied and then sighed, "While I do not condone her marrying without the king's consent, and doing so so shortly after my father's passing," Mary said pensively, "I must admit I am pleased to hear the news," she admitted, while simultaneously feeling a pinch of jealousy at Catherine's good fortune to have been queen of England *and* be able to marry for love and bear a child, "She always was a wonderful mother figure to all her stepchildren, including the two from her second husband, Lord Latimer, and though we were of a similar age, even to me," then she cleared her throat, "I will not say that I forgive her. But I can admit Catherine will make a wonderful mother to her baby. I shall write to congratulate her," and she walked over to her writing desk.

As she put quill to parchment, she almost forgot about what had irked her the year before and she wished her former stepmother nothing but love and happiness.

As Mary handed the sealed letter to her messenger and watched him ride off in a cloud of dust, she revelled in the hope that she too would one day have such luck as to bear a child, despite having surpassed her best childbearing years. If Catherine's journey had taught her anything it was that it was never too late to fall in love, marry and even to conceive, and that she may yet find the happiness she had been denied for so long.

September 1548

Though they had not seen each other since Mary had stormed out the night that Catherine had announced her marriage to Sir Thomas Seymour, Mary's world came crashing down when she received the news of lady Catherine's passing.

Her friend, confidant and favourite stepmother had died of childbed fever just days after giving birth to her much longed-for baby girl, whom she had named for Mary in her final moments of consciousness.

Mary sunk into a deep sorrow upon hearing the news, engulfed by the guilt she felt for the way she had reacted at Catherine's marriage announcement, and for never having visited her during her pregnancy.

Catherine had always been a loyal and caring friend, one whom had stood by her and spoken for her, and who had always had Mary's interests at heart; and despite not having seen her in over a year, the world felt darker and colder without her in it.

She had not deserved such a fate as to be left to die a peasant's death, which according to the mutterings of servants, could have been avoided with proper postnatal care. The former queen of England, whom the king himself had ordered to keep the queen's jewels upon his death, would have had excellent care provided for her, if only her husband and master had arranged it.

Mary's mind took a dark turn during her state of depression, and as she lay wallowing in her darkened bedchambers, her mind began to suspect the worst. For perhaps Frances had been right? Perhaps this had all been Seymour's plan all along... to inherit Catherine's fortunes as Dowager Queen and achieve a higher rank upon marrying her, then to leave her to die at his earliest convenience...so that he may marry Elizabeth?

But Mary could only speculate, her anguished mind desperate to find someone to blame for this appalling affair. But there was no one to blame, and her death was ruled as a faultless tragedy, for to the world, Sir Thomas Seymour was an anguished widower, left to raise a daughter alone after the loss of his dearest wife.

It took Mary a long time to come to terms with her loss, a long time in which she prayed and reflected. And as she asked for God's guidance, Mary was left with no other explanation than that it had been God's wish, and that He had decided that it had been Catherine's time.

For when God calls on you, there is nothing left to do, but to answer.

January 1549

It had been two years since Mary had been to London to see her little brother, the king.

Ever since Edward's coronation and the rise to power of his Lord Protector – his uncle Edward Seymour – Mary had felt pushed aside and belittled for her staunch belief in the

Catholic faith, and even though she had retreated to her new estates to remain out of sight, it seemed there would be no escaping the terrible things that were developing throughout the country, and Mary had begun to secretly consider if perhaps she would be safer elsewhere entirely.

"There is rioting in Cornwall," Frances told Mary softly as they made their way through the halls of Hunsdon House on their way to Mass, "There is open hostility towards the new prayer book."

"Of course there is," Mary whispered back, "It is blasphemous! To replace the Bible with that Book of Common Prayer as the sole legal form of worship is...*ungodly!*" Mary shook her head, "My father left the door to reform ajar during his reign and we all saw the chaos it created. But now... Edward has blown it wide open, and I fear for what is to come next."

"The king's Act of Uniformity is giving me greater fear than anything your lord father ever did," Frances added as she crossed herself at the entrance of the chapel, "I cannot believe the king would allow for the Lord Protector to abolish Catholic Mass!"

"The king is too young to have an opinion on religious doctrine," Mary whispered, "This is all the work of the Lord Protector and his council. I will write to my cousin the Holy Roman Emperor and ask that he intervene on my behalf on this matter. I cannot simply lay down and allow these heretics to destroy all that I have left to treasure."

It was not long before Mary received a reply from her cousin, King Charles V, Holy Roman Emperor, that he had done as she requested and had written to the Lord Protector, that any attempt to prevent Mary from hearing Mass would not be tolerated by him or any of her other relatives. It gave Mary great pleasure to know that she still had some support after losing everyone else she had held dear. And as she waited to hear from the king's council, she continued to attend Mass at her leisure, while the rest of the country was being punished with immediate imprisonment upon doing the same.

March 1549
Greenwich Palace, London

"It could amount to a war," the Lord Protector, Edward Seymour, insisted to the king's council, "If we do not appease king Charles V on this, England could be faced with a war with Spain, and we are not strong enough to fight back," his piercing green eyes searched the faces of the young king's advisors.

"Over this matter there really cannot be any exception," John Dudley said calmly, "The lady Mary has always been stubborn," to which he looked around the table and observed as some of the members of the Privy Council nodded in agreement, "She and her mother enjoyed holding an axe over our heads of the power of Spain. And they never came to Katherine of Aragon's rescue, so why should we fear them now over this?"

"Because," Edward Seymour replied as he pressed his thumb and forefinger into the corners of his eyes in frustration, "The king is but eleven years old. He has no betrothed and certainly no heir to follow him soon. The Tudor line is weak! We must contain our people and avoid an invasion at all costs. Even if the chance of it going forward is slim, the repercussions of a war with Spain now would be too vast," he shook his head, "I cannot risk it. I shall write to the lady Mary and to king Charles with my decision."

John Dudley nodded slowly in agreement but watched through narrowed eyes as the cowardly Lord Protector quivered visibly at the slightest threat of invasion.

Hunsdon House, Hertfordshire

Mary received a letter from the Lord Protector himself that made it abundantly clear that though she was not to be exempt from the new laws of the land, there would be no close investigations made into what might be occurring in her own household.

"Frances!" Mary called as she raised her head, smiling in triumph over this small win, "I have something I need you to do for me."

"Yes, my lady?" Frances asked and she watched as Mary's expression change into a mischievous grin, clearly beginning to enjoy her newfound power over the king's council.

"I will be hearing Mass this Sunday at my chapel," she said casually, "and I would like it known by anyone who cares to listen that they would be most welcome to join me."

If the Lord Protector would give her permission to attend Mass at her residence, then surely any Catholics who would care to practice their faith would be able to do so with her within the safety of Hunsdon House and without fear of conviction. And if she could do this one small act of kindness for the good Catholic people of England, then she would.

"Is that wise, my lady?" Frances asked as she furrowed her brow, "It would make you a target."

"I already am a target, Frances," Mary said as she waved the comment aside, "With Edward an unwed young king, and with me being next in line – especially being a catholic – I will always have a target on my back."

"Then," Frances asked, "Why would you willingly put yourself within their line of sight?"

Mary cocked her head to one side, "Don't you see, Frances," she said, "This is why God has granted me this permission – so that I may shepherd the people of England towards the light in any way that I can during these dark times. My standing

329

firm in my belief gives them hope that the true faith is not forgotten, and by opening my doors to those who wish to attend Mass with me, I am showing them that they will always be safe with me.

Frances smiled but it did not reach her eyes, "Do you not fear for your life? The Lord Protector may yet arrest you for breaking their new laws."

Mary chuckled, "My dear Frances," she said as she stood from her seat, "I survived my father's tyranny for all my thirty-three years. This Edward Seymour could not scare me if he turned up at my doorstep dressed up as the devil himself."

But though she stood tall and spoke bravely, a little voice inside Mary's mind continued to niggle at her deepest doubts and she found herself wondering yet again, after all that time and all that she had overcome, if her life in England had run its course.

May 1549

Mary's open disobedience and abuse of the act of compassion Edward Seymour had bestowed onto her by allowing her to attend Mass although it had been lawfully forbidden all over the country, was now known across all of England, and she soon received multiple letters from the king's council insisting that she obey the law.

Though Mary was clearly engaging in a dangerous discussion in which she denied the king's authority, she seemed surprisingly at ease throughout, standing firm in the belief that she was ultimately within her rights to continue to worship as she always had.

"I fear for the lady Mary," Frances whispered to Cecily one morning as yet another messenger arrived, carrying yet another letter written in the king's name.

They both watched as Mary casually glided towards her writing desk and forged a reply in which she responded that the new law was not valid, being as king Edward was not of age to make mature decisions upon the matter, and that Parliament had no authority in the matters of religion.

"I do not believe her façade," Cecily replied, "She is scared," and she continued to fold the linens she had abandoned moments earlier.

"Then why put up such resistance?" Frances whispered back.

Cecily shrugged, "She is the only Catholic heir to the throne," she replied wisely, "Mary signed her father's oath all those years ago which proclaimed himself as the Supreme Head of the Church of England and denied Rome. I simply do not think she could ever go through that again. The guilt she felt over it likely still haunts her to this day."

Frances looked over to Mary as she continued to write, "The inner turmoil she has always faced must be exhausting," she remarked.

Cecily raised her eyebrows, "I just hope she knows what she is getting herself into with this," Cecily said, "And that she won't be run out of England as a result for her disobedience."

Frances nodded slowly in agreement.

In reply to Mary's cleverly composed letter, she received a collection of Protestant books, this time sent to her by the king himself, to try to show her the error of her ways.

Preachers were sent to her home in an effort to get her to conform. But of course, all were in vain, for Mary had learned her lesson through her past faults, and she would never denounce her faith.

Each insult that came her way only strengthened Mary's resolve to remain true to her mother's catholic teachings. She took it as the ultimate test from God, and with every attempt that failed to convert her, Mary grew stronger in the belief that she would one day be rewarded for her devotion to the true faith.

December 1549

Edward Seymour had governed as king in all but name for three years, but his increasingly stubborn and over-bearing attitude towards the council had begun to alienate the very men whose backing he needed. And when their patience with him had finally run out, he was removed from his position as Lord Protector in a coup led by his own councilman John Dudley.

Perhaps even more surprisingly, the late Dowager queen's widowed husband, Thomas Seymour, had been arrested for attempting to kidnap the young king, to try to force an agreement for the king's betrothal to Seymour's ward, Mary's cousin – the lady Jane Grey.

"Needless to say," Cecily said as she helped Mary undress, "He was not successful."

"What is to become of him?" Mary asked, though she knew the answer, and her heart ached for Catherine's poor baby girl who would become orphaned due to her father's reckless behaviour.

"He as well as his brother, the former Lord Protector, Edward Seymour," Cecily said, "Will be executed on Tower Hill on the morrow."

"Edward Seymour to be executed too?" Mary asked, frowning at the information, "What has he done since being demoted from his position within the council?"

"Rumour has it," Frances chimed in as she unpinned Mary's hood from her hair, "That he planned to have his replacement, John Dudley, murdered."

Mary raised her eyebrows, "Is it true?" she asked curiously.

Frances simply shrugged, showing no interest in the truth.

Mary sighed as her ladies readied her for bed, and watched through the mirror as Frances brushed her long red hair while Cecily pulled back the bedsheets, "How do you feel about Seymour's replacement at the council, my lady?" Cecily asked then.

"John Dudley?" Mary asked rhetorically.

"I hear he has already been made Earl of Warwick," Frances interjected, "And he is not to be called Lord Protector but President of the Council."

"President of the Council?" Mary echoed and then rolled her eyes, "Well, regardless, I can only hope that this new *President of the Council* will continue to allow my household to hear Mass as Seymour had done. But I have a bad feeling that will not be the case," she shook her head and sighed deeply, "I would hate to have to bring the Holy Roman Emperor into this matter again," she said as she climbed into bed, "but I will use all the means at my disposal if I am cornered."

May 1550

As expected, things did not improve and John Dudley, Earl of Warwick, could not simply ignore Mary as his predecessor had done.

"He is like a dog with a bone!" Cecily said irritably as she read the letter from over Mary's shoulder that he had sent, demanding she abandon her Catholic beliefs.

Mary sighed and threw the letter into the fire, "It is during times like these that I miss ambassador Chapuys' advice," she said as she watched the letter burn, "His wisdom had always guided me through difficult times before."

Mary's greatest ally and dear friend, Eustace Chapuys, had been released from his services to the crown four years prior due to his failing health. His departure from England to retire

333

in Louvain had ached Mary's heart greatly, but she knew that he deserved the rest above all others after all the troublesome years he had endured as Imperial Ambassador to her late father. But nevertheless, Mary missed his fatherly affection as well as his wise advice, which he had always offered her readily throughout her darkest moments.

"Can you request the new imperial ambassador speak to the Earl of Warwick on your behalf?" Cecily asked, stirring Mary from her thoughts.

"I could," she replied with a sigh, "but I have a feeling it will not improve the matter. All he can hope to achieve is to delay the inevitable."

"But what can the Earl of Warwick do?" Frances asked with a shrug.

"Don't be dense, Frances," Mary snapped, suddenly irritated by Frances' naivety, "Now that he is in power, he can *do* whatever he likes!"

And Mary had been right; not one week after she had received that final letter, John Dudley the Earl of Warwick sent priests to her home at Hunsdon House yet again, to increase the pressure for Mary to conform, shaming her for her beliefs and lecturing her in ways suitable only for base born children. Their unwelcome scolding had been far worse than any other sent by the late Edward Seymour, and it had left Mary's head pounding with frustration and – dare she admit it – fear.

In fact, it had distinctly reminded her of the time she had her life threatened by the duke of Norfolk to sign her father's Act of Supremacy all those years ago.

It had been the final straw; and that evening, once the undesirable guests had left defeated, Mary sent a letter to her cousin King Charles V of Spain requesting his help for her to escape from the intolerable country that was England.

Chapter 17

April 1550
Hunsdon House, Hertfordshire

"I can no longer remain here," Mary whispered to her ladies, "It has become too dangerous."

It was true. Her father, king Henry, had been a slow and reluctant reformer on the matters of the church – his ever-changing policies fluctuating over the years between Catholicism and Protestantism – while her brother's reign had proven to mark a clear difference between Mary and the government, his Protestant upbringing shining through in his rule.

In truth, Mary knew that she had been dealt with leniently compared to others who had faced imprisonment for refusing to conform with the new religious regime, for she had the backing of King Charles V the Holy Roman Emperor behind her to keep her safe from prosecution.

Upon Mary's very first intimidating visit from the king's priests to attempt to convert her, King Charles V had sent a message directly to king Edward's council via his ambassador, Francois van der Delft, that he would not tolerate Mary to be forced to change her religion. The Holy Roman Emperor's power being vast and ever-increasing throughout Europe made him someone that king Edward's council could not afford to affront.

His message had kept Mary safe for some time, and while others were being imprisoned and punished for crimes such as merely owning rosary beads, Mary was able to attend Mass at her residence up to four times a day.

But even Mary knew that her cousin's patience and ability to intervene on the matters in England would run out soon enough, and when that day came, what would become of her?

"My life is at stake," she continued, "My cousin king Charles has done what he can, but I cannot trust my little brother to protect me. Deep down I think I always knew my father would not have wished me dead – I was too valuable as a spare heir. But my brother has no such affection. We are different creatures, from two different worlds, and I cannot trust that he would not arrest and try me if his council told him to."

"What will you do?" Cecily asked.

"I have invited the imperial ambassador, Francois van der Delft, to meet with me," Mary admitted, "And I am hopeful we will come up with a solution."

When the ambassador arrived the following afternoon, he bowed grandly to Mary, "My lady," he said, his grey moustache so large Mary hardly saw his lips move.

"Ambassador," she replied in greeting and sat down by the fire, offering him a seat opposite her with a wave of her hand.

"I will speak bluntly," Mary said as she ambassador took a seat, "For I fear my time to act is running out."

The ambassador nodded and sat forward in his chair, intertwining his fingers together as he listened.

"I know that I am in danger from those who surround the king," she said, finally letting her composed mask slip, "They are particularly malevolent towards me, and I believe it would be foolish to continue on this path and wait till the blow falls."

The ambassador's moustache twitched, and Mary wondered what expression was hiding underneath those great whiskers.

"Forgive my forwardness," Mary continued, "But I must ask you of your opinion. While I would gladly remain in England if I were able to serve God as I have done in the past, I fear that if my brother were to die childless, that his council would

336

seek to end my life before I could ascend to the throne as a catholic monarch and undo all their Protestant regimes. So I must ask you this: What should I do?"

Van der Delft crinkled his eyes in thought, "If you are serious about wanting to leave the country of your birth," he said slowly, his moustache bouncing as he uttered the words, "Then by summoning me I assume you would leave to reside in *Espana*?"

Mary nodded, "My family there will help me," she said.

The ambassador sat back in his seat and crossed his legs, "Then I suggest for you to be collected from the coast of Maldon in Essex and taken to an imperial warship which I can easily arrange to be at our disposal."

Mary stared as the reality of the situation was taking form, and then she nodded.

"I will make arrangements," the ambassador said as he rose to his feet, "My lady," he said as he bowed his head in farewell and walked out of Mary's chambers.

June 1550

"When does the Spanish ship arrive?" Cecily asked as she packed Mary's corsets.

"King Charles has sent it," Mary replied as she thought of the secret letter she had received the day before from Francois van der Delft informing her to be prepared, "It should be at the coast within the week, and I have a messenger on the lookout to fetch us as soon as it arrives."

Frances sighed, "It is hard to believe it has come to this."

Mary shook her head, "England has become poisoned," she said, "And there are few left who see it clearly for what it should be: with Catholicism as the true religion, England loyal to Rome and the Pope, and I as a princess. To be alone in this world with such a belief is a dangerous thing."

337

"But can you truly abandon everything you have ever known?" Frances asked, "Give up the *throne?"*

Mary shook her head in frustration as though the idea of one day becoming queen of England must not be allowed to re-enter her mind, "My brother is king" she said logically, "Soon he will be married and produce his own heirs. I cannot risk my life for the slight chance that he may not accomplish that. Even to speak of it is treason," but as Mary spoke the words she felt a tight knot in the pit of her stomach and she momentarily wondered: Was she giving up too soon?

But she shook her head and scolded herself for her dark and sinful thoughts.

Not only was it treason to imagine the death of the king, but she would also never wish such a fate onto her beloved little brother and godson, whom she has loved and watched grow into the noble king he now was.

And above all else, the young king was not to blame for where her life had led her. The advisors that surrounded him were heretics and sinners, poisoning England's people and sinking the country deeper into depravity and immorality by forsaking catholic laws and believing themselves to be above the teachings of God. And at the age of thirty-four Mary was tired of living within a sinking ship, and of swimming against the tide. Now, with a new life in Spain on the horizon, she could hope for a better future, one with options beyond waiting and praying.

One where she would live as a legitimate princess, surrounded by a family that would appreciate her and care for her well-being. A future where she may find happiness.

And yet, the idea of giving up everything she had been born to be still stung like a thorn in her side, just as it always did whenever the path towards happiness presented itself to her.

A few days later, Mary inhaled deeply to quash the heavy feeling in her chest as she stood by the window, her mind reeling as she watched the rain falling heavily onto the gardens below.

She had heard the commotion outside indicating that the messenger had arrived with news of the Spanish ship's arrival, and her heart skipped a beat as the doors to her chambers opened.

"The carriage is ready, my lady," her guard announced, "to take you and your ladies to Maldon."

Mary nodded and followed the guards through the candlelit hallway and down the stairs, her chest growing tighter with each step. But she climbed the step into the carriage with unfaltering grace, and held her head high throughout the entire journey, willing herself to believe that this was the right thing to do.

Her ladies sat beside her in silence, neither of them looking at each other throughout the entire journey for fear of giving away their opinion on their mistress' plan to flee.

When they finally arrived at the coast of Maldon, Mary's carriage stopped on the road so as not to get stuck in the wet sands below, and they one by one emerged from the carriage, the wind whipping their skirts about as they looked out over the rough waters.

Frances' stomach churned, and at the sight of the Spanish warship in the distance she could no longer contain her opinions.

"My lady," she said earnestly as she turned to Mary and took her hands in hers, "are you sure this is what you want?"

Mary snatched her hands away as if she had burned her, "What I *want*?" she repeated harshly, her expression one of stone as she looked around herself, her eyes darting from her guards to the Spanish ambassador as he approached slowly, his feet struggling to walk on the sand, "I do not *want* this!

339

England is my home! I was born to be the first queen regnant of England. Fleeing is the last thing I ever wished to do."

Mary raised her hand over her eyes then as the wind blew sand into the air, and she stepped aside awkwardly, the reeds that whipped at her ankles adding to her frustration.

"Then why do you allow yourself to be pushed out like this?" Frances asked, her doe eyes pleading with Mary.

Mary stared at her friend, her anger dissolving suddenly into pity for the little fool, for even as such a close bystander, Frances had no idea what it was truly like to be a bastardised princess with a target on her back. She sighed and took her lady's face in her hands.

"My dear Frances," she said, "nothing that has happened to me has been by my own choice or volition. I have endured many moments such as this, never knowing from one day to the next if it is safe to welcome the new dawn. But I am *tired* of living in fear, and I can no longer allow anyone to make me fear the rising of the sun. This time it is not like the others. My father's need for every surviving child was the only thing that kept me alive then, but my brother's new council have no such need for me. They fear my catholic faith and what I would do if I ever came to power. To escape now, is my only hope of survival."

Frances sniffed and wiped the tears from her cheeks, but she nodded her head in understanding, "Perhaps you will meet a handsome Spanish prince," she said then with a smile in an attempt to lighten the sullen mood, "and live the life you have always deserved."

Mary smiled.

"My lady," ambassador van der Delft said beside her then, having finally made his way through the sands, "The ship approaches," and Mary turned to look over the water as the Spanish ship grew nearer.

"No doubt you will be wed and with child within the year once we arrive," Frances said dreamily beside her, "Perhaps it is for the best…"

Mary smiled tightly at her friend, the nervous feeling within her growing as the ship inched closer. But perhaps Frances was right. Perhaps this new venture was indeed for the best.

Mary closed her eyes and inhaled the salty air deeply into her lungs as she allowed herself to envision her life in her mother's homeland. An image came to her easily, and she could see herself happy, her belly swollen with child as her faceless husband took her hand and kissed it. Her other children running around her legs, chasing each other, their laughter echoing in her mind. She could feel the warm Spanish sun on her pale skin, and soft grass beneath her bare feet. She could see herself without worries or fears, and she was safe.

But then Mary opened her eyes and she found herself back on the English coast, watching as the ship that would take her to that future approached lazily, and she all of a sudden knew that the future she had seen must never come to pass.

The faceless love she had envisioned must never be, and the children she would have must never be born. For however wonderful it had felt, it had not felt *worth it.*

"I – I can't do it," she stammered then, "I have changed my mind, I can't do it."

Cecily and Frances looked at each other, their mouths agape in utter disbelief, "My lady?" Cecily said.

"But the ship," the ambassador said, "It is here!"

Mary shook her head violently, "No," she said, "I cannot abandon my fate."

"But you said yourself that you are not safe here!" van der Delft exclaimed.

"What has changed your mind so suddenly?" Cecily said as she took Mary's hands and gently pulled her away from the disgruntled ambassador.

"I saw the future I could have had," Mary said quietly, her face twisted in sadness, "a future I might have if I get on that ship. And it was beautiful," she whispered, "But it would never replace the void in my heart that I would create by fleeing my destiny."

Cecily squeezed Mary's hands, "Mary! Listen to me!" she commanded, desperate to regain Mary's composure, "If you stay here you will die!"

Mary shook her head and swallowed down her tears, "I cannot give up now," she said, "Frances was right, I cannot give up."

Cecily looked angrily at Frances, who averted her gaze, and then she let go of Mary's hands, "You cannot be serious!" Cecily said, her tone hard as stone, "We are so close to safety!"

"I cannot explain it, Cecily," Mary declared, throwing her hands in the air, "I saw the life I have dreamed of for so long. I saw it, I could *feel* it. And somehow, though it brought me such joy, it felt…wrong."

Cecily put her hand to her forehead and turned away from her mistress, "As always," she said steadily, her back to Mary, "we will stand by you, no matter your decision. But I have made my opinion perfectly clear. I do not think it safe for you to remain here."

"No matter the bliss I may find if I were to escape today," Mary explained, "I would be throwing away everything my mother died for to protect, and everything I have given up so far to keep. God would never forgive me if I strayed from my true fate now."

"Even if the king may have his own heirs soon," Cecily said icily, playing the devil's advocate, "and you would never attain the throne?"

Mary stared back at her, her expression hardened as she raised her chin, "Even then."

July 1553

Three years went by much the same as every other year of Mary's mundane existence.

She remained secluded at Hunsdon House for most of her days, visiting court only when explicitly invited by the king, and as each year ticked by, Mary's uncertainties that she had made the wrong decision grew more and more undeniable.

Her health continued to fluctuate like the seasons, feeling perfectly well one day to being bedbound and unable to sit up without feeling faint the next, and her ladies noticed that her ailment had become increasingly more regular and severe as she aged.

With each year that had passed since Mary's change of heart over her escape from England, she had also begun suffering from intense toothaches which had resulted in four of her teeth turning black and rotten, two of which were her incisors and were therefore unable to remain hidden whenever she spoke or smiled. Yet Mary could not bring herself to allow the physician to pull them, for though their appearance was unpleasant, Mary would prefer to keep her rotten teeth than to be known as the toothless lady Mary.

As an unmarried virgin – to everyone's better knowledge – of thirty-seven years old, Mary knew that her prospects of finding a match were becoming increasingly non-existent, and the images of what her future could have been haunted her dreams most nights.

Yet she would never voice her growing concerns to anyone, knowing already that Cecily would have no sympathy after having expressed her opinion openly to Mary.

Her royal cousin, Charles V of Spain would also likely never wish to aid her again after she simply did not board the ship he had so gallantly sent for her at his own risk.

Mary was therefore stuck in a rut of her own creation, cursed to wander the gardens at Hunsdon House, or to hunt in the woods nearby, or to stitch yet another embroidery; forever waiting for a day that many never come.

It was a strangely ambivalent feeling then when a letter arrived one day from the newly appointed imperial ambassador Simon Renard with the terrible and premature news that her little brother, beloved godson, and most gracious king, had died at the tender age of fifteen, unmarried and without an heir.

Though he had been ill since the start of the year, Mary had recently been reassured that he had since recovered almost completely, which made the news of his sudden passing all the more unexpected.

"How do you feel?" Cecily asked calmly as she poured Mary a cup of small ale.

"I feel," Mary began but then stopped and looked down at the deck of cards before her, "I am not sure," she admitted and then picked up the card from the top of the deck and began picking at its corner.

"It must be a rather troubling concept?" Cecily deduced.

"Yes," Mary agreed, "It is troubling, as you say. My mind cannot quite comprehend how to feel the thrill of *finally* becoming queen of England, while simultaneously knowing that I attained it due to the death of my dear brother."

"The physicians did what they could," Cecily said then, hoping to ease Mary's mind and lift some of her guilt.

"Mm," Mary mumbled as she took a sip of her ale, "I know. And I believe in God's plan."

Though her time had come sooner than she had expected with the death of her young brother being so sudden, Mary had considered this moment for quite some time. Edward's council making it difficult for her to attain the throne had always been a likely outcome, and in that knowledge, Mary had begun to secretly weigh up what would be her best move in such an event.

She had inherited many castles from her father of which she could choose from, but not all offered everything that she would need to fend off a potential army. What she needed now was somewhere close enough to London to put pressure on her late brother's council, threatening them with her proximity, but also one which offered great defence in case they sent a force to capture her.

They sat in silence for a while as the realisation of what was to come dawned on Mary and she stood up slowly from her seat and cleared her throat.

"Pack up my things, ladies," she commanded, "We must move my household to a more fortified residence."

"Where to, Mary?" Frances asked.

"Suffolk," she replied, "Let the country know that the Queen of England is to convene at Framlingham Castle, and for all who wish to show me their support to meet me there."

Framlingham Castle, Suffolk

Support for Mary flocked by the hundreds as it became common knowledge throughout the country that the President of the Council, John Dudley, had been preparing to seize and detain Mary before she could claim her rightful throne. Her household's immediate move to the well-fortified Framlingham Castle having perhaps been the sole reason why Dudley had not succeeded gave Mary immense pleasure, knowing that she had begun her reign with a tactically successful move.

And in the days that followed, many had joined her cause, offering their services in any way they could.

One such supporter that soon joined her was Edward Mone – the tax collector of her late brother king Edward VI. He had been a loyal servant to the monarchy and had not agreed with the Privy Council's plan to overthrow the rightful heir on their quest to maintain their power.

With the young king now dead, Edward Mone's loyalty shifted to whom was next in line to the throne, as he believed was expected of any faithful servant to the royal lineage.

And with the royal finances in Mary's control, she had a well placed first step to attaining more. Not long after that, Cardinal Reginald Pole, who had spent the last twenty-one years in exile in Padua, Italy, returned to England to serve his queen as Papal legate to England. He entered Framlingham Castle proclaiming his support for Mary and she swiftly appointed him as one of her chief advisors.

But she knew that the late king's council would not make it easy for her to simply claim her throne. Mary knew that she had to act carefully to keep her head, and though she had been kept well informed of the court's goings on over the years, she was about to learn that there was so much more to uncover.

"It will be difficult, my lady," Cardinal Reginald Pole said as he, Mary and Edward Mone sat at a long wooden table in Framlingham castle's great hall, "but the people of London will rejoice at your return, of that I am sure."

"There is much I am yet to understand," Mary said calmly, her mind feeling soothed despite the chaos, "To my knowledge the king was recovered..." she said suspiciously.

"The President of the Council," Edward Mone replied, having been the only one present enough at Edward's court to have had insight, "and indeed all of the protestant advisors to the king, informed me as such," he said, "But while he was unwell, no one but they were permitted to see him, and all matters of estate were conducted behind closed doors. I had my suspicions, but then news of his regained health broke all over court."

"The king's council have always been snakes in the grass," Mary said sourly, "Nothing they say or do is to be trusted," and the men nodded in agreement, "What can you tell me of John Dudley's actions since the king's death?"

"I do regret to share this news with you, my lady," Mone said as he met her gaze, his dark eyes conveying his anger at the betrayal to the king's memory, "But before the king's death, the duke had drawn up a final act of succession which declares you and Elizabeth not suited to inherit the throne upon king Edward's death due to being declared as... illegitimate by your father, Henry VIII."

Mary blinked, "But the document does not hold any power," she said frankly, "My father's will was law. Illegitimate or not, the line of succession is clear."

"Nevertheless," Cardinal Pole said then, "the protestant council were not accepting of my lady's religious beliefs."

"There were even brief rumours," Mone added as he raised his dark eyebrows, "that you yourself had poisoned the young king – all fabricated by the council of course..." and he chuckled lightly.

Mary did not even flinch at hearing the ludicrous rumours, and Mone continued.

"The duke of Northumberland, John Dudley, has taken matters into his own hands. Shortly before the king's death he had his eldest son marry the protestant lady Jane Grey –"

"My own cousin..." Mary added quietly.

"—precisely," Mone continued, "And the king amended his will on his death bed to proclaim the lady his heir..."

At that Mary scoffed and rose from her seat in one fluid motion. Her advisors watched her as she walked over to the window and inhaled deeply, "What else?" she asked bluntly.

347

Cardinal Pole cleared his throat and Mary turned her head towards him, "The lady has been proclaimed queen, my lady," he said and looked Mary straight in the eyes, "I hear she is awaiting her coronation in the Tower of London."

She raised her eyebrows briefly and chewed the inside of her cheek as she contemplated the information.

"It is of little consequence," she said after some consideration, "The duke may marry his son to whomever he pleases, and he may verbally proclaim anyone as the new monarch. It does not make it so. My father's Act of Succession was clear – the lady Grey is not to succeed the throne unless all king Henry's children die without heirs. That gives a clear indication that I, as his daughter, come first in the line of succession after Edward, which is primarily what concludes this state of affairs. The people of England will support me in my claim – I have faith in that," she said boldly.

"Hear, hear," Pole said as he nodded his head, and he reminded Mary of his late mother, her former governess Margaret Pole.

"Now," Mary said after a brief moment, "Let us discuss our next step," and she resumed her seat at the head of the table with her head held high and a faint smile upon her lips as she watched the men before her.

Her time had finally come.

Mary decided that – for the time being – she would act graciously and allow the Privy Council a chance to rectify their wrongdoings against her, even though they had made her recent years unbearable.

She wrote them a letter stating clearly and concisely what they already knew to be true: that by the terms of the legal Act of Succession of 1544 she was now queen. And she called for their obedience and loyalty.

The people of England expressed their support throughout the country, acclaiming Mary as their true queen. But John Dudley would not give up on his power, and he left London at the head of a force to capture Mary.

But Mary's support had been growing every hour, and before the duke's force had arrived at Mary's stronghold, her troops had grown threefold, including the simple Catholic folk of the surrounding counties, as well as several catholic lords of the lands, one of which was Sir Henry Jerningham, a former courtier of her late father's, who had rallied troops in Suffolk on Mary's behalf.

Upon John Dudley's arrival at Framlingham Castle, it became instantly clear to his troops that they would be on the losing side of the battle, and they, as well as members of the Privy council who had previously backed the lady Jane Grey, abandoned him.

And he was left with nothing more to do than to surrender.

Following the surrender or disappearance of the lady Jane Grey's supporters, Mary and her household made their way from her estates at Framlingham Castle towards London.

They were followed by hundreds of her people who steadfastly walked behind their horses and carriages simply to witness their new monarch's ascent to the throne.

One afternoon the procession arrived at the outskirts of London and Mary decided to spend the night at Wanstead House, a royal hunting lodge, so as to enter into London the following morning with the rising of the sun.

It was at Wanstead House that Mary would be greeted by her half-sister Elizabeth who had travelled from her home, Somerset House, to congratulate her older sister and to show her undying support. And that evening, as Mary prepared for her formal entry into London as the new Queen of England, she gave the arrest order for the lady Jane Grey and her husband Guildford Dudley, to be imprisoned in the Tower of London and to await their queen's judgement.

3rd August 1553
London

Mary's entry into London would be etched into her memory as the most joyous and fulfilled day of her life. After decades of waiting and never daring to hope, she had finally achieved her purpose, and once all the traitors were properly dealt with, Mary knew exactly what her first order of business would be.

The trials for John Dudley duke of Northumberland, his son Guildford Dudley, and the lady Jane Grey, were over extremely quickly, with there never being any doubt that their intent had been to steal the crown out from under the rightful heir. They were all three executed without another thought.

And with their execution came the end of all of Mary's opposition, leaving the path clear for her to undo her father's greatest mistakes. While preparations were underway for her coronation, Mary introduced two new pieces of legislation, the first of which proclaimed that the marriage of Henry VIII and Katherine of Aragon was and always had been legal and undisputed, asserting Mary as a legitimate princess.

Parliament passed the legislation instantly, legalising what Mary had known to be true all her life. The second piece of legislation called for the reversal of all Protestant laws passed during king Edward VI rule, which was met with a little more resistance from Parliament as they considered its outcomes.

"Many were married under your half-brother's reign, your majesty," Sir Henry Jerningham said, having been appointed Mary's Vice-Chamberlain of the Household, "are they all now to be separated or lose their districts?"

"Precisely," Mary replied icily.

"The people will not be accepting of this," Jerningham replied.

Mary turned to glare at him, "The wrongs that were done must be righted," she said plainly, "This is the first step to returning England to its former glory and to flush out those that would poison it."

"Forgive me, your majesty," said Stephen Gardner, "But the people will not accept these rulings easily."

Stephen Gardner had been a loyal member of king Henry's council for years, and though he had supported the royal supremacy and separation from Rome, he had been a thorough opponent to the Reformation. He had survived Mary's father's ever-changing doctrines throughout the years, much like Mary herself had, but had been imprisoned during her brother's reign for opposing Edward's Protestant reforms, dubbing them to be theologically wrong and unconstitutional.

Mary had released him from the Tower the very day she had arrived in London and due to his strong Catholic beliefs and loyalty to her father had appointed him Lord Chancellor of her Privy Council.

"Those that will not take it easily," Mary replied, "Are precisely those that we hope to find so that we may lead them onto the path of righteousness."

Gardner bowed his head and said nothing further on the topic, moving swiftly on to the next matter of discussion.

"The restoration of the Six Articles of 1539," Gardner said, "including the celibacy of the priests shall be restored without much opposition, I believe."

Mary nodded once and rose from her throne, watching in awe as all the men followed suit, relishing in the fact that none shall ever sit in her presence again unless she allowed it, and the power and respect she now held in the palm of her hand felt intoxicating.

"Very well gentlemen," she said, "I shall leave the matter to be discussed. I trust the right decision will be made in due course," and with a rustle of fabric from her rich dress of cloth of gold, she exited the Queen's chambers.

1st October 1553
Greenwich Palace, London

The day had finally come.
Her ladies rushed around her in a flurry of fabrics and shoes as the servants brought in water of lavender and rose.
Mary was seated before her mirror as she was dabbed at the neck and arms with the scented water, totally oblivious to the chaos that surrounded her as she watched the woman staring back at her from inside the looking glass.
The woman she saw reflected back at her was quite clearly happy because her pale blue eyes were shining with excitement and joy, even though her thinly lipped mouth was only smiling slightly.
Mary watched herself as she moved her head from side to side as she observed the finer details: the lines on her forehead and the handful of greying hairs that had sprouted among her fiery red mane some years ago. The woman staring back at her was not striking to look at – never had been – and yet – though she had looked at herself every day for thirty-seven years – on this day she appeared almost beautiful.
There was no longer any fear in her eyes or worry etched across her brow. No more clenching of the jaw or squinting of the eyes in suspicion.
This new woman was strong. She held a power in her hands that only a man had ever before possessed, and her claim was utterly undisputed.
The people of England loved her and supported her, more so than she had ever dreamed possible, and it was on this feeling

of acceptance – which she had been searching for her whole life – that she would nourish herself, and she hoped it would fuel her for a lifetime of success.

For finally Mary could understand what it felt like to be adored.

Westminster Abbey, London

Mary entered Westminster Abbey wearing a rich dress of blue velvet stitched with cloth of gold, her auburn hair pinned elegantly under the same gold circlet that she had worn on her entry into London not two months earlier. The streets had been covered in flowers; and men, women and children alike filled the streets, craning their necks to catch a glimpse of the first Queen Regnant in England's history.

Mary's heart soared as she entered the beautiful abbey and she breathed in the rich scent of the incense that filled the air, to calm her nerves.

God really was smiling down upon her this day, and it was almost as if she could feel His presence within her soul guiding her forward, for with each step that she took towards the altar, she could feel her nervousness fading away.

"If any man," Stephen Gardner the Bishop of Winchester called as Mary reached the High Altar, "will, or can, allege any cause why Mary should not be crowned, let them speak now!"

And before Mary could even take a breath, the people before her, as well as outside the abbey, called in unison, "Queen Mary! Queen Mary!" and she believed in her heart that her life until that moment had meant nothing in comparison to the one she had yet to live.

Everywhere Mary went, people bowed.

As she made her way through the Palace or to give alms to the poor, everyone – whether they be high-born or a peasant – expressed their deepest respect to her, and her chest filled with a pride so great that she could say with certainty that everything she had gone through had been worth it for this feeling of acceptance.

"How does it feel?" Frances asked excitedly the following morning as she and Cecily got their queen dressed in a rich gown of black velvet stitched with gold threat.

"It feels," Mary contemplated, "Normal. As though I have been queen all my life."

Frances sighed with relief and Cecily smiled.

"You have waited a long time for this," Cecily said, her voice cracking with emotion.

"But now that it has finally come to pass," Mary said, suddenly serious, "there are two main matters at hand."

"A *husband*?" Frances squealed as she jumped up and down, her juvenile outlook on things living on though she was a lady of thirty-seven herself.

"That would be one of the matters, yes," Mary admitted as her cheeks blushed a deep red, "It is imperative that I produce an heir to succeed me. But primarily is the matter of the country's religion."

Cecily nodded, "There are only few Protestants among the people," she said as she tightened Mary's corset.

"How do you know of the numbers, Cecily?" Mary asked.

Cecily shrugged, "It is common knowledge that the people are rejoicing the return to the Catholic faith."

"Yes, but they fear for their lives," Mary pointed out as she sucked in her belly, the corset feeling tight around her waist, "People will lie about anything to keep their heads," and she fell silent as she remembered her own lapse in judgement when she had signed her father's Act of Supremacy.

She shook her head clear of those memories, "Call a meeting of the Privy Council," she told Frances, "There is much to be discussed," and Frances hurried away.

It did not take long for Parliament to pass the legislation for Catholic practices to be reintroduced, and almost immediately thereafter, the banned relics and altars that had been hidden away during Edward VI's reign reappeared, and a Latin Mass was sung throughout London.

It seemed that Cecily had been right about the population being in the majority for the Catholic ways, for there was much enthusiasm for the processions, as well as the prayers for the dead to return, something that had been forbidden during Edward's Protestant rule.

However, Mary soon found that though her people welcomed all the old practices, they did not understand the need to return to Papal Supremacy.

"Most of England cannot even remember a time where they paid taxes to a foreign power," Bishop Stephen Gardner said, who had been a supporter of Royal Supremacy despite his strong Catholic beliefs, "It is an unnecessary expense at a time where we should be concentrating on what our country needs, which is to regain footing under a new rule."

Cardinal Pole shook his head disapprovingly, but Queen Mary was disappointed to see many other council members to be nodding in agreement with Gardner.

"I understand your concerns, Lord Chancellor," Mary replied slowly as she considered her council's opinions, "and I am prepared to accept it given that all catholic practices have been restored. Perhaps once England is stronger, we shall return to this matter."

Mary had learned from experience that the best way to deal with men was to be gentle and calm, but inside she was raging.

Papal Supremacy mattered. It was at the very heart of the catholic religion itself, and unified Christendom under the Pope's leadership. To deny that was an act against God.

But Mary knew that not all matters could be rectified in one fell swoop, and she decided to appease her council on this point for now.

"A much more pressing matter at hand is the matter of marriage, and an heir," said the imperial ambassador, Simon Renard. At the abrupt change in topic all eyes were suddenly on him, and yet he seemed completely at ease, "Has your majesty given the matter of a husband some thought?"

In one united motion, all heads turned to look at Mary, and though she raised her chin stoically, her cheeks burned red with apprehension.

"I have indeed given it some thought," she replied icily, not wanting to give away her true feelings – that the idea of marriage at her age frightened her despite her hope for it, "I have considered the possibility of Prince Felipe of Spain, son of the Holy Roman Emperor."

At the announcement, some members of the Privy Council looked sideways at one another, while the imperial ambassador raised his dark eyebrows and nodded in appreciation at the mention of a possible union with his country.

"A unity between our two countries once again?" he stated rhetorically.

"Forgive me, your majesty," the Lord Chancellor Stephen Gardner said as he wrung his hands together before him, "Perhaps it would be wiser to consider a suitor closer to home?"

"Who did you have in mind, Lord Chancellor?" Mary asked, feigning intrigue, for she had already very much made up her mind about a match with Spain.

"The Earl of Devon, Edward Courtenay," he replied carefully, his old eyes shining with hope for a match within England to strengthen the country, "He would be a splendid match. He is the last of the Plantagenets, and great-grandson to Edward IV. He is said to be very good looking, charming, and his noble birth would, of course, make him suitable for your highness."

Mary sighed, "I believe I remember his parents," she said slowly as she thought, "They supported my mother during the king's Great Matter I believe?"

Gardner nodded enthusiastically, "Yes, I believe so, your majesty."

"And I am grateful to them for that," the queen said after a moment's thought, "However," she continued, "I do believe a match with Spain would strengthen England significantly, which is what is ultimately our joint objective, is it not, councillors?" she asked as she looked around the room.

The members of her council mumbled and nodded in agreement.

"Very well," she concluded and turned to look the imperial ambassador in the eyes, "Ambassador Renard, I ask you to convey the message to my cousin king Charles V, and present Spain with my proposal."

Then she stood from her gold painted chair at the head of the council table and exited the room, leaving her advisors bowing behind her as her face burned with anxiety at the prospect of marriage.

Chapter 18

"I am a woman of thirty-seven," Mary later exclaimed in private to her ladies-in-waiting, "What if I am too old? What if I cannot please a man in such a way so as to produce an heir?"

Cecily quickly slammed the door to the queen's chambers closed to ensure her outburst would not become court gossip. Then she hurried to Mary's side, who had slumped onto the ground beside her bed in a heap of velvet.

"Every lady has this fear when their wedding approaches," she soothed.

"Prince Filipe is eleven years younger than I," Mary added, "I fear he will not be happy with me."

"You have yet to hear a response from Spain," Frances added as she approached, "They may not accept."

"That in itself is another worry!" Mary threw her hands in the air, and Cecily shook her head at Frances, who bit her lip and shrugged.

"Mary!" Cecily said as she took the queen's hand, "You must remain calm. This is what you have always dreamed of. What you have prayed for!"

"But now that it is becoming reality," Mary admitted, "I fear it," she whispered, like a scared little girl.

Cecily smiled, "You fear failure," she deduced, "Which, given your experiences, is understandable. But you must produce an heir. Think of your people, think of England. They *need* a catholic heir from your womb. The alternative –"

Mary groaned angrily, interrupting her friend, "I do not need reminding of the alternative," she said, then she swallowed her tears and rose from the ground, "You are right," she admitted with a sigh, "I cannot let England fall back into

Protestant rule. Too much is at stake," and then she inhaled deeply and straightened her back.

"I shall do what I must for my country," she said as she supressed her fears, "Whoever it may be, I am to be married. And I shall give England their new catholic heir."

December 1553
Greenwich Palace, London

"We have received word from Spain," imperial ambassador, Simon Renard announced, "that they have accepted the betrothal between your majesty and Prince Felipe. The Holy Roman Emperor is convinced that his son would be a stable and mature suitor, and able to offer protection to your majesty's kingdom."

Queen Mary inhaled deeply at the news, her heart fluttering in her chest as she sat upon her throne, "I am pleased to hear such news, *senor* Renard," she said and then dismissed him with a wave of her hand.

Renard bowed and turned, leaving the English queen to greet the noblemen and ladies that had begun to arrive throughout the month for the Christmastide.

Upon leaving the throne room, he began making his way to his chambers so as to convey a letter to his master, king Charles V of Spain, when he crossed paths with Stephen Gardner, the Lord Chancellor.

"Is there news?" Gardner asked as he approached Renard in the corridor.

"Indeed," Renard replied, closing the space between them, "I have just come from her majesty's presence to announce Spain's acceptance. The queen and the Spanish prince shall be wed."

The Lord Chancellor nodded but looked down at the ground before him, clearly dissatisfied with the development.

"It is good news," Gardner answered tactfully, "Spain will offer England much support, and no doubt help to guide the queen in certain matters."

Renard smiled, urging Gardner on with his silence, and Gardner took a step towards the ambassador.

"As you well know," he said quietly, knowing from his many years at English court that even the walls had ears, "there has never been a queen regnant before in all of English history," he whispered.

"I do," Renard replied coolly, continuing to feel at ease though Bishop Gardner towered over him menacingly.

"Then you must agree that this marriage is imperative for the future of a catholic England," Gardner continued.

Renard frowned, "Of course."

Gardner nodded, "But something does trouble me, ambassador," he added, his voice having turned threatening, "Will the Spanish prince be happy to settle for an older queen, in a country where he must be condemned to play the queen's consort?"

The imperial ambassador looked up and met the Lord Chancellor's gaze, his implication becoming suddenly clear, "The news is fresh," he replied slowly, "In due time I am certain the details shall be discussed. The queen will be advised, I am sure, as to what is best for her country."

"Indeed, she will," Gardner replied, raising one bushy eyebrow, suggesting that he would not stand to have Spain barrage into England and take control over Queen Mary's kingdom, "But it is your prince who will need to be properly briefed as to what his role shall be. He shall never rule England through our queen. Have I made myself clear?"

Renard bowed in mock respect, "Completely," he replied with a sly grin. Then he cleared his throat, "May I be excused?" he asked sarcastically, and he walked away, leaving the Lord Chancellor to collect himself.

*

Shortly after news broke that their new queen was arranging to marry the Spanish prince, her subjects grew alarmed, fearing that England would become part of Spain through their union.

The people's worries created civil unrest throughout London, causing Mary to fear she had made a terrible mistake.

"Is it unwise to wed prince Felipe?" she asked her council one morning as news had reached her that the people's discontent was mounting, "My people are outraged at the prospect!"

Renard rose from his seat, "I can assure your majesty," he said cooly, his short stature forgotten with his commanding tone, "that the people's anger will fade as they learn that England shall remain as its own country. The union between prince Felipe and your majesty is entirely logical, and the prince is delighted to wed your majesty."

Mary inhaled deeply as her chest tightened in fear of losing her people's love for the sake of a man she had never met.

"I must be clear," she said as she met the ambassador's gaze, "I have no intention of turning *my* country over to the prince – nor to any man! A union between myself and whomever it shall be is to be made primarily to produce a catholic successor," she said, her tone aloof, "If Spain can reassure me that the prince's intentions are pure and noble in that respect, then we can discuss formalities."

Renard nodded, "The Holy Roman Emperor has made it abundantly clear," he promised, "that a match between his son and your majesty would be as Queen Regnant and King Consort. Prince Felipe has agreed in writing," and he produced a document from his pile of papers before him.

The queen took it and handed it straight to her Lord Chancellor, who smirked triumphantly at the imperial ambassador before reading through it.

"It is signed and has the prince's seal, your majesty," Gardner said in confirmation of the ambassador's words.

Queen Mary nodded her head and considered the situation, "Very well," she replied after a moment's deliberation, "Then my subjects must learn to live with their monarch's decision. In time they shall thank me for my choice to marry a foreign prince. With the power of the Holy Roman Emperor behind me, the catholic faith will be triumphant, and a catholic prince will soon follow to put aside all their fears."

January 1554

It seemed that, just months after her coronation, Mary was suddenly falling from favour when the announcement of her engagement to the prince of Spain was met with a hostile reaction from her people.

"This is why," Mary exclaimed, her eyes blazing, so similarly to her father's, "We should have irradicated the Protestant vermin before any other matter! They are causing widespread unrest through their manipulative propaganda and creating a smear campaign against their monarch! It is treason!"

The imperial ambassador, who Mary had begun entrusting over any other of her councillors, gazed silently ahead as the naïve queen rambled about the unfairness of her situation.

It had become widely believed throughout the country that Charles V of Spain was planning to use the queen's feminine inferiorities to his advantage by tempting her with promises of wedded bliss and security, while cleverly using their unity to drag England into Spain's ongoing war with France.

The French king, having heard along with the rest of Europe, that England and Spain were considering a union, began to fear exactly that, and he sent orders to his French ambassadors at English court to secretly do all in their power to interfere with the match.

They had begun by spreading rumours to anyone who would listen that Spain was planning invasions of France with English troops for fodder, and it did not take long for the people of England to be in uproar.

"Our match is causing civil unrest," Mary continued to rage in private to the imperial ambassador, "Perhaps it would be best not to continue on this route, after all."

Renard looked at the queen's face – strained and haggard from an emotionally distressing life – and he contemplated his response carefully.

He knew that Mary put a lot of faith in him, for she clung to the belief that Spain would always back her and put her interests first. He also knew, that while the lady was educated as a child on how to rule, she had spent the majority of her life confined to various castles and had very little experience of politic and life. With this insight he knew to take advantage of her naivety, for it was not Queen Mary I of England whom he served, but king Charles V of Spain, and though the union between England and Spain may cause unrest to her people, it brought great advantages to his master.

"The king has sent his envoy to discuss the details of the marriage contract," he said calmly, having learned early on in her reign that she admired his coolheaded nature, "My king is not interested in a war with France, but do not take my word for it alone... the contract will have in it the specifications what he truly wants."

"Which is?" Mary asked, baffled.

"He wishes to take control of the sea between Spain and the Netherlands," Renard said honestly, "and to open the trade route between the two countries."

Mary raised her eyebrows and nodded, "Ah," was all she said.

The ambassador continued quickly, "The king is prepared to be very generous to put your people's mind at ease," he said as he shifted in his seat, "He is extremely eager to secure this match. He believes it to be of great interest to you and him, both."

Mary nodded but was not entirely convinced.

Her people's love was of extreme value to her, more so perhaps even than the love of a husband, since it had been the people's support that had raised her to attain the crown, and without them she would be queen of no-one.

"I shall await the king's envoy," Mary said diplomatically, "to learn of the more specific details of the marriage contract." Then she stood, concluding their conversation.

The imperial ambassador rose from his seat before her and bowed, "Your majesty."

Then he exited the queen's chambers, leaving Mary to wonder if marrying the Spanish prince would be a reckless move on her part.

But her time to consider all her options had run out.

Queen Mary was a woman of thirty-eight and quickly approaching her seniority in terms of conceiving a child.

The production of a catholic heir to succeed her was imperative for England's future as a catholic kingdom, and though her people continued to display hostility at the union, she saw no other valid reason to object to the marriage with Filipe of Spain.

"It aches my heart," Mary called out as she sat upon her throne in the great hall, "to know this decision will enrage my subjects so profusely. But I hereby announce that the marriage contract between myself and the prince of Spain has been agreed," and she looked upon the faces of her court, "With this union England gains more than it loses. I have been assured that Spain seeks no invasion of France, and I give my solemn vow that they will certainly have no luck in gaining any English troops if king Charles V changes his mind in the future on that matter."

The noble ladies and gentlemen of the court cheered and clapped at the announcement, giving their queen the distinct impression that they were indeed happy to hear the news.

Just a few days later, however, when the prince of Spain was due to arrive at the English coast, an uprising ensued to try to prevent his arrival.

The rumours spread by the French Ambassadors, as well as those who secretly practiced Protestantism within London, had been enough to cause widespread belief that Spain would indeed lead England to certain war with France, despite the fact that their queen had publicly announced Spain's signed declaration that they would not.

"What do we know of the traitors?" Mary asked her council as news of the uprising reached the Palace.

"At the head of the uprising," Vice-Chamberlain Jerningham replied, "is the Protestant Sir Thomas Wyatt, as well as the father to the late Jane Grey, Henry Grey the Duke of Suffolk. The queen's own potential suitor Edward Courtenay," he glanced at Gardner who had suggested the match, "is also involved."

"They must be found," Mary declared icily.

"I can assure you, your majesty," Simon Renard replied, "That they will be."

"They are gaining much support," Jerningham added, "It is said their numbers are growing by the hour."

Mary nodded as she stared straight ahead, unable to think of a suitable reply to such treacherous news.

"Are their numbers large enough for an overthrowal?" Cardinal Pole said, giving voice to everyone's concern.

"Not before we find them and put them to justice," Jerningham replied passionately as he banged his fist upon the council table.

Ironically, it was indeed their large number of followers that inevitably ruined the rebels' hopes of remaining secret, and just a few days later Gardner learned, through his personal spies, of Edward Courtenay's location.

The Lord Chancellor wasted no time in relaying a message to Courtenay that it would be in his best interest to meet with him.

Courtenay, being young and foolish, met with Gardner eagerly and without his accomplices' knowledge, and it did not take long before all important details had been extracted from the boastful and thoughtless young man.

The local leaders of the uprising, having heard of Courtenay's betrayal to their cause, quickly panicked and fled towards France, their fifteen thousand supporters fleeing with them in hopes of regrouping for a swift return. But as they travelled, their forces learned that it proved almost impossible to flee to France during the winter, and they did not remain loyal for long, most of them deserting their leaders Thomas Wyatt and Henry Grey.

Those few that did remain, returned with Wyatt and Grey to Westminster in hopes of procuring a pardon, but they were met by forces loyal to their queen.

"What is your ruling my queen?" Mary's captain of the guard asked as the traitors approached in the distance.

Mary blinked, keeping her expression hardened, "There will be no pardon for such treason against the crown," she replied, "If they fight, kill them. If they surrender, arrest them."

The captain of the guard bowed and hurried away to give the command to his men to be prepared for a battle.

As Wyatt and Grey made contact with Mary's forces, a brief exchange of words occurred where their pardon was denied, and, as Mary had predicted, a battle ensued.

But the three thousand remaining men of Wyatt's rebellion could not withstand the queen's twenty-five thousand, and it was not long before they surrendered.

All three thousand men and their leaders Wyatt, Grey and Courtenay were hereby arrested and taken to either the Tower of London or to the Fleet Prison by the River Fleet, to await their trial.

March 1554

For the weeks that followed, prisoners were tried every day, the punishment for their treason being death by hanging.

Since the rebels' capture and imprisonment, prince Filipe and his household had arrived upon the shores of England, and while their arrival had not been met with much animation from the people, the Spaniards nonetheless made their way into London with as much flourish as would be expected from a prince of Spain.

"He has arrived! He is here," Frances said excitedly when news came that Prince Felipe was on his way.

Mary looked up from the bible on her lap, "That is great news," she said, but her tone did not suggest that she meant it.

Frances frowned, "Are you unwell, your majesty?" she asked as she approached.

Mary looked around herself to gauge whether the servants were out of earshot, "No more so than usual," she said tellingly, and Frances knew that Mary was referring to her ailment, the strangulation of the womb, as the physicians called it.

"Do you wish me to close he shutters?" Frances asked quietly as she turned towards the open windows.

"No, it is not too bad," Mary said as she raised her hand, "I was in much pain last night, but I am well now," but she shifted uncomfortably in her seat.

"Let me loosen your corset to aid with the swelling," Frances suggested as she so often had done in the past when Mary's inflamed belly would bulge uncontrollably.

"No," Mary said then, feeling suddenly flustered, "I must endure. I cannot be seen with loosened attire. I am the queen now."

Frances chewed her lip in worry but nodded, "Do you wish me to fetch the physician?" she whispered.

Mary looked up, "Perhaps that would be a good idea," she agreed, "But do not fetch him to me, I only need a vial of my remedy making."

The lady-in-waiting smiled, glad to be of service, "I shan't be long," she said and hurried away on her errand.

As Frances made her way through the halls, she contemplated Mary's chronic ailment.

For decades she had suffered with the strange symptoms, never showing any signs of improvement, and yet, since she had been crowned queen, Mary had shown incredible restraint when it came to keeping her suffering hidden from the world.

Her newfound strength in containing her pain was undoubtedly a show for her courtiers' sake, for to suggest any sign of weakness in a monarch would surely mean the beginning of the end, as it had done with her father's wounded leg.

Frances knew that by simply being at the age of thirty-eight years old, unmarried and childless, Mary was already at an enormous disadvantage as a ruling monarch, that adding a mysterious and unrelenting illness to the mix would have nothing good come of it.

Upon arriving at the apothecary, she quietly requested the queen's physician to blend her majesty's special mixture, and as she waited Frances said a silent prayer that Mary would be in good health by the time the prince arrived to meet her in a few hours' time.

For England's future as a catholic nation hung in the balance, and nothing aided the path of love less than a bloated and flushed middle-aged woman, clinging to life by the skin of her rotten teeth.

Mary swallowed the vial's contents whole and lay down in her darkened bedroom as she awaited the arrival of her betrothed at Greenwich Palace, hopeful that when she woke that she would feel something beyond intense nervousness and nausea.

Surprisingly, when Frances gently shook her awake just an hour later, Mary awoke clear-headed and ready to finally meet the man that would be her husband, and as she sat up in bed, the memory of her very first betrothal at the age of just two-years-old flashed in her mind.

How long had she awaited this moment? It seemed almost as though all those other betrothals had happened in a former life, to someone else entirely.

The great hall and the throne room had been decorated with tapestries of cloth of gold and silk, to welcome the prince with England's best, and Mary thought it only fitting that she too would be adorned in her finest.

To meet her betrothed she chose to wear a dress of black velvet and covered herself in jewels befitting her station, and as she glanced at herself in the mirror, she thought briefly how pretty she looked, and what a shame it was that so many of her teeth were stained with decay.

But there was little time to ponder things she could not change, for as soon as she was decent there was a knock on the door, and the prince of Spain was announced by her usher.

Flustered to be meeting him in a much more personal setting than she had initially planned, Mary froze as she found herself face to face with a tall, handsome young man, displaying a full beard and dark eyebrows, dark eyes and full lips.

Mary felt her heart skip a beat at the handsome figure before her and felt suddenly ashamed that he would no doubt be feeling nothing of the sort at the short, aging lady before him. But before she could sink deeper into her shallow pond of self-worth, prince Felipe leaned forward and kissed his betrothed in accordance with English custom, and Mary was taken aback by his high sense of decorum and protocol.

And though not a word had yet been spoken between the two of them, Mary believed she and Felipe of Spain would make a fantastic match.

Thomas Wyatt and Henry Grey's trials were concluded quickly, their treason giving them no escape, and they were condemned to die by beheading.

One hundred and fifty of their supporters had also been executed in accordance to their betrayal. And yet, when Mary's future husband suggested they show the remaining two-thousand-eight-hundred-and-fifty traitors mercy, Mary was relieved to see he had a forgiving heart.

"It would bring me much peace," Filipe said slowly, his Spanish accent noticeable as he considered his words, "If your majesty would consider showing the remaining prisoners mercy."

"You do know," Mary replied, "That they are imprisoned for their rebellion against our union."

Filipe nodded, "*Si,*" he said, "But I believe that is precisely why we should be lenient. Show them that you are a forgiving mother to her children, and let our union begin with compassion."

Mary smiled up at him as they strolled the gardens, "I appreciate your benevolence for my people," she said, "Perhaps you are right," and she dropped her gaze as if to contemplate his suggestion, though she had already decided that it would be exactly what she would do.

Chapter 19

May 1554
Greenwich Palace, London

The royal couple spent much time together, often strolling the palace gardens hand in hand or deep in conversation, and it was noted by many courtiers that the pair seemed to get on very well indeed. Their wedding would be the first royal wedding England had witnessed since Henry VIII's last one to the late Catherine Parr over ten years ago, and though there had been much outrage at the prospect of this day, the people could not help but gather excitedly at the church of Winchester to await the arrival of their queen and her king consort.

That morning, Mary was standing by her open window, gazing out over the city, as she tried to calm her unsteady breathing.

Her wedding day had finally come after nearly four decades of waiting and countless failed betrothals; and yet she did not feel as fulfilled as she had imagined she would.

The prince treated her kindly and was clearly well versed in the forms of etiquette, and though he was young and handsome, she could not shake the thought of the first Phillip she had almost married.

Mary's throat closed at the thought of the duke of Palatine-Neuburg, and she swallowed hard to keep from crying on her wedding day.

Mary groaned at herself in exasperation. Those days had been lustful and sinful, and she should not be thinking of them on the day of her marriage to another.

And yet she could not stop herself from comparing the two Phillips, and the different ways in which she felt about them.

Mary squeezed her eyes shut and threw her head back in frustration as she tried to calm her thoughts.

When she eventually opened her eyes, she watched as a seagull soared in the sky above her, cawing thoughtlessly, and she allowed her mind to go blank. She closed her eyes again and breathed in the summer air and it dawned on her yet again that perhaps she had simply not been born for happiness.

But this marriage was not intended for love.

It was not intended for companionship or for any matters of the heart.

This match had been created for the sole purpose of the production of a catholic heir, one which would have the strength of Spain behind him, and which would keep England safely within the catholic practices for all the years to come.

It did not matter that Felipe did not make her swoon; it did not matter what they thought of one another at all. It only mattered what would come of their union.

Mary smiled then as she realised, like a bolt of lightning to the brain, that her life's greatest achievement went hand in hand with great loss. But also, that she would gladly give it all up again to be where she stood this day.

No, Mary reminded herself as she inhaled deeply, she had not been born for happiness. She had been born to rule.

The wedding night went by quite contrary to the wedding day.

Where the day had been long and slow, with many traditions, speeches, feasting and dancing, the night went by quickly and without much ado.

Mary, having had to pretend to know nothing of the goings on between husband and wife in the bedchambers, lay motionless on her back while the inebriated young Spaniard thrusted urgently above her. Mary had tried not to take it to heart that he had had his face buried in the pillows over her shoulder

373

throughout the two-minute incident and was simply glad when it was over, for it meant their marriage was officially concluded and a prince may be within her womb shortly thereafter.

Once Filipe had rolled off her, Mary had lain back motionlessly, staring up at the ceiling as she waited patiently for the steady snoring that signified a deep slumber.

When she was certain Felipe was asleep – or perhaps simply passed out from all the wine – she slowly slid out of bed and pulled a small knife out from underneath the mattress which she had stored there the night before.

In one swift motion she sliced a small but deep cut into the heel of her own foot, then quickly stashed the knife back underneath the mattress, climbed back under the sheets beside her husband and listened intently for any change in his breathing.

As the sound of Felipe's steady snoring continued, Mary lay on her side with her knees tucked up against her chest in the hope that the cut on her foot would bleed enough for the sheets to feign for those that had been lain on by a former virgin.

And she prayed to God for forgiveness.

September 1554

"Your majesty," Cecily whispered to her queen one morning as they were getting her dressed, "do you wish me to close the shutters?"

Mary looked at her lady-in-waiting and frowned, "No, Cecily," she said, "I am quite well."

Cecily nodded at Mary but gave Frances a confused look over her shoulder and Frances frowned questioningly in reply.

Cecily responded silently by raising her eyebrow and looking down at Mary's corset, which would not fasten properly as it often did when she was suffering from her illness, due to bloating.

Frances shrugged her shoulders briefly to which Cecily *tsked* under her breath and widened her eyes in provocation, to urge Frances to understand her silent exchange.

Mary, having noticed her ladies acting strangely behind her back, turned to face them, "May I know what all this is about?"

Cecily cleared her throat while Frances and Mary both looked at her confused, "Your majesty," Cecily said, "Forgive me but do you not feel unwell?"

"No," Mary answered simply.

"Then may I be so bold as to ask if you have had your courses this month?" Cecily said with a knowing smile.

Mary took a step towards her, "You know my courses have always been irregular."

"Yes," her lady admitted, "But do you recall when you had your last one?"

Frances suddenly gasped in realisation as Mary considered the question.

"Not since before king Felipe arrived, your highness!" Frances squealed excitedly.

"What of it?" Mary asked, "It is not unheard of for me not to bleed for several months," she replied.

"No," Cecily agreed, "But you have been wedded and bedded and your belly has grown. If you are not suffering your usually aches and sensitivity to the sunlight, then the only other explanation may be -"

"—That I am with child?" Mary said incredulously as she put a hand to her belly, finally understanding what her ladies were suggesting.

Frances clapped her hands excitedly, "Your majesty!" she exclaimed in congratulations.

375

Mary looked up and smiled, "Call the physician, Frances," she ordered, "I shall know for certain before I announce it."

The old physician came at once and, after asking some questions and examining the queen's swollen belly, he nodded, "You are indeed with child, your majesty," he said with certainty.

His confirmation was so confident that Mary instantly burst into tears, "It is a miracle," she sobbed as he packed up his instruments, "I have never been so happy!"

Immediately, Mary ordered for dresses to be made to fit her expanding shape, and rumours were flying across the court that a new heir was underway. Mary walked around the palace with her head held high and her hands cradling the little bump before her, while her smile never faded.

King Felipe was of course informed, to which he reacted accordingly by congratulating his wife and queen with a kiss, but Mary could tell that he was not as overjoyed as she.

But Mary did not let the man's ego dampen her mood, for she understood that the implications of creating heirs with her as queen regnant of England, meant that their first child would be an heir for England, and not for Spain, which would be difficult for a foreign prince to accept.

But his reaction did not vex her, for he was completing his purpose, that was all that mattered.

Queen Mary's pregnancy did anything but soften her.

As queen of England in her own right, and therefore supreme leader of her country, Mary had no time to rest as former queens with child had been able to do.

She had the task of both a man and a woman upon her shoulders, being solely in charge of the production of an heir as well as the running of the entire country.

But Mary did not mind, for it was in her blood to do just that.

In fact, the official confirmation that she was indeed with child only spurred Mary on to continue her quest of leading her people back to the true faith. It was suddenly imperative that, by the time she had borne England an heir, it would be cleansed of all its impurities and be ready for her child to inherit as a pure and catholic kingdom.

Mary thought long and hard about how she would go about the sudden change for her people, but if the rebellion led by Wyatt and Grey had taught her anything, it was that it would not be enough for her people to love her. Wyatt's rebellion had been spurred by simple rumours and protestant propaganda, and within days it had gathered thousands of people to rebel and plot against her.

It was something she could not risk happening again.

For her reign to be as long as her father's had been, Mary would need to incite not only love, but also fear; and what better way to do that than by reintroducing some of the old laws of the land.

Queen Mary put forth a bill that called for the revival of the Heresy Act, which had been repealed by king Henry VIII. The Heresy Act proclaimed that to be a Protestant was a crime punisheable by death, and that all Protestants who refused to convert to Catholicism were to be burned.

"The nobles that have gained vast riches from their Protestant faith will not easily be quashed," the Cardinal Pole pointed out.

"There is also the matter of you own sister…" imperial ambassador Renard added slyly, his small eyes narrowed as he observed the queen's reaction.

"Half-sister," Mary reminded her councillors icily.

"Nevertheless, she will not be easily converted," Renard continued, "Nor will the Archbishop Cranmer for that matter."

"Cranmer is a heretic," Mary stated the obvious, "He, like every other protestant, will have to convert by the time the reinstated laws come into effect if they wish to remain on this earth. According to all of you there are not many in the land who still follow the Protestant faith. So, there should not be much opposition. However," she added as she looked down at the table before her as she tried to avoid making eye contact with her advisors, "I will deal with Elizabeth myself."

"What will you do, your majesty?" Gardner asked, curiously.

"She is stubborn," Mary admitted, "Just like her whore mother before her. But she is no fool. My hope is that she will listen and make the right choice. For no one shall be exempt from these laws, not even my own flesh and blood."

January 1555

The Heresy Acts had officially become part of the law of the land, and the outcome was utter terror among the people.

Catholics and Protestants alike feared their new queen for the way in which she had chosen to rule her subjects, leaving England in a nervous and unsettled state.

It began with the arrests of the bishops that represented the extreme reforming party of England, John Hooper, John Rogers and John Cardmaster were all taken to the Tower and condemned by bishop Stephen Gardner after they refused to give up their heretical beliefs.

They all burned at the stake.

The next to follow was her father's long-time advisor, the Archbishop of Canterbury, Thomas Cranmer.

Queen Mary hoped that his arrest would be enough to deter the Protestants from their sinful paths, fearing in her heart that her subjects were all doomed to Hell if they did not accept the catholic faith into their souls.

Never in all her years had she envisioned her reign to be so troubled and dark. After all the adoration she had received upon her coronation it felt almost as though she were living within a terrible dream.

But nonetheless, Mary told herself that monarchs would never be loved by every subject, and that her determination for the ultimate good of the realm, meant the unfortunate demise of a chosen few.

After all, she had given all of them the chance to right their wrongs, and to accept the true faith to guide them away from their profane beliefs. But unfortunately, there would always be those who would not listen to reason, and before they could continue to corrupt the rest, they would need weeding out.

But her actions triggered growing hatred among the people towards their queen.

People of both faiths felt suddenly unsafe in their own homes, never knowing what act or word would be deemed as heresy or not.

Many destroyed or hid their books, fearful that one may be misconstrued as a heretical item and would condemn them to their fiery end.

Fifty-eight of the queen's own subjects, both men and women, had already been burned alive, and it was not long before the people who had welcomed and adored her, now referred to their queen as 'Bloody Mary'.

"*Bloody* Mary?" the queen screeched in disgust, "How dare they?! I should have them all arrested for such disrespect!"

"You must not exert yourself too much, your majesty," Cecily pointed out from behind her as the queen and her advisors sat around the council table.

Mary frowned and sighed, "What other news is there, Lord Chancellor?" she asked in an attempt to change the subject and relieve her tightening chest.

"The king consort has begun making plans for the succession," Gardner said as he looked down at his documents, "In case of your majesty's –"

Mary waved her hand, "Yes, yes in case I die in childbed," and she sighed angrily, "As queen regnant it is rather tasteless is it not? Being as it imagines my death."

The councillors looked around at each other, the situation being completely new to all of them who had never before served a queen regnant.

"Indeed," the imperial ambassador braved, "However it is imperative that the line of succession is clear if it were to happen."

"Once my son is born," Mary said as she placed her hand upon her heavily swollen belly, "there will be no doubt as to who will follow my reign."

"There is the question of your half-sister," Renard mentioned boldly.

"What of her?" Mary prompted, almost as if to provoke the ambassador into admitting his disapproval over Mary not yet having convicted her Protestant sister as a heretic.

"Well, she has not converted to Catholicism –" he voiced brazenly.

"Argh!" Mary exclaimed angrily, cutting him off with a wave of her hand, "The stubborn girl will say one thing and do another. She expressly promised me to my face that she would attend Mass, then has a stomach sickness every time. What am I to do?"

The question was rhetorical, yet every one of her council members looked down or raised an eyebrow, each of them silently suggesting that the only action left to take was the one so many others had suffered. But they all knew the queen would not sentence her little sister to such a fate, no matter how many threats she spewed in anger.

"The other option we have," Gardner added from his seat beside the queen, "is to surpass your half-sister and declare the young Scottish queen your heir. As your father's grand-niece she would be accepted, and she is a catholic –"

"But she is engaged to marry the dauphin of France!" ambassador Renard exclaimed in horror, "That is not an option."

"It is an option, *senor* ambassador," Mary interjected, "If I so choose it. But I will have to discuss things with my husband on the matter before any decisions are made today."

And with a slight nod of her head, her ladies emerged from the shadows behind her and helped Mary up from her seat at the head of the table. Then the men before her stood up, bowed, and exited the room.

Shortly after they left, and Mary had taken a seat by the hearth to warm her swollen feet, there was a swift knock and the door opened.

"Felipe," Mary said in greeting as he entered and walked towards her.

"My queen," he said as he bowed, took her hand and raised it to his lips, his rough beard scratching at her skin.

"Sit with me a while," Mary offered with a closed smile, self-conscious of her black teeth, "We must discuss the line of succession."

"I have some thoughts on the matter, your majesty," Felipe said, his voice nonchalant, "The queen of Scots is out of the question."

Mary flinched at his bluntness, "You forget yourself, my love," Mary said with a laugh, "It is not your decision."

Felipe instantly frowned and looked down at the ground as he mumbled in Spanish.

Mary raised her eyebrows, "I urge you to speak up," she warned.

He raised his head and looked at his wife, his queen, his superior, "*Siempre me recuerdas quien es el verdadero rey.*"

Mary breathed a short laugh, "Well, yes," she said, "It seems I must remind you who England's true 'king' is, when you come in here declaring decisions as though your opinion alone is what matters! *You* are the king, my love. But in this union, I as queen, am still above you, as this is *my* country."

"Then what do you propose we do!" Felipe retorted acidly, "Your cousin the Scottish queen is to marry France's prince. She is to inherit England too? Then what is to happen to *Espana*?!"

"I agree it would not be preferrable," Mary said carefully, "but it is my decision to make."

Felipe stood up in one fluid motion, throwing his hands in the air and began pacing up and down in agitation.

"It will not matter," Mary said then in an attempt to soothe her hot-headed spouse, "I am healthy and will survive childbed. Then we will have our very own heir for the throne of England."

Felipe stopped in his tracks, his hand over his bearded chin in thought, "And what if you do not?"

Mary scoffed in shock, "I will convince my sister to convert to Catholicism," she said, her voice giving away how uncertain even she was in her own promise.

It was Felipe's turn to scoff, "That little girl will not do as you say, *my queen*," he said, and Mary pressed her lips together to contain the rage she felt over his tone, "She is as poisonous as an adder, and no matter what she promises you, she will not keep it."

Mary nodded in thought but did not reply, the acidity in his tone leaving a bad taste in her mouth.

"Aha!" Filipe suddenly exclaimed, "We should have her wed."

"Elizabeth?" Mary asked, dumbfounded.

"Si!" he replied as he sat back down beside her, "If we were to wed her to a Catholic, perhaps even to an ally to the Holy Roman Emperor himself, we could control her better."

Mary released a breathy laugh, unsure as to whether her husband was jesting or just mad, "She will not accept," Mary pointed out.

Felipe took Mary's face in his hands and looked her straight in her pale blue eyes, "You are the queen of England, are you not?" he said forcefully, "You will make her."

May 1555
Hampton Court Palace, London

Preparations were being made for the queen's confinement, and she and her household travelled to Hampton Court Palace where she wished for the birth to take place.

The birthing chamber was prepared, as well as the nursery, where a beautifully carved cradle was made for England's new heir, and many women, including wet nurses and maids were hired in preparation for the royal baby.

Mary decided to invite her half-sister Elizabeth to be with her during her confinement, as it would mean spending six weeks in close proximity with one another without the distraction of other courtiers, and Mary was convinced that she could get through to her little sister on the matter of her faith if she just had enough one on one time to help her see the light.

But there never did come a time in which Mary and Elizabeth could speak freely, for almost as soon as the queen was confined to the dark and airless chambers, her mind began to spiral into alarming depths of melancholy, which no one, not even Mary herself, could explain.

Days would go by during which Mary could do nothing but sob uncontrollably, curled up in a ball on the floor and her ladies could do nothing to aid her. It was as though she could not see nor hear them, and they feared that their queen had indeed gone deaf, blind, and mad.

After several days of little eating and uncontrollable crying, her ladies called the midwives to examine the queen, fearing that perhaps she had lost the child and had been unable to utter the words.

"What if she has miscarried?" Frances asked Cecily quietly as the midwives flocked around the queen's bed.

"There would be blood," Cecily said, her voice completely emotionless.

"What if the baby is… dead?" Frances whispered in horror, her doe eyes wide in fear.

"What if there is no baby," came a sing-songy voice behind them and they both turned to curtsy to the lady Elizabeth.

"Your grace," Frances mumbled while Cecily remained silent.

"There may not be a baby at all," Elizabeth repeated.

The lady was now a beautiful woman of twenty-one. Her skin was as pale as snow except for her pink cheeks and she too had inherited their father's red hair, although hers was not auburn like Mary's but a much brassier tone which Cecily noticed looked almost like flames dancing upon her head.

"Of course there is a baby," Cecily said monotonously, "The queen has all the signs."

Elizabeth shrugged, "I am only making conversation," and she turned and left, her walk so light she may as well have been floating.

Frances watched her leave, then turned to Cecily, "Do you think she may be right?"

"How would that even happen?"

Frances raised an eyebrow, "Perhaps God has taken the child away…" she thought aloud.

Cecily looked at her from the corner of her eye and replied while hardly moving her mouth, "Never say such a *stupid* thing again, Frances, if you value your life."

Frances nodded, aware of the recklessness in her statement, "The babe will be making Mary sad. Once he is born, she shall be recovered."

Cecily inhaled deeply as she watched the midwives try and fail to soothe the hysterical queen, "Let us pray you are right."

One night, as Mary's ladies read their bibles by the hearth and Elizabeth embroidered by the window, Mary suddenly sat bolt upright in her bed, and wailed like a wild animal.

Immediately her ladies jumped up and raced to alarm the midwives.

"It is coming," Mary said through gritted teeth, "The baby is coming."

Frances laughed breathlessly in relief – it seemed her queen had been expecting after all – and she crossed herself quickly before attending to Mary.

The room was filled with midwives in an instant, all of which fluttered around the queen, mopping her brow and whispering calming words in her ear, while the eldest midwife peeked beneath the sheets.

"Has your majesty been feeling any pains?" the old midwife asked.

Mary nodded, "Yes, it comes and goes. Is that normal?" she asked, her voice breaking with fear.

The midwife laughed, her cheeks wrinkling with delight at the naïve question, "Very normal, your majesty. Remain calm. All will be well."

Another pain ripped through Mary and the old midwife between her legs popped her head up suddenly, her face ashen, "Your majesty must push right away!"

385

"Already?" one of the other midwives replied, horrified.

Mary looked around the room in search of a kind face and found her sister by her side, "Elizabeth," she said, and Elizabeth took her sister's hand, "Do not leave my side," Mary said, her plea so raw and vulnerable that Elizabeth could not help but suddenly fear for her older sister.

"I am here," she said calmly, and smiled.

Just then another pain washed over Mary and the midwife urged her to push. Mary inhaled deeply and pushed with all her might as her body shuddered in shock.

Suddenly there was a surprised exclamation from the old midwife at the foot of the bed, and a loud gush as Mary's waters broke and her baby fell out from within her. Mary looked up at the midwife and searched her wrinkled face for a positive reaction as to whether it was a boy or a girl, but all she saw was panic.

"What – What is it?" Mary stammered as she tried to sit up.

The other midwives moved closer to observe the new-born baby and at once recoiled or gasped, covering their mouths in disgust.

"What is it? What's wrong?" Mary cried, her face twisted in devastation, for surely their reaction could only mean the babe had not been born alive, like so many of her mother's babies.

The old midwife swallowed and bundled the babe in the prepared blanket, her face never changing as she walked towards her queen, "Do you wish to see?" she asked, her voice suggesting Mary would not like what she saw.

Mary nodded and stretched out her arms, "I wish to see my baby," she said boldly.

But when the bundle was placed in her arms she recoiled in horror, "What is this?" she whispered in horror as though someone had handed her the wrong creature.

The bundle felt fleshy in her arms and when nobody replied Mary placed the bundle down beside her on the bed and

386

unwrapped the blanket from around it to reveal a large, oval shaped mass. It was the size of a cantaloupe, but pinkish in colour with patches of thick, wiry black hair and teeth that protruded out of it on one side. It was not breathing nor was it moving, its appearance suggesting it was never alive to begin with, and suddenly Mary began to see black all around her. Her head fell back onto the pillows, and she could hear the midwives rushing towards her, shouting at one another. Then she closed her eyes, her last thought before she fell into a deep sleep being that this must be God's punishment for all her past sins.

Greenwich Palace

"The people are celebrating!" Stephen Gardner fretted, "Rumours have spread of a healthy birth. What are we to do?"

"I cannot say," the imperial ambassador said, leaving Gardner dumbfounded by his lack of words.

They remained silent for a while as they contemplated the grotesque news they had received earlier that same day.

"We must announce that the pregnancy was false, and that there was no baby," Gardner then said as he chewed the nail on his thumb.

"No baby?" Renard echoed as he narrowed his eyes.

"I have heard it can occur," Gardner replied as he stared ahead unseeingly as he thought.

"Surely the people will not believe that," Renard argued.

"They will believe whatever we tell them."

The ambassador frowned and ran his hand through his thick hair in uncertainty, "I am not sure," he admitted.

"We cannot allow the kingdom to know of this... this *thing* the queen birthed," Gardner said passionately, "To do so would condemn her as a witch and all of us as her sycophants. Catholic England would fall!"

Renard nodded slowly, "You are right. No one must know," and they both fell silent once more.

"I assume the creature has been… disposed of?" Renard then asked after a long silence.

The Lord Chancellor nodded, "It was thrown into the fire as soon as it was born. The queen is yet to recover from the shock."

"We must pray she regains her strength and may attempt to conceive again. We must have a catholic heir to the throne. Preferably one who is not married to the Dauphin of France, or one who is deformed beyond human recognition."

Gardner shuddered, "I heard it had horns sprouting from it."

Renard shook his head, "We shall never know for certain," he said emphatically, "But I am glad to not have seen it with my own eyes. To have that ingrained in one's memory… it must not be an easy burden to bear."

August 1555

Queen Mary emerged from her confinement in complete silence, and it was clear to everyone who set eyes upon her, that their queen was furious.

She returned to Greenwich Palace utterly humiliated over her public failure and days went by in which the queen did not eat as self-punishment for the disastrous incident, and in the hope of cleansing her rotten soul.

While she had grown impossibly thin, Mary still maintained an arduous workload, fuelled entirely by her rage. She summoned her council every day since her return from her confinement to discuss matters of state in secret, without even her ladies to attend her.

But it was on one such day, while her ladies dressed her in preparation for the day ahead, that Mary would share her woes with them as her anger boiled over yet again.

"Even from the grave my father continues to devastate any scrap of happiness I might have had," Mary spat out angrily as her ladies went about tightening her corset and tying her skirts.

Cecily gave Frances a look and shook her head slightly, urging her not to reply.

But Mary did not wait for an answer and continued ranting in hatred, "He kept me waiting – frozen – for decades!" she exclaimed, "Betrothed to one man, then another, never *actually* marrying. Always just there *in case* I could be of use! And let's not forget everything he did to have a precious boy – ha! –the irony of it all does not escape me... his cherished son, whom he moved mountains to obtain, never even grew old enough to produce heirs, and now his eldest daughter is... *too* old! His ego has ruined countless lives, and for what? Now neither of his first two heirs have been able to continue his line, and Elizabeth – God only knows what will happen if that stubborn little fool inherits my throne!" she stomped her foot then like a petulant child and balled her fists at her sides as she let out a ragged, animalistic screech, "Even in death his actions haunt me! That accursed man!"

Her ladies continued in silence, tying the sleeves to her dress, and putting on her shoes.

"This should be *my* moment," Mary continued, "the one I have been waiting and praying for my entire life! I was going to prove him wrong, but now what am I left with?!" and she fell silent then and sat on the edge of her bed in a heap of fabric.

"You may try again, your majesty," Frances mumbled bravely.

Mary scoffed, "The king will not even look at me, Frances," she admitted, "And he is set to sail to the Netherlands on business for Spain this coming week. So tell me, you stupid girl, how is one to conceive without a man's intent?"

389

Frances looked down at the ground, "Forgive me, your majesty," she mumbled.

"Go away," Mary ordered Frances, and she curtsied and hurried out of the rooms.

Mary sighed heavily once the door was closed behind her, "I know it is not her fault, but I no longer care for her enthusiasm. It irks my very soul."

"What will you do next, your highness?" Cecily asked casually as she brushed down Mary's other dresses.

Mary walked over to the open window, "Do?" she said as she looked out over the city, "There is much to do, Cecily. Come," and she waved a hand for her lady to join her at the window, "Do you see them all down there, running around like ants?"

Cecily pretended to pay close attention to the people below, as she knew Mary would want her to, "Yes."

"Like my father, they too are to blame," Mary said, her tone icy.

Cecily turned to face Mary, "I do not understand," she confessed.

"Had they only accepted my decision to wed Filipe sooner," Mary explained through gritted teeth, "and had they not *rebelled* and defied their sovereign queen's word, he would have come to England much earlier and we could have conceived a healthy child. The intense pressure my own people put me under not even a year into my reign... it burdened me. Their rebellion left me drained and fearful. It is something I did not expect to feel anymore after finally acquiring the crown. I always believed becoming queen would finally soothe that frightful feeling, that it would keep me safe."

Cecily fell silent and looked down at the city once more, this time taking in the sights of the common people below as they went about their day selling their goods, some shouting at their children to behave, some even whoring in the dark alleys. And Cecily suddenly felt a shiver run down her spine in dread for them as she considered Mary's intent.

"I know you have not been the same since those days, your majesty," Cecily replied tactfully, "But they are not all to blame for it."

"No, you are right, Cecily," Mary agreed with a nod of her head, "They are not all to blame. It is not all of my people who make me fear the future. But there are those who seek to supplant me. They are hidden in the shadows, but their whispers are the loudest of them all. They are the ones who try to turn my catholic subjects against me. They are the ones who spread the idea to call me *Bloody Mary*."

Cecily swallowed and watched her old friend's face grow twisted with hatred as she spoke.

"The traitors and heretics must all be dealt with," Mary uttered bitterly, "Upon my death, if I am to forfeit my crown to another who is not my own, then I must make sure that my country is cleansed of its heresy. They have no idea the lengths I will go to to protect the true faith, and if they wish me to become this Bloody Mary, then so be it."

October 1555

And so it came to be.

The burning at the stake of Protestant priests and common folk alike became a daily fixture in the city of London, a total of two-hundred and thirty-seven having been condemned heretics to burn alive for their sins and more being arrested every day.

The people of England were in distress, fearing for their lives each day, being unable to trust even their friends or neighbours for fear they would be thrown to the wolves for even the slightest misstep.

There had not been such civil unrest since the Cousin's War nearly a hundred years earlier, when the Yorks and Lancasters had fought over the throne for three decades.

But Mary would not be deterred. She believed that once the core of the disease was eliminated that the remainder of her reign would be glorious, and though she knew better than to hope for a miracle that would bring her an heir, she now simply hoped to leave England healed from the years of poisoning her brother and father had inflicted.

Mary could feel her anger fading with the burning of each heretic and in its stead, slowly but surely, the sadness crept in.

Though she had suffered a great loss on that frightful day, she had not yet allowed herself to mourn, and with the country in complete ignorance about the birth, Mary felt unable to grieve for her child that no one would even know had ever existed.

She had agreed with her council on their plan to hide the truth of the deformed babe – for nothing good would have come of it if her people knew the truth – and thankfully, the initial news that had spread like wildfire across the country of a healthy boy suddenly dispersed into the wind, and no one ever mentioned it since.

The midwives who attended her during her confinement had been paid off to secure their silence, while her ladies and Elizabeth were likely to be trusted and were therefore the only ones who truly understood what trauma she had endured that day.

But Mary did not wish to speak of it. The thing had been tossed into the fire without giving even a sound of protest, and it had very likely never even been a human child.

The memory of it twisted Mary's stomach into knots and she would often lay awake at night heaving at the thought of it growing within her for all those months.

And yet she mourned its loss. For it had been a ray of hope, and while it had grown inside her, she had loved it as her child. It had also given her great pleasure to believe she could provide England with a catholic heir, and to prove everyone who had doubted her for her gender, wrong.

But it was not meant to be, and Mary would have to live with that notion.

She had tried her very best to do as was expected of her, but now it was time to let it go.

November 1555

"The king will not be returning to England," Mary announced to her council, her voice lifeless, "His father, King Charles V and Holy Roman Emperor, has abdicated his throne, leaving his crown to his son, my husband. He is to be crowned King Filipe II of Spain in the near future."

Her council looked around at one another as they mumbled their concern, "What about an heir for England?" Cardinal Pole asked bravely, "We must consider our options."

"There shall be no child from my womb," Mary pointed out, "But I am not of ill health, and there is no suggesting that I may not reign for decades to come."

Bishop Gardner nodded and smiled, but no one else reacted.

"My heart is broken at my husband's absence," Mary admitted then, "But we must not falter. Your queen is strong, and I will not abandon my country."

"Well," Sir Jerningham said then, "we must mention the growing complications throughout the land. Your majesty's subjects are not happy, and there are uprisings throughout the country."

"Anything serious?" the imperial ambassador asked cooly.

"No," Jerningham replied, "But small groups can grow quickly," and he met Mary's gaze.

"We have cleansed the city of its most radical Protestants already," Mary said, "If these new rebels wish to join them in hell, I may aid them in that."

"There is no reason to believe they are protestant rebels, your majesty," Gardner replied, creasing his bushy eyebrows together.

"Who are they then?" Mary asked Gardner, but he turned away to cough into the crook of his elbow.

"They appear to be protesting against the deteriorating conditions that plague the countryside and cities alike," Jerningham cut in on Gardner's behalf, "The harvest season has not been plentiful, and there is famine in many parts of the country."

"What can be done?" Mary asked her advisors as she glanced at them one-by-one through lifeless eyes.

All of them began looking at one another, some cleared their throats while others rummaged through their papers.

Mary raised an eyebrow and groaned in annoyance, "You may leave me," she commanded, "Come to me if any of you have a suggestion," and they all stood and exited the rooms.

"Gardner," Mary called to her Lord Chancellor before he had a chance to leave, "Stay a moment."

The bishop moved towards her slowly, "Your highness?"

Mary smiled up at him, "How goes the burning of the sinful?" she asked casually, as though she were asking about the weather.

The bishop bowed, "Very well, your majesty," he said, and she noticed his voice sounded ragged, "The once daily burnings have decreased vastly in recent days! Over three hundred heretics have now met their fiery fate, none of which had agreed to convert to the true faith."

"I am saddened they would not save themselves," Mary said, "But to deny the true faith is to deny God. Their souls could not be saved."

"Indeed," Gardner agreed, and then coughed into his closed fist.

Mary frowned, revealing deep creases which had developed over recent weeks, and cocked her head to one side, "Are you unwell, Lord Chancellor?" she asked.

Gardner smiled a gap-toothed smile at his queen, "No, your highness. I am well," he lied.

Mary nodded, "You may leave," she said as she waved her hand towards the door.

Stephen Gardner bowed deeply, "Your majesty," he said, and then he turned and slowly left the room.

January 1556

"The Lord Chancellor, bishop Gardner," said the young messenger as he entered the queen's chambers, "has died."

"Died?" she echoed aghast.

"Yes, your majesty," he said as he stared straight ahead.

Mary's eyes glazed over in shock, unable to process the news. The messenger, seeing his queen in quiet distress, took the opportunity to leave before she could unleash her unpredictable rage onto him, and when Mary finally looked up she found that he was gone.

She called her ladies to her, who had been reading their bibles by the window.

"What news, your highness?" Frances asked, always eager to know everything.

"The bishop is dead," Mary said quietly, "and I have news from Spain I must discuss," she sniffed and cleared her throat, willing herself not to cry but finding it increasingly difficult to deal with all of her never-ending sorrow.

"Call a meeting of the council," she said, and Cecily hurried away.

Once all had gathered in the great hall and Mary took her seat on her throne, she inhaled deeply and made sure to speak clearly, knowing that the news she had yet to share would not be taken well. "Gentlemen," she said eloquently, "As some of you may already know, our most beloved friend and ally, the Lord Chancellor, bishop Stephen Gardner has died," and the members of the council began to mumble and hang or shake their heads. Mary continued, "I am deeply saddened by this news, as I am sure are many of you. He was a loyal subject, and a most faithful ally to our catholic cause," she allowed some time in silence, and then continued once more, "I have called you here, not only to share this sad news, but also to tell you that my husband, King Filipe II of Spain, has called for aid from our country."

"Aid?" Jerningham asked from among the crowd, "For what, your majesty?"

Mary inhaled deeply to quench the burning anxiety in her chest, "It pains me to speak the words, but Spain has called England to arms, in their war against France."

"War?" Jerningham echoed, dumbfounded, "But why should England go to war with France now?"

"We cannot afford a war," another voiced, and suddenly all were speaking and shouting above one another.

Mary watched from her throne as the men squabbled and waved their hands in anger, and her heart felt heavy with guilt.

"My lords!" she called when it was clear the shouting would not cease on its own, "My lords, it pains me to even speak of it, and while I know I promised this day would never come, I gave that promise as Queen Regnant of England who had power above that of the king consort. But as King of Spain my husband has equal, if not more, power than I. To leave Spain without its English allies now would be detrimental for England if we ever were to need aid from Spain in the future. I must consider everything, and I must think of the long-term wellbeing of my country."

"It is preposterous," called one voice from the members of the council.

Mary raised an eyebrow, "I beg you to redirect your anger," she called passionately into the general direction the voice had come from, "for it would be unwise to focus it on me. I have reflected upon all options, and this is the safest one for my people – their safety always being at the forefront of my mind! We must do our part. And in return we shall be protected."

The Privy Council's initial distaste over the new development did not last long, however, when yet another plot against their queen was discovered, led by a Sir Henry Dudley, a protestant cousin to the late John Dudley duke of Northumberland. It was discovered that he had been directly financed and encouraged by the King of France himself to achieve this scheme to overthrow Mary. And with that the council's rage towards the French grew enough to agree with their queen's order to join forces with Spain in their war against France.

The plot did not reach its full potential, however, when Mary sent her spies to infiltrate the group and soon enough, she was informed of the ringleaders' whereabouts.

The cowards attempted to flee towards France once word broke that their plans had been botched, but all were arrested with the exception of Dudley, who had managed to escape.

The traitors were racked for information before their executions, and it did not take long for them to admit that the plan at the heart of their treachery had been to replace Mary with her own half-sister, Elizabeth.

"Send guards to search the lady Elizabeth's estates," Mary ordered as soon as she heard the awful news, suddenly feeling sick to her stomach at the prospect that she could no longer trust even her sister, "Arrest her household. None are free of suspicion."

As soon as her guards left, Mary doubled over and expelled her stomach's contents into her chamber pot as her fear consumed her entirely.

Was her own little sister behind this plot to usurp her? The same little Elizabeth whom she had begged their father to consider when she had outgrown all her clothes? The same Elizabeth whom she had tried to shield from the knowledge that her mother had been gruesomely beheaded? The one she had loved and protected throughout her entire life, even when her council had suggested she should be burned along with all the other heretics?

Mary could not fathom it; it would be too much of a betrayal.

She shook her head to clear her thoughts, and she took herself to the chapel, where she spent all night praying to the Almighty God that at least one person in her life would not abandon or betray her.

"The lady Elizabeth has had no incriminating letters on her person or her chambers," Imperial ambassador Simon Renard informed Mary the following day, "her governess, Kat Ashley, however, has been arrested. She had incriminating heretical literature hidden in her rooms and is being interrogated as we speak."

Mary relaxed visibly in her chair as she learned that her sister had likely not been involved in the scheme to depose her, "I am glad to hear it," she admitted.

"It is great news," the ambassador replied monotonously, "It does, however, reopen the matter of your sister's religion."

"The king has already expressed his opinion about this, ambassador," Mary replied icily as she pressed her thumb and forefinger into her closed eyes, "The only other option we have is our cousin the Queen of Scots."

"And we have discussed why she cannot be considered," Renard replied, "as future queen of France, it is simply impossible."

"I must admit," Mary replied abruptly, "I do agree with that now."

"Your majesty," Renard said as he fidgeted in his seat, "To marry your sister to king Filipe's ally, Emmanuel Philibert of Savoy –"

"I am no longer interested in discussing this further!" Mary interrupted angrily, "A more important issue at hand is the war on France," and she stood up angrily, her temper suddenly boiling over, "I will not allow the French to make a mockery of me and to undermine me by funding and supporting plots and harbouring traitors! England will join forces with Spain and make war on France. There is undoubtedly no avoiding it now!"

"Your majesty," Cecily said quietly as she entered Mary's chambers just a few days later, "I bring news."

Mary did not look up from the letter she was writing angrily at her writing desk and instead only grunted for her to continue.

Cecily cleared her throat, "Uh," she began, "I am not sure how else to tell you other than to simply say it…"

Mary continued scrawling hastily.

"Your majesty," Cecily started again, then took a step towards her, "I regret to inform you," she said slowly as she fretted over how her queen would react, "that the former imperial ambassador, Eustace Chapuys, has died."

Mary's quill stopped abruptly, and she froze in shock, the ink in the quill's tip creating an ugly blotch on the parchment before her.

"Your majesty?" Cecily mumbled after a long silence.

Mary blinked and turned to look at her lady, "Yes?" she said as though she had not heard a word said before then.

"Did you hear the news?" Cecily asked as she narrowed her eyes in confusion.

"The news?" Mary parroted; her eyes glazed over like that of a portrait.

"About ambassador Chapuys?" her lady replied carefully.

Mary raised her eyebrows, "Oh, yes!" she said with an eerie smile, flashing her rotten teeth, "I hear he has died! God rest his soul," then she turned back to her writing desk and picked the quill up before dipping it into the ink pot.

Cecily watched; her mouth agape as she considered what she ought to say.

"Do you wish me to fetch you some wine, your majesty?" Cecily asked, "Do you wish to speak of it for a moment?"

"Hm?" Mary simply said as she continued writing.

"Mary?" Cecily asked as she took another step closer and peered over Mary's shoulder, and her heart sank as she saw the letter her queen had been writing was not meant for anyone but herself, as she scribbled over and over *Forgive me mother, I have failed. Forgive me mother, I have failed.*

And Cecily was no longer able to convince herself that her friend and queen was okay, for it seemed that all the pain and suffering she had endured over the years had finally made her a little insane.

April 1557

"Members of the council," Mary called as she addressed the room, "I have summoned you here today to request your approval of the declaration of war against France," and she looked around at the men before her who did not seem entirely willing, "The two new war ships I had commissioned are ready for battle and we have raised over six-thousand men and six-hundred horses. England is ready."

400

The members of the council visibly shrunk in their seats, all desperate to avoid the wrath they knew was to come.

"We have spent two days," Jerningham said, his normally confident voice suddenly less sure of himself, "deliberating this request we knew would come from you, your majesty. And we have our answer for you now."

"Well," Mary replied, her impatience rising, "What have you decided, councilmen?"

Jerningham cleared his throat and looked at Mary, "My queen, while we initially agreed with your majesty, it has been decided that the request be rejected," he said as he bravely looked up into his monarch's face and then looked away when her face reddened and contorted with rage, "We are in unified agreement," he quickly continued, "that England will support King Filipe with the ships and with money, as is in accordance with your marriage treaty. But to involve England further with this war on France would lead to economic disaster."

The room filled with a soundless buzz, Mary's rage vibrating through the air, and as they knew she would, she began bombarding them all with insults and disparity for their open disloyalty.

"What of the troops we have raised?" she finally asked when she fell back into her throne, out of breath.

"They may return to their homes. Live their lives," a council member replied.

Mary scoffed, "I am deeply unsatisfied with this news," she spat in fury, "And I can guarantee that the king of Spain will be too."

July 1557

Mary had been right. The king of Spain, having heard that his wife's council would not approve of England's declaration of war on France, immediately set sail to England.

401

Upon his arrival he did not waste time with words, but instead raised a force of a thousand English commoners and mercenaries by bribery, offering great rewards to any man who joined his cause, and then departed the country once more in direction of France and in pursuit of glory in a foreign war.

Mary received daily letters of the achievements of their joint Anglo-Spanish troops and shared the news of success smugly with her council, "I have news of a resounding victory at St. Quentin, gentlemen," she said one day after yet another successful letter arrived with news, but none dared reply.

January 1558

Mary's arrogance was quickly slashed when a messenger arrived bearing news that would change everything, and as Mary read through the fateful letter, she suddenly collapsed to the floor and wailed a long and torturous bellow, as though her heart were ripped from her chest and torn in two.

"We have lost Calais," Mary announced monotonously to her council later that same day, "Our last English foothold in France."

Jerningham banged his fist down upon the table, "Damn that rotten king!"

"Mind your tongue!" Imperial ambassador, Renard replied dangerously as he stood up sharply.

"Calais has been ruled by monarchs of England for more than two hundred years!" another council member exclaimed in outrage, "Your Spanish snake has used England for his own causes and left Calais undefended!" he added in reply to Renard's outburst.

"Calais was nothing but a practical nuisance to your country," Renard remarked, "A drain on your resources!"

"Enough," Mary said but no one heard her.

"It is not up to you or any monarch but *our own* to decide whether Calais was worth defending or not!" Jerningham exclaimed as he stood up, his shoulders broad and tense.

"I cannot claim to know what my master did or did not do for the good of the war –" Renard spat out, his eyes blazing with fury.

"Enough!" Mary then cried out, and the men fell silent, slowly resuming their seats as they looked around at one another, "The loss of Calais will haunt me until my final breath, gentlemen. And I heartily wish now that I had considered your warnings, but there is no money or leadership to regain it," she paused as the members of her council grumbled in anger, and she took the moment to place a hand over her heart as it ached, "While there is nothing left that I can do, I can assure of this: That when I am dead and opened, you shall find Calais engraved on my heart."

May 1558

Mary became miserable in a way she had never felt before.
She no longer saw any light in the sunshine and heard no melody in the birdsong. The world looked bleak and grey, and no amount of praying or entertainment could lift her broken spirit.
Her continued lack of purpose and misfortune played heavily on her mind, and there was no longer anything anyone could say or do to breathe life back into her.
She would walk the halls of her palace like the ghost of her former self, floating from duty to duty, seeming neither interested nor motivated, and spent many hours on her knees praying in her private chapel.

403

She would fast for days, feeling sick at the mere thought of swallowing the food brought to her, and only taking small bites when her ladies begged her to eat.

She could no longer see even the slimmest sliver of hope in her future and began to lose all interest in living. For what was the point of life if one dreaded the very rising of the sun?

Her final wish of being a good queen to her people had slipped through her fingers when she had agreed to aid Spain in their war, and Calais had been scattered in the wind along with the ashes of the three-hundred heretics she had burned alive. There was nothing left for Mary to do but to admit that her fate as queen had not been as glorious as she had anticipated.

She had failed her country and her subjects – there was no other way about it – and Mary I's reign would be remembered as nothing but failure after failure.

Though she had survived all who had wished her harm and had endeavoured and eventually achieved the fate her mother had pushed onto her, it was now clear that it had been an entirely wasted existence.

Every chance at happiness and love, had been exchanged for the glittering prospect that the crown would be her happy ending. Yet no one had warned her that the price she would pay for power and glory were not limited to her misery *before* acquiring it.

The restoration of the true faith throughout England was, however, a great success. One that she would often console herself with at night when her thoughts kept her from sleep. But as each day went by without any hope of a catholic heir to succeed her, it became less and less of a victory, as it too would surely end in failure when her Protestant sister would be the only able to succeed her.

It was this thought that gave Mary one last push to attempt to save her only success, and she called the messenger to fetch the lady Elizabeth to court.

Mary would have to try one last time to convince her sister to convert to the Catholic faith so that she may rest easy at night knowing that her hard work to restore England back in favour with Rome and God would not collapse under Elizabeth's rule.

Her young sister arrived the following day and greeted her queen warmly, curtsying grandly before the court as Mary received her in the throne room, "Your majesty," she said with a beaming smile, one Mary could not help but notice included all her beautifully white teeth, and she subconsciously ran her tongue over her own, cursing her failing body.

"Lady Elizabeth," Mary replied icily, "I have invited you here in the hope that we may speak plainly with one another."
Elizabeth looked up at her half-sister and smiled sweetly, "I am but your humble servant, your majesty."

Mary's face twitched at the sarcastic tone, "You may not choose to be so insolent when you hear what I am about to say," and she inhaled deeply and raised her chin, looking down at the pretty young lady before her, "I have summoned you here to insist that you relinquish your heretical faith in favour of the one true and Godly path of Catholicism. There will be no discussing it. You are here today to either accept or refuse. And your answer will lead you to your future," Mary paused, then continued, "I urge you to choose wisely, Elizabeth. For today I make my ruling as your queen, and not your sister."

Elizabeth stared wide-eyed at Mary, her perky breasts heaving up and down as she breathed in anger, "Do I have a moment to consider, or must I speak now?" she asked.

"Now," was all Mary replied as she watched her through tired eyes.

Elizabeth dropped her gaze and the queen watched as her sister – whom she had always loved and cared for as she would have imagined she would have cared for her own daughter – as she balled her hands into fists at her sides and her cheeks blotched in anger, so similarly to herself. And for a moment her heart ached for her, knowing the terrible position she was putting the young lady in: the impossible choice of one's life over that of one's religion.

Just as Catholicism was to Mary, Elizabeth's hold onto her Protestant faith held a deeper meaning than simple belief. Protestantism was what had paved the way for her mother's marriage to the king and had been the key to the validity of their marriage. It secured the knowledge in Elizabeth's mind that she had always and would always be a true and legitimate child of the former king and queen of England. And Mary knew from her very own experience just how important that was.

It was this final similar detail that Mary hoped would make her sister see the light, as she herself had – much to her regret – chosen her life over her faith when her father had threatened action against her had she not signed the Act of Supremacy all those years ago.

But Mary should have known that her sister would not be so easily manipulated, and she utterly underestimated Elizabeth's stubborn nature, "I have made my choice, *sister*."

"Speak it," Mary whispered, fearing what she knew would be her answer.

Elizabeth raised her chin defiantly, "I say nay," and the court behind her gasped, "You shall have to burn me alive for my sins."

Mary sat slumped in her seat at the head of the table, as the members of her council squabbled and argued, some banging their fists and pointing their fingers in each other's faces, but she could hear nothing. It was as though the world was spinning in slow motion, and she raised her head to observe as the men argued passionately over things Mary no longer cared about.

For what did it matter? Once she was dead and buried none of it would make a difference. All the pain and heartache, the loss and the hate she had endured, all of it would have been in vain.

Which is why she could do nothing but watch as her council raged before her, fighting to prove their own point more important than another.

Mary's eyes glazed over, and she focused on a small hole on the wooden table. She was unaware how long she stared at it for, but then she felt a hand on her shoulder, "Your majesty," Cecily's voice whispered in her ear, and suddenly Mary was out of her trance, and her mind assessed the chaos.

She stood up slowly from her seat in the hope that it would be enough to alert the councilmembers of their crassness, but their angry shouting continued.

"Gentlemen!" she called gruffly, and immediately all eyes were on her, "I beg you to cease the incessant fighting," she said as she resumed her seat, as tired as a mother to bickering young children.

The men looked around at one another, most of them still frowning, and took their places in their seats.

Once all were seated, Mary continued, "I shall hear from imperial ambassador Renard," she said, "What matter needs discussing?"

Renard cleared his throat, "The matter of your sister, your majesty."

Mary sighed, "What of her?"

"She remains locked up in the Tower of London," Renard said.

Mary waited but when he did not continue, she said, "I am well aware of that. Is there a point to this?"

Renard shifted uncomfortably in his seat, "My master the king of Spain brings up the issue of marriage for the lady Elizabeth once more –"

"Tell your master, *my husband*," Mary interrupted, "that the matter of marriage for the lady is not up for discussion," she replied, "I shall not wed my sister to someone and have her shipped out of the country."

"Then it begs the question of your successor, your majesty," Renard continued.

"My successor will be whomever I choose when God calls me to Him," Mary replied, her words slurring slightly as her head felt suddenly heavy, "Until then it shall remain... a mystery."

"What about the Lady Margaret Douglas?" Cardinal Pole interrupted pensively.

"My aunt Margaret's daughter with the Earl of Angus?" Mary replied, frowning.

"Well, why not?" he replied, "she is a catholic, and as niece to the late King Henry VIII she has a strong claim."

"Not as strong as the late king's own youngest daughter," Renard chimed in, "Elizabeth is a threat to Catholic England. She must be dealt with."

Mary ignored the imperial ambassador's interruption, "It is a fine idea, Cardinal," she said as she nodded her head, "I shall think on it."

But Mary never did think on it, for suddenly the country was once again in turmoil.

408

She received reports from various counties that though the areas were not afflicted by plague, people were dying by the thousands from a new, unknown sickness.

It spread quickly throughout the north of the country and many farmers died, leaving large amounts of grain unharvested, and by mid-September over eight-thousand people had died from the mysterious flu, followed by thousands more as the unharvested crops led to widespread famine.

And all the while, as her people died or sickness or starvation, Mary could do nothing but pray.

She spent hours each day begging God to spare her people, but each day came another rising number of reported deaths.

And very soon, as they all knew it would, members of the court began to fall ill, and Mary was advised to make her will.

October 1558

Mary's stomach began to bloat once again as it had so many times before, but this time she cared little for the appearance of things and allowed her ladies to dress her with loosened corset.

It only took one day for rumours of pregnancy to be whispered throughout the court.

"What can they possibly think?" Mary asked her ladies one morning, "That it may be an immaculate conception?" and she scoffed and shook her head, fighting her inner thoughts to not even consider the possibility, "How can people believe me to be with child when the king and I have not even been in the same country?"

Frances shrugged as she pinned Mary's hood to her thinning hair, "People choose to overlook the obvious when they wish for something hard enough."

"Yes," Mary agreed, "But I know better than anyone that wishing and praying for something hard enough does not make it reality."

Frances smiled at Mary's reflection, "You achieved the crown through wishes and prayer," she pointed out in one last ditch effort to cheer her queen.

"I'm beginning to think that perhaps it was not God that had anything to do with it," Mary mumbled as she rubbed a hand over her swollen belly.

"Do you need me to fetch your remedy from the physician, your majesty?" Frances asked as she noticed Mary's discomfort.

Mary returned her friend's smile, "No, I have very little pain," she lied.

"You have not suffered from this in some time, your majesty," Frances realised then, "Perhaps you are finally overcoming it after all these years!"

Mary looked at her excited expression, "Perhaps," she agreed, though deep down she knew that rather than overcome this ailment, it would likely be the death of her.

Frances curtseyed to her queen and stepped aside as Mary rose awkwardly from her seat and made her way to the throne room to commence her daily duties.

The mysterious flu that had engulfed the country had not yet ceased, but as the number of daily deaths finally began to slow significantly, Mary and her council were able to agree that the worst was behind them, and that restoring the country's former strength was now of primary importance.

Mary eased herself into her throne, and the usher announced the entry of her advisors.

"Gentlemen," she greeted them, and they all bowed quickly in response, "What news?" she asked automatically, to begin the meeting.

"Your majesty," the Queen's Secretary, Sir William Petre said, "Your will has been amended at your request."

"Good," she said curtly, then cleared her throat, "Read it," she commanded.

"The will remains much the same, except for the matter of your successor…"

"Yes…" Mary said impatiently.

"As requested," Petre continued, "and approved by the lawyers, it now no longer states a specific heir, but rather 'a successor by the Laws and Statutes of the Realm'."

Mary inhaled and jolted suddenly as a stabbing pain shot through her stomach, "Excellent," she mumbled through gritted teeth.

Her council nodded in agreement.

"With the lady Elizabeth still imprisoned in the Tower," Imperial ambassador Renard said, "no doubt the people will call for the Lady Margaret Douglas, your cousin, to succeed your majesty."

"But your sister's support is growing," Jerningham added carefully, "Her imprisonment has evoked sympathy towards her."

"She will stay where she is until she accepts the true faith," Mary said monotonously, "With time to do nothing but reflect, perhaps she may yet be my heir."

Her advisors nodded back at her.

"On another matter," Mary continued, "I wish to add one last thing," and she frowned slightly as another pain shot through her, "Upon my death, I wish for my mother's body to be exhumed and to be laid to rest with me."

"Your majesty –" Petre said.

"It shall be my final command," Mary interrupted, "I insist it be added as soon as possible. I know I will not rest in peace without my mother beside me for all eternity."

411

The councilmen looked at her, then at one another before all either smiled back at Mary or nodded their head in agreement.

"If there is nothing further to discuss, then I shall take my leave," Mary said as she began to rise.

Her ladies, seeing her struggle to stand, hurried towards her and as Mary slowly walked through the members of her Privy Council, she could see in their eyes that they too saw what she already knew: That death was becoming an increasingly blatant reality for England's very first Queen Regnant.

17th November 1558
Tower of London

Lady Elizabeth awoke early one morning, before even the first ray of light and before the birds had begun singing their song.

She was startled from her sleep by a dream she suddenly could no longer remember, and yet it left a knot in her stomach and a sour taste in her mouth. Her gut was warning her that something would happen this day.

Perhaps her sister had finally sentenced her to die as she had so long threatened to do, and Elizabeth wondered what it would feel like to be burned alive. It surprised her to realise she did not fear it.

She lay back down on her musty bed covers, curled up into a ball and closed her eyes, hoping to go back to sleep, when suddenly she heard a commotion outside her door.

The lady sat up and stared at the door, willing it to open so that she may finally be released from this prison and meet her destiny, even if it meant certain death.

The heavy footsteps came closer as they climbed the stone stairs of the Tower of London. She held her breath as she counted each heavy thud as they climbed the eighty-seven steps, and suddenly she could see a sliver of light shining from underneath the heavy wooden door to her cell.

She swung her legs off the bed as the keys jingled from behind the door as her jailor tried to open it, and Elizabeth was swiftly reminded that she wore nothing but her nightshift. But there was nothing to do about it now, their unexpected arrival granting her no time for modesty, and so she raised her chin bravely as her heart began to beat quicker in her chest, and she braced herself for her sentencing.

The door swung open, and two guards walked in holding torches, which they used to light the burnt-out candles on the cell walls. Elizabeth watched them as her breathing grew shallower and she was ashamed to realise she feared the unknown far more than she feared death.

"What is the meaning of this?" she said, her voice trembling slightly.

The guards stood by the candles they had lit and ignored her question as another set of footsteps ran up the stairs. Elizabeth looked from the guards to the open cell door and wondered for a brief moment how far she would get if she ran. But before the thought could even develop, Sir Henry Jerningham, Queen Mary's trusted advisor and member of the Privy Council, stood in the doorway. Elizabeth stared at the man wide-eyed as he stared back at her. He then cleared his throat and nodded at one of the guards who swiftly offered Elizabeth his cloak.

She took it and wrapped it around herself, baffled by the kindness, and wondered if this was a plot to lower her guard.

She looked back at Henry Jerningham and noticed a sadness in his worn face, "What is the meaning of this, my lord?" she asked again as her stomach flipped.

Jerningham took a step towards her, and Elizabeth prepared herself for the inevitable. Her time on this earth had come to an end.

But then suddenly the great lord bent the knee and bowed before her, followed immediately by the guards beside them, and as he raised his head he spoke, "Queen Mary is dead," and he presented Elizabeth with a ring as proof.

"My sister's ring," Elizabeth said dreamily as she took it carefully from him.

Like a bolt of lightning, realisation suddenly struck her, and Elizabeth fell to her knees, shaken by the knowledge that her death had been evaded by her sister's own, and that today would not be the day in which her life would end, but rather when it would begin.

End of Book 1

Author's note:

While most historical events mentioned in 'The Saddest Princess' remain factual, some have been altered and/or dramatized to accommodate the fictional side of the story.

Since this book focuses on Mary and her perception of the world, some character depictions, such as Anne Boleyn's, are created based on *her* view and opinions of them.

Most of the characters mentioned are based on real people who historically lived through the events, while some others are completely fictional – I leave it up to you to decide who those characters may be.

Printed in Great Britain
by Amazon

29261377R00235